Just Right

Look for these titles by
Erin Nicholas

Now Available:

No Matter What
Anything You Want

The Bradford Series
Just Right
Just Like That
Just My Type

Just Right

Erin Nicholas

SAMHAIN
PUBLISHING

Samhain Publishing, Ltd.
577 Mulberry Street, Suite 1520
Macon, GA 31201
www.samhainpublishing.com

Just Right
Copyright © 2011 by Erin Nicholas
Print ISBN: 978-1-60928-004-8
Digital ISBN: 978-1-60504-947-2

Editing by Lindsey Faber
Cover by Scott Carpenter

First Samhain Publishing, Ltd. electronic publication: March 2010
First Samhain Publishing, Ltd. print publication: January 2011

Dedication

To Lindsey, who gave me a shot, who likes my books almost as much as I do, and who can look past the overuse of my favorite words and punctuation to the story and characters underneath.

Chapter One

It was not a good day to go low-carb.

Not that any day was a good day to go low-carb. But as she struggled to hold the bloody, pissed-off drunk down on the trauma room table, Jessica Bradford *really* missed the double-chocolate jumbo muffin that was a part of her usual Wednesday morning routine.

"Get off me! Let me go! Get *off* me, you bitch!"

She didn't think she'd been called a derogatory term this early in the morning before. Great, a new record.

It was going to be a long day.

She sighed. As the first nurse into the room as the gurney rolled in, Jessica got the questionable privilege of getting to hold the guy's hand. Kind of. She somehow wrestled the man's arm down again, thumping it against the examining table with more force than was strictly necessary. Dan, another of the ER nurses, got a firm grip on his wrist.

"Okay, Linda, now," Dan said to another nurse. "Get it in *now.*"

Linda's hands were admirably steady as she inserted the needle to deliver a potent sedative into the man's forearm.

"Ow! You bitch!" The man attempted to bring his hand up alongside Linda's head.

His arm rose only a couple of inches as Jessica and Dan held strong, but Jessica's arms burned with the effort and she knew she couldn't hold him much longer.

Amazing. The man looked like he'd been in a minor scuffle—and had come out the winner—instead of a head-on collision on the expressway. Not to mention that he had been acting like a pain in the ass since he'd been brought in. That *had* to use up some energy.

Linda focused on her task and managed to get the needle taped down securely before the man could rip it free with his thrashing. Fortunately, his other arm was broken in at least three places and he was unable to use it to do more damage to himself or the staff working to help him.

"Please let it work quickly," Jessica, prayed.

The crash of metal against the hard tile floor was earsplitting as the man's right foot kicked over the tray near the bed and the array of instruments hit and scattered. But he'd been aiming for the nurse who was cutting open the leg of his blue jeans.

"Get off of me!" the man bellowed. "Goddamn it!"

"Not quickly enough," Dan replied dourly.

Jessica had to put all one hundred and twenty pounds of her body weight against the man's arm to keep him from yanking the IV out before the sedative could work.

"Turn the drip up," Jessica muttered.

The man tried to thrash his other arm, but instead moaned loudly. Of course, the alcohol content of his blood likely dulled the intensity of the pain somewhat. Including the pain from the gash on the top of his head that was spurting blood even as the ER physician, Matt Taylor, labored to stitch it shut. The man's head jerked from side to side and he continued to swear at everyone who came into his line of vision.

Nearly three minutes later, he finally began wearing out, or the medication was kicking in, or both, because he started to calm. Jessica slowly released her hold on him, then carefully stepped away from the table, rolled her head and rubbed the back of her arm. Wrestling a man with three times her muscle mass and ten times her adrenaline levels had definitely created some knots.

Just then, the exam room doors banged open.

And Ben Torres walked in.

Jessica froze mid-knead.

The genes Ben had inherited from his half-Hispanic father were gloriously evident in his tanned skin, dark hair and deep brown eyes. But even without the eyes, he took up space in a confident, graceful, solid way that made Jessica think about things she hadn't thought about in years. Things like large hands and proportionate other body parts. And other thoughts entirely inappropriate in a place where things truly were life and death.

It wasn't her fault she got distracted. Dr. Ben Torres was magnificent. Even when he was upset. As he obviously was now.

He was scowling as he stalked into the room.

"How are the kids?" someone asked.

"Dead in the ambulance," Ben said flatly without looking at anyone but the man on the table.

A nurse automatically handed Ben gloves, which he pulled on as he came toward the man.

"What about the mother?" Dan asked.

"In a coma. Bleeding profusely," Ben said shortly, stopping at the foot of the table the man lay on. "She won't make it."

No one responded for a moment and all sexual thoughts fled Jessica's mind as she stared at Ben. It wasn't just the news he'd delivered. It was tragic, but unfortunately not an uncommon report for an emergency room. It was the way Ben said the words. There was a coldness in his voice that Jessica had never heard from him. The rest of the staff responded similarly, shrinking away as he passed them. Ben was always serious in the ER, intent on his work but calm and composed. Now he looked furious, barely holding on to his anger.

Then the relative silence was interrupted by, "Son of a bitch!"

The man on the table suddenly tried to sit upright. Matt's hands still held the end of the thread that was partially keeping the man's scalp together. The man howled in pain as the thread in his head pulled and his mangled arm shifted.

People around the table lunged to restrain him again and someone yelled, "Give him more!" Someone went for a syringe and Jessica went for the wrist with the IV. But as she leaned in, the man grabbed the front of her shirt and jerked her forward.

"Damn it! Get me out of here! Get them off of me!"

She wrapped her hands around the man's arm and opened her mouth, but before she could respond, Ben pushed in next to her and grabbed the man's wrist. He twisted and the man yelped and let go. Jessica stumbled back as Dan came forward too and pushed against the man's chest, forcing him back down on the table.

"Calm down," Ben ordered the man.

"Screw you."

"These people are trying to help you," Ben said, through gritted teeth.

Jess was close enough to see the tension in his face.

"Screw them!" the man shouted. "I don't want their help."

He pulled hard against the arm Ben held, then grimaced in pain as Ben squeezed his wrist.

"Don't you remember me, Ted?" Ben asked, his jaw tight. "I put your sorry ass back together two months ago when you plowed your car into that tree."

The man didn't look any happier, but his struggling slowed a bit as he stared at Ben. "That's right," Ben went on. "Thanks to me you were able to get up this morning and appreciate the beautiful sunrise and get ready for work at a rewarding job where you help people and contribute to society. Oh, wait."

He leaned in closer to Ted, his expression dark, his tone cold. "That was the woman lying on that table in the next room. But the breakfast she made and the hugs she gave her kids and the latte she bought today were all her last. Because of you."

Jessica wasn't breathing and she knew no one else in the room was either. She couldn't tear her eyes away from Ben and the intensity of the emotions on his face.

Ted squirmed on the table and tried to turn his head away from Ben's stare of contempt, but Ben caught Ted's chin in his hand and forced the man to look at him.

"Look at you." Ben's voice was low and angry. "You're barely scratched up compared to those kids, but these people still have to stay and help you. But I know you're wasting their time, just like you wasted mine. I spent four hours in that operating room making sure you would live. But when you got in your car this afternoon you were basically telling me to fuck off, weren't you? And this time you took three people with you."

Ben looked like he'd like to take the man's head off. "That woman and her kids would still be alive if I hadn't done my job so well. It's probably a good thing you don't need surgery today. I might not be having as good a day."

Jessica wanted to gasp at Ben's implication, but she couldn't force any air into her lungs. And she couldn't look away to see how the rest of the staff was reacting.

"You're a waste of time. And you *are* going to jail for this."

Ted's eyes went wide and he struggled in Ben's hold, thrashing his head side to side.

"This is crap! Get me out of here! Goddamn assholes!"

The man's bellowing jerked Jessica out of her daze. Thank goodness, because she was close enough to Ben that she found herself flinching away as he pulled his arm back. She jumped when his fist came forward quickly and connected with Ted's face.

Ted howled and struggled to lift a hand to where blood was now running from his nose. But the staff stood frozen for several seconds.

Dan reacted first, pivoting and putting his shoulder into Ben's chest. "Back up, Torres."

Dan had to let up on the pressure he was exerting to keep Ted down and the man thrashed, rolling side to side. Dan gritted his teeth and turned back to subdue the patient, unable to deal with both men at once.

Jess recovered, sort of, and stepped in front of Ben. "I've got him," she said to Dan, putting both hands on Ben's chest.

She pushed him back, aware of the pounding of his heart under her palm and, inappropriately, aware that she'd never touched Ben other than brushing against his arm or hand while they were working.

"Dr. Torres," she said, willing him to look at her when he resisted the pressure on his chest.

His six foot two inches to her five foot six was a significant difference, not to mention his solid two hundred pounds of muscle to her slim build, which was mostly from good genes versus good exercise habits.

She pushed harder. "Ben!"

He looked down at her and backed up a step. She followed him as she glanced over her shoulder at the man who continued to moan and complain.

"You could have broken his nose," she said for Ben's ears only.

"I did."

She looked up quickly. His tone was so flat she could only assume that cracked cartilage had been his intention. She swallowed, not sure what to say to that. And completely unable to fully pull her attention from the body heat soaking into her palms.

Ben stared down into the eyes of the woman he'd purposely been *not* touching since he'd come to Omaha. She looked so damn good. She smelled delicious. And her hands were on him. Finally.

Ben glared at the man writhing on the table and the rage tightened his chest again. He wanted to concentrate on something *good*, something pleasurable and sweet, like the woman in front of him.

But Ted Blake had to get into his car this morning instead of sleeping off his drinking binge.

Ben wasn't sorry he'd hit Ted. He wanted the selfish, stupid bastard to feel at least a measure of the pain he'd caused. The blood from Ted's nose couldn't come close to equaling the amount of blood the five-year-old and two-year-old in the next room had lost because of him. But the feel of his fist connecting with the cartilage in Ted's nose had been at least slightly satisfying. Ben knew it meant he'd stooped to Ted's level, that two wrongs don't make a right and all that bullshit. But hitting Ted had definitely felt good.

And *damn*, Ben wanted to feel good. It had been a long time since things had been that simple.

He especially wanted to kick his obsession with fixing things—things that didn't stay fixed in particular.

Ben focused again on Jessica, who still had her hands braced on his chest and who was still looking at him like...he was a successful, respected surgeon who'd punched a patient in the face.

He just wanted to feel good. And he had an excellent idea about how to make that happen at the moment.

He grabbed her by the upper arms, pulled her up onto her tiptoes and kissed her, eliciting as many gasps from the ER staff as when he'd hit Ted.

This felt *so* much better.

Hell, he was going to get suspended anyway. Might as well add sexual harassment to the list while he was at it.

Not that Jessica was responding like a woman being

harassed. Her hands gripped his shoulders and she tipped her head to the right, making the fit of their mouths more absolute. She pressed her chest and hips against him, parting her lips for his tongue to invade the silky heat of her mouth.

In fact, the only reason Ben didn't back her up against the nearest wall and make things really interesting was the security guards who showed up.

One cleared his throat. "Dr. Torres, we've been asked to escort you off of St. Anthony's campus."

Ben released Jessica, finally feeling some of the long-sought satisfaction when he saw her lift her hand and press her fingers against her lips, her green eyes wide, a long strand of her dark hair slipping from the ponytail she always wore neat and tight.

"Okay." He had no intention of resisting.

"The patient is finally under sedation," he heard a nurse report to Dan.

Perfect.

"Let's go." Ben turned and led the way out of the trauma room, more than ready to leave.

The truth was, he should have walked out of the ER and not come back a long time ago.

There were five words that Jessica hated to hear from her brother.

"Jess, I need a favor."

Yep. Those were them.

She closed her eyes. "Come on, Sam. I had a long day." She wanted to prop up in bed, watch Seinfeld reruns and eat a pint of Peanut Butter Passion.

"It's important, Jess," Sam said, his tone the one he used for coaxing shy women out onto the dance floor. "I tried to handle it, but I need your help."

The tone always worked on curvy blondes.

Jessica was not a curvy blonde.

"I'm...busy."

"Dry your hair and get dressed," he said. "I told you—it's important."

Jessica paused with the comb halfway through her straight

brown hair and stared at the phone receiver in the mirror. How had he known her hair was wet? That was weird.

"I said I'm busy."

"No. You said *I'm*, then there was a long pause before you said *busy*."

She scowled. "So?"

"So, that pause means you were trying to think of a good excuse because you can never quite bring yourself to lie about it. You're at home. It had to be taking a shower, doing laundry or cleaning the apartment."

Jessica bristled. "I do other things here than...wash things."

"Yeah, but if you were really doing anything important you would have actually *been* busy and you would have just told me what you were busy doing instead of using the noncommittal, generic *I'm busy*."

Jessica was thrown off for a moment by her brother using the word *noncommittal.*

Showing off her own impressive vocabulary, she replied again, "So?"

"I need your help. It should be enough that I say it's important," Sam said, moving on from the "busy" conversation, probably bored by now with the topic that wasn't directly about him.

Of course, *important* could mean almost anything with Sam.

It could mean he was a few dollars short of getting in on a poker game. It could mean that he needed a place for a couple of buddies from out of town to crash for the weekend. It could mean that one of the girls he'd flirted with had taken him too seriously and he needed an emergency wife to get the girl off his back. Jessica sighed. She hated playing Sam's wife. He always wanted her to be bitchy and she always ended up feeling bad for the girl.

"It was a *really* long day at work."

And it was all because of Ben Torres.

Rumor had it he had been suspended by the Chief of Staff and the hospital attorneys were riled up trying to figure out how to troubleshoot the situation. There were charges pending as well. Manslaughter for Ted. Assault for Ben.

Not that any of it affected Jessica directly. She was an ER nurse. There were more surgeons, there would be more accidents and more patients. But she couldn't get Ben out of her mind...or suppress her insane urge to make sure he was all right.

"I heard," Sam said.

Of course he had. Sam was the head paramedic on the best ambulance crew in the city and he not only worked with the ER staff regularly, he was also friends with many of them, including Ben. Matt Taylor, the ER doctor on Ted Blake's case, was a poker buddy of Sam's.

"I'm tired and—"

"Shame on you, Jessica Leigh Bradford," Sam broke in. "I'm your little brother. Your *only* brother."

The *only* part was right. The little part not so much. Sam was younger than Jessica by five years, but she didn't even come up to his chin.

"I'm *not* in the mood for this." But she knew that she didn't sound convincing. She'd always been a sucker for the little brother bit. Because he was right. He was her younger brother and she felt responsible, even now when he was twenty-five and definitely a big boy.

"Too bad."

"What is it?" she asked, trying to soak a cotton ball with skin toner with one hand while holding the phone with the other.

"A babysitting job."

She frowned, forgetting the cotton ball for a moment. "Did you say babysitting?"

"Well, first, do you have a sexy dress?"

Jessica forgot about the toner, cotton ball and everything else. "Excuse me?"

"You're going to need to borrow one then," Sam said. "And high heels. Do you have high heels?"

His tone suggested that he sincerely doubted it.

"Of course I do." They were way in the back of the closet somewhere, but she was pretty sure she still had them.

"What about the dress?"

"I have a dress, Sam."

"But is it sexy? It will have to be sexy. Maybe you should

call Marcy."

This called for a dress from her friend Marcy? Marcy didn't dress in anything that didn't reveal cleavage and lots of it. What in the hell was going on?

"Sam, maybe you'd better define *babysitting*," Jessica said grimly.

Jessica tugged at the dress where it hugged her hips so closely that she hadn't been able to put even a pair of panties between it and her skin. The scrap of black material that was supposed to be a dress was ridiculous. It wasn't practical for any purpose whatsoever.

She frowned. That wasn't completely accurate. It was useful for one purpose: to attract attention.

And it was a good thing she was trying to get Ben Torres' attention. He was the *only* man she would ever consider wearing the thing for.

She hiked the too-large-to-be-fashionable red purse that she'd needed to bring along back up onto her shoulder, sighed and squinted up at the neon sign above the door to the tavern she now stood beside. As a *C* and an *E* were the only letters that still worked, Jessica wasn't even sure of the name of the bar where Ben was supposedly getting drunk and stupid. But she paused long enough to give one last attempt at getting the dress down to at least mid-thigh.

It was futile.

There simply wasn't enough material.

"It's for Ben. It's for Ben," she muttered as she walked over the pieces of broken concrete that she supposed had been a sidewalk at one time.

It took about two steps to figure out that broken concrete and high heels didn't go well together.

Jessica was swearing under her breath by the time she crossed in front of the big, black SUV parked facing the sidewalk. As she passed, the headlights flashed on and off three times.

Jessica wobbled once, but kept walking...and swearing under her breath.

She was a woman, alone in a strange part of town. Avoiding

trouble was always easier than fighting it off.

As she reached for the thick, wooden door handle to the bar, however, the SUV's horn blasted.

She jumped nearly a foot and swung around to face the truck. The lights came on again, spotlighting her up against the door. A man leaned out of the driver's side window.

"Damn, girl, you look like a wet dream in that dress."

Her breath whooshed out. "Dooley, what are you trying to do to me?"

She approached the side of the truck walking gingerly on the gravel in the heels that simply refused to provide a stable platform for her to move on. She heard male laughter from inside the cab as she arrived at the window and glared at Dooley, one of her brother's best friends. He grinned unapologetically, his tan skin and shaggy blond hair making him look more like a California surfer dude than an ace paramedic who'd grown up on a farm in Nebraska.

"Jessica, if I'd known that you had *that* underneath your clothes I would never have agreed to send you in to Ben." Mac Gordon, head shaved bald, sat in the backseat behind Dooley, grinning widely over his goatee.

"Hi, Mac," Jessica greeted the big ex-firefighter turned EMT. She had always thought of these guys as brothers, but she couldn't help but feel good about the compliment. And she knew it was sincere, though none of these guys would ever make a move on her.

She met her brother's eyes, then looked at Kevin Campbell, the dark-haired paramedic sitting behind Sam.

"What are you guys doing here?"

"Making sure Dumbass Torres didn't try to drive himself home before you got here," Kevin said, turning to look at her. He was holding an ice pack against his right eye.

Her eyes widened. "What happened to you?"

"Dumbass Torres," he grunted.

"He *hit* you?" Jessica couldn't believe it.

Had Ben lost his mind? First a patient, now one of his best friends. And a big friend at that. Ben was solid, but Kevin was NCAA-Division-I-Defensive-Lineman solid. He was bigger, taller and a more experienced fighter than Ben. Hitting Kevin would have been stupid. For anyone.

"If he'd hit me, he'd be the one black and blue," Kevin said with a scowl.

Sam grinned at his disgruntled friend. "I was trying to get Ben's car keys away from him and an elbow ended up in Kevin's eye."

Kevin muttered something under his breath and Sam chuckled.

"Ben wasn't real apologetic, though, so Kevin's bent out of shape."

"Why did you guys bring him here?"

Mac coughed and grinned. "Uh, we didn't exactly bring him. We followed him here."

Sam nodded, his mouth now set in a grim line. "He's been trying to lose us. Unsuccessfully."

"Lose you?"

"He took us to a country dance club. He knew Dooley would hate it."

Dooley shuddered and Jessica laughed. "You okay?"

"Barely."

"The hot cowgirls in short skirts helped," Mac said.

"And he brought you here because?" Jess asked.

Dooley gestured to the flashing pink neon female silhouette in the window. "Exotic dancers."

Jessica looked quickly at Kevin, who definitely looked unenthusiastic. In spite of his willingness to bruise Ben if he started a real fight, Kevin had become a Christian two years ago and now tried to live an upright, moral life. Including avoiding nearly naked dancing girls. In fact, Kevin's only reason for going out to bars with his buddies was to serve as a designated driver, and he was likely with the guys tonight out of true concern for Ben.

Jessica hid her smile by turning her face away from the dim glow of the streetlight. Kevin was a good guy, but she could imagine the mini-sermon he'd given the guys to keep them in the truck and out of the bar.

"So, you're sitting out here waiting for me?"

"Pretty much," Dooley said with a shrug.

"It's interesting that you call in one woman to do something that four guys couldn't."

"It ain't our fault that you got the boobs, honey," Mac said from the back seat.

"Well, if boobs are Ben's thing, I can compete." She laughed. "I've got them even if I haven't used them like this in a while."

Mac and Dooley both laughed and even Kevin spoke up with an, "I'm not worried."

"Speaking of boobs," Sam said, definitely not laughing. "Is that one of Marcy's dresses?"

"No, it's mine."

"Of course it is," Sam muttered. He looked over his shoulder at Mac. "This is why I didn't ask Sara. She doesn't even have that kind of a dress."

Jessica's eyebrows rose at the mention of her and Sam's little sister. She was not only concerned about Sam sending Sara into a bar like this, but the idea of *any* other woman trying to entice Ben didn't sit well with Jessica, even if the other woman was Sara. "You were going to ask Sara to do this?"

"No," Sam said firmly. "You were definitely the one."

Dooley laughed. "He said—"

"Never mind," Sam interrupted.

"What?" Jessica asked. "What did Sam say?"

"*Nothing.*" Sam gave Dooley a firm look.

Which Dooley ignored.

"Sam said you could definitely hold your own in a place like this."

Jessica raised her eyebrows at her brother. It had been ten years since she'd been in a bar, period.

None of these guys had known her prior to her dad's death, so they only knew the in-charge, bossy, dependable ER nurse and big sister side of her. That was who she was now. But there had been a time when she'd been a regular in places worse than this, wearing less.

"He also said you'd be very interested in where Ben spends the night."

Jessica felt her cheeks heat. She glared at the brother who never seemed to be paying attention, but knew her too well.

"Yeah, because I need to know where to drop him off," she said, meeting Dooley's eyes directly, challenging him to make more of it than that.

Until an hour ago, she never would have guessed that there

would be a chance for her to make more of it than that. And she was certainly nervous about the fact that Ben might not want to turn it into anything more.

Dooley grinned and said, "His apartment. I don't want him puking on my couch."

Jessica shook her head. "If he starts puking, you guys are getting a phone call."

"You clean up worse than that every day in the ER," Kevin said, his tone still grumpy. "You're a nurse. Why do you think we called you?"

"Because you would look stupid in this dress," she shot back. "He's *your* friend."

"I bet he gets pretty friendly with you when he sees that dress," Mac said.

Jessica hoped so. Not just because she had a major thing for Ben, but also because it would make convincing him to let her drive him home a lot easier.

"Unless she stays out here all night talking to us," Sam broke in. "And Blondie takes him home."

"Blondie?" Jess asked.

"One of the hot cowgirls who drove him over here," Dooley said.

"*One* of them?" Jessica repeated.

Dooley's grin grew. "The other one's a redhead."

Jessica pulled her purse up on her shoulder determinedly. "I'd better add a brunette to the mix."

There were no exotic dancers in the bar.

In fact, there were only two other females in the place besides Jessica, and they occupied the tall stools on either side of Ben. The dilapidated stage in one corner may at one time have had a pole with half-naked women wrapped around it, but those women were now undergoing hip replacements and playing Canasta at the nursing home. The hunch-backed, gray-haired bartender, who barely spared her a glance away from the tiny black-and-white TV he was watching, was older than the stage. And about as good-looking.

The smell, a combination of cigarette smoke, mildew and beer, was the most distinct characteristic of the bar. But it was only the first thing Jessica hated about the place.

The beautiful blonde and heavily made-up redhead with Ben were easily the next two things. The tall table in front of them was littered with beer mugs, bottles and shot glasses. The pool table nearby was surrounded by large, hygiene-deficient men, its perimeter covered with dollar bills and ashtrays with cigarette butts and still-smoking stubs.

Ben stood out in khaki pants and a black, knit shirt, while everyone else was dressed in worn denim and T-shirts with various tasteless slogans. But the pool cue he balanced against his knee and the half-full mug of beer he held fondly did give him something in common with the other patrons.

She watched as the biggest, sweatiest of the men crossed the space between the pool table and where Ben sat.

"That's the third time you lost. Pay up."

Ben passed the man a huge wad of bills with nothing more than a smile. The man chuckled as he quickly counted the money, then pocketed it. He called out, "That's two hundred bucks off of him so far. Who's up next?"

Jessica shook her head. Obviously Ben's skills were limited to the OR.

Her eyes narrowed when the blonde leaned in, pressing her breasts against Ben's bicep as she reached for the pretzel bowl at the edge of the table. Jealousy, worry, impatience and just the tiniest bit of doubt hit Jessica in a wave that stopped her feet.

She frowned. It was very possible that this whole thing was just another of her brother's bad ideas.

She wasn't worried about how she filled the dress out. That was one of the few things that hadn't changed in the past ten years. But push-up bras and high heels were only part of strutting in a bar. The other, bigger part was the attitude. Jessica was afraid that she'd lost the attitude somewhere in the midst of her crash-course in planning a funeral, attending parent-teacher conferences at age twenty and learning to pack a lunchbox, call the electric company and unclog the shower drain all at the same time.

Becoming an overnight orphan and mother to her two younger siblings had definitely taken a bit out of her strut.

Jessica scowled at Ben harder as he leaned in and said something near the redhead's ear, causing her to seductively toss her hair over her shoulder and laugh.

This was all Ben's fault.

The blonde leaned in again, brushed her fingers through his hair and pressed her lips against the side of his neck.

Quick, hot, irrational anger coursed through Jessica at the sight...and at Ben not pushing her away.

Ben was a doctor, a *surgeon* for heaven's sake. He saved lives. He was the best trauma surgeon in three states, probably in the entire Midwest. He was sharp, responsible, well-respected; practically a Boy Scout.

In spite of current evidence to the contrary, she thought grimly as she watched Ben throw back a shot and set the glass on the table with an audible *thunk*.

She wanted to stomp up to him, grab him by the ear and drag him out of here.

But if the direct physical approach would work with Ben, Sam wouldn't have needed to call her.

She headed for Ben, not bothering to pull her skirt down this time.

"Ben? Wow, it's great to see you!" Jessica slid in between him and the redhead, rose on tiptoe and kissed him on the cheek, inhaling the scent of him the way she'd been wanting to for almost six months. She flashed back to the surprising, full-on French kiss from earlier that day. She had wished ever since that she hadn't been quite so shocked. She'd barely had time to enjoy the kiss itself.

Ben met her eyes, no sign of surprise evident at all in his face or body language. Then, slowly, his eyes roamed from the top of her head, over her bare shoulders, lingered on her black-satin-hugged breasts, then continued past her waist and hips and down the length of her legs to the tips of her deep burgundy-painted toenails.

She ignored the tingly places—though it was hard to ignore pretty much her whole body—and went on with her charade. She gestured at the two girls he was sitting with. "I guess you're doing well in spite of the problem with the surgery." She smiled at the two other women and rounded the table to the only unoccupied stool, determined to make it clear she was here to stay. "I told him that he would eventually find a woman who wouldn't mind."

"Wouldn't mind what?" the blonde asked in exactly the

sweet voice that Jessica had guessed she would have.

The stool was directly across from Ben. Jess slid up, aware of his gaze on her. She kept her eyes on the blonde. "Oh, you know. That the implant didn't turn out."

The redhead frowned. "Implant?"

Jessica dropped her voice to an exaggerated whisper. "Penile."

"Penile?" the blonde repeated, frowning hard enough in confusion that Jessica was afraid she was going to hurt herself.

"As in penis," Jessica clarified before the girl's brain cramped. She turned to Ben. "You didn't tell them?"

Ben was watching the conversation as if he was an uninterested third party. He kept his arm along the back of the blonde's chair and his other hand wrapped around his beer mug. He met Jessica's eyes, one eyebrow going up.

The blonde looked at Ben. "What do you mean it didn't turn out?"

"Oh, it was awful," Jessica gushed. "They got the wrong size. Can you believe it? Too big. Then had to take it out. Try another one. Still too big. Then there was the infection."

The girl's eyes dropped to Ben's lap. "Oh," she said weakly.

"She knows a lot about your penis," the redhead said to Ben.

"She sure seems to," he agreed, looking directly at Jessica when he finally spoke. "Apparently, she's spent a lot of time thinking about it."

Jessica worked on not blushing, but definitely broke eye contact. Which she was sure entertained him.

"She your girlfriend or something?" The woman looked more curious than concerned by the possibility.

"No," Ben said, still looking at Jessica, the tiniest hint of a smile on one corner of his mouth. "I do believe Jessica is my chaperone."

The redhead looked confused while the blonde looked disappointed.

"Um, he can't...?" the blonde asked, looking at Jessica.

Jessica shook her head regretfully. "No. But he's very open to adopting, so don't worry, you can still have children."

"Children?" the blonde choked. She looked at Ben, then back at Jessica. "But we're not involved. I mean, I just met him.

I don't even know his last name."

"Oh." Jessica tried to look sheepish. "I'm sorry. I assumed that you were together."

"Uh, no." The blonde scooted away from Ben's arm.

Jessica tried not to smile. "You're single, then?"

The blonde nodded hurriedly. "Definitely single."

"Oh, then maybe you're the girls they were asking about," Jessica said thoughtfully.

Both women looked at her. "They?" the redhead asked.

"There are these four guys outside in a truck. They said they were waiting for a couple of girls they'd followed from some country bar."

"Do you know who they are?" The redhead straightened on her stool.

Jessica shrugged. "Some people outside were talking about them. I guess the guy in the backseat behind the driver is in the new Matt Damon movie that's shooting here." She was reaching, but remembered reading something in the paper about the star being in town for a few days this month.

The blonde perked up. "Who's he with?"

"All I know is that the driver is loaded. I mean, insane amounts of money." Jessica gave a dramatic eye roll. "Probably a producer or something. And the guy in the backseat with the icepack on his eye is a stuntman in the movie. He's supposedly *huge*—in all the good ways, if you know what I mean."

The girls definitely seemed to know what she meant.

"What about the fourth guy?" the redhead asked.

"The one in the front passenger seat is gay," Jessica said apologetically. One of the girls would have to go one on one. "But three out of four ain't bad, right?"

Jessica had never seen a quicker, or more contrived exit in her life.

Ben watched the girls as they left, then he drained the rest of his beer and met Jessica's eyes.

"Who's the gay guy?"

"Sam."

Ben's mouth curved up. "Sam doesn't deserve some action?"

Jessica settled back in her seat and crossed her arms. "Knowing Sam, he'll somehow convince the girls that they've always want to do a gay guy."

Ben smiled outright then and Jessica had to take a deep breath. He was so good-looking, and when he smiled she almost couldn't keep from climbing up on his lap and kissing him senseless.

"And of course you had to scare them off with a dysfunctional penis story," he said, as if they were talking about the weather.

She smiled and lifted a shoulder. "First thing that came to mind."

"My penis is the first thing that came to mind?"

To hide the hot, fast blush she felt stain her cheeks, she ducked her head to dig in the huge purse she'd carted in with her. "Don't forget the dysfunctional part," she muttered.

"Jessica," he said. He waited until she looked at him. Then said, "Let me take this opportunity to assure you that my penis is in no way dysfunctional."

She resisted the urge to look at the topic of conversation. She had no doubt that Ben's was functional in all of the ways penises were supposed to be. And yes, it was one of the first things that came to mind. So what? Why did that have to mean anything? It was a just body part. All men had them. She could have just as easily said something about his eyes.

Sure.

"Good news, Ben," she said, changing the subject and setting out her supplies.

On the table in front of Ben she put a bottle of water, two white capsules, four orange tablets, a banana, a bottle of Gatorade and a box of condoms.

She paused and looked at the box of condoms for a moment. So much for changing the subject.

"I guess we took care of the need for these." She picked the condoms up, prepared to drop them back into her purse.

"Oh, keep 'em close," Ben said.

Her head snapped up, but he sat casually, turning the empty beer mug slowly with one hand, one ankle crossed over the other knee, watching her as if he was testing her. Jessica decided to pretend she hadn't heard him. Or at least that she didn't know what he meant—or what she wanted him to mean. Or at least that she didn't care.

She dropped the box into her purse. "The good news is," she went on, twisting open the cap on the bottle of water. "I'm here to keep you from wrapping your car around a pole, getting a drunk driving citation, losing all your savings at a game..." she glanced over at the pool table, then back at Ben, "...that you obviously suck at, *and* from waking up in the morning with a sexually transmitted disease."

He didn't even blink.

"These are vitamin B tablets," she said, indicating the white tablets lying between them. "Especially good for hangovers." She'd done a lot of studying on the ways to reduce and treat hangovers and had tried most of them herself long before she'd even met Ben.

He didn't say anything.

She held out the bottle of water to go with the capsules he was ignoring. Water was the *key* to treating hangovers. She was sure Ben knew that.

He ignored the bottle.

She narrowed her eyes. "I assume that means you'll be very cooperative and pleasant since I'm doing you such a big favor."

Chapter Two

Ben couldn't believe that Sam had sent his sister. The bastard.

Just when Ben thought Sam Bradford was too laid back, too concerned with having a good time, too self-centered to notice one of his buddies lusting after his older sister, the jerk sent her into the bar dressed like she knew how to use all those delicious parts God had given her.

But Ben knew better. Jessica Bradford was a lot of things: well-respected, dependable, bossy, intelligent, compassionate, fiery and highly moraled. She was not, however, any of the things Ben wanted tonight. Like horny.

The real problem was that two months ago Jessica had bent over during a trauma in the ER, and he couldn't forget the glimpse of red lace he'd seen through the thin material of her pale pink scrub pants.

The petite woman the ER staff affectionately called "the little general" wore bright frickin' red thongs.

Sam was a manipulative SOB. No man could resist Jessica in this dress, least of all the guy who could get hard in the middle of a trauma looking at her in hospital scrubs. But Sam was also smart. He knew Ben wouldn't turn Jessica down, even when she was trying to do exactly what Sam and the guys had been failing at all night.

Jessica was smart, too, and seemed pretty smug right now. She sipped politely from the water bottle she'd brought and waited for Ben to respond.

The woman had brought him ibuprofen, a banana and Gatorade, for God's sake. She'd managed to lecture him without even using an impatient tone of voice. It didn't take too many minutes around Jessica in the ER to know she liked to have things her way.

She obviously thought she was here because it was the noble thing to do—saving him from himself or some self-righteous crap like that—and Jessica definitely struck him as the type that stepped up for noble causes.

Well, she was going to enjoy this one. He'd make sure of it.

He'd wanted her for a long time. Before tonight, he'd liked what he knew about her and wanted to know more, but he couldn't do anything about what he wanted to do *to* her. When he was at work he wasn't filing tax claims, or harvesting corn, or teaching algebra or asking if people wanted to Super Size things. He was saving lives. He simply couldn't—*wouldn't*—be distracted by a nice body and some sexy underwear when he was supposed to be putting *people* back together.

Of course, that was before he quit putting people back together a few hours ago.

Now he could pretty much do whatever the hell he wanted.

He came off his stool and rounded the table. He grasped the edges of Jessica's seat in both hands and turned her to face him, then moved in until his belt buckle touched her knee. "So, what do you want in exchange for this huge favor you're doing for me?"

She didn't pull back or even stiffen in response to his sudden nearness, and he was inordinately pleased, but she did look mildly surprised. He could see her lips fall open slightly as she pulled in a long breath.

He'd never dared test if the chemistry he felt was reciprocal. He and Jessica were colleagues in a stressful environment that required concentration, quick thinking and skills that were practically reflexes. The last thing he needed was the distraction of trying to get a bullet away from a spinal cord or patching a bleed in a major artery while his girlfriend stood across the table from him fuming about their latest argument.

"I get the satisfaction of knowing that you're safely home," Jessica finally said.

They needed to be very clear on a few important points. "Is Sam paying you?"

She looked offended by the suggestion. "Of course not."

"Do you feel sorry for me, Jessica?"

She snorted. Actually snorted. "No, Ben. I do not feel sorry for you."

He moved closer, a centimeter at best, but enough to fill more of the air around him with her scent and body heat. Her eyes widened a fraction and if he hadn't been watching for it—or for any reaction at all—he would have missed it.

"Are you worried about me?"

She wet her lips before answering and Ben thought about just kissing her and finding out if her response to him that morning had been a product of shock or true attraction.

"Sam's worried about you," she said.

Her voice sounded breathy, if he wasn't mistaken. He grinned and crowded closer, propping an elbow on the table beside her hand. Still she didn't move. But her breathing got faster.

"I don't give a damn how Sam feels." He finally gave in to the desire and opportunity to touch her. He lifted his hand and drew the pad of his thumb along her lower lip. "But I'd love to know how *you* feel."

Up against him. Naked. On a bed.

Or a pool table, he thought, aware of the closest horizontal surface.

Jessica's lips fell open under his touch and Ben felt the jolt of satisfaction go through him. He thought it was noteworthy that the conservative, always-in-charge, always-knew-what-she-was-doing ER nurse—who always smelled like cotton candy—was suddenly looking flustered. He wondered if it was her response to him that surprised her or his response to her.

It was very likely that she'd had no idea that he was sexually aware of her before this. He was good at a lot of things, and focusing on his job, in spite of distractions like beeping monitors, distraught family members and sexy co-workers, was one of them.

In truth, he'd been attracted since day one. He'd watched Jessica run the ER staff like a drill sergeant, do the dirtiest, hardest jobs herself, then later cry with the mother of a patient after he delivered the news that the woman's son would live.

But then there was the day he'd seen her bend over to get more towels. He'd seen the cherry red edge of her thong and just like that, in the midst of trying to clamp off a torn pyloric valve, he'd gotten hard.

For several seconds all he could do was wonder how many

other colors she had in her underwear drawer.

It was those several seconds that concerned him. Several seconds in the ER could be life or death.

Now, however, there was no table—or critical patient— between them. No hospital rules. No bad consequences to him touching her the way he'd been aching to for six months.

He leaned in. "How *do* you feel?"

"I feel like..." She swallowed. "I feel like helping you."

"Well," he drawled, his thumb trailing off her lip to her jaw. "Let me give you a short list of ways you can help me tonight."

She swallowed again, harder this time. "Is getting you some good carbohydrates and strong black coffee on that list?" she asked.

Her smile made him want to pull her up against him and show her number one on that list right here and now.

"Maybe with breakfast."

He saw in her eyes that she knew exactly what he was talking about.

"Ben, I came to drive you home. Period." She sighed. "I'm just the taxi service."

He took her hips in his hands and pulled her off the stool and up against him. Then he turned her until her shoulder blades pressed against the table, making sure she felt his erection...and making sure he felt *her*.

"If you're just the taxi service, why did you wear this dress?"

"Sam..." She had to stop and clear her throat. "Sam thought it would get your attention."

His hand caressed her hip. "Sam is a very good friend."

Ben leaned in to kiss her, intending to take her mouth and not let her up for air until she was ready to give him everything—at least twice. It was time he did something about this crazy obsession with Jessica.

He saw Jessica's eyes close, her deep intake of air, but missed seeing her hands come up to his chest. He felt the pressure of her pushing against him, though.

"Ben."

He pulled back.

"How about you sober up first, and then we'll talk?" Jessica asked.

"I don't want to talk."

She opened her eyes and looked...hesitant. Which was a weird look for Jessica. Ben had never seen her anything but confident and steady. It was also clear that she wasn't used to *feeling* hesitant.

"I want to get naked. With you. Right now."

"In total silence?" she asked, her smile a bit wobbly.

"I'll let you talk dirty," he said with a slow grin.

She crossed her arms between them, difficult as it was in the nearly non-existent space. "I am not talking dirty to you, Dr. Torres."

She sounded convinced...almost.

"If you want to stick to moans and groans of pleasure, I'm fine with that."

She pulled in a long breath. "You're drunk."

He leaned back to look at her. "Maybe."

"That's why you're acting like this."

"Like I want to take you to bed?" He chuckled softly and pressed closer. "I can honestly tell you that the beer has nothing to do with this."

She narrowed her eyes. "Little hard to believe."

"Why?"

"Gambling, fighting with your best friends..."

He felt the lecture coming on. He'd been chewed out today by his boss and his friends. He was not going to listen to it from her too. All he wanted to hear from Miss Jessica was her begging him to make her come.

Ben moved in quickly, captured her chin in his hand, tipped her face up and covered her mouth with his.

The kiss was hot and hard and *so* sweet.

Jessica seemed to melt instantly. She pressed closer, her hands sliding up to his shoulders and then behind his head. Ben increased the pressure, slanting his head slightly, encouraging her to open her lips and let him truly taste her.

She was his new favorite flavor. He lessened the pressure, wanting to savor her, but she pressed closer, moaning in protest, digging her fingers into his hair.

Well, okay. If she insisted.

He bent his knees, pulled her up against him and wrapped his arms around her, one hand in the middle of her back, the

31

other cupping her left buttock. He pressed her against his throbbing shaft and ground into her, eliciting another moan, though this one was hardly one of protest.

The heat continued to build and Ben felt frustration building with it. Frustration with the layers of clothing between them, frustration with the lack of good leverage against the table, frustration with the feeling that kissing Jessica was the best thing he'd felt in practically forever, and very possibly the stupidest thing he'd ever done. This was only kissing and he never wanted to stop. How would making love to her be?

Suddenly, Jessica pulled back, sucked air into her lungs in a large gulp and withdrew her hands like he was a hot stove.

"We have to stop."

Ben leaned in and kissed her neck just behind her ear, and felt a tremble go through her. She definitely didn't push him away.

"You taste even better than I imagined," he said in her ear.

She jerked in surprise. "You've imagined it?"

"Often and in great detail."

She looked stunned. "But you never even flirted…"

"Generally, when we're together, there are people losing blood from critical places. When would I have flirted?"

She frowned and nodded. "I know. But you never asked me out. I never caught you looking at me…" she frowned deeper, "at all. Not to mention looking at me unprofessionally."

"You want men to look at you unprofessionally?"

"No. Just you." It was instantly clear that she regretted letting that slip.

He grinned. Now they were getting somewhere. "Oh, I promise you that I've been looking. And imagining. Why don't you let me show you all the things I've come up with?" He rubbed his palm in a firm circle on her hip.

She shook her head. "I can't do this."

Oh, yes she could. And she wanted to. *That* he would put a whole bundle of money down on.

"Why not?"

"You've had an…unusual day. You're not yourself."

He felt more like himself than he had in a long time. "How do you figure that?"

She looked at him as if she was questioning if he had a

head injury along with alcohol intoxication. She pushed against him once more and he finally released her enough for her to settle her full weight back on her own feet. He kept a hand on her hip, though, and didn't step back.

She tucked a strand of hair that had escaped her twist behind her ear and pulled the hem of her dress down. It didn't go down very far. This dress wasn't made to cover things.

"Let's see..." she said, her tone of voice suddenly conservative. "You punched a patient in the face and got suspended from the hospital. You hit one of your best friends and told the others to fuck off. And now you're attempting to seduce a co-worker that you've barely noticed before now. Not to mention that your blood alcohol level is well above the legal limit. I'd say it's a pretty safe assessment that you're not yourself tonight. So, thank you for the offer, but I'm going to decline getting naked with you."

The sheer prissiness of her voice was enough to amuse him. The haughty tilt to her chin, her arms crossed over her stomach, the rigidity in her spine and the way she looked like a woman who didn't like to get her hair messed up made him want to mess it up good.

He also sensed her disappointment, not so much in how he was acting, but in the fact that she couldn't bring herself to go ahead with the things she wanted. He didn't think the things she wanted were a completely new concept to her. This felt more like passion that had been simmering; sizzling its way down a long fuse rather than a sudden, out of control, who-would-have-guessed kind of lust.

Jessica was responsible, dependable, steady, self-controlled...all of those good, conservative adjectives. Ben knew them well. He'd lived them his whole life.

"At least admit you want to go home with me."

She sighed. "Fine. I do. I have a little thing for you. But I guess I pictured a first date differently from this." Her hand gesture encompassed the bar, the five beefy guys playing pool, the geriatric bartender and the floor that hadn't seen a soap bubble in a long, long time.

Ben smiled. Jessica was stuck. She had to take him home. She couldn't leave because she truly believed he needed her and she couldn't throw him over her shoulder and forcibly take him out of the bar.

"If I'm not going to get any, that leaves only two other things I'm interested in," he said.

"Which are?" she asked.

"Liquor and pool." He stepped back from her. "Who's in?" he asked the mediocre players he'd been losing game after game to all night.

Not that Ben cared. He'd come here to blow off some steam and make the night go faster, without having to hang out with the friends who wanted to know what was wrong, how he was, what he was going to do and on and on.

Ben didn't want to talk about it. He didn't want to explain himself to anyone. And he shouldn't have to. He was tired of medicine, tired of dedicating more time and energy toward people's health and well-being than they did themselves, tired of the responsibility and the fact that no matter what he did, illness, injury and death could never be stopped. What was the point?

He tried to relax his grip on the triangle as he positioned it to rack the balls for the next game. It didn't matter now. He'd quit. Walked out. Gotten suspended. It was all over.

"*I'm* in."

Ben turned to see Jessica standing with her shoes off, holding a pool cue.

"Do you know how?" Ben asked, smiling at the picture she presented. This wasn't the type of place he'd ever imaged her in, but she seemed to be adjusting...almost getting comfortable. Interesting. Very interesting.

"As bad as you suck, I'm not sure it matters if I know how," she said. "But yeah, I've played."

"By all means," Ben said, gesturing at the table. "Show me what you've got."

"I think we need to establish what the stakes are." Jessica rubbed the little blue square of chalk over the end of her stick as she watched him.

He shrugged. "I've only got about fifty bucks left."

Jessica moved into position to break. She leaned over the end of the table, her skirt riding up on the backs of her thighs, positioned the cue between her first two right-handed fingers and lined up her shot.

And he might let her win if it kept her standing like that.

"If I win, you let me take you home, finally." She looked at him over her shoulder and smiled knowingly when she caught him studying her posterior assets.

"Okay." This pool game suddenly seemed like the best idea he'd had in a long time.

Jessica looked smug as she turned back to line up her shot again.

"Don't you want to know what I want if I win?" Ben asked, blatantly taking in the view.

"Sure. What do you want?"

"The next forty-eight hours with you."

She stared at him over her shoulder, then straightened and faced him. "What?"

"If I win, you spend the next forty-eight hours with me."

"Just like that?"

He shrugged. "Yeah. You drive me home and then you stay."

"I've...um. I've got...stuff to do."

"Call in sick."

She didn't hesitate. "I'm not sick."

Ben shook his head. "And you won't lie about something like that, right? It would be irresponsible."

Jessica raised her eyebrows. "Of course it would be."

Ben sighed. It was typical that the first woman he wanted to sleep with in far too long to remember was a good girl.

Ben rested a hip against the pool table and regarded Jessica. "What happens when you want to spend the whole day in bed?"

That annoying little flippy-thing happened in Jessica's stomach again. It had been a long time since she'd wanted to stay in bed for the reasons Ben was implying. But, yeah, he had a point. If that happened, what would she do?

She cleared her throat. "I could put the stuff off until later, I guess."

"I want you to spend the *whole* day with me," Ben said seriously. "Two days, actually. Forty-eight hours." Then he shrugged. "I can probably find someone else that would be interested though. Since you're too busy."

Jessica frowned. Come to think of it, she did feel ill when she thought of Ben with any other woman.

"Fine. My stuff can wait."

Ben straightened and looked at her for a moment before he asked, "But you won't lie about being sick, right?"

"I'm not sick," she repeated. "But I'll take care of it."

"I'm sure you will," he said, almost to himself. But before she could ask him what he meant he said, "So, it's an enthusiastic yes?"

"It's a reluctant *fine*."

He grinned. "Good enough."

Jessica broke the triangle of balls apart with a resounding *clack*...and went on to sink five of her seven balls before even pausing to survey the table.

Ben was staring at the pocket into which yet another striped ball had fallen when she turned to smile at him smugly. It was worth all the irritation to see that look on his face.

She walked around the edge of the table to position her next shot. As she pulled her cue back she was confident that she would only need one more shot after this. But as she started her forward motion, Ben leaned over.

"Look at this picture," he said softly. "A long stick, hard balls, you bent over the table..."

She missed.

Jessica stared at the ball that had bounced off the edge of the table and rolled back toward her. Damn. That should have been an easy shot.

Ben laughed and came around the corner of the table. He nudged her aside with his hip against hers.

"Okay, big shot. Let's see if you can win without me letting you." She slid over only enough to let him line up his shot and crossed her arms.

He lined up the shot and Jessica watched and heard the balls smack together, then the dull thud of them falling into the pockets: two balls in the same shot, in two corner pockets on the opposite end of the table. It was a brilliant shot. The shot of someone who had played a lot. Not the shot of someone who had been losing money at the game. Not the shot of someone who had been drinking heavily.

He continued shooting until no solid balls were left on the green surface.

"Game over," Ben announced as the eight ball was still

rolling down the chute. He tossed his pool cue onto the table and lifted the beer mug.

She was still staring at the table.

"Let's go." Ben took her hand and started toward the door without a word to any of the people he'd spent the better part of his time, and wallet, on.

"You could have done that all along, couldn't you?" she asked, grabbing her purse off the sticky tabletop as they passed and then tripping along behind him.

He glanced back at the table. "Yeah, probably."

"Why didn't you? With those guys? Why drop all that money?" she asked as he pulled her out the door and into the parking lot.

He shrugged. "No motivation to win."

Jessica suddenly realized that she might have her hands full with Ben Torres. Still stunned over how he'd finished the pool game just as she'd been completely convinced he could barely walk a straight line, Jessica stopped at her car door and inserted the key to unlock it. She might have her hands *too* full with him, she amended. And not in a good way.

"Jessica."

She turned and he immediately pressed in close, backing her up against the car.

He dipped his head, his lips moving toward hers and Jessica thought her heart would stop. She leaned closer, her lips parted and she felt his breath on her lips.

And the smell of beer hit her.

She pulled back, as difficult as it was up against the car. She felt hot all over; at the same time feeling the sharp stab of disappointment that this moment wasn't exactly as she'd pictured it. She fought the urge to sigh as she stared into those brown eyes and wanted desperately to let it all happen.

It would be good. And what was the harm? One night with a great guy. She deserved that, didn't she?

It was just one night, anyway. A few hours. It wasn't like she would be completely reverting back to everything she'd managed to escape. She wouldn't be smoking and drinking and partying all night. It wasn't illegal or dangerous. She wouldn't wake up with any piercings or tattoos she couldn't account for. They'd use a condom and everything would be okay. She could get right back on track in the morning.

At the latest tomorrow afternoon.

For sure by evening.

Ben leaned in and kissed her neck, behind her ear and Jessica's knees went weak. She felt the clasp in her hair release and the twist tumble free. Ben tossed the clip on top of the car's roof before his fingers threaded through her hair and tipped her head to the side. His lips followed the curve to her collarbone and back up to her ear.

"I've wanted you for so long," Ben said gruffly, running his hand through her hair from her scalp to her shoulder blades over and over.

"You never..." She trailed off, knowing, of course, why he hadn't said anything or acted on it.

"We worked together."

She bit her bottom lip and nodded her understanding.

He dipped his head. "But now we don't have to worry about that."

Oh, yeah, the little detail of his suspension. Which reminded her of the little detail of him acting completely out of character tonight. And the fact that if she hadn't shown up tonight he would be out here pressing a blonde or a redhead or both up against a car.

She'd wanted Ben since she'd worked that first trauma with him six months ago. He'd been bold, confident and skilled in the ER, but he'd really done it to her when she'd gone with him to talk with the victim's family afterward. He'd been straightforward but compassionate, patiently answering questions, admitting that he couldn't work miracles, but assuring them that he'd do all he could. There was something about the way he met their eyes and the body language he used, or the tone of voice, or all of the above, that calmed them and gave them the trust that they needed to let Ben do what their son needed him to do.

That was the Ben she wanted. The sexy, charming hero of the ER. Not this trouble-making playboy.

"Ben, when I get you home it will be to *sleep* only."

"Can I at least kiss you one more time?" His voice was low and husky.

Jess had never wanted anything more in her life.

"Can you pass a breathalyzer test?" she asked.

He thought about it for a second. Then shook his head. "No."

"There's your answer."

He watched her closely for a moment and she felt that if he kept staring at her like that he'd eventually be able to read her thoughts.

"Do you always do the right thing?"

Oh, boy. Always? As in every minute of her life?

She stood up straighter. "I try to." Which was completely true. In the past several years, she had expended more energy on doing the right thing than on anything else.

"Doesn't that get exhausting?" he asked.

In that moment he seemed as sober as she'd ever seen him.

"You have no idea." She sighed.

"Do you ever have any fun?" He seemed concerned.

She frowned at him. "Of course."

He tipped his head to one side. "Are you sure?" he asked, clearly not believing her at all.

He had no idea.

She lifted her chin. "Perhaps your idea and my idea of fun are different."

He chuckled then. "Maybe. But I don't think so." He trailed a finger down her arm from shoulder to wrist. "At least, not in *every* respect."

She couldn't suppress the shiver of delight his touch created. "You can be sure that I prefer fun I'm going to remember in the morning."

He continued smiling at her. "You'll remember it tomorrow. And for the rest of your life."

Oh, the confidence. The sexiness.

She narrowed her eyes at him. "I meant *you*."

He didn't reply right away, but watched her as if trying to decide the best way to convince her of something. Then he asked, "What's the right thing to do right now?"

"To ask you to get in the car so I can take you home." Not that it was exactly what she wanted to do, but it was the *right* thing.

He nodded slowly. "Okay."

She looked at him in surprise. "So, you do know how to

take advice."

He leaned in until their eyes were level. "I do want a few things from you, Jessica, but advice is not one of them." He clamped her hair clip onto the strap of her purse, then turned and strode around the front of the car and got into the passenger's side without another argument or comment.

Jessica pulled in a long breath before getting behind the wheel. She wasn't sure how she was going to survive the next several hours with Ben. She was either going to end up vowing to never speak to him again, or seducing him. Or both.

Thankfully, Ben didn't seem inclined to converse on the drive. He rested his head against the seat and closed his eyes.

Jessica, on the other hand, felt like she'd just finished a marathon.

Her heart rate and the spinning thoughts had started slowing when she saw movement on the right hand side of the road a few yards ahead. She slowed and peered into the darkness. As they approached she could tell it was a man. He was waving his arms furiously, trying to get their attention.

"Ben? Are you awake?" she asked as she checked the mirror. There was no one behind them.

"Mmm-hmm."

She glanced at Ben. He didn't look very awake.

"Ben? There's somebody up there, flagging us down."

Their headlights arched over the back of the man's compact car, him and...

"Ben!" Jessica hit the brake and threw the car into park. "Call 9-1-1!"

Ben sat upright quickly and fumbled in his pocket for his cell phone. "What's going on?"

"There's a woman beside the road."

Jessica was out of the car and slamming the door by the time she finished the sentence.

The woman lay on her right side, one leg bent awkwardly underneath her. She was unconscious, the left side of her face covered in blood.

Jessica knelt beside her.

"What happened?" she asked the man.

"I hit her," he said.

His voice wobbled and Jess looked up. His face was pale in the illumination of the headlights and Jess realized that if he went into shock she would have two patients on her hands.

"Sir, you have to calm down. And sit down," she said in her most forceful voice. If he fainted and fell on the pavement he could get hurt. She didn't need two patients.

"I didn't see her... I didn't..."

"Sir!" Jessica said loudly. "Sit down!"

"Is she..."

"I'm a nurse," Jessica told him as she felt for the woman's pulse. "I'm going to help her. *You* have to sit down."

She couldn't feel a beat at the woman's wrist. Jess bit her bottom lip and put her ear next to the woman's mouth. She didn't dare move her, not knowing her status, but she had to determine if the victim was breathing.

The man slumped to the grass at the side of the road and immediately started sobbing. "She was jogging, or something. I didn't see her."

"They're on their way," Ben said, joining Jessica beside the woman. "What do we have?"

Jess didn't answer, holding her breath as she tried to determine if the woman breathed. She placed a hand on the woman's chest, trying to feel for the rise and fall of her chest, as it was far too dark to make out something so subtle. Jess felt her adrenaline pump through her veins as she realized the woman wasn't breathing.

"How long ago did it happen?" Jess asked the man sharply.

He looked up at her blurry-eyed and didn't answer.

"When?" she shouted at him.

"A few minutes ago. Right before you came along," he choked out. "Just now."

"I'll steady her neck," Jessica said to Ben. "You roll her." She had to start CPR.

Jess steadied the woman neck by sandwiching her head between her forearms. It was an awkward position, but she couldn't leave the woman lying there with no pulse or oxygen intake.

Ben log-rolled her easily and Jessica quickly got into position. In the distance she heard a siren.

"I need light," she said, trying to see what was going on with the woman's face, particularly her mouth. Hopefully there were no injuries that would prevent air exchange during CPR. "There's a flashlight in the glove compartment."

Mere seconds later Ben knelt beside her again with the large flashlight.

He shone the light on the woman's face, knowing what Jessica needed without her instruction.

The left side of the woman's face was bloody, a gash in her temple was oozing and several abrasions showed from ear to chin. There were tiny pieces of gravel in the wounds as if she'd scraped her face along the side of the road. The outside of her mouth was clear.

Jessica parted the woman's lips and Ben angled the light into her mouth. It also looked clear.

She bent to breathe into the woman's mouth, then began chest compressions. She was in the middle of the cycle when they heard the sound of something hitting the ground.

She kept count as she looked over her shoulder. The man had crumpled.

"You take care of him, I've got this," Ben said, moving in next to her, ready to take over at the next cycle.

Jessica paused and breathed, then looked up at Ben sharply. "No. I'm fine."

The sirens grew nearer and Jessica recognized the sound as a police car.

"Jessica, I'll help." Ben insisted, positioning his hands on the woman's chest next to Jessica's.

"No!" She pushed against him with her shoulder, but had to immediately return to the compressions.

"Why not?"

She paused and gave the woman two breaths.

"You've been drinking all night!"

"I'm fine."

She finished the third cycle of compressions and bent to breathe again and his hands positioned where hers had been. She delivered the breaths, then tried to put her hands back on the woman's chest. "No, Ben." She fought the panic. She couldn't trust him now. This woman's life was at stake and he was intoxicated.

"For God's sake..."

She shoved against him. "No!" she shouted.

He removed his hands and sat back on his heels. She didn't look at him. Couldn't look at him. She didn't want it to be this way. But this woman's life was her responsibility.

Ben went over to the man and checked on him. He was, evidently, breathing because Ben returned to her side. But he said nothing. Just sat there, a heavy presence. It was good that these tasks were routine for her.

The police car arrived a few minutes later, siren blaring, lights flashing.

"What's going on?"

Two police officers approached with flashlights as Jessica finished another cycle. Ben said nothing and the silence from him seemed louder than anything he could have shouted.

"I'm a nurse," Jess said. "We came upon the accident a few minutes ago. Pedestrian hit by the truck. No pulse, no breathing. CPR times four minutes."

"What's with the guy?"

"Truck driver," Jess answered. "Fainted about a minute ago." She glanced in Ben's direction. "His vitals are strong." She assumed Ben would correct her if it wasn't true.

"You okay there?" one of the cops asked her.

She heard Ben shift behind her, but didn't look at him. She delivered two breaths, then answered, "Yes."

One officer moved toward the man and knelt to pull the guy's wallet from his back pocket, while the other went to examine the truck.

The ambulance arrived a minute later, the crew bailing out immediately.

Derek Williams was the first to the victim.

"Jess?" Her brother's friend was clearly shocked to see her. He dropped his gear. "Ben?"

"Hi, Derek." Jessica continued the compressions as Ben got to his feet.

"What's the story?" Derek asked Ben. In spite of his surprise, and interest, in seeing Jessica and Ben together, it was business first.

"You'll have to ask Jessica."

Derek looked at Jessica as she raised her head from the

victim. The woman still wasn't breathing.

Jessica gave him the scenario, after gratefully surrendering the CPR to one of Derek's crew members, Mike.

"Lookin' good, Jess," Mike commented as he took over.

"Thanks." She got to her feet and rolled her neck.

"What's up with the driver?" Derek asked Ben, obviously assuming they had each taken a victim.

"He's fine," Ben said shortly. "Received no treatment."

"Any orders, Doc?" Derek asked, gesturing toward the woman.

"Jess?" Ben asked, looking at her.

She glared at him. "Ben's been drinking. I'm not sure he's in a position to give orders about medical treatment."

Derek's eyebrows nearly disappeared under his hairline and his eyes were wide with surprise.

"Oookay," he said slowly.

"You weren't involved...in the accident, I mean?" one of the police officers asked as he approached.

"No. I was driving," Jess said.

"You were on your way...?" the cop asked.

"To his place."

Derek said nothing, but looked at them each thoughtfully. That's when he seemed to notice his friend's sister fully.

"Nice...dress."

She sighed. Derek was just one more person who she'd only known in the past ten years, and who couldn't imagine the Jessica Bradford he knew owning or wearing something like this. She was sure Derek was going to have all kinds of questions and comments for Sam later. "Thanks. Can we go?"

"Yeah, we've got it," Derek answered.

They were already hoisting the woman into the back of the ambulance on a stretcher.

"Let me know how she turns out."

"Sure thing."

Ben and Jessica each gave statements to the police, then were free to go.

They went back to Jessica's car and she started to climb in. She was dreading the drive now. Ben was obviously angry with her. But dammit...

She paused with one foot in the car, one still on the ground and pointed a finger at him over the top of the car. "You were in no condition to treat that woman and you know it!"

Ben didn't seem surprised by her outburst. "I'm a physician," he said coolly.

"Who had too much to drink." She pulled her foot from the car and put it securely on the ground.

He stared at her. "I've *operated* after thirty-two hours with no sleep, with a head cold, and a sore thumb. CPR is like reciting the ABCs for me; I can do it while juggling and balancing on one leg."

She was shaking her head by the time he finished. "No. That was all that was keeping that woman alive, Ben. The second I pulled over on the side of the road, she was my responsibility. Believe me, I would have *loved* to have your help, but you could have screwed it all up. Thank God one of us was sober."

Ben stared at her. "Why are you so pissed off?"

"Because part of being an emergency professional is knowing when you're not up to it," she snapped.

"Why are you so pissed off about this whole night? You've acted..." He frowned and leaned his forearms onto the top of the car, watching her carefully. "You've acted disappointed, all night. Like my mother used to when I stayed out past curfew or cussed in front of my great aunt."

Jessica crossed her arms and fought to keep her expression composed. He'd hit it right on the head. She was disappointed in him. Not just in how he'd been acting, but in the fact that she couldn't depend on him in a situation so like the ones that had put him on her pedestal in the first place.

"You certainly didn't act like a brilliant young professional who saves lives for a living tonight, did you?"

"You're talking about my *job*. Not who I am twenty-four hours a day."

She looked at a spot over his right shoulder. She didn't understand that. Being a physician, the sacrifice and dedication that took, was a part of him. Maybe Ben wasn't who she thought he was.

"Your job is pretty much full-time, all the time, for you though, isn't it?"

She still didn't look at him. "So?"

He sighed. "So, I want a break once in a while. Once in a while I want to let loose, get drunk and not worry about it. What's wrong with that?"

"You never know when someone might need you," she retorted, gesturing toward the spot where the woman had lain just minutes before.

"Exactly!" he said, somewhat triumphantly. "I *don't* want to be *needed* all the damn time."

She stared at him. What was going on with him? This didn't sound like the man she thought she knew.

She frowned at him. "You don't mean that."

"The hell I don't," he shot back.

"Well." She wasn't sure what to say to him. She didn't know what was going on tonight, but tomorrow would be different. It would be better in sober daylight after a good night's sleep.

"You're obviously still drunk." She slid behind the wheel and slammed her car door shut. By the time Ben joined her in the car, she had the engine running and the radio loud enough that talking was impossible.

Twenty minutes later, Jessica pulled up in front of Ben's apartment building. She hadn't asked him for directions. Sam also lived in the complex and had pointed Ben's place out to her once when she was dropping him off.

She and Ben hadn't spoken again. She was both mourning and celebrating that the evening was almost over.

She'd had high expectations for the night with Ben. With the flirting and innuendos it had felt almost like a date at some points inside the bar. But the celebration was in knowing that as of tomorrow Ben would be back to his normal self and she could return to her state of infatuation. Granted, the crush would return to being from afar but better that than...disappointed.

She kept the car running in the parking spot.

"Do you have your key?" she asked.

Ben pulled it from his front pocket and jingled it for her. "Of course." He paused, then asked, "Have you ever forgotten your key to anything?"

What a weird question. "Sure." She shrugged. "But I have

spares for everything."

"Spares," Ben repeated. "As in more than one?"

She gave him a puzzled frown. "Two."

"For each thing?"

"Yes."

He stared at her.

"*What?*" she exclaimed.

"Have you ever had to use your spares?"

Jessica thought about that. "I don't think so."

Ben shook his head with a smile, but didn't comment.

So, he thought she was...fastidious. It was nothing she hadn't heard before. Still, she wondered how Ben felt about it. Did he honestly like wild and free or was that the beer talking?

Irritated for some reason she couldn't fully explain, she asked, "Do you remember which apartment number is yours?"

"There're lots of pretty girls in this building that would let me in if I get lost."

She was absolutely certain he was right.

"Then I won't worry about you." She knew she sounded huffy.

He had one leg swung out of the open car door, but turned back. "You're coming in, right?"

Surprised, she shook her head. "No."

He brought his leg back into the car. "Forty-eight hours. You promised."

"You still want me to do...that?"

"How else am I going to prove to you that I'm a good guy in spite of the beer?"

Oh, she wanted to stay. "I don't know if I should..."

"Jess, you always do the right thing. The right thing to do is keep your word. You can't go back on a promise. Can you?"

She did know he was teasing her. It was just an excuse to get her to do what he wanted her to do.

But it was a pretty good excuse.

"Okay." She shut off the car and reached in the backseat for her duffle bag.

Ben was watching her curiously when she slammed the door shut.

"You keep a bag in your car in case guys ask you back to

their places?"

"I had planned to go to the gym after work but opted for a mound of ice cream instead."

Her tendency to eat instead of exercise when stressed had turned out to be fortunate. Not a big motivation to kick up her workouts to five days a week, but at least she had a change of clothes and all the shower supplies she would need. She didn't wear much makeup anyway. Besides, Ben had seen her at work, covered in blood and mud...and worse. And he'd seen her tonight. She hoped the dress, makeup and hair she'd put on for that evening would linger in his memory for at least a few days.

Ben took the bag from her without another comment and started toward the building.

"Jessica?" Ben asked as they climbed the steps to the front door.

"Yeah?" She was half holding her breath as she followed him. She was going to be spending the night in Ben's apartment. Not exactly the way the scenario had played out in her imagination, but still...

"Have you ever gone home with a guy from a bar?"

She froze mid-step. His hand was on the handle but he didn't move to open it.

"Does it matter?" she asked, hoping her voice sounded funny only to her.

"You mean is there anything you can say that would make me *not* want you to come inside?" He smiled without waiting for an answer. "No way."

How he managed to make her melt each time he looked at her that way, she didn't know. But it happened again.

She shrugged. If she lied to him and the truth came out later, would it ruin something that might start tonight? But if she told the truth, would it ruin something before it even had a chance to start? He said there wasn't anything that she could say that would make him not want her here. She decided to test him.

"Yes, I have gone home with a guy from a bar before."

He leaned in and looked at her closely. "I'm not talking about being the designated driver."

She wrinkled her nose at him, hiding the fact that she was relieved his assumption about her wholesomeness was going to save her from a full confession. "You didn't specify the reason."

He laughed and pulled open the door, ushering her in. It looked like all the time and effort she'd put into portraying herself as a principled, conservative prude might have paid off. Not only did Ben believe the best of her morals—for now—but the idea of tempting her to the dark side seemed appealing to him.

"Hi, Jerry," he greeted the doorman.

"Hey, Dr. T," the older black man greeted.

At this time of night, the elevator was not in high demand, so the ride up to the fifth floor only took a few minutes. Ben opened the door to his apartment and flipped on a light before stepping back to let her precede him.

"I need to get some aspirin," he said. "Make yourself at home."

He headed down the hallway, toward what she assumed to be the bedroom or bathroom.

She turned into the living area and surveyed the room with surprise.

Ben's apartment was different than she'd expected. She'd tried to picture it before, but hadn't known Ben well enough to truly imagine what environment he would create at home. But she'd pictured expensive taste for some reason. Probably because he was a doctor and could afford it. She'd also pictured a big-screen TV, a Nintendo and a small beer fridge in the living room, but that was likely because Ben was a friend of her brother's.

Interestingly, Ben's apartment had a relative lack of...well...stuff. He had one large sofa, a stereo system that looked like he bought it in college and a coffee table that could have easily been a hand-me-down from his mother or a garage sale. It held a huge stack of *Newsweek* magazines and medical journals.

In the eating area there was nothing. Not a table, not a chair, not even a coaster. The kitchen was similar. She assumed there were dishes in the cupboards but there were no small appliances, not a cutting board, not a dishtowel.

The only thing that even remotely decorated the apartment was a collection of art pieces and masks on the largest living room wall.

She'd seen similar displays at museums but never in a

person's apartment.

"You can have my bed."

She whirled to find Ben standing in the arched doorway into the living room.

"What did you say?"

"You can have my bed. I have two bedrooms, but only one bed."

Jessica's heartbeat sped up just thinking about sleeping in Ben's bed. Imagine what would happen to her vitals if he was going to be in there with her.

Wait a minute...

"Where are you going to sleep?"

He raised an eyebrow. "Well..."

"Ben," she said warningly.

He grinned. "The couch. It pulls out into a bed."

So, she'd be alone. In Ben's bedroom. In his bed. Where he slept. Maybe naked. Surrounded by his stuff, his scent...

"I'll take the couch," she said quickly.

"No way. You are not sleeping on the couch."

"You might...need to get to the bathroom quickly in the night." She could *not* sleep in Ben's bed. For one thing, there was no way she would be able to *sleep.*

"Jessica, I am *not* hungover. I'm not going to have to run to the bathroom."

"Still, I would prefer the couch," she said firmly.

He pulled himself up to his full height and looked offended. And determined. "Women who sleep in my apartment, sleep in my *bed.* Unless we're related. Which you and I are not. You, of all people, will be sleeping in my bed."

She didn't ask, or let herself wonder, what the *of all people* meant. "Ben, I—"

"Then again, I probably should sleep in the bed. With you. What if I need you in the middle of the night?"

That stopped her. Having Ben talk about needing her at all, but especially in the middle of the night, brought all kinds of fun things to mind.

Then she frowned. Maybe he was talking about all of the not-so-pleasant possible side effects of the alcohol in his system. He could have trouble breathing, his heartbeat could become erratic, he could even have seizures. Sure, *that* thought was what she needed to ensure she wouldn't get any sleep at all.

"You could..."

His low chuckle brought her eyes to his face and she realized by the look in his eyes that he was *not* referring to needing her to hold his head while he threw up in the toilet.

"Ben, I am *not* having sex with you tonight!" Unless he kept asking. And kept looking at her like that.

"So you keep saying," he said as he headed for the kitchen. "You hungry?"

"No. I'm fine." She turned back to look at the art again. "Where did you get these?"

A minute later, he emerged with a Pop-Tart in one hand and a glass of water in the other.

"Africa." He took a bite of the strawberry pastry.

"You got them in Africa or they're from Africa?"

"Both. I got them when I lived there."

Jessica turned to look at him. "You *lived* in Africa?" How did she not know that? She'd made a point of finding out everything she could about Ben. Maybe Sam didn't know.

Ben's gaze remained on the masks. "My father was a missionary in Africa. I lived there from the time I was twelve until I was eighteen and came back to the States for college. After medical school I went back and worked until I had to come back here for...my mom."

She had known that Ben had come to Omaha after his mother passed away to take care of the funeral arrangements, her estate and all of the other things that kids, unfortunately, were left to do when their parents passed away. She also knew that Sam didn't know why Ben had chosen to stay in Omaha after everything was settled. But Sam wasn't a guy to push or prod. If Ben had said he didn't want to talk about it, Sam wouldn't have talked about it.

"You lived in Africa right before you came to Omaha, then," Jess said. "I didn't know that."

"I don't talk about it."

He put the rest of the Pop-Tart in his mouth.

"You regret coming back to the States?"

He swallowed and shook his head. "Of course not. I had to take care of things for my mom."

"Do you plan to go back now?" She'd had no idea that Ben leaving was a possibility. He'd just gotten here.

"No," he said shortly.

"Not at all?"

"There's no point." He tossed the Pop-Tart wrapper on the breakfast bar between the kitchen and the eating area. "Goodnight, Jessica."

He stood watching her, obviously expecting her to turn and head down the hallway to his bedroom. She did turn, reluctantly. He seemed upset and she didn't have any idea why, but she felt compelled to make him feel better.

"If you need anything, you'll call me?" she said, turning back.

The melancholy expression was gone in a heartbeat and he gave her a sexy grin.

"If I need *anything*?" he asked, suggestively.

She rolled her eyes, but couldn't help her smile. He was incorrigible. "Let's run down the list of things you can call me for. Vomiting," she listed, ticking the items off on her fingers. "Shallow breathing, cold clammy skin, hypothermia or mental confusion."

"Basically I can call you only if I experience any of the symptoms of alcohol poisoning?" he asked wryly.

"Basically."

"Got it."

She smiled and reached out to touch his forearm. He seemed surprised by the touch, some of the water in the glass he held sloshing over the rim. She smiled, letting herself enjoy affecting him—and knowing it—this way.

"And Ben?" she said gently.

"Second thoughts already?"

The question was blasé, but the roughness in his voice proved that he was not any more casual about even this minor touch than she was.

"I want you to know..." She trailed off, having fun teasing him.

"Yeah?" The huskiness was even more pronounced.

"I..."

He stepped closer. "What?"

Jessica quickly realized that she had to quit the game

before he ended up convincing her that his intoxicated state didn't matter. In fact, she knew in her gut that Ben was in complete control of his reflexes and compulsions at this point and would remember anything that happened in Technicolor detail. Still, she couldn't go back on her avowal *not* to go to bed with him tonight or he would never believe anything else she said again. The need to maintain some control between her and Ben was strong and she could only assume it was because she also knew, in that same spot in her gut, that once she lost *any* control around Ben, she would lose *all* control.

"Ben, I am..."

He moved closer, trapping her hand between her breasts and his forearm. "Yeah?"

She licked her lips and gathered her resolve. "*I* am sleeping on the couch. No arguments."

He didn't argue. He sighed.

"You're very bossy, you know that?"

"I've been told something like that once or twice."

He stepped back from her. "And you always think you know what's best for everyone."

She couldn't deny it. "I'm very often right."

He sighed again. "Fine. There's only one activity I'm interested in staying up for tonight and it isn't arguing."

She fought a smile. "Good. Go to bed. I'll see you in the morning."

He leaned in before she could react and pressed a not-so-quick-but-nothing-erotic kiss to her lips.

"If you need me, I'm down the hall and to the left," he said, stepping back and smiling with satisfaction.

Jessica could only assume it was in response to the look of surprised arousal on her face.

"And I mean if you need me for *anything*," he added.

"I don't intend to be in need of anything," she said, somehow.

He gave her a wink. "And I intend to get to work on changing that first thing in the morning."

Then he pulled his shirt over his head, pausing long enough to give Jessica an eyeful before he turned down the hallway, unbuckling his belt and unzipping his pants as he went.

Jessica almost ended up on her nose leaning around the corner to keep him in sight as long as possible.

Chapter Three

Jessica's nipples were perfect. The entire left breast was damn nice. He was assuming the right matched, but it was still covered with terrycloth.

Even if it didn't, Ben was currently the happiest man on earth.

The towel she'd wrapped herself in had slipped as she reached overhead for the bottle of mouthwash in his medicine cabinet. Ben was glad he'd put the bottle up high. The more she reached, the lower the towel slid. She was, of course, unaware that the mirror in front of her reflected to the mirror on his dresser, which he could see perfectly from the bed. He'd never noticed it before but was now very thankful for the way he'd arranged the room.

Jessica in his bathroom, in nothing but a towel, warm and still wet from her shower, was a fabulous way to start a day.

She reached up again, retrieving dental floss, and Ben knew exactly what to do.

Jessica was known as a non-dater, a non-flirter, a non-partier. It wasn't that she wasn't friendly to the staff and downright magical with the patients, but she didn't go out. Period. She wasn't nasty about it or judgmental about those who did. She just always said *no thank you.*

Well, he was in the mood to do a whole bunch of stuff definitely including flirting and partying, and Jessica was, for some reason, the only person that he wanted to do it with. It didn't make sense, but he'd had a lifetime of trying to make sense of things and he was tired of it.

If his attraction for Jessica didn't make sense, it certainly didn't mean that he couldn't enjoy it.

He was going to try something new—he was going to just go with it.

Ben pushed himself up out of bed, pausing only long enough to drop his boxer shorts near the clothes hamper.

His major morning erection would impress Jessica, or scare her. Either way, there was no time like the present to start getting to know each other better.

"Good morning."

Jessica sucked in a quick breath and grabbed the top of her towel. The fact that the top edge of the towel came *below* her left breast registered in the next second.

She yanked the towel up and spun to face him, her face red.

"Good—"

Her gaze dropped, her cheeks got even redder and she pulled her eyes back to his face. But her eyes dropped to his jutting erection again.

Ben grinned. This was going well.

"I..." Jessica croaked. She stopped to clear her throat, lifted her gaze again and blinked a few times, then turned her eyes up toward the ceiling. "Good morning."

"You look great in the morning."

"Um, thank you." She continued looking up.

"Your neck is going to get a kink in it," Ben told her, amused.

"You could use a good duster," she replied conversationally. "There are cobwebs all over that light."

He glanced up, never having noticed the fixture before, not to mention the cobwebs. "I certainly wouldn't be offended if you reached up there and tried to brush them away," Ben said.

She looked at him and frowned, opened her mouth, then glanced down at her towel. He watched as her mind put the pieces together. Reaching up, towel sliding down, breast exposed, him here in front of her...

He wondered if her imagination went as far as his did. Like to him taking her nipple into his mouth, sucking, making her moan.

A certain part of him liked the idea a lot. He grew harder. Not that Jessica noticed. Her eyes were back on the ceiling.

Ben crossed his arms and leaned a shoulder against the

glass shower door. He decided to let it go. For now. He had no doubt that he would eventually be very familiar with Jessica's nipples. "Are you finding everything you need?"

Her eyes remained trained on the light fixture overhead. "Yep. Yes. Um, yes. I'm fine."

"Don't need anything at all?"

Without looking where she was going, Jessica began inching toward the door.

"Coffee," she said. "I definitely need some coffee."

Ben grinned watching her, and vowed to make Jessica more comfortable being naked around him as soon as possible. Practice made perfect, after all.

"I'm going to shower and I'll be right out."

"Gre—" Jessica's response was cut off when she slammed the door behind her.

Jessica was dressed in record time. There was no coffee pot so she was now searching Ben's cupboards for something, *anything*, other than Pop-Tarts that would pass for breakfast food. She was trying to keep her pulse at a normal, steady rate too. Which she might have been able to accomplish if she could quit thinking of Ben standing in the bathroom in all his glory.

It wasn't her fault that all of the food in his kitchen reminded her of him. Naked. Aroused. *Largely* aroused.

That guy was simply made to be naked. It wasn't fair to cover all of that up with clothes.

She opened the cupboard near the fridge. It held a jar of peanut butter. *Only* a jar of peanut butter. Peanut butter that would look good smeared all over Ben...for her to lick off.

Jessica groaned, slammed the cupboard shut and yanked open the drawer by the fridge. The Twinkies were penis-shaped. She stared down at the three individually wrapped cakes. Okay, they weren't *exactly* penis shaped. But in her imagination, at the moment anyway, it didn't take much.

She stomped to the fridge but it held only beer and bottled water. The beer reminded her of the bar last night and the way Ben had pressed her up against the car. The water made her think of the shower he was taking right now. Naked. The bread on the counter could be used for... Jessica frowned. She couldn't think of anything specific, but as long as Ben was there and naked, it would be fun.

"What are you doing?"

Jessica jumped and spun toward Ben, who stood in the doorway. At least now he was dressed.

She wasn't sure if she was relieved or disappointed.

"Quit sneaking up behind me!"

He grinned. "I'm not apologizing. The view from back there is awesome."

He'd been awake for all of thirty minutes and he was already making her hot and bothered. She could only imagine what he would do when he got some caffeine in his system and got warmed up.

"To answer your question," she said, changing the subject quickly. "I'm trying to make you breakfast. But you have no food."

Ben leaned against the counter behind him. "I eat at the hospital."

"All the time?"

"Unless I go out. Or have something delivered."

"You don't know how to cook?"

"I don't want to cook."

"Ever?" Jessica asked. "You never get the craving for a home-cooked meal?"

"I got away from home-cooked meals living in Africa. Not a lot of meatloaf and chicken pot pie down there."

She hadn't thought of that. "Don't you get sick of the hospital food and going out?"

"I don't worry about food too much. I eat when I get hungry because if I don't, eventually I won't be able to function. In the past, food's simply been a requirement. Whatever is there is there."

"What do you mean *in the past?*" she asked.

"I'm turning over a lot of new leaves," he said. "I'm going to enjoy life more, savor things, not let my work be everything. One of the things on my list is to eat once in a while just because it tastes good."

She made a mental note to make him her famous lasagna and fudge brownies soon. That would win him over. Then she frowned. Why was she trying to win him over anyway? Win him over for what?

"Why are you frowning?" he asked, lifting his cup again.

"I was wondering where I could get some eggs. I'll cook for you."

"Nah. I'll take you out."

"You want to go out?" She crossed her arms. "I figured you'd be hungover."

He didn't look hungover, she conceded. In fact, he looked...sexy.

He had stubble along his jaw, having obviously chosen not to shave. He was barefoot and was dressed in a green, slightly rumpled T-shirt and a pair of khaki shorts.

"I feel fine," Ben said.

"Not even tired?"

He shrugged. "No."

"Headache?"

"No. Which is disappointing. I'm sure you'd hold my head in your lap and rub it for me. Then fix me tea and nurse me all day."

It did sound nice. "Self-inflicted syndromes don't get that kind of attention," she told him.

"If I was actually sick, you would stay?"

"If you asked nice, I might."

He grinned and stepped closer. "I could ask *really* nice." His hand stroked the back of her arm right above the elbow.

She cleared her throat as she tried to ignore the sparkles of heat that were suddenly dancing through her.

"I'm a good cook," she said, a bit breathlessly.

Ben looked her directly in the eye. "Jess, I am absolutely sure you're a good cook. Just as I'm sure you're good at everything you do."

"Good at everything?" she repeated, surprised. "Why do you think that?"

"Because you do everything a hundred and ten percent."

She didn't answer. He and Sam must have talked about her. How else would Ben know so much?

"It's a compliment," he said, squeezing her arm.

"You sure?" Sam had never appreciated her perfectionist tendencies.

"How is giving a full effort to something a bad thing?" he

asked, removing his hand from her skin.

"I tend to expect everyone to give one hundred and ten percent," Jessica admitted. "It annoys people."

He chuckled. "I haven't found you annoying so far."

Her stomach did the flipping thing that was becoming familiar already. "But you don't want me to cook for you?"

She wanted to, which was completely stupid. She'd learned to cook by trial and error, and had generally hated every minute of it. Cooking healthy was a pain in the butt when drive-thru burgers and fries were so easy and quick, but even she had known that kids needed vegetables and milk. She hadn't even known how to pick good fruit when she'd first started putting food on the table for her siblings. Now, thanks to determination and an ability to learn quickly, she was practically Betty Crocker. For some reason, she wanted Ben to know that.

"Sometime I do," he promised. "But I have some quick business this morning, so I thought we could have breakfast out. I'm buying."

He looked so different, Jessica thought as they went out to the car that his friends had apparently dropped off from the bar at some point.

Before today, she'd seen Ben only in hospital scrubs and the slacks and shirt from last night. Now he looked...relaxed and casual. Even his eyes looked different. Usually his expression was concentrated and serious. He laughed at the hospital, of course, but he always had an intensity about him, like he was ready to jump in and operate on someone at any moment and be totally competent at it.

But since she'd seen him at the bar last night, that had been missing. It was as if he was any other average guy on the street with no clue how to resect or repair any given internal organ.

She rode beside him to downtown Omaha without paying attention to where they were going, still pondering the change in him. Maybe it was because of his suspension. There wasn't any chance work would page him so he didn't have his usual I'm-ready-for-anything edge. Maybe when the suspension was over he'd get back to normal.

Ten minutes later, they pulled up in front of a coffee house that occupied the middle of a series of shops. The shops lined the north side of one of the old brick streets in the part of downtown known as The Old Market. The area had once been the distribution center for goods shipped out of Omaha on the Union Pacific Railroad. The multi-block area was made up of restored warehouses that were now shops and restaurants on brick streets with a variety of street performers, vendors and horse-drawn carriages.

The coffee shop was adorable. Jessica loved the restored wood floors, and the twelve-foot ceiling in front of windows nearly as tall. Multiple round tables with two to four chairs each were clustered throughout the middle of the huge room along with couches, easy chairs and loveseats gathered in cozy sitting groups around the outer perimeter. A long counter ran along the wall at the back of the shop and doorways behind the counter led to what Jessica assumed to be the kitchen area. A large chalkboard hung on the wall between the two doorways and had the menu printed on it in multicolored chalk.

The shop served breakfast and simple lunches and was open six a.m. to ten p.m. in order to cater to local college students who might find it a pleasant study or meeting spot.

The woman behind the counter lit up when Ben came in.

"Benjamin Torres! I missed you two mornings in a row."

"Sorry, Dolly." Ben gave her a sheepish grin. "I've had some stuff going on."

Jessica almost rolled his eyes at the understatement.

"Dolly, this is Jessica Bradford." Ben looped an arm around Jessica's shoulders. "Dolly owns Cup O' Joe."

"Hi, Jessica."

Dolly was probably sixty-ish and reminded Jessica of what Santa's wife should look like, complete with apple red cheeks, white curls and a quick, warm smile.

"Hi, Dolly. It's nice to meet you." It was also nice to have Ben's arm around her.

"You too. 'Specially if you're the 'stuff' that Ben's had going on."

Jessica felt her cheeks heat and tried to correct the older woman, but Ben laughed and hugged her against his side.

"And if she isn't then you just got me into big trouble," he said. "You ever think of that?"

"Yeah, I did think of that," Dolly said, swatting at Ben with the end of her dishtowel. "And if you're bringin' her in here, it's at your own risk, Mr. Doctor-man."

Ben and Dolly laughed and Jessica smiled, feeling bemused by the interaction between Ben and the coffee shop owner. They seemed to know each other well enough to have already established the kind of friendship that would stand up under good-natured ribbing.

They placed their orders and Jess handed Ben a ten-dollar bill to pay for hers, then went to find a table, leaving Ben to talk to Dolly about whatever had brought him down here rather than eat her cooking.

She picked a table near the window. There were four other occupied tables. Three tables away two women were engaged in the intimate type conversation that happens between best friends. A table in the corner was surrounded by three twenty-somethings and held two open books and three more stacked to one side. The other two tables were of only one each. An older woman sat sipping idly from her cup, staring out the window, obviously lost in thought. A man in a suit, who had the biggest cup of coffee Jessica had ever seen, was tapping away at a laptop between sips.

Jessica smiled at Ben as he joined her, setting her cup of coffee in front of her. "This place is nice."

He looked around. "I think so." He tossed Jessica's ten-dollar bill down in front of her as he took the chair beside her.

She frowned at the money but decided not to pursue who was paying for what. "You come here a lot, I take it."

"Nearly every morning. Besides great coffee, Dolly has great advice."

Jess laughed as she stirred her coffee. "Most guys get advice from bartenders, don't they?"

"Most bartenders don't know how to get lipstick out of carpet or how to make lemon meringue pie from scratch."

She did not want to know why Ben needed to get lipstick out of carpet.

"Sounds like you need a..."

Jess stopped and felt her cheeks burn.

"A mother?" Ben asked.

Jess couldn't believe she'd almost said that. How

insensitive. She knew Ben's mom had died from liver failure a week before Ben had come back to Omaha. "I'm so sorry."

"It's okay."

"I know what it's like to have those kind of questions and no one to ask," she said, honestly. She had no idea how to get lipstick out of carpet even now. "My mom left when I was ten."

"And your dad died when you were a teenager, right?"

So Sam *had* talked to Ben about their parents. He'd at least mentioned his dad to his friend. That told her a lot about how much Sam liked and trusted Ben right there. Her brother only talked about their father by accident when words like "Remember when..." or "Dad..." slipped out before he thought better of it. But evidently he hadn't told Ben *how* their dad died. Or that it was her fault.

Jessica sipped from her cup to soothe her suddenly tight throat. "I was twenty," she said after she swallowed. Not exactly a teenager. But certainly not an adult.

"My dad was killed in a plane crash when I was eighteen," he said.

"I'm sorry."

"Me too."

They sat in silence for a moment.

Finally, Ben shifted on his chair and pulled a piece of paper folded lengthwise from his back pocket.

"Do you have a pen I could borrow?"

"Sure." Relieved to have something to do, she opened the front zipper of her purse and withdrew two. "Blue or black?" she asked holding them up for him.

He shook his head and selected the black. "Always prepared for anything?" he commented.

She couldn't deny it so said nothing.

Ben began filling in blanks on the paper.

"What's that?" She sipped the delicious blend of coffee, caramel and cream.

"Job application." He continued writing.

She swallowed, sure she'd heard wrong. "For you?" she asked, though the answer was obvious on the first line of the application labeled *Name*.

"Yes."

"You have a job," she pointed out. "Once your suspension

is over I know they will welcome you back with open arms."

But she didn't think doctors filled out written applications picked up at the front desk, anyway.

"Yeah. Probably." Ben kept his head bent over the application. "I just don't want it anymore."

That got her attention. "*What?*"

"Yeah. The doctor thing's not all it's cracked up to be."

"What are you talking about?" she asked, staring at the top of his head.

"What's the point?"

"What's the point?" she repeated. "The point of what?"

Now he looked up. "The point of what I do."

"How about saving lives and healing the sick, and little things like that?" she asked, deprecatingly.

He frowned at her. "Except that saving lives and healing the sick doesn't always happen."

She couldn't think of a thing to say to that. How could he not want to be a doctor anymore? It was a *calling*. He made the world a better place through what he did. She decided to try that approach.

"Ben, all doctors lose patients sometimes. You can't heal them all. But what if all doctors felt the way you do? Where would we be then?"

His frown was still firmly in place. "That's not my problem. Besides," he pushed his chair back and handed back her pen. "The money's too good. There will always be doctors."

She watched him go to the counter and hand his application to Dolly.

Jess felt like she was the butt of some stupid joke. She wavered between disbelief and anger at Ben. He had a God-given talent for healing. He was not taking that seriously enough. He was overreacting to the suspension. And the ego— did he think his suspension was unfair or undeserved? He'd broken a patient's nose, for heaven's sake! She was agitated by the time he returned to the table.

"How are you qualified to make coffee?" she asked as he took his seat. "You don't even have a coffeepot in your apartment."

"I make the coffee at work sometimes."

"There you go," she said, trying not to sound panicked or

hysterical. "That coffee is terrible."

"Not when I make it," Ben said, resting his forearms on the table and daring to look amused. He seemed so calm about giving up everything he'd worked and trained for, abandoning the patients who would need him in the future.

"That's not the point," she told him crossly. "You probably won't get the job anyway." Which was a stupid thing to say. Why wouldn't he get the job? He and Dolly were obviously friends and how hard could the coffee thing be, anyway? The man could repair lacerated spleens, for God's sake.

"I already have the job. The application was a formality. For audits and stuff like that."

"How long have you been planning to quit?" she asked.

"About a week."

She took a deep breath. "Ben," she tried for a sweet, cajoling tone of voice. "Why do you want to work in a coffee shop? You have ten years of higher education, you're a Board certified physician, you're the best surgeon in a four-state area. People need you."

He looked thoughtful as he answered. "Because it's simple here," he said. "People come in for coffee, I make it, they give me the money, I give them the cup. Everyone's happy. I've met their need and nobody dies."

"Nobody dies?" she repeated, dumbfounded. "*That* is your criteria for choosing a profession?"

"I'm not going back to the hospital."

She opened her mouth to reply but the sound of a pager suddenly split the air.

She looked at him questioningly as she reached for her purse. He held up his hands.

"I'm on suspension, remember?" He looked happy to make the announcement.

It was her cell phone. She had a text message.

Call me immediately. Dr. Edwards.

"Oh, sh...great," she muttered, catching herself short of swearing, which she was sure would have delighted Ben. As it was, he was grinning when she looked up.

"I need to return this call," she said.

Russ Edwards was the Chief of Emergency Medicine at St. Anthony's. He was Ben's boss. He wasn't directly over Jessica or the rest of the nursing staff, but he had a lot of pull and was certainly higher up the proverbial food chain than she was. Which made it very weird that he was calling her. It couldn't be about anything good.

"Russ Edwards," he answered on the first ring.

"Hi. It's Jessica." She tried not to sound hesitant or worried.

Ben looked at her questioningly and she smiled, knowing instinctively that Ben should not hear the conversation she was about to have and that he couldn't know she was talking to his boss.

"Is Ben with you?"

Obviously he expected her to know exactly who he was talking about. She had to be careful about how she answered Russ's questions so that Ben didn't pick up the fact they were talking about him.

"Yes."

"He's been with you all night?"

"Not...like that. I...um..."

Jessica had a hard time defending herself adequately without saying his or him or Ben's name.

Ben appeared interested in her sudden verbal stumbling. She looked at the huge coffee mug in front of her rather than the subject of her conversation.

Russ seemed to take pity on her. "You know where he was all night?"

"Yes."

"Did he get into any trouble?"

She frowned. "What do you mean?"

"Sam told me he had a scuffle at a bar, but that it was with a friend. No police or anything involved."

"Right."

"Was there anything else?"

Ben had drunk too much, attempted to seduce her, and had tried to do CPR on a patient while under the influence. However, he'd not done anything illegal and hadn't even been hungover.

"No. Nothing else." She took a sip of coffee, keeping up the pretense of a casual phone conversation with a friend Ben didn't know.

"Great," Russ said with relief.

Jessica smiled at Ben and rolled her eyes, trying to be convincing about the rambling girlfriend that was supposed to be on the other end of the phone.

"I'm depending on you," Russ said. "Keep him with you and out of trouble."

"*What?*"

Ben raised an eyebrow at her exclamation. She looked away.

"We've got the lawyers working on this thing with Ted Blake, the patient from the ER. But in the meantime Ben can't get so much as a speeding ticket. He's got to keep clean. You're the girl to ensure that happens."

She gritted her teeth over Russ's condescending *girl*. "What do you want me to do?"

"Whatever it takes."

Her eyes flew to Ben as her imagination celebrated Russ's choice of words.

"You can't... There isn't..." This keeping the conversation as one-sided as possible was challenging. "Why me?" she finally asked.

She picked up her mug and sipped again. She was drinking coffee, chatting with a friend on the phone, no big deal, nothing for Ben to be interested in.

"Sam said you were very influential with Ben last night."

Hot coffee down the wrong pipe.

Jessica coughed and tried to breathe at the same time, basically unsuccessful with both things. She coughed hard twice and sucked air in through her nose deeply.

She had a pretty good idea how Sam had explained the situation to Russ.

"I can't believe he said that!"

She didn't need two siblings. A sister was enough. She couldn't kill Sam, but she could probably disown him. And change all of her phone numbers. And move.

With Ben sitting right there, she couldn't get into a true argument with Russ.

"Sam informed me that you are the perfect person to keep

an eye on Ben. And I tend to agree. You always go above and beyond...with extremely admirable results," Russ said smoothly.

Uh-huh. She wondered if Russ realized how far above and beyond she was willing to go with Ben.

"Flattery isn't going to work," she muttered.

"But endorsements will," Russ said. "I'd think a recommendation from the head of the ER would go a long way in helping you get the job you applied for last month."

Jessica sat up straighter. Russ evidently knew about her application for the position of ER Department Director. The promotion would put her in charge of the entire ER staff and day-to-day operations. It was a position she deserved. It was a huge responsibility, requiring tremendous organizational skills, unwavering confidence, the ability to mega-multi-task, and the gumption to order lots of people around all at once... Hell, she'd practically been made for the job.

A recommendation from Russ would guarantee she got the job. The jerk.

"And this is how I'm going to get it?" she asked.

"Exactly."

She supposed she had to respect the fact that he didn't sugar-coat things or make her guess.

"I see."

Russ obviously heard the coolness in her tone.

"Ben has to stay out of trouble. The Board of Directors is still pissed about what happened with Dr. Thomas last summer. Now I have another ER physician in trouble. I have to control this or it's going to look like I'm not handling my staff. *My* job is on the line here. I don't like that and I'll do whatever I have to so that this isn't a problem."

She knew that Dr. Thomas had been investigated after a family filed a lawsuit against him. They alleged he'd given their father the wrong medication and caused severe kidney damage. The suit hadn't held up and Dr. Thomas was still practicing, but the Board didn't like bad publicity, interviews with attorneys or writing press releases for damage control. Understandably.

"Hitting a patient is bad enough, but we can handle that if this guy doesn't press charges. Ben can *not* get into any more trouble and this is all so out of character I don't know what to expect. No scandal, nothing illegal, nothing unethical. I don't want him doing anything risky."

Jessica understood that the whole situation was hugely problematic for Russ and potentially the whole hospital, so she should cut him some slack. But the only thing saving Russ from her ire was that she wanted to do it.

She wanted to spend time with Ben and this seemed like a more moral reason than because kissing him was like every erotic fantasy she'd ever had rolled into one.

Russ was correct to believe that Ben needed someone looking after him. It was clear Russ would assign someone else to the task if she didn't agree to do it. And she *really* didn't like the idea of someone else, no matter who it was, doing it instead of her.

"Fine," she said to Russ.

"Jessica." Russ's voice had lost its edge a bit. "Take care of him."

And once again she was reminded of the biggest problem with the plan. She didn't know how the hell she was going to do this.

"What are you doing the rest of the day?" Ben asked as she disconnected.

"I was going to...visit my sister," she said. Russ clearly felt that she was going to need to keep an eye on Ben for at least a few days. That meant there would be time to tell him about how she spent most of her free time outside of work. Later.

"I'll come too." He pushed his chair back from the table.

She did too, in surprise. "You want to visit my sister?"

"I do if that's what you're doing."

He stood and Jessica followed.

She stared at him, feeling the tug at her heart intensify. He wanted to be with her? Or was that her pathetic crush twisting his words into something romantic and sweet when he simply meant that it was a way to kill some time? After all, his friends were all *working*.

Ben glanced at his watch. "Or I guess I could go see if Charlie's is open yet."

"No," she said quickly at the reminder of the bar she'd found him in. She grabbed his hand without thinking. "No. Sara would love to meet you. But I'm not seeing her until four."

He turned his hand over and tugged her closer to him, his eyes full of mischief.

"Gosh, how could we pass all that time?"

Jess pictured herself as a cartoon—drawn with voluptuous curves of course—melting into a multicolored puddle at Ben's feet.

"Um..." was all she came up with.

"Just a guess," he said turning, her hand still in his, toward the door of the coffee shop. "But you generally spend your time off cleaning your house, doing errands, working out, organizing closets, productive stuff like that, right?"

She frowned, not sure where he was going with this. "Pretty much."

"Have you ever just blown off a day?" Ben stepped out onto the sidewalk, pulling her with him.

She followed him to his car.

"Blown off?"

Ben opened the passenger side door for her. "You know, done a ton of stuff that's not toward any purpose and doesn't accomplish a thing except having fun."

"Are you implying that I don't seem fun?" she asked. She often worried that was exactly the case.

He chuckled. "I'm sure you're fun. But I bet you feel guilty having a good time, right? Like you should be doing something more constructive?"

Admitting that would definitely make her seem like no fun.

"There's lots to do," she said.

He hadn't let go of her hand. Now he squeezed gently.

"Do you feel like you could give up some of that control and spend the day having fun with me?"

The only answer that even occurred to her as an option was, "Sure."

It was for the good of the entire hospital after all. She *had* to spend the day with him now.

"Where should we go?" Ben asked as they backed out of their parking spot and headed west.

Somewhere fun. Somewhere fun. Jessica wracked her brain. "The zoo?" she finally suggested, as she saw the sign directing tourists to one of Omaha's best attractions.

Ben sighed. "No, no, no. The zoo is too educational for what we're talking about. No learning or expanding horizons or being a better person today. We'd probably end up having an interesting *conversation* about the importance of conservation efforts in the rain forest. What we're going for is something that produces nothing worthwhile in the end."

"A movie?"

He shook his head. "There might be a hidden moral or social message in it. Better not risk it."

She sighed and shook her head. "I guess mindless wastes of time are going to have to be your department."

He chuckled. "I can do that. And," he said, looking both ways and then pulling into the left turn lane, "I have just the place."

The funny thing was that her heart thumped when he pulled up in front of the arcade. She hadn't played video games in years.

Her eyes were wide taking in all of the lights and colors while Ben changed bills into quarters. With the roll of coins, he also handed her cotton candy.

"No nutritional value whatsoever," he told her. "Eat up."

She did so, with a nearly embarrassing amount of enthusiasm.

"The rules are that you have to use every one of those quarters," he told her. "And not only on junk food," he added, eyeing the already half-eaten mound of pink sugar she held.

She nodded. "No problem." She fully intended to play some games. She just didn't know where to start.

Ben headed toward the back of the arcade while Jessica wandered up and down the aisles in between machines, checking everything out. After a few minutes of looking, she found the perfect one. Extreme Racing Star was complete with steering wheel, gas and brake pedals. She had to put her cotton candy down, so she stuffed a huge bunch in her mouth at once, then slid behind the wheel and started plugging in quarters.

The time flew by. *New High Score* was flashing on the screen when Ben leaned into the little car shell.

He whistled. "You have many hidden talents."

She smiled up at him.

"But I bet you always drive the speed limit in real life, don't you, Jess?" He smiled when she blushed.

"I've seen up-close the effects of careless, fast driving," she told him.

"Working out some pent-up aggressions here, or are you a closet NASCAR fan?"

"You're just jealous because I got the new high score."

"Maybe," he agreed, tugging her out of the car. "How many quarters do you have left?"

She dug in her pocket and pulled out her remaining stash. "Only two." She was actually disappointed.

"That's all I have left too. What do you say we play something together?"

She might not know much about mindless wastes of time anymore, but she could have easily come up with something to play with Ben.

He led her to a game she'd never seen before. "I've never played this one."

"Good," he said good-naturedly. "The object is to collect the treasure chest and, of course, not let those monsters eat you."

"Sounds straightforward."

They each took a control and for several minutes fought valiantly back and forth for the lead in points. They shoved playfully and gloated over the other's mistakes. But soon it was clear that Ben was going to go from level seven all the way, leaving her far behind...the loser.

"Oh, look, isn't that Tom Cruise?" she asked.

Ben didn't even blink. Right, he was a guy. "I think that's Britney Spears over there," she tried.

"I don't like blondes," Ben muttered, skillfully avoiding a particularly mean monster.

She tucked her brunette hair behind her ear with a smile. He was tough to distract. That focus made him a great doctor. As did his obviously superior hand-eye coordination.

But she had a very wide competitive streak.

She got close to him and rubbed her hand up and down his forearm.

He bit his bottom lip. Still, he had advanced to level eight.

Jessica wasn't sure what came over her then, but she pressed closer, her breast against his bicep.

"That's cheating," Ben said, without taking his eyes off the screen.

"It's called defensive strategy," she said. Besides she was rubbing his left arm and he was right handed.

"If it wasn't such a nice strategy I'd argue the point harder," he said, somehow managing to jump over two monsters as he said it.

She unbuttoned the top button of her shirt and ran her hand up his back.

"Keep unbuttoning and I'll let you win every time," he said, just before the orange monster ate him in one gulp.

She laughed, feeling free and something that felt suspiciously like *sexy*.

"Are you going to concede the game to me, or do you want to take your last turn?" Ben asked.

She left the button on her shirt unbuttoned and stepped up to the game control. "Oh, I don't give up that easily."

He chuckled. "Good. Because I'd like to try out some defensive strategy myself."

Her heart rate went into double time. She wasn't sure she could take much distraction from Ben without turning into a blathering idiot.

"But you're ahead by fifty thousand points and four levels," she protested.

"And I'd like to keep it that way," he said.

Fine. She was a competitor. She had a brother who had specialized in cheating and distracting in order to win even a simple game of checkers. She had to focus on the game and not let Ben get to her. Which was a great plan for winning the arcade game, but also for not letting Ben realize his influence on her. For that matter, it would be good to prove to *herself* that he didn't affect her that much.

She pressed the button to start her round and was thirty seconds into the game when she felt Ben move in behind her. He braced his hands on the game console on either side of her hips and took a long slow breath near her right ear.

"You smell so good," he said huskily.

Jess felt his body touching hers from her upper back to her derriere.

Autopilot and superb physical reflexes were all that kept

her from being obliterated by the purple monster.

Ben kissed the side of her neck where it curved into her shoulder and she somehow continued to play simply because she was afraid he would stop if the game ended. His hands moved to her hips and pulled her more firmly back against him. Delicious sensations licked every nerve ending in her body— though some more than others.

She miraculously executed a brilliant move that took her to the next level and Ben evidently decided to pull out the big guns. His right hand moved from her hip to cup her right breast.

She sucked in a surprised gasp, and as his thumb flicked over the instantly pert tip, she didn't even care about the bright yellow monster that gobbled her character up in one bite.

The *Sorry, you lose* music played for a few seconds before Ben pulled away. "Okay, my male ego is restored. I like this game and I'm obviously good at it."

She whirled around, embarrassment burning her cheeks. "That was a dirty trick."

He laughed and failed to step back. "A dirty trick that *you* started."

She frowned. He was right. Dammit. She was never that easily distracted. "It seemed like a good idea," she said.

"It *was* a good idea," Ben assured her. "I've been wanting to feel you up since I saw you half-naked in my bathroom this morning."

"I... But..." she spluttered, turned on, shocked and well, turned on.

"How about a batting cage?" he asked.

"You probably won't get a chance to feel me up if I'm holding a big wooden club," Jessica grumbled. But she hadn't minded it at all and Ben knew it.

"Then we'll go to the climbing wall," he announced.

She glanced at her watch. "I have somewhere I have to be in a little over an hour." She was surprised by the intensity of her disappointment. She'd never been disappointed to go to her volunteer job before.

"So, let's go there."

"You want to come?"

"As long as you're going to be there, I can't see why not." He bent his knees and looked directly into her eyes. "Unless it's the hospital."

She rolled her eyes. "I've got the point already." But she did want to take him with her. It might be good for him. Not to mention a great way for her to spend more time with him. "Let's go," she said.

"Name the place."

Twenty minutes later they pulled up in front of the Bradford Youth Center.

"I don't suppose it's a coincidence that this place has your last name?" Ben asked.

She smiled as she shut the car off and reached for the door handle. "No. It's named after my father. He started it up and we used his life insurance money to add a huge addition and a bunch of programs after he died."

Ben got out and followed her up the front walk. "You spend a lot of time here?"

She nodded. "My sister, Sara, is the administrator. She's got a degree in social work. Sam and I both volunteer time here and run programs. So do a few of our friends and a couple of Dad's friends."

"I'm impressed," Ben said. "Not surprised, but impressed."

Jessica led him through the front doors and down the hall immediately to the right. She knocked on the doorframe as she turned into the first room on the left.

Ben heard a female voice say, "Hi, Jess," as he stepped in behind Jessica.

Jessica gestured to the pretty woman standing at the desktop copier gathering the pages the machine slid onto the tray in front of her. "This is my sister, Sara."

"Hi, Sara," Ben greeted the woman he'd heard so much about from Sam.

"Hi."

When Sara smiled Ben saw the resemblance between the sisters, but on first glance they didn't seem to look much alike. Jessica had rich brunette hair, with reddish gold streaking through it. It was thick and straight.

Sara on the other hand had long, blond hair that coiled

perfectly like the long ribbons his mother used to curl by pulling the scissors along them quickly.

She had a sweet air about her. Some of it was perhaps the ten years that separated the sisters, but Ben knew from things Sam had told him that some of it came from Jessica having worked hard to keep Sara innocent and protected, while Jessica dealt with all of the burdens after their father had died.

"Sara, this is Ben. He's..."

Ben turned toward her with interest. He wanted to hear how Jessica chose to explain who he was and what he was doing here with her.

"He's a doctor at St. Anthony's," Jessica said. "And a friend of Sam's."

Ben waited for four heartbeats, while Sara looked from him to Jessica and back.

"I'm also the man who is going to be sleeping with your sister," he said, extending his hand toward Sara.

Sara looked surprised, then amused, her smile wide as she took his hand. They both ignored Jessica's outraged gasp.

"Well, thanks," Sara said. "Sam keeps saying that's what she needs."

Ben laughed, instantly liking her. Not that it should have surprised him. Sara was more than Jessica's little sister. Jessica had raised her, after all.

"Sara," Jessica said tightly.

Sara rolled her eyes. "See, this is how it always works. I tell her what Sam has said or done and *I* get yelled at."

"Sa-ra," Jessica said again, firmer and louder.

"Is he lying?" Sara asked, turning to her sister.

Jessica's mouth opened but nothing came out.

Sara propped a hand on her hip and tipped her head, unconcerned by Jessica's sudden inability to utter a syllable. She smiled. "That's definitely not a denial."

Ben kept from laughing but could see why Sara was enjoying this. The look of frustration on Jessica's face was great. Jessica Bradford, in control, bossing everyone else around all the time, didn't get that look easily.

"We haven't slept together," Jessica said. "Not that it's your business anyway."

"Yet," Ben inserted.

Sara laughed. "I'm sorry."

Jessica frowned hard. "He's fine." Then shook her head. "I've got to talk to Sam about his influence on you."

Anxious to direct the conversation away from her sleeping with Ben, she moved toward the door. "I'm going to show Ben around the center."

She simply didn't talk about guys and sex and stuff like that with Sara. It was amazing that Sara was as innocent as she was with Sam for a brother. But Sam took protecting her as seriously as Jessica did. Having her mom walk out and her father die suddenly, all before she was ten years old, was enough to deal with.

"Sara seems great," Ben said as they stepped into the hallway.

Jessica grimaced. "Except for the delight she and Sam get from having her say things that shock me."

Ben put his hand at her back and she wanted to stop and lean into him. She knew she couldn't act on all of the things Ben stirred up in her body and imagination, but that didn't mean they'd gone away.

"Sara is a compliment to you," Ben said, ambling along beside her, his hand on her back seemingly just to touch her.

Jessica looked at him quickly. "What do you mean?"

"From what you and Sam have told me about your past and your dad and everything, I know that how Sara turned out has a lot to do with you."

She couldn't sleep with him, but wow, when he said stuff like that, how was she supposed to resist throwing herself into his arms?

"Thanks," she said past the tightness in her throat.

Ben smiled down at her as he pulled the door in front of them open. "It must have been tough."

"Becoming a mother to a girl right after her father was killed and just before she became a teenager? Yeah." Jessica laughed. "Tough is one word. But I had to do a good job." Jessica bit her bottom lip. That had sounded pretty dumb.

"You wouldn't have done anything less than a good job," Ben said matter-of-factly as they stepped into the game room.

Jessica recognized that Ben was complimenting her but it hit her that this was who Ben thought she was. It would be, because this was who she wanted people to think she was. With Ben, though, she wanted him to know the real her, and this woman she'd put on for ten years was only a small part of that.

But would he like the real her?

He thought she was the type to step in, take over and do a great job. He had no idea that simply making breakfast for Sara and getting her to school on time had taken Jessica a month to master. Bigger things, like remembering to pick her up after Girl Scouts and pay the mortgage on time, had taken longer.

And that was only the beginning of the things that would shock Ben about her.

Chapter Four

Jessica was turning out to be more than just a great body.

Ben wasn't sure that was a good thing. Of course, he already knew that she was a fantastic nurse. The best he'd ever worked with, in fact. He would have been blessed to have had her in Africa. Jessica would have been able to stand next to him and do the job under even those sometimes horrible conditions. And she would have appreciated the moments when things clicked, like when a mother learned that keeping herself well was as important as keeping her child well; when a child finally measured at the appropriate level on the growth chart; when a man successfully used a piece of equipment that would help the entire village. Yes, Jessica would have been good there.

And he would have taken her to bed a long, long time ago.

Ben took in the details of the rooms they were walking through with only a fraction of his concentration on the center and the rest on the woman beside him.

The large room was filled with three ping-pong tables, two pool tables, four TVs complete with Nintendo game systems and a multitude of mismatched tables, chairs and couches. The wall opposite of where they stood was painted bright yellow with black letters across it that read, *"When we treat man as he is, we make him worse than he is; when we treat him as if he already were what he potentially could be, we make him what he should be." Johann Wolfgang von Goethe.*

The wall to their right was a pale green and said, *"...to know even one life has breathed easier because you have lived. This is to have succeeded." Ralph Waldo Emerson.*

Finally, the words, *"Always do right. This will gratify some people and astonish the rest," Mark Twain,* ran across the bright blue wall to the left.

Ben smiled. This was where Jessica spent most of her time outside of work. He could tell the place was like a second home by the way she straightened things as they passed, the way she walked around things without needing to look to avoid bumping into them, and the way she *seemed* while she was here. There was pride and contentment on her face. She was comfortable here, relaxed, at home. He liked it. A lot.

He grabbed her elbow and spun her around, pulling her against his chest. He loved the way her breath caught as his lips came within centimeters of hers.

"Have I ever told you that you're the best nurse I've ever worked with?"

Her eyes went wide. "No."

"Working with you for the past six months should have taught me that you can turn me on just by being in the same room. But evidently it's not limited to the hospital. Part of the turn-on is how much you love your work there. The same is true here, I guess."

Which was something he hadn't realized until right then.

Her passion and competency were as exciting to him as her red thong. Because he could relate to her, could feed off of her energy in the ER, could share the exhilaration and burdens that came with their jobs. He respected her immensely. Which made the fact that he wanted to do all kinds of dirty things to her...different. And more confusing, because he didn't intend to have anything about the ER in common with anyone anymore.

"You turn me on with anything that excites you. Like the arcade. Now this place."

Wow, he was in big trouble. Because what he said was true. Anything that made Jessica's eyes sparkle was going to make him want her even more.

Her cheeks got pink with his words. "I do love the ER. But this is..." She turned her head to survey the room and Ben reluctantly released her. "This is...so big," she said, stepping back and sweeping her arm wide. "I mean, there are lots of ERs. But there is only one Bradford Center."

"Does it matter so much because of the center itself, or because of your dad?" he asked, truly curious.

She didn't answer him directly. "I don't remember a time in my life when my dad wasn't working on this center."

"You spend so much time down here because you want to carry on his work?" Ben asked.

Jessica nodded.

"Did he ask you to?" Ben asked. He supposed he should be more sensitive but he wanted to know about her and it was easier to jump right in.

She met his eyes again. "He didn't have the chance." Tears sparkled in her eyes before she focused on his shoulder instead of his face. She shook her head. "He wouldn't have asked, anyway."

That made no sense. Jessica was perfect for being in charge, taking a vision and making it huge. "Why?" Might as well dig in deep as long as he was digging.

Jessica took a deep breath. "I spent a lot of time doing things for myself before he died." Her chin went up. "In fact, I didn't do anything for anyone else, unless it benefited me. I wouldn't have been a very good choice to run the center back then."

She seemed serious. Ben had an incredibly hard time believing any of it.

"*You* were selfish?"

"That's one adjective my father used," she agreed.

"Give me two more."

"How about three more? Like defiant, cynical, obstinate."

Ben chuckled. He couldn't put those words in the same *thought* with Jessica.

"I—" she started and he found himself holding his breath.

"Jessica! They're here!"

Sara's voice interrupted. Jessica glanced at the doors leading back toward the office, where Sara had just poked her head through. "Um, they need us."

"Need us?" Ben asked.

"Come on." Jessica was already jogging across the rec room.

They met Sara outside of her office and she opened her mouth to say something, but the double doors at the end of the main hallway banged open. The sound of the metal door handles hitting the concrete wall echoed through the hall, followed immediately by the chaotic sound of multiple voices all taking at once. Eight teenagers stumbled through the wide doorway. Two of them carried a kid she knew only as David.

Jess knew the moment Ben saw the blood because he surged around her toward the boy, his instincts obviously moving him. The confusion wouldn't slow him down. He was used to the ER.

"What happened?" he demanded as he tried to touch David's bleeding face.

The two who held David up looked at Jessica and one asked, "Who's this guy?" She put a hand on Ben's arm to stall him.

"He's out," Corey, one of the boys, told her grimly. "Only lasted six minutes."

"Take him to the rec room," she said.

"What the hell..." Ben started.

"You can help," she said, starting off behind the boys. "I'll need sutures, Sara."

Her sister went for the supplies and the other kids followed Jess and Ben down the hall.

"He was in a fight," Jess told Ben as they walked, trying to keep the explanation simple for now.

"Evidently," he said dryly.

The guys laid the unconscious boy on one of the couches.

"I'd guess he lost," Ben added.

"Third time this month," she said, moving in to examine David's face.

Ben was right beside her.

David's lip was cut on top and bottom and he had a laceration along his cheekbone as if a ring had cut him. Rings or other jewelry were illegal in the fights but there weren't exactly referees either. One of David's eyes was blackening over the spot that had barely begun to heal from the week before. And David was indeed out cold.

"You don't seem surprised by this," Ben commented as he took the first aid supplies from Sara and pulled on rubber gloves, then started cleaning the wounds as Jess felt for any fractures along his jaw and cheeks.

"It's why I had to be here tonight. Tuesdays and Thursdays are fight nights." She found no broken bones so took the gauze pads from Ben and handed him the suture kit. "Here, you're the surgeon."

He refused it for a moment, quickly doing his own exam including blood pressure check and listening to David's heart and lungs with the stethoscope Jess had included in their box of supplies. "You're sure there're no other injuries?" he asked, looping the stethoscope around his neck.

Jess was struck by how great he looked with it on. In charge, confident, commanding. She glanced at the other teenagers. "Anything else go on?"

They all shook their heads. "It was only six minutes," Mario said. "I think he was still hurting from last week. He looked terrible."

Jess turned back to Ben. "Guess not. They're not supposed to hit below the belt."

"They watched?" Ben asked, gesturing with his chin toward the boys.

She nodded. "We always have people there. Mario pays close attention."

Ben looked like she was speaking a foreign language to him. He looked over at Mario. "He didn't take any shots in the stomach or ribs?"

"One or two," Mario reported. "But that's not what knocked him down. It was his head."

Mario had been involved with the fighting as more than a spectator in the past. He knew what to watch for and what could happen. Nobody stayed down long before Mario and his buddies picked them up and brought them in.

Still, Ben sighed. "One or two." He lifted David's shirt and examined his ribs and abdomen. "Okay," he said finally satisfied with the assessment. "I'll stitch him up while you explain."

Jess agreed, but this was so hard. She wasn't sure why she'd thought bringing Ben here was a good idea. Part of it was because this place was so important to her and because she thought he would understand, or at least accept it.

"These fights have been going on for a couple of years. The boys meet downtown at an abandoned building. We're here to patch them up afterward."

"You don't try to stop it?" Ben asked, his voice angry.

"That's not our role. We send people to bring them back

when they're hurt. We try to recruit them, though. We've gotten a few."

"Recruit them?"

"To the center, to come here instead and be a part of this group. To find other ways of fitting in."

"Is it a gang thing?" Ben asked as he applied perfect stitches to David's cheek with ease.

"Dammit!"

Jess and Ben both jumped.

"Why's it gotta be a gang thing?" Mario was glowering at Ben. "All us losers don't have anything better to do than fight?"

"Mario," Jess tried to interject. "He doesn't…"

"So what's the story?" Ben asked, meeting Mario's stern glare directly and not looking even slightly apologetic.

Jess knew that Mario would respect that Ben didn't back step. But the seventeen-year-old was tough and would defend his friends, and himself, to anyone.

"They are fighting for something," Mario said. "They need something. They're proving something. But they're doing it the wrong way." Mario rose from the arm of the couch. "But that doesn't mean it's a gang, or that they're all delinquents."

Jess couldn't help but smile at the boy who, at one time, had been here for similar stitches.

"And do they ever prove whatever it is?" Ben asked, unblinking.

Mario and Ben stared at each other for a long moment and Jess had to wonder what kind of male ego competition was going on.

Finally, Mario said, "Not this way."

"So, what happens?" Ben returned to the stitches on David's head.

"They keep trying." Mario watched him work on the boy. "Or they realize there are better ways."

Ben finished the stitches and sat back. He glanced up at Mario. "Ways like what?"

"Like here." Mario straightened and propped his hands on his hips, challenging Ben to question or disagree.

Jess hid her smile this time. Mario was tough. There was no doubt about it. But he was no longer violent. He had a quick mind and a sharp tongue and could easily hold his own with those weapons alone. He also knew exactly who he was and what he wanted and no one was going to be able to argue with him or convince him of anything different from what he knew. And Mario knew that this center was the best place for him and the other kids who came here.

Ben rocked back on his heels and then stood. He faced Mario squarely.

Jess prayed that he wouldn't say anything that would offend Mario or the rest of the boys. He was a smart man. She could see that he admired the way the boys brought David in and he admired Mario's confidence. But she wanted Mario to see that. She wanted the boy to trust Ben. He could use a man like Ben to look up to.

Unfortunately, Mario went on the defensive easily. He was fiercely loyal once he let someone close, but it took a lot to earn his trust.

"You used to fight?" Ben asked.

"Yeah."

"Why?"

"Money mostly."

Ben frowned. "Money?"

"The rich kids place bets on the fights and pay the winners."

Ben shook his head in disgust. He looked at Jess. "I don't suppose the authorities know?"

"The best way to stop it is to convince the fighters that they don't want to do it anymore," she said calmly. She'd been through all the emotions that Ben was feeling. But she had to pick the battles that she could win. One kid at a time.

Ben stripped off his gloves in a brisk, angry movement. "Does that work?"

"Ask Mario." She gestured to the other boys in the room. "Or Brian. Or Tony."

Ben glanced at the boys sitting and standing around the room. They all met his eye confidently.

"They were all fighters?" he asked.

"Yes, and now they're all here," she said proudly.

"And even without those three, they're still having fights," Ben said.

"But *they're* not."

Now she was the one to meet Ben's eyes confidently.

"You can't save them all like that," Ben said angrily.

"But the ones we do save are worth it."

Jess looked at the boys on the couch again. Her heart filled. They were good kids. They'd taught her as much or more than she'd taught them. They needed someone to tell them they could do more than fight, that they were worthy of praise regardless of the outcomes of the battles they faced...*all* the battles. Jessica knew it was her role to be their cheerleader. She believed in every one of them.

"It's like the ER," she said, turning her eyes back to Ben. "We can't, and don't, save them all. But we still show up every day and the ones we do save are worth it."

Something flashed in Ben's eyes and Jessica knew that he was thinking about Ted Blake. The man who Ben did not feel had been worth his efforts. Jessica held her breath, waiting for him to say it. But he didn't.

"And what about him?" Ben asked, gesturing toward David, instead.

"We'll keep trying," Mario said.

Ben turned. "Why?"

Mario shrugged. "*We* don't have anything to lose."

"We're another option for him," Jess added. "But he'll have to ultimately make the choice."

"And the next time he fights?" Ben asked.

Jess frowned at the pessimistic comment. "Maybe tonight will be the last time."

"And if it's not?" Ben pressed.

"Then we'll be here to fix him up."

Ben shook his head. "Doesn't it get discouraging?"

"Sure," Jess admitted. "But the one thing most of these kids have in common is that no one has ever shown them that they are worth the effort. We're giving that effort."

Having seen that David was patched up and safe for the time being, the kids had started to disperse around the room. One television was turned to a movie, four boys racked balls up on a pool table and three girls took over a table covered with scrapbooking materials for the baby book they were making for Sophie, the pregnant sixteen-year-old.

Ben sighed. "I don't know how you do it."

Jess didn't like that. Ben was supposed to be the kind of guy who would jump into something like this wholeheartedly.

"Want to get something to eat?" Ben asked.

Jess shook her head. "I told Sara I'd stay until seven when Mac gets here."

He looked around. "I'll wait."

"You don't have to." But she wanted him to.

"I know." He looked around and stretched. "What will you do until then? Stitch more up?"

"If they need it."

"If not?"

"Play basketball, talk, help with homework, stuff like that."

"Is that what I should do?"

Her eyes found Sophie at the table of girls laughing and talking as they glued the scrapbook together. "I might have a better idea."

Ben's eyes followed hers to the beautiful young girl who was, unmistakably, very pregnant.

He looked back at Jess, both eyebrows up. "You want me to deliver a baby?"

Jess smiled. "Not tonight. I hope. But it'd be great if you could talk to her about the pregnancy, make sure she knows how important it is to take care of herself, things like that."

"Can't you talk to her about the pregnancy?" Ben asked, obviously not thrilled with the request.

"You're the doctor," she said simply.

"I'm not an obstetrician."

"Surely they covered pregnancy and delivery in medical school," she said stubbornly. "What happens if you're stuck in an elevator or a taxi with a woman in labor?"

"You want me to talk to her about having her baby in an elevator?" he asked, his tone mild.

Jess smiled. "As long as you include how important her prenatal vitamins are you can talk to her about whatever you want."

"I could tell her how to remove a gall bladder, but I'm not sure about contractions and such," Ben said. "What if I tell her something that's wrong?"

He needed to put more vulnerability into his voice if he wanted her to believe that he was worried. Instead, it sounded like nothing more than an excuse. A weak excuse.

Jess could tell he'd already resigned himself to doing it, but she went along.

"You won't," she told him.

"You put a lot of faith in me."

"More than you do in yourself, evidently."

He frowned. "And you're pushy."

Jess shrugged. "So I've been told."

"Give me one good reason to do this."

"It's your moral and professional responsibility as a physician."

"Try again."

Jess frowned now, frustrated with the reminders of his sudden lack of dedication. "Because you have the initials M.D. after your name and that carries more weight than anything I can tell her."

"Even if it's the same stuff?"

Jess sighed. "How can you not get this? Those two letters matter to people. They convey a certain understanding that you have advanced training and a commitment to helping others. People know you know what you're talking about and assume that you automatically care about them."

"You realize that many physicians go into medicine for the power and the money," he said flatly.

"But not you."

His eyes narrowed as he looked down at her. "How can you be so sure?"

She couldn't totally answer that, other than to say that she had a feeling about him. Many factors played into that, including her brother's friendship with Ben and observing him at work for so long. But some of it was an instinct. A twinge of awareness she had for him that she'd never felt for another person.

And she could not forget the first day she'd ever seen Ben. He'd paced into the ER like a general into a war room. In the midst of the chaos and adrenaline, the noise and flurry, Ben brought calm confidence. She'd never even heard his name before that moment, but the feeling that everything was going to be okay now that Dr. Torres had arrived was something that she remembered distinctly even now. She loved calm and confident. She wanted someone who could quiet the storms, who knew in a heartbeat what was needed—and could provide it.

Her faceless fantasy man suddenly had a face, name and personality.

But she wasn't going to tell him that.

For one, he'd think she was crazy.

And two, if he continued on the path he was on, it would no longer be true.

"You walked out," she finally answered. "If money and power were all that was important to you, you wouldn't be giving them up."

"There are hundreds of girls like Sophie," Ben said. "Why should this one matter to me?"

"Because she matters to me," Jess said, with no idea whether that made a difference or not.

He bent his knees to put his eyes on the same level as hers. "Are you asking me for a favor?"

The way he was looking into her eyes made it impossible to blink. She licked her lips, strangely restless under his gaze.

"Because, if so," he said before she could answer. "You'll owe me."

She tried to frown even as her heart thumped. "You're a doctor. You should *want* to check her out."

He moved closer. "But I don't. What I *want* is about another woman all together."

And suddenly she wanted to owe him—and have him cash the debt in soon. In spite of the fact he was committed only to avoiding commitment.

This was going to be a problem.

She couldn't sleep with a guy she was disappointed in. Could she?

Jessica cleared her throat. Didn't matter. She wasn't going to sleep with him. She was pretty sure. "So, you'll talk to her?"

"If you go out with me after you're done here," Ben said with a sexy grin.

"Out where?" Not that it mattered.

"Dancing."

That wasn't at all what she had been expecting. "Seriously?"

"Unless you just want to go back to my place and have sex."

She really wanted to do just that. But she shouldn't. And she had will power. Somewhere. Or she had at one point. Before Ben. "Um..."

He grinned. "Yeah, I figured dancing was a good way to get up against you but not make you nervous."

She stood up straighter. "Why would I be nervous?"

He cocked his head to one side. "You seem like the type to get nervous about an affair."

An affair. The words echoed in her head. Casual sex. Short term. That was all he wanted with her?

While her pride wanted to tell him he was crazy to think he could walk away after a night with her and her heart protested anything so simple, part of her felt a whisper of relief.

If it was just a fling, brief and minimally emotional, then she could have the amazing sex she was sure Ben would deliver—and that she deserved, dammit—but she didn't have to worry that he would eventually let her down. She would know going in not to expect anything more.

Could she have an affair and not want more?

She could admit that she'd wanted more than an affair. But that had been with the old Ben, the Ben she'd built up in her mind as the perfect guy. She wasn't so sure this Ben could give her anything she needed beyond the best orgasm of her life.

Not that a mind-blowing orgasm was anything to dismiss lightly.

She rubbed the middle of her forehead. This was crazy. She could not sleep with him. She wasn't the laid-back, unbelievable-sex-is-enough kind of girl. She would have expectations outside of the bedroom. Already did in fact. Expectations that she couldn't shake.

She really had three problems. One, she still wanted him—every damn inch of him—whether he was saving lives or not. Two, the more time she spent with him, the more she liked him—even unemployed and taking nothing seriously, Three, she had to spend time with him. Her future at the hospital depended on it.

"Yeah, I'm a prude at heart," she said weakly. Maybe that would turn him off.

"I didn't say you're a prude," Ben said, running his hand down her arm.

"*I* said it," she said firmly.

If he believed it maybe he wouldn't even try to seduce her and then she wouldn't have to work at resisting him.

"I could change your mind."

"I'm...abstaining." Yeah, that sounded good. Not sleeping with the guys she'd met over the past year wasn't technically abstaining. It was more like a no-brainer. But telling Ben she was abstaining was far less complicated than admitting to him that he was the first to make her happily wax her bikini line in a very long time. Maybe he would respect it and quit touching her so much. Which made her forget every good intention she had regarding the hospital and Ben's future. And her own.

Yeah, he definitely needed to stop touching her. That would make everything easier.

Respectful wasn't exactly how she would have described his expression. Mildly surprised was more like it. But interested too.

"Why are you abstaining?" he asked.

Because my vibrator has been doing a fine job and doesn't make promises it doesn't intend to keep. "I'm a role model." She gestured at the kids. She'd never needed a reason before, so hadn't thought of that, but it sounded good.

He moved in closer and his voice dropped. "You don't act like you want to abstain."

She felt her blush. Yeah, no kidding.

She evidently didn't reply soon enough because Ben added, "In fact, you seemed to like having my hands on you today."

The memory of his hands, especially on her breast, zinged through her as if he was touching her right then.

As her blood hummed and her nerves sang, she also felt strangely comfortable.

"Well, I..."

He chuckled. "Then again, I'm not sure I've ever gone out with a virgin before so how do I know how they act?"

Jessica froze, just resisting a large guffaw at Ben's mistaken assumption. He gave her a wink and then turned and crossed the room toward Sophie. Thank goodness. The fact that she was dumbfounded was going to get hard to hide.

He thought she was a *virgin*? How had that happened?

Apparently her no-dating-guys-at-work policy and her luck with only meeting men outside of work that she didn't want to sleep with had resulted in some interesting assumptions.

And apparently Ben wasn't intimidated or turned off by seducing a supposed virgin.

She watched as Ben approached Sophie and introduced himself.

He smiled at the girl and Jessica's heart tripped. That damn smile. It was going to be the death of her. Or at least of her heart.

Well, dancing with him was much less dangerous than everything else she wanted to do with him, and if he was going dancing, then she was going dancing. Russ wanted her to keep an eye on Ben. Ben out at a nightclub was precisely the type of situation that would make Russ nervous.

Jess shook herself out of the Ben-induced stupor and went over to join Ben and Sophie.

"You're really a doctor?" Sophie asked as Jess arrived beside Ben.

The way the girl's eyes took in Ben's shorts and T-shirt and ratty tennis shoes told Jess that the absence of a lab coat and stethoscope made Sophie suspicious.

"Ben is a doctor. He's a friend of mine," Jess inserted.

Ben raised an eyebrow at her introduction. Okay, maybe friend wasn't entirely accurate but was he more than a friend, or less?

Either way, he certainly wasn't *just* Ben.

"He works in the ER at Saint Anthony's."

"I used to," Ben added. "And I still have a medical license, for now anyway, and I was wondering if there was anything I could do for you?"

Jess frowned at his explanation of his career status, but he didn't look at her.

Sophie shrugged. "I went to the free clinic for a checkup."

"That was three months ago," Jess said gently. "In pregnancy a lot changes every month."

"Um…"

Jessica could tell that Ben wasn't inclined to insist or even persuade, and that annoyed her. "Please let him give you a quick checkup," she said. "It will make *me* feel better."

"I guess," Sophie finally answered.

Jess showed Ben and Sophie to the dining area off the rec room and got him the blood pressure cuff, stethoscope, tape measure and the glucose test strips they had in their supplies, thanks to her ability to sweet-talk the hospital.

When they were set, she headed toward her sister's office, still thinking about Ben's insistence that he was *not* an ER doctor. Why was he being so adamant about it? He *was* a doctor and it was clear that the ER was his domain. That didn't disappear with a few days off. Perhaps he was considering not going back to St. Anthony's, but surely he wasn't permanently going to leave medicine all together. Doctors didn't do that. Men who were dedicated to helping others, saving lives, didn't suddenly stop being dedicated. That wasn't heroic. And Ben Torres—in her experience and especially in her dreams—was first and foremost a hero.

Ben emerged from the small conference room and his talk with Sophie feeling strangely tired.

It hadn't been easy. Sophie was sixteen and not at all ready for, or even aware of, what labor and delivery would be like. He'd had to start at the beginning. To her credit, the girl had asked questions. They were painfully naive questions, but at least she was trying to learn.

He was ready for a big break. In the form of dancing and letting loose with Jessica.

His eyes were drawn to her immediately when he stepped into the rec room. She was shooting pool with a couple of the guys and was laughing as she lined up and took the next shot. Which was a tough, brilliant shot and reminded Ben of how he'd underestimated her in the bar last night. In more ways than one.

But though she was obviously beating them badly, the boys were laughing with her. It was clear that she took her role here, influencing these teens, seriously, but she wasn't faking the enjoyment or the caring that he and the kids saw.

Ben propped a shoulder against the doorjamb and watched her.

He remembered thinking she was beautiful the first time

he'd ever seen her. She'd been holding a teenager, like the ones here, away from the body of her injured brother. The foot-long shard of window glass that had pierced the boy's lower abdomen was the reason Ben had been called into the ER.

He didn't let Jessica distract him every time they were in the ER together, but he was always aware of her. He knew where she was, what she was doing, what she wore and when she left.

Which was why punching Ted in the ER on his last day was an easy, instinctive reaction. The man was one of the fools Ben had to patch back together nearly every day. He'd been out getting drunk and then treating the highway like his own personal racetrack. Ben had wanted to punch him the minute he saw him. The rage grew when Ben heard the two-year-old pronounced dead in the next trauma room. But when the man had grabbed Jessica, Ben couldn't hold back. Sure, he'd been looking for a reason, but Jessica was a damn good reason.

And it had felt so good.

The pent-up aggression that had been building against all the villains, all the bad guys of the world that hurt others through their selfish actions, all came pouring out in that one decision. He would not try to fool even himself by pretending it hadn't been a very conscious choice. He'd known as he'd moved, as if in slow motion, that he was going to get suspended. And he hadn't cared. Still didn't.

In fact, he hadn't cared about much since the phone call from Africa...

Ben shook off the memory. It did no good to replay it. He couldn't change what had happened.

Instead, he strode toward the only thing he'd been able to work up any enthusiasm for in days. And she was, oddly enough, a perfectionist virgin that disapproved of his career choices. Go figure.

He took her arm when she stood from her last shot. "I'm ready to go."

She turned and gave him the smile that felt like a soothing balm on his wounds. "I have to put in some more time."

He wondered if she could put that time in somewhere a little more private. With him. With fewer clothes on. "I'll stay, too."

"You sure?"

"Why not?" He certainly wasn't going to get to kiss her, or touch her, or talk her into going dancing if he left.

"Then there's something else I could use your help with."

"What's that?"

She pointed a finger at something over his left shoulder.

He turned and saw a woman of about sixty sitting next to one of the teenage boys who had helped carry David into the center. She wore a blue dress and panty hose, clunky patent leather shoes with a slight heel, and even a strand of pearls around her neck.

"Who is she?" Ben asked.

"Tony's grandmother."

He heard Jess take a deep breath, then rush through the rest.

"She's got a bad infection in her foot. Tony ran home as soon as he realized you were a doctor to tell her so she could come get it checked."

Ben pursed his lips. Complicated. That's what all of this was turning into. Which was precisely what he wanted to avoid. But this was Jessica and he *was* going to take her dancing. At least. No sense in ticking her off yet. No doubt Tony's grandmother got to Jessica as much as Tony did.

"She looks like she was on her way to church," he said, turning to face Jess.

"She dressed up to see you."

He snorted. "Right."

Jessica looked exasperated. "Ben, I realize the ER is different, but it surely isn't so hard to believe that doctors are important? That people respect them?"

"They dress up to go to the doctor and church?"

"Two very important appointments with people they want to make a good impression on."

Ben huffed out a breath of frustration. Great. Expectations. Expectations that came to see him with pearls.

"Fine. I'll see her," he agreed. "But not for free."

"Ben!" Jess protested. "These people don't have any—"

"I don't want *her* to compensate me." He moved in close to her and his gaze dropped to her lips. "And I don't want money."

He knew the moment she understood his meaning. He watched her suck in a quick breath and her tongue darted out to wet the bottom lip he'd just studied.

"What..." She had to stop and clear her throat. "What do you want?"

Oh, what a question. Ben's imagination took it and ran. What he wanted involved an awful lot of naked on Jessica's part. But he didn't think she was quite ready to hear that.

"We're already going dancing," she said when he didn't answer right away.

"That's an excellent decision, by the way."

"So there's more?"

Ben looked at her, her breaths coming quicker than they should for casual conversation.

"I want you to spend the day after tomorrow with me too."

Her eyes got wide. "The day after tomorrow?"

"Yeah. You still owe me tomorrow, from the initial forty-eight hour deal, but I want the next day too."

"All day?"

"Yes. Like we did today."

He saw her cheeks flush slightly and realized she was thinking about the arcade. Which pleased him.

She hesitated.

Ben glanced at Tony's grandmother. "I bet her foot hurts."

"That's low," Jessica said.

Ben knew, however, that Jess didn't believe that he'd walk away from the woman. And he wouldn't. As much as he wanted to.

"That's the deal," he lied.

"Fine."

"The whole day," he clarified.

She smiled and Ben realized that this was a very good idea.

"Go check her foot already," Jess said. "I want to go dancing."

Tony's grandmother spoke softly and politely to Ben, of course, but requested that Jessica be present for the examination. Ben didn't mind. Having Jessica around was nice. Distracting to an extent, but nice. He liked her laugh, which he'd heard a lot since coming to the center.

Ben stopped his thoughts right there.

"Let's take a look at that foot," Ben said, forcing himself to concentrate on the older woman in front of him and not as much on the younger woman to her right.

"It's been bad lately," Mrs. Wilson told him as Jessica assisted her in pulling off her knee-high panty hose. "It throbs."

Ben could see why. The entire forefoot was purple and swollen, including the toes. In fact, her first three toenails were becoming blackened. The portion of the foot from the mid-arch and up to the ankle was also reddened, though looked healthier than the rest. Farther up the ankle and leg became less and less red and swollen, to a point below the bulk of her calf muscle.

Jessica handed Ben a pair of latex gloves before he could ask. He probed the area, finding a few sore spots, but others where Mrs. Wilson didn't react at all.

"Can you feel that?" he asked, pressing on her middle toe.

The woman shook her head. "Not really. Some pressure is all."

She had nerve damage.

"You're diabetic, aren't you Mrs. Wilson?"

The woman glanced at her grandson, then at Jessica, then nodded to Ben.

"And are you controlling it?" Ben asked.

The woman looked down at her foot. "I forget to check my blood," she admitted. "And supplies are expensive."

"There are lots of ways to get help with the money," Ben told her, though he suspected she knew that. "But you have to remember to check your blood sugars. Diabetes is a serious condition."

The woman nodded.

"Have you ever had an actual diabetes education class?" Ben asked her as he lifted her foot to inspect the bottom.

"No."

"I'm going to set you up to attend the class at St. Anthony's. It's free," he added.

"How will I get there?"

Ben held back a sigh. "The bus stops right across the street from the hospital, Mrs. Wilson. You'll need to attend five nights, but it's only once a week."

"It's at night?" the woman asked. "I don't like going out at night."

Ben didn't hold this sigh back. "There's a class that meets

before lunch as well."

He watched her try to find another excuse. "Mrs. Wilson," Ben interrupted as she opened her mouth. "You have to be in charge of your diabetes. I can't help you if you're not going to help yourself."

His voice was firm and he could see the older woman's eyes widen. She was probably regretting getting dressed up for a jerk like him.

"Ben," Jessica said.

He didn't look at her. She was probably disappointed that he'd talk to a patient like that. She had no idea that this was minor.

Man he was sick of trying to help people in spite of themselves. Why should he? If she didn't care about her foot, why should he? She'd let it get this bad. Obviously, she wasn't overly concerned.

"I'll help her get to the classes, Doc."

Ben looked up at the woman's grandson. "If she's going during the day, you'll be in school."

"Isn't this more important?"

Ben stood up quickly and frowned down at the boy. "*Nothing* is more important for you than school."

"But her foot..."

"There are other options." Ben turned and looked at the boy's grandmother. "Aren't there, Mrs. Wilson?"

The woman bit her bottom lip, but nodded.

"Okay." Ben was satisfied. The woman also needed treatment to her foot, however. "Jessica, could you get Mrs. Wilson the phone number for the wound clinic at the hospital?" he asked.

After the door had shut behind Jessica, Ben dug into his back pocket, extracting his wallet. He pulled a fifty-dollar bill out.

"I'd like to have you see an WOC nurse," Ben said, referring to the nurses specializing in wound care. There were no open areas on Mrs. Wilson's legs yet, but a consultation would be good for her. If she would see a friend of his, he'd have Valerie scare the woman with what could happen if she didn't take better   care of herself.

"This is for bus fare," he explained, handing the money to the older woman. "I want you to go to those classes, but I understand things get in the way sometimes."

He watched as Mrs. Wilson hesitantly took the money, her eyes wide. "Thank you, Doctor."

"There are only two things you have to do to thank me."

She looked up at him expectantly.

"Go to the classes," he said simply. "I will check to be sure you do."

She nodded.

"And don't tell Miss Bradford that I gave you the money."

He would do what he could for this woman. Hell, he would have easily blown the fifty bucks eating and drinking at a bar and grill with his buddies. Giving the money to this woman to improve her health was better for him too. But he didn't want Jessica to know. She'd blow it out of proportion, assume it meant he was coming around and would be heading back to his scalpel and scrubs any minute. No sense in getting her hopes up.

The door opened and Jessica came in. And, for a moment, Ben felt like he'd already had those beers he was going to blow his money on. He felt light and happy and, if he wasn't mistaken, like doing some karaoke. Something mushy like Sonny and Cher's "I Got You Babe", maybe.

He knew he was probably smiling like a twelve-year-old with a crush, but she made him feel good. And made him want to make her feel good. Her hair looked freshly brushed and he wondered how often she freshened up in a day. She was obviously the type to take pride in her appearance. Even with blood all over the front of her in the middle of a trauma, she looked collected. He liked that about her. Jessica wasn't someone he'd have to worry about or take care of. She could certainly take care of herself.

But damn if he didn't have the very strong urge to mess up her hair.

Chapter Five

"Thank you for talking to Sophie and seeing Mrs. Wilson," Jess said sincerely as Ben joined her at the center's front doors after washing up.

Ben ignored her appreciative comment.

"You're still voting for dancing rather than going to my place for a night of mind-blowing sex?"

It was *so* tempting.

She sighed as he took her hand and they stepped out into the night. She wasn't a gambler by nature. Anymore. She liked things as orderly and predictable as they could get. Not everything in life could be planned, but that only made it more important to plan the things she could control. And who she gave her body, heart and life to was certainly one of those things.

"I think I'm in the mood for dancing," she said.

"That's only because you've gone dancing before and you know what it's like. If you knew what sex was like you'd vote that way."

She wanted to tell him the truth about her sexual history, just to see the stunned look on his face, but she bit her tongue. She didn't know how he'd react, and she didn't feel like giving him up yet.

"Still, I think it's dancing."

They stopped by his truck and he unlocked her side. "I was hoping you'd say that," he told her as he opened her door for her.

She raised an eyebrow. "Oh, really?"

He pressed close and she stopped breathing for a moment.

"Yeah, because I'll get to be up against you longer this way. I have a feeling the first time we make love it won't last too long."

Jess took that as a compliment. Ben was nothing if not controlled.

She took a shaky breath. "Well, that's...good."

Of course, being up against Ben for any period of time, clothes between them and vertical, or not and horizontal, might be the death of her.

"Should I change clothes before we go?" she asked, looking down at what she wore. It was appropriate for the arcade and the center, but not for a club...or a fancy restaurant? She looked at him. Maybe this would be a romantic date, with a candlelight dinner after dancing and—

"Nah, you look fine," Ben said.

Oh.

A few minutes later they pulled up in front of a club called Black and Blue.

"Should I be worried?" Jess asked as they walked toward the front.

Ben moved in close to her. "I'll protect you." His arm slipped around her waist and his hand settled on her hip.

Okay. She didn't need candlelit dinners.

The club's entrance was on the street level, but she saw a long flight of stairs leading down into the darkness.

The sound and vibration from the music grew steadily as they descended, Jess in front of Ben, but holding hands.

She reached the huge wooden door at the bottom of the steps and pulled. The noise and heat hit her all at once. Ben nudged her from behind when she paused in the doorway, and she moved forward with him pressing in close.

Light was not a part of what bombarded her senses. The club was dark, the carpets, walls, tabletops, everything in a blue and black checkered pattern.

Jessica took a deep breath and felt herself smile. The heat soaked into her, the music seemed to reach into her, and the thump of the bass felt like it was coming from within her bones. The energy in the room, the passion, the adrenaline, seeped into her bloodstream, making her veins feel like they were carrying carbonated soda.

It had been a long time, but her gut hadn't forgotten.

It was clubs like this where she'd gone to let loose, to untangle everything from her thoughts and feelings to the actual muscles that carried the tension of trying to live up to her dad's high standards.

She hadn't even realized she'd missed it.

Her eyes adjusted as they moved into the interior of the club and she found the dance floor.

The first thing to come to mind was the movie *Dirty Dancing* and the thought *Oh, yeah, baby.* Couples covered the floor, but in most cases she would have been hard pressed to say where one person ended and the other began. There wasn't a millimeter of space between them. "Do you want a drink?" Ben asked near her ear.

She shook her head slowly as she watched a beautiful Latino woman in a deep red dress that barely covered her breasts dip back over the arm of her partner. The man blatantly ran his palm up over her rib cage and over one breast.

Jessica's skin heated, remembering Ben's hands on her earlier, then heated further realizing that they would be again soon.

"Jess?" Ben asked.

She turned and faced him. "Yeah?" Her gaze zeroed in on his mouth and she craved those lips on her skin. Any skin. Or all of it.

She moved closer.

He let her, but asked again, "Do you want a drink?" His voice was husky now.

She shook her head. "Let's dance."

He didn't argue. In fact, they were barely on the dance floor before he twirled her and pulled her up against him. His hands settled at the base of her spine, holding her against him.

As if she'd even think of moving.

Ben moved against her, pressing hips to hips, belly to belly. And she rethought that whole not-moving idea quickly.

The music was a Latin beat, the bass deep, throbbing through her body. The heat in the club was pure sexual energy and it was clear that foreplay was the reason everyone came here. There wasn't even much drinking going on. Or talking. Any verbal exchange between partners was in the form of whispers, lips to ears. Most exchanges, however, were in good old-fashioned body language.

"You know why I brought you here, don't you?" Ben asked against her ear.

His breath on her skin created goosebumps down her neck and arm.

"I have a pretty good idea."

He chuckled. "Not that, believe it or not."

She pulled back and looked up at him. "No?" She wasn't sure if she should be surprised, or relieved, or disappointed.

His eyes darkened. "Oh, Jess, I want to make love to you. Don't doubt that for a second."

She forgot to breathe for a moment.

"But I could pursue that any number of ways. I brought you *here* because I was sure you'd never been here before."

"Hmm," she said vaguely, resting her temple against his chin.

"And I think it's going to be fun showing you some things you've never done before."

Her heart sped up in response to the tone of his voice even more than because of the words. "Oh?"

"There's something about you that makes me want to get you wrinkled and confused," he said low in her ear, his breath tickling her neck again.

"I..." She swallowed. "I don't like confusion."

His laugh was more of a low rumble. "You're an ER nurse. Isn't what you do all about confusion?"

She nodded, her cheek brushing against his shoulder. She felt mellow, in spite of the way Ben made her blood sing. "I'm there to help restore order, to some degree."

"Ah." He turned her to avoid another, more energetic couple dancing near them.

Though what they were doing was hardly dancing. It was more swaying. Slowly.

"Like what you do at the center, right?" he asked.

"Right." What was the point in lying or downplaying it, really? The sooner Ben understood what made her tick—and vice versa—the sooner they could get on to deciding if they could be together or not.

"Where's that come from?" he asked.

"Life," she said simply, then sighed as he trailed an index finger down the length of her throat. "When Dad died I had two choices: take control or let the chaos win."

She knew some people admired what she'd done. But she didn't consider it all that amazing. She'd had to do it. She certainly couldn't have let her brother and sister go to foster care.

"No interest in confusion...at all?" Ben asked, his finger running back and forth across her collarbone bringing her effectively out of her reminiscing.

She sighed again. "Can you better define confusion?"

She probably should be asking him if he'd decided to go back to the hospital, or if he'd thought about private practice. But instead she wanted to know how he was going to induce confusion in her life. Great.

"I could show you," Ben said.

She was coherent enough to know that *that* was a dangerous idea. "Start by telling me."

He turned her again, but she quickly realized it was to get her back against the closest wall. He leaned in, his forearm resting on the wall, even with her forehead. His index finger traced down the length of her throat, then kept going down her sternum to where her top buttoned between her breasts. He ran his finger back and forth across the top edge of her shirt as he talked.

"When I say confusion, I'm talking about turning a few things upside down for you, making you try a few new things, maybe making you feel some things you haven't felt before."

Already there, Jess thought.

Ben leaned in slowly until his lips were right against her neck and she felt him inhale deeply. "I can't get over how great you smell."

She met his gaze

"It's vanilla."

"Vanilla," Ben repeated slowly. "My favorite flavor."

Flavors brought to mind tasting and tongues and Jess felt a delicious shiver dance over her.

Hell, she'd wear Tabasco sauce if it got *that* look from him.

"Do you have it back here?" he asked, the tip of his finger brushing the sensitive skin behind her ear lobe.

She nodded. He bent his head and she felt the touch of this tongue in the same spot.

She was pretty sure he heard her moan.

"Tastes even better than it smells," he said. He watched her, his eyes heavy. "Where else?"

She licked her lips, which he watched intently, then lifted her right wrist. He caught the wrist and lifted it, her palm up. He breathed deeply, then she watched, heartbeat thundering, as his tongue flicked over the pulse point. The sensation zinged straight to her stomach, then instantly dropped lower to another spot that throbbed.

"Where else?" he asked gruffly.

She was afraid her hand was shaking as she lifted a finger and indicated the base of her throat where she was sure he would see her heart pounding.

He dipped his head and his lips touched the spot gently. She let her head fall back and, the permission given, he increased the pressure of his lips, then sucked slightly, before lifting his head to look at her.

The urge to take her clothes off for him was nearly overwhelming.

"Anywhere else?"

She nodded, unable to speak once she saw the heat in his eyes. She pointed to the valley between her breasts.

"I am a very happy man," he declared, with a crooked grin. Then he bent his knees and tasted her again.

He had his hands on her hips—thank goodness—because he helped to keep her upright.

But it was nearly a lost cause after that.

Ben rose slowly, but he didn't ask her permission this time.

His lips claimed hers in a lusty, hot, wet kiss that wouldn't have been complete without his hands all over her, especially cupping and teasing her breasts and at her hips, bringing her more fully against the part of him that clearly wanted her as much as she wanted him.

They could make love right here in this dark corner of this club and it was doubtful any of the other patrons would notice—or care. More skin was showing and being touched on that dance floor than they would need to expose to get the job done.

Ben's hand cupped her buttock and one finger slid between her legs and over the sensitive skin aching for him. Even with the material of her pants between them, Jess felt a sob of pleasure catch in her throat. He was so good at this. As she'd known he would be. Ben would make sex glorious.

And that was the thought that yanked her back to earth like an anchor dropped into a puddle.

Just as she'd built Ben up as the perfect guy, she'd created an amazing fantasy around having sex with him. It had to be perfect. Which was unfair to him. And scary for her. Because at the same time her imagination was creating fantasies, her conscience was reminding her that perfection was unattainable.

But geez, when she was letting the fantasy build, she had never believed she would actually have sex with him.

She pushed against him, pulling their mouths apart first. He looked down at her, questions in his eyes. His breathing was heavy and he didn't seem inclined to move his hands anytime soon.

"What's wrong?"

"This isn't how I want to do this," she said unsteadily.

"Tell me what you want and I'll do it," he said, moving a finger and making her moan.

"No," she gasped. "I don't want to do it here, like this."

Ben studied her with a frown. "But if I let you go right now, you'll decide not to do it at all, anywhere."

"Not tonight," she agreed.

"I could change your mind." His lips came close and his finger moved again.

"I know," she sighed, giving in to the sensations that she knew no other man would ever produce in her.

"And you think for some reason that I'm this big hero and wouldn't think of pressing my advantage, right?" he asked against her lips.

"You are a hero. It's not a matter of opinion. You're a good guy."

"What if I told you my heroics don't extend to gorgeous virgins who go soft in my hands?"

It probably wasn't a good thing that he knew his effect on her so well.

"It does," she said with confidence. "You don't want to

pressure me."

His hips moved into hers. "Don't I?"

But she could see him already resigned and it only made her infatuation with him stronger. She knew as well as he did that he could easily make love to her tonight and she wouldn't even be upset tomorrow.

The fact he was not going to push proved that he was truly one of the good guys—the kind of guy who saved strangers' lives for a living.

"I need a drink," he said as they stepped apart. "I'm obviously thinking too clearly."

Jess readjusted her clothes. "Thinking clearly is not necessarily a bad thing."

"I'm not making love to you right now. *That's* a bad thing."

She was so happy he'd backed off with a simple request—and with the fact that she'd been coherent enough to make the request—that she followed him to the bar.

He ordered a glass of whiskey and downed it in one swallow. She ordered only a soda. They sat on two stools with Ben's knees on either side of hers, claiming her as his territory with a possessive hand on her thigh.

That she didn't mind. His third whiskey she did.

"I'm driving you to drink?" she asked when the third glass was set in front of him.

"Gotta fill my free time somehow." He shot the drink back.

"No other ideas at all?" she asked dryly.

"Yeah," he said, looking toward the corner they'd been making out in. "But you said no."

"Sex and drinking are your only options?"

"Pretty much."

"You could...oh, I don't know, *work*."

He gave her a half smile. "Nah. That sounds too responsible."

"That's one word, one of many, like respectable, rewarding..."

"I know all about working," Ben interrupted. "I've been working since I was fourteen. I've put in thirty-two hour shifts, I've seen more than my share of blood and guts and pain. And I've also got nothing to show for it."

She gasped. "How can you say that? You've saved lives!"

"Yeah." He shrugged. "But we're talking about *me*."

Her eyebrows shot up. He was *not* this selfish. She hoped.

"You get *nothing* out of it?" she challenged.

He narrowed his eyes as if considering the question. "Nope," he said finally.

"The feeling of satisfaction, being needed, being someone's...savior?"

"Dammit, Jessica," Ben snapped. "You make it sound like these people have pictures of me on their mantels and bring me sacrifices and pay homage."

She opened her mouth to protest, but Ben wasn't done. He jabbed his index finger against the wooden top of the bar, emphasizing each point.

"Nine out of ten of the people I work on don't know my name and remember me only because of some scar on their body. Not to mention that most of them are going to leave the hospital and immediately do something stupid. One of them will light up a cigarette on the ride home. Another will decide that strapping on his seat belt is too damn much work. Someone else will decide that it's a lot easier to get to sleep at night if she takes a few pills. Some other asshole will beat up his kid because he got beat up by his old man and he thinks that's how he's supposed to handle the fact that his life sucks." Ben's hand slapped the top of the bar loud enough to make the woman sitting behind him jump, then scowl at him. "Basically what I do is for absolutely nothing in the end. I put people back out there where they can screw things up worse."

He was breathing hard and the wonderful mouth that had done such awesome things to her only a few minutes ago was now set in a hard, cold line.

She didn't know what to say. If that was how he saw things, could she change his mind? He couldn't have been a doctor—the doctor she'd watched all these months—without knowing what he did was good.

"So, you get to walk away when things get tough?" she demanded. "You think things always have to be clean and neat and have happy endings and you have to always be the hero and always do the right thing? What's the real deal? If you can't win, you're not even going to try?"

Ben felt a hot anger that he would have never believed he could feel toward Jessica. It was so unfair. What she was accusing him of was total crap. But she didn't know that, because he hadn't told her. He hadn't told anyone what had driven him out of the ER.

"I've had plenty of pain and blood and death on my caseload," he said caustically. "I know more about bad outcomes and defeat than any other surgeon in this city."

He wanted to tell her all of it, he realized. He was disappointing her and God knew why it mattered, but it did. Maybe if he told her about Africa she would understand, and forgive him for falling short of her standards.

Jessica thought she knew what was best for everyone else and he wanted to believe that he only wanted her for a good time. Her expectations were way too much for him to worry about living up to. She was way too demanding for where he was in his life right now.

But part of him wanted to lean on her. Jessica was led by firm internal directives. She didn't waffle or flounder over what to do in any circumstance. She knew what to do and she did it.

He was so tired of having his life turned upside down and not knowing which way to go when the spinning stopped. Maybe she could tell him how he could get over this.

"I was a missionary in Tanzania for five years," he finally started. "I led a team that was assigned to the poorest of poor small villages."

He took a deep breath. Memories were never far away. During his five years there he'd become part of the community. The people of the village and his team had become his surrogate family.

"We treated the people medically, of course, but we also worked on prevention and teaching them to treat themselves and each other. We also gave them supplies and equipment and taught them how to use and maintain it."

Jessica was watching him with a combination of open interest—which touched him because of how much his missionary work had meant to him—and admiration. The admiration he didn't want. He hadn't gone to Africa for any kind of praise or prestige. He'd gone because his father had ingrained in him that those with plenty were called to share with those without. Ben had plenty—money, health, resources and talent. He'd felt drawn back to Tanzania where he'd spent four years with his missionary father. So he'd gone. Three weeks after finishing his surgical residency. And he'd stayed two years longer than he'd planned.

"What happened?" Jess asked, obviously having grown impatient during his reflection.

Bitterness rose from his gut through his chest and into his throat. He swallowed and said hoarsely, "A month ago I found out the entire village was wiped out by a rebel army trying to control the region. There weren't any survivors."

Emotion choked him for a moment as faces flashed through his mind, villagers and missionary team members alike.

He'd lost a lot of people in that one event. Friends, colleagues, people who'd trusted him.

"Oh, Ben..." Jess reached out and touched his arm.

He didn't pull away, but he didn't want her sympathy either. He wasn't feeling sorry for himself. He was feeling guilty. To his very core.

"I worked to save their lives for five years and then they were all wiped out in a day and a half. It was all for nothing."

"Ben..." Jess started again.

He could see her eyes were glossy as if full of tears.

"Don't you see?" he asked harshly. "I taught them how to prevent and treat diarrhea, dehydration, infections; all of these things that were killing them off, but in the end I couldn't keep them alive."

"You don't blame yourself for what happened?" she asked, her tone shocked.

He blamed himself for leaving them. Not that he could have defended them, but at least then he wouldn't have been the only one to escape. He also blamed himself for getting into a profession where there was more grief than gratification. He'd seen how it had consumed his father and how his father had given the ultimate sacrifice for it. Why hadn't Ben known better?

He shook his head, struggling to put it into words. "I didn't kill them," he said, "But I didn't save them, either. I went in thinking I was going to change their world. I was so full of myself and what I was doing. But in the end, nothing I did mattered. Training midwives to safely deliver babies who would grow up and be slaughtered instead? Did I do them a favor? How about the babies *I* delivered?"

He went on before she could interrupt with an attempt at consolation. "I was so self-righteous. I was saving the world. But those babies were almost four when that army came through. They had to watch their village burn and their neighbors and families be killed, feel the terror and then the pain as they were killed. Did I do them a big favor?"

Jessica seemed to be breathing as hard as he was and he felt her touch on his arm tighten as if holding on to keep him from running away from her.

Which he considered.

She was making him face all of this again, when all he wanted to do was forget. And he'd been doing okay at that. Mostly. Some of the time. She was also challenging him to return to the work in spite of knowing better now. He should resent her for making him miss it, for making him consider trying again, in spite of the fact that he knew there would be more bad days than good, more stress and helplessness and unsolvable questions. But he didn't resent her. In fact, he couldn't get enough of her.

Jessica swallowed twice before she said, "But those babies... Their mothers had four years to love them and teach them
and—"

"And then they got to know the pain of losing them, of not being able to protect them. In the end, what I did amounted to nothing."

She looked at him for several long seconds. Finally, not sure what else to do, she went with her heart. She slid off of her stool, stepped forward, wrapped her arms around his waist and hugged him.

Ben grabbed her tightly, holding her against his thundering heart. She closed her eyes and simply felt him—and let him feel her.

He seemed to be content to just hold her. His chin rested on the top of her head and he sighed deeply. Jess felt the sigh clear to her soul. She reveled in giving him comfort.

They were touching in every possible place they could with clothes on. There was nothing at all sexual about the embrace. Jess also reveled in that.

After several minutes of breathing together, Ben pulled back and looked down at her. The pain in his eyes had eased somewhat.

"This is what I need," he said gruffly. "Life, pleasure, happiness. It's selfish but I can't do it any other way. Not anymore. I gave up a lot of comforts in Africa. I missed out on time with my mom. And in the end it was all for nothing."

"Ben, sacrifice is part—"

He put a hand over her mouth. "I want to enjoy now. I put my time in. I did my part."

"And now you're going to party your life away?"

"I'm going to celebrate life, the good things, the fun things."

"Booze?"

"I was thinking more along these lines."

He bent and kissed her.

It was a gentle, sweet kiss and she certainly had no reason to protest. Ben needed healing, affirmations of life and goodness. She got that. He needed a break. She could understand that.

But the fact that the village and the events in Africa had meant so much to him spoke volumes about him as a person. A person like Ben wouldn't hide from those who needed him for long.

Would he?

She pulled back, pressed her lips together and looked into his eyes. He had some major issues to deal with. Not only did she *not* want a man with issues, she wanted one who had some goals that went beyond wasting as much time and money as possible in bars. She needed focus. She needed purpose. And she needed to be with someone who supported that. Not someone who made it his personal mission to distract her from that focus and purpose whenever he could.

In fact, right now was a perfect example. She was in yet another bar, trying to get Ben to behave, when she should be working on plans at the center, or picking up an extra shift at the hospital or...cleaning her refrigerator. *Anything* that she might succeed at.

But she couldn't leave him here. Lord knew what kind of trouble he would get into.

"Let me take you home," she finally said, pulling back from

the embrace.

He looked at her for several seconds and she could tell he was trying to read her expression.

She understood that he was deeply affected by what had happened, but she wasn't going to let him use it as an excuse to walk away from everyone who still needed him.

"Part of winning is getting up no matter how many times your ass hits the ground," she said. "It's easy to stay down. It definitely hurts less. But anyone can stay down, Ben."

He took a deep breath, then nodded wearily. His eyes dropped to the empty glass in front of him. "It's especially easy if you don't have someone constantly pushing you back up."

There was no question about who that someone was and he didn't exactly sound appreciative.

"Let me take you home," she said again.

"Nah." He looked up at her, a new determination in his eyes. "I've only had three drinks," he said. He looked her up and down. "And I'm not gonna get lucky. At least not with you."

Jessica bristled. He was being difficult and contemptuous on purpose. But he wasn't going to get lucky with anyone else either if she had anything to say about it.

"Ben, you do not need any more to drink. Let's go."

"Not unless you're going to sling me over your shoulder and carry me out of here."

He motioned to the bartender and Jessica fought a surge of frustrated tears.

She didn't want to leave him. He could wrap his car around a tree. He could plow his car into someone else. He could pass out and get robbed. He could get into a fight. Or he could pick up some woman. Basically they were right back to where she'd found him last night.

But she couldn't stay. She was falling for him already. It would get harder and harder to remember that all of this was what she *didn't* need. She'd had her time of aimlessness and idleness. If that was the direction Ben wanted to go, he'd have to go without her.

She fought back the tears and picked up her cell phone, punching in Sam's number. Russ was going to have to be okay with someone else keeping an eye on Ben for a while. She wished that angering Russ was her biggest concern right now.

Yes, she wanted the promotion, but she wanted Ben even more—in spite of knowing better. She was potentially walking away from both tonight.

When her brother answered, she said simply, "It's your turn to babysit," and gave him the address. Then she motioned the bartender over. "If this guy—" she pointed at Ben, "—tries to leave before his friend gets here to drive him home, call the cops and report that this car—" she scribbled Ben's license plate number on a napkin, "—is being driven by a drunk driver." She handed him a twenty for his help.

The bartender agreed and pocketed the money with an interested look in Ben's direction. Ben glanced at him, but said nothing to him or to her.

"Try not to do anything stupid," she said as she leaned in and kissed Ben's temple. "Goodbye, Ben." She pulled back and looked at him for a long moment. She didn't want this to be goodbye. But just in case it was, she had to say it.

As she walked out of the club she couldn't help the glance back.

He sure didn't look like much of a hero sitting hunched over the bar with four empty glasses in front of him.

"You know that you don't have a clitoris, right?"

Ben strolled into the kitchen where Sam was preparing grilled cheese sandwiches.

Sam turned away from the stove, an incredibly funny expression on his face. "Excuse me?"

Ben tossed him the bottle he'd found when looking for a towel in the bathroom. "Thought I should fill you in, just in case you were wondering why this stuff wasn't working for you."

Sam looked at the label that claimed the oil inside had a warming and arousing affect on the clitoris if applied prior to sexual activity. He grinned when he realized what it was. "Oh, it worked for me—indirectly."

"Better than the leopard print panties?" Ben had also seen those in the lid-less shoebox in the cupboard under the sink.

Sam set the bottle on the counter and turned to flip the sandwich in the pan. "I do my best work when panties are *not* involved."

Ben chuckled and grabbed a banana from the bunch on the counter. "What is that collection?"

Sam shrugged. "Stuff people have left here."

"People? As in, how many?" Ben bit off a huge hunk of banana.

Sam slid the golden sandwich onto a plate that already held two others. "However many are in there."

"Three panties, a bra, a garter and the oil."

"So, six," Sam concluded.

"They were each from a different woman?" Ben asked.

"Probably. I don't remember which is which anymore, though."

"They didn't ask for their underwear back the next time they were here?" Ben asked.

Sam shrugged again with a large grin as he added cheese to yet another piece of bread. "There's no *again* around here. One night, that's all they get."

Ben shook his head and bit off another bite of banana. Wow. Sam certainly didn't have a problem getting wrapped up in other people's lives. If his friends were getting too drunk in some bar, he sent someone in to get them. If a woman came up for some fun and left anything behind, he just chucked it in the shoebox.

Sam didn't get too attached to his patients either. He'd told Ben once that he'd chosen being a paramedic partly because he could work the overnight shifts he preferred and partly because he didn't have to do anything more than keep them alive, however he could, until they hit the ER. Then the big decisions, the tough choices and the hard work were someone else's responsibility. Like his.

"I need to be more like you," Ben said, shaking his head. Sam pushed a plate with two sandwiches toward him. "You have to show me how. Give me lessons or something."

Sam even used paper plates. No washing, no worrying about breakage.

"The warming oil has directions on it, man. I am *not* showing you how to use it." Sam took a huge bite of bread and cheese and yet still managed his unapologetic grin.

"I'm talking about the way you get by without anyone expecting more of you." Ben bit into his sandwich too.

Sam washed his food down with a big swig of milk. "That sounds like maybe I should be insulted."

"No, you should appreciate it," Ben said emphatically. "You can do your thing your way and everyone accepts it."

Sam finished off his first sandwich, watching Ben contemplatively as he spoke. "Basically I'm irresponsible and inconsiderate."

Ben scowled at him. "I'm *commending* you. I want to be like you."

Sam laughed. "I wasn't offended. I was clarifying what you were saying."

"I'll give you an example," Ben said, on a roll now. "I can remember the names and birthdates of all but one of the women I've slept with. How about you?"

Sam looked amazed. "Hell, no. Are you *kidding*?"

"I've had one one-night stand. And I do remember her name. Otherwise, I've slept with three women, all of whom I had significant relationships with."

"It's not necessarily *bad* to have only slept with a few women, most of whom you really cared about," Sam countered. "You're what they call one of the good guys."

"I'm guessing the woman who owned the warming oil thought you were pretty good," Ben said dryly.

Sam grinned. "Sure. Yeah. For that. At the time. But I can also assure you that she didn't call begging me to come home and meet her parents."

"You're a good guy," Ben said. "You just don't take things too seriously. You know when to say when. You don't try to fix everything for everyone else. You know that you can't always make everyone happy so you don't worry about it."

"And you're not like that," Sam said, nodding. "Yeah, you're right. I get that. It's not that you don't know when to say when... You don't even know that there is a when. Especially with work. Right?"

Because his dad never said when.

The thought flashed through Ben's head before he could stop it, or brace for it.

His father had been all about his work. Being a missionary had been Michael Torres' calling and he put his heart and soul into it. Everyone he had ever known respected him and was inspired by him. But none of those people had lived with him. None of them knew what it was like to always have the work, the calling, the mission put first. Ben had been loved, but he had never been prioritized. Neither had his mother. They were expected to be self-sufficient enough, emotionally strong enough, smart enough to not require Michael to take time or resources away from his work.

Michael had known that he would give one hundred percent to his work. He'd never intended to have a wife and family. But he'd accidentally fallen in love with Ben's mother. Then they had accidentally gotten pregnant. Not that Ben ever believed Michael regretted being a husband and father. But he couldn't focus on it. His work was what he lived for and what he taught his son to value. Work, service, sacrifice. Those were the ideals Ben had inherited from his father. And even though he knew how it felt to be an afterthought, Ben had felt guilty, lazy and selfish any time he'd entertained ideas of focusing on something other than his work.

There had been no such thing as free time, blowing off steam or frivolity in Michael's life, and he'd managed to take those out of his son's imagination as well.

Even when he was watching a football game on TV at home, Ben had a medical journal open in his lap. If he was having a beer with the guys after an especially hard day in the ER, he was still replaying cases, and planning for the next day. Even with women he was always only partially there. They didn't know it, of course, but he couldn't remember one woman he'd ever given one hundred percent of his attention to.

Until Jessica.

Until the one woman who constantly tried to get him to focus on other things.

It was perfect. Perfectly frustrating as hell.

"I want to learn how to say when," Ben announced.

"It's not that hard," Sam said. "Hell, you just need to hook up with people who have the expectations that you want to meet."

Sam's words hit Ben direct in the gut. Quitting his job at the hospital was a step in the right direction in getting away from some of the people who expected so much of him.

The only thing he wasn't sure of was what to do with the people he didn't want to get away from.

"You look like hell," Sam observed as he turned back toward the refrigerator.

Sam tossed a can toward Ben.

Ben caught the can and started to protest, his system rejecting the idea of any further additions of alcohol to his blood stream. He knew how to avoid hangovers, but he'd also drunk more in the past week than he had in the past five years. He thought he could possibly feel his liver cells dying even now. It was a nerdy reaction to the morning after a binge, but he'd always been much more the studious type than the party type.

He realized it was a soda before he turned it down, though, and went ahead and popped the top before acknowledging his friend's comment.

"That's about right."

He wasn't hungover and he'd gotten nearly nine hours of sleep, but he was feeling pretty damn lousy about how he'd left things with Jessica last night. Not to mention that Jessica was not waking up beside him this morning, a fact his libido continued to protest.

In short, he was crabby and horny.

"How about you?" he asked.

Sam loved to go out and Ben knew that his friend rarely saw the hours between about four a.m. and noon. That's why he preferred the late ambulance shift. Sam was a night owl by nature.

Sam shrugged. "I'm okay." He took a swig of Coke and glanced through the open archway at the television in the living room.

Ben shifted and took a drink as well, watching as the shortstop scooped up a line drive and threw the runner out at first.

"Are you pissed that I sent Jess after you in the bar the night you quit work?" Sam asked.

Abrupt changes of topic were not unusual with Sam, so Ben barely blinked. Paramedics, ER doctors and nurses and anyone else who dealt with mere minutes separating life and death learned to cut to the chase. It was a work habit that very often spilled over into other aspects of socialization.

Ben looked across the countertop at his friend. Was he pissed that Jessica had come to get him?

"No. Not at all."

Sam nodded. "Didn't think you would be."

"You didn't have to send her, though," Ben added.

"Yeah, I did." Sam ambled into the living room and settled into a chair.

Ben frowned. Not because Jessica had been the one to come for him, but because he hadn't needed a babysitter.

"I was doing fine," he felt obligated to say as he sank onto the end of the couch.

Sam laughed. "I doubt it."

Ben scowled. "What the hell does that mean?"

Sam grinned at him. "You're a fun guy. I like going out with you and everything. But I'm not sure you're up to partying on your own."

"I wasn't on my own."

"Right, you were with a couple of girls that thought you filled your pants out well and a couple of pool sharks who thought you filled your wallet out well. You were on your own, man."

"I wanted to be on my own."

"Yeah, well, friends don't leave friends to their own stupidity," Sam said. "We've all seen too many of the consequences of driving yourself home mad, drunk or both."

Ben didn't want to thank Sam. The other man was younger, had a reckless streak four times the size of anything Ben was capable of and had a reputation with the women that made even a few of the paramedics blush.

But Sam was a good friend and had been looking out for him. Plus, he'd sent Jessica.

"I appreciate your intentions," he finally said. "But..."

"Forget it," Sam said, stretching out his legs and propping his feet on the coffee table. "I figure you're paying me back. For one thing, Jessica is worried about you right now, which means she's letting up on me. Besides, she needed to have sex."

Ben frowned at Sam, but his friend's eyes were on the television. It wasn't fair that Sam got to be so laid back and comfortable and worry-free all the time. Work and women didn't rile him up, but Ben thought maybe he knew something that would. Maybe the only thing.

"Sam, you remember the waitress that you took home from

Eddie's bar two months ago?"

"Jennifer." Then he pulled his eyebrows together. "Or was it Jill? No, it was Jennifer. Jen. Or Jan. Anyway, I remember her," Sam said, with a large smile, his eyes back on the baseball game.

"You remember the things you told us about her and what all she was willing to do?"

"Sure." Another big grin.

"Sam, I want to do all of those things to your sister and then some. At least twice." Ben paused and let that sink in.

That did get Sam's attention. But not for the reason Ben anticipated.

"Are you telling me that you and Jessica *haven't* slept together yet?"

It was official—nothing could get Sam Bradford's blood pressure up.

"No. We haven't slept together *yet*." Ben frowned. "But I can assure you that it won't be a problem much longer."

"What the hell have you been doing all this time?" Sam asked, incredulous. "Damn, man, no wonder you don't have anybody leaving sex gel at your place."

"Doesn't it bother you to be encouraging some guy to sleep with your sister?"

"You're not just some guy."

"I don't have to worry about you coming after me to defend her honor?"

Sam laughed. "I don't think it will surprise you that Jessica doesn't need a lot of defending. But of course if she needed me. I'd step in. Then again, you're not exactly hurting her."

Of course he would never hurt Jessica. But... "I'm not doing *anything* to her, Sam."

"Oh, yes you are," Sam said. "You're helping her have fun. You're reminding her that she doesn't have to push and worry and prepare and watch her back all the time. You're making her happy."

Ben didn't need to hear that.

That was what he *wanted* to hear. He wanted to hear that he was important to her. At the same time, it complicated everything. It meant that she was important to him too. And that meant that his attempt at reckless and just-for-fun was failing miserably.

Which ticked him off.

He didn't fail things. Ben was good at, and gave his best to, everything.

Besides, hearing Sam talk about emotions was creepy.

"Listen, Sam, I want to—and fully intend to—sleep with your sister. In every position I know and a few I intend to make up as I go."

That sounded good to him, especially out loud. It was a solid plan. It certainly met *his* goal. His *only* goal, he assured himself. Complete and utter physical satisfaction...for both of them.

There was a pause before Sam asked, "Then what?"

Ben looked at his friend. "What do you mean?"

"What then? When you've run out of positions?"

"Then..." Ben meant to say *that's it.* In fact, for a moment he thought he had said it. It was what he *should* say. But the two words simply wouldn't come forth.

"Then?" Sam prompted after a long moment of nothing but silence.

Ben finally managed to find an honest answer to give his friend that seemed to know him too well at times.

"I'm not looking for anything long-term or serious, Sam."

That was the truth from the bottom of his heart.

Of course, him not looking for it didn't mean that it hadn't found him anyway.

Sam whistled low. "They let you cut people's bodies open and mess around inside?"

Ben frowned. "What do you mean?"

"They let you use a scalpel on people, but you're stupid enough to think that this thing with Jessica is only about sex." Then Sam laughed. "That will make this even more fun to watch."

Ben didn't appreciate his friend's enjoyment of his situation, but he was out of defenses. "Hey, Sam, you know that sixty bucks I owe you?"

"I'm never getting it back, right?"

"No way."

Chapter Six

Late that afternoon, Ben was greeted enthusiastically by the five boys surrounding the long table at the far end of the room. The four large pizzas and case of soda he carried were a big part of that, of course.

Except for Mario, who always seemed suspicious of him.

"What's this?" Mario asked, taking the lead as usual, though not even shifting an inch from the posture where he had an elbow on the table, an ankle crossed over a knee and his back so slouched he appeared four inches shorter than he was.

Ben gave the boy direct eye contact. "Thought I'd be more welcome if I came with food."

Mario acknowledged the truth of the statement with a single nod. "Why do you care about being welcome?"

"I need to make Jessica happy with me again, it makes her happy if I hang out with you guys and I thought pizza would convince you guys to let me hang out with you."

"And why do you care if Miss Bradford is happy?" Mario asked.

Because he'd screwed up big time the night before. Ben put the pizzas down and took a chair. "It makes it a lot easier to kiss her."

He didn't feel bad about sharing the somewhat private truth. These kids had seen a lot of real life and he was sure the fact that men and women liked to kiss hadn't escaped them. It wouldn't surprise him if some of them had even noticed that Jessica was kissable, though he thought Mario saw Jessica more as a big sister.

None of the boys commented. Most of them were already munching pizza but Mario was watching Ben as if trying to figure something out.

"Is she happy now?" Mario asked, jutting his chin toward something over Ben's right shoulder.

Ben turned to find Jessica standing across the room. She was talking to Sophie, the pregnant girl Ben had counseled the night before. But Jessica was positioned strategically so she could see everything Ben and the boys were doing. He knew that wasn't an accident.

He turned back around. "You know her pretty well. What do you think?"

The boy's eyes glanced to Jessica again, then returned to Ben. Ben detected a hint of satisfaction over his acknowledgement of Mario's relationship with Jessica.

Mario shrugged. "She's seemed different lately."

That got Ben's attention. "Yeah?" He forced himself to not react.

No sense in both of them thinking he was pathetic over Jessica.

He didn't know what Mario meant and it might not matter. In fact, it shouldn't matter. "How's that?" he asked anyway.

Mario glanced at the other guys at the table. Three were gathered around some handheld device with a screen, one bobbing his head up and down to the beat that was emanating from the device. The other boy at the table was leaning back in his chair, his eyes closed and his hands clasped over his stomach.

Mario turned back to Ben. "She seems more relaxed, I guess."

"Is she usually tense?" He could see it. Jessica seemed to know what she wanted and how to get it. Perhaps the determined focus he appreciated in her in the ER was really who she was.

Mario sat up straighter and leaned in. "Why do you care?"

Ben thought about that, his eyes again returning to Jessica. She was now on hands and knees rummaging in the bottom of the storage closet. His body responded like it was programmed, evidently not minding a bit that she now wore denim instead of scrub pants. Or that she was royally pissed at him.

Ben looked into the intense brown eyes staring him down.

"Told you—kissing," Ben said.

"You don't have to *know* her to kiss her," Mario replied without missing a beat.

The kid had a point.

"I don't really know her."

"But you want to."

Mario was right. Ben tried to tell himself that it was sex-driven. He wanted to know every inch of her body, know how she sounded and looked as she orgasmed, find out what she fantasized about.

"Yeah, I want to," Ben agreed, knowing the sex stuff was only part of it even as he spoke.

"Do you think she wants to know you?" Mario asked.

Ben nodded. "Yeah, I do." Which was a surprising turn-on.

Mario paused, watching Ben, then sat back in his seat. "All right." He drummed his fingers on the tabletop for a few seconds. Finally he said, "I think she likes to goof off. I think that's more who she is. But she thinks she has to be the serious, in-charge type. And she has to work at that...and to make others believe it."

Ben knew in his gut that Mario was right and he was amazed. He'd have to remember that Mario was not just bright; he didn't miss a detail, obviously cared a lot about Jessica and was frighteningly good at analyzing people.

Ben was also jealous. Sure, Mario had known Jessica longer, but he wasn't supposed to *know* her. It was okay if Mario knew how she liked her pizza or that she wore a lot of green. But Mario had noticed things that Ben suspected Jessica didn't even consciously realize.

Ben wanted to be the one noticing things and tuning into her.

So much for not getting too involved.

Hell, he hadn't even slept with her yet.

"Incoming," one of the boys muttered.

Another slipped the device into his jacket pocket and the third flipped open the paperback book he'd been holding. They stayed huddled together but now it looked like they were studying—and had been all along.

The boy who had been dozing surreptitiously pulled another copy of the book from his jacket and propped it open on his stomach. He opened his eyes and focused on a page without moving his head, making it seem from behind—where Jessica was coming from—that he'd been reading the whole time.

Mario slid yet another copy from under the pizza box lid, already open and kept it flat against the table and Ben knew from where Jessica had been across the room she wouldn't have been able to see the book, or lack of it, on the table top.

"Twelve o'clock," Mario muttered with a faint smile at Ben.

"How's it going over here?" Jessica asked

Ben turned and smiled at her, wishing he could pull her down onto his lap.

"It's going great," he said.

"What are you guys talking about?"

Jessica tried to act casual but she'd already been good about keeping her distance and letting Ben get to know the kids.

Having him here made her jumpy, though she couldn't say why for sure. Ever since Ben had walked into the center, casual as you please, as if nothing had happened last night, she'd been waiting for...something. After last night, she had convinced herself that not only did she not expect to see much more of Ben personally, she didn't care. Thinking about giving up the promotion in the ER made her stomach hurt, but not as much as Ben made her heart hurt. He'd been a jerk the night before, spouting off about how unrewarding his work was, and she had realized on the way home in the cab that she didn't want to be around him if that was how he felt.

She also didn't like how sorry he was feeling for himself. What he'd been through with losing everyone in Africa was horrible. She could understand what he was feeling; she'd lived with guilt and regret long enough to recognize it easily in someone else. But she didn't like his moping and pouting. When she'd regretted her choices, she'd jumped in and *done* something, tried to make up for them. Ben was running and she didn't like that characteristic at all.

The problem with walking away from him because of those things was that she didn't think he liked those things in himself any better than she did.

And now he was here. Voluntarily. Spending time with the

kids. If he was here because he'd had a change of heart and realized the good that could be done here, great. If he was here simply to butter her up after last night, well...it was working.

It seemed that Ben and Mario could be friends—or a bad influence on each other. They both drove her crazy in the same way by not realizing their full potential.

At least for Mario there was some justification with his sorry excuse of a mother and no positive male role model. Ben was acting like a spoiled brat.

But Ben could be someone Mario could look up to. And that was what made her decide to talk to him again after all.

"Ben's helping us with our American Lit class," Mario said.

Ben turned back to face the boy and Jessica could no longer see his expression.

"What are you reading?" she asked.

Mario held up the front of the book. *Lord of the Flies.*

She crossed her arms. She'd read it. She wondered if Ben had. He was obviously a smart guy, but she had the sneaking suspicion that American Literature was not the topic of his conversation with Mario. Jessica moved to the side a couple of steps so she could see Ben's face.

He glanced at the other boys, who were watching him as well. If they hadn't been discussing the book, Ben might confess and keep himself out of trouble.

"Yeah, but I think we should finish the discussion after they read the waterfall scene. It's my favorite," Ben said.

"Waterfall scene?" Mario asked.

"Yeah, with all the naked native girls," Ben said pushing back from the table. "It's hot."

Jessica checked Mario's reaction to Ben's comment. He simply quirked an eyebrow. He didn't say anything, though, and Jessica couldn't help but admit that Mario must like Ben.

Ben took her elbow and steered her away from the table. She enjoyed the way his large hand engulfed her arm and the heat of him against her side. Ben wasn't even attempting to be subtle about touching her. She was amazed by how at ease he was putting his hands on her—and how much she enjoyed it—considering what little amount of time they'd known each other.

"I'm on to you, Torres," she said when they were across the room from the boys.

"What do you mean?" he asked, leaning in and pushing open the door leading into the hallway.

"I've read *Lord of the Flies.*"

"Great book."

She smiled as she stepped out into the hallway. "Ben, there are no naked native girls in that book."

He grinned the grin that always made her want to start taking her clothes off. "I know. But they won't know it until they've read the whole thing looking for it."

The door swung shut behind them, leaving them alone in the hallway between the rec room and the office.

She laughed. "I don't know that you'll get invited to any more book club meetings after they figure out what you did."

Ben smiled. "Maybe they'll forgive me when they see their test scores." He looked around. "Want to make out?"

It took her a second to catch up with his change of topic. "Yes," she answered.

He looked surprised for an instant, but moved closer quickly. "Great."

"But we can't," she said, putting a hand up against his chest to keep him, literally, at arm's length. "Anyone could walk out here at any time."

"Have you seen Sophie, the little pregnant girl in there?" Ben asked, still crowding closer in spite of her hand. "I have a feeling a lot of these kids are familiar with making out."

Jessica laughed, sounding and feeling breathless as Ben braced a hand on the wall behind her. "I have to be a good role model. Show them that you can say no to things even when you really, really want them."

"I have a feeling you've said no more times than anyone I know."

"And you want to be the one that teaches me yes," Jessica said. *If he only knew.*

"I prefer 'yes, oh, yes Ben', but we can start slow."

She laughed again in spite of the fact that her heart was racing and her blood was heating.

He leaned in until their lips almost touched. "I'm sorry about how last night ended."

She nodded. "Me too. I'm glad you got home all right."

"I felt bad enough after you left that I didn't have anything

more to drink. And Sam showed up about ten minutes later."
Ben brushed his lips across hers in a not-quite-a-kiss.

"Thank you for coming here today," she whispered.

"Did it help get me back on your good side?"

"Is that the only reason you came?"

"Yes," he said. "But now it's not the only reason I'm glad that I came. How's that?"

She smiled. "Good enough."

"Let's practice that yes word," he said, his hand bringing her hips closer to his. "Do you want to make out?"

"Yes."

He looked pleased for one second, then frowned suspiciously. "*Will* you make out with me?"

"No."

He sighed and leaned back resignedly. "I guess you're going to go miniature golfing then."

"Miniature golfing?" Jessica repeated. What a strange alternative to making out. "Why am I going miniature golfing?" And could she convince Russ that this was an important step in getting Ben back to work?

"Because you want to spend time with me and I'm going to be miniature golfing. If I can't make out with you, that is."

"Does the miniature golf course have a bar?" she asked.

"Concession stand. But no bar."

After last night, that was all she needed to hear.

Ben was really just a big kid, which Jessica would have never guessed from how he came across in the ER. Her vision of him was more that of a military general: thinking clearly and quickly on his feet, commanding respect because he was the first to charge into the middle of the situation, not only willing but preferring to be in the trenches with his people. At work he was intensely serious, focused and thorough. He was also somewhat demanding of the staff he worked with and was saved from being considered a jerk by the fact that he worked longer and harder than anyone, demanding more of himself than he did of those around him. And the fact that he was downright funny when the trauma was over.

The miniature golf course was entirely different. He didn't

concentrate or focus at all. He was very preoccupied with touching Jessica every chance he got, consuming as much junk food as he could and singing along—badly—with the oldies played over the loud speakers.

Jess was trying to line up a shot on the last hole, visually measuring and calculating the angle of the shot.

Ben was behind her and she could feel him studying her backside. She missed the shot by at least two feet.

She turned on him with a scowl. "You ruined my concentration."

"It's miniature golf, Jess," he said chuckling. "It's supposed to be fun."

"Which means you're not supposed to even try to do a good job?" She felt pouty. She hated to lose.

"You try to do the *best* job on everything," he said.

"So?"

He shrugged. "So, I don't."

"You still won," she pointed out.

He grinned. "I know. Maybe there's a lesson in there for you."

Yeah, like not miniature golfing with Ben anymore. Cavalier attitudes bothered her.

They turned their clubs in and Ben headed for the snack bar.

"You ever heard of high cholesterol, Dr. Torres?" Jess asked as she watched him scoop a sinful amount of nacho cheese sauce onto a corn chip and shove the whole thing into his mouth. There was a little boy's birthday party going on across the room, but they were alone in the immediate area at the corner table.

"You ever heard of a thing called relaxing?" he asked, thankfully *after* he swallowed.

She wiped a glob of cheese off the tabletop near Ben's elbow with a napkin. "You seem to be in good health," she said. "I figured as someone who's seen what a poor diet and lack of exercise can do, you would watch it better."

"I used to care about that," he said. "Do you know, though, that there are places in the world that don't even *have* cheese?"

"I'm not even sure that what you're eating actually is cheese."

He washed another mouthful down with a large swig of his third soda. "Appreciating what you have, even *indulging* once in a while is good." He swiveled on his stool, took aim and launched the empty soda can into the trashcan a few feet away. It was a perfect shot.

She looked at him closely. "Are you still trying to get me to sleep with you?"

He laughed, another chip partway to his mouth. "In general, yes. At this moment, with this conversation, no. Good to know where your mind is though."

She blushed and stood up, crossing to the trash can. She retrieved the aluminum can from the top of the garbage and transferred it to the recycling bin. Back in her chair, she dug an anti-bacterial wet wipe from the packet she carried in her purse and wiped her hands.

She looked up to find Ben watching her.

He glanced at the wet wipe, then back at her face, but said nothing about it.

"Why did you think I was trying to get you to sleep with me just then?" he asked.

Because she liked it when he flirted and liked the idea that he was pursuing her. But just because she felt the chemistry between them every moment didn't mean that he did, and she would do well to remember that so she didn't embarrass herself.

"The word indulgence made me think you might mean *I* should indulge."

"You should." He polished off the last chip.

"With you?"

"Yes. And at the lingerie store."

She tried to hide her smile. "So it *is* all about sex."

"Sex is one of my favorite features of life on earth, but there are other good ones too."

It was easier to be disapproving when he reminded her of the women who had shared his bed.

"Drinking is one of those things?"

He rolled his eyes. "Sleeping in, ice-cream sundaes, vacations, staying up late, great books, great movies. There are a thousand things. You can't spend all your time on only one or two things and you can't live by the rules all the time."

"Rules keep things in control, make things predictable and

keep things fair," she said.

"And occasionally breaking the rules makes things interesting."

She huffed in frustration. "I notice you didn't mention your work as something that makes life good."

His face hardened almost instantly. "Mine hasn't."

"I don't understand how you can say that," she protested.

He scowled. "Doctors work often horrendous hours, are deeply in debt because of medical school loans, are terribly sleep-deprived and deal with illness, depression and death every day. Every time we heal someone, two more people get sick. Not to mention that that first person will also get sick again eventually. What's the point?"

She stared at him. "Wow, you have got a serious ego problem, you know that?

He frowned at her. "An *ego* problem?"

"Yeah, you think that you've got it rough, don't you? You think all the crap in the world keeps getting dumped into *your* lap. Poor Ben, right?"

He felt offended, but also...strangely intrigued. "What the hell are you talking about?"

Ben watched Jessica shake her hair back from her face and look at him with an expression he hadn't seen before and didn't like. She looked angry, and determined, and resigned.

"You're not the only one who's had shitty things happen to them." She took a deep breath, and said on her exhale, "My mom walked out on us when I was twelve and my dad got shot protecting my apartment from three young punks who were looking for drug money when I was twenty."

Ben felt the globs of cheese he'd eaten and the bucket of soda he'd drunk mix and congeal in his stomach. Maybe he'd overdone it. "God, Jess, I—"

She held up her hand to stop him and took another shaky breath. "Let me tell you this."

He nodded. He didn't want her to, because it wasn't going to be good. But he'd dumped on her last night, told her all about his grief. And it had felt better. Not immediately, but later. Later he'd felt like maybe there would be a time, sometime, in the future, when it would be okay. Or at least not quite so bad.

He wanted to do that for her. If hearing her story would help her at all, he'd listen. "My mom left us when Sara was two. I was twelve, but it took me years to connect all the dots. When I was sixteen, my dad's sister told me the whole story. My dad was eight years older than my mom and she was a runaway when they met."

Ben watched Jessica's face. She was staring at her hands, which were spread flat on the table in front of her. But he knew she wasn't seeing them.

"Dad took her in, got her cleaned up and then married her. To save her. I mean, I think he believed that he loved her, but she was just another one of his projects. My dad believed very strongly in purpose...in having a *reason* for doing things. So he gave my mom a purpose. He made her a mother. To me. And then when she got restless and unhappy, he got her pregnant with Sam. And then later, with Sara. Finally, it was too much."

Jessica looked up at Ben. There were no tears in her eyes. The sadness seemed to go deeper than that. "My dad was an intense guy. I can feel sorry for my mom, because I know what it was like to live with him. I hate to say that he didn't believe in pleasure but...he didn't believe in having or spending extra money, for instance. You made what you absolutely had to have and that was it. If you had any extra, you gave it away. Same thing with your time. You used your time on the basics—school for us, work for him—but extra time, free time was to be donated, spent making the world a better place."

"You grew up poor?" Ben asked, fascinated and relieved to be given this look into Jessica and her past.

She nodded. "You could say that. But my dad made good money. He was a lawyer. Of course, he did lots of pro bono work. But he gave lots and lots of money away too. I mean, we had electricity, heat, air conditioning, that stuff. But we didn't have television or video games. We had books. We had a radio, but not tapes or records. See what I mean? The basics only. The rest went to those less fortunate."

Ben was amazed. He'd never heard of anyone living like that. "And your mom couldn't take it?"

Jessica shook her head. "And I didn't blame her." She laughed. "When I was old enough to know that she'd left and why, I understood. And it made me mad at my father. It was his fault she left. I mean, he couldn't have bought a stupid TV to keep his wife happy?"

"Do you really think she left because she didn't have a TV?" Ben asked gently.

"Of course not. It was the whole thing, the whole philosophy that she had to live with. That everyone else is always more important and that having fun was selfish."

"What about you and Sam and Sara?" Ben asked. "What did you do?"

"I stepped in and did a lot of the stuff around the house. Dad hired a woman to help take care of us. Sara doesn't remember any of it and Sam barely does. And we didn't know what we were missing. Sure, our friends had TV and stuff, but we didn't spend a lot of time anywhere else. We had chores and charity work to do as soon as we were old enough."

Ben frowned. "Sounds very strange."

"It was. I didn't realize it until later, though." She took a deep breath. "The thing is, we were well cared for. He loved us. He spent time with us. He read to us, took us on hikes, to museums, sang to us... We learned a lot and never missed what we didn't have. The problem was when I started blaming him for not having a mother to help me with all the things girls need moms for. And I didn't stop blaming him until I was almost twenty. Then he died before I could tell him that I forgave him."

Jessica's eyes dropped back to her hands. "That's what's been driving me for ten years. The idea that I have to make it up to him. He wasn't *wrong*. He was passionate about his beliefs. He was eccentric, but he was a good person. I mean, he helped so many people. He was so generous."

"You were young. You didn't have a mother. Your life was...weird," Ben said. "I don't think you were wrong to be upset and confused."

"Maybe not." She shook her head. "But I never got to talk to him about it. I never heard his side. I never said I was sorry."

She sniffed and wiped the wetness from her bottom lashes. "I had moved into that stupid apartment only a month before. He hated it. It was in a bad neighborhood, and it was a complete dump. But I was trying to show him that I finally understood the minimalist ideas he'd promoted. I had nothing in there worth anything. I had twenty-one dollars in cash and no credit cards. But he came to see me one afternoon and came upon those kids trying to break in. When he tried to defend my worthless collection of stuff, they shot him and ran off. When I found him, he was still alive but unconscious."

Her voice broke and Ben reached out to cover one of her hands. She didn't move to hold his hand, but did let him touch her, which helped Ben more, he suspected, than it did her.

"He never woke up. He died before I could tell him I was sorry, or that I loved him, or goodbye."

A tear did slip down her cheek then. "I've been obsessed with goodbyes ever since then." She raised her eyes and smiled at him. "I can't leave anyone I care about without telling them goodbye, and I always try to say something important. It annoys my brother and sister."

"I doubt that."

She shrugged. "It does. But I don't care."

She smiled again and he felt relieved. She was okay. She was sad. She had some baggage. But Jessica was strong.

"You said goodbye to me at the bar last night," he recalled all of a sudden, a warmth spreading through his chest.

Jessica looked surprised for a moment. "You remember that?"

"Of course. You also told me not to do anything stupid." She cared about him, Ben realized. She couldn't leave him last night, even as disappointed as she was in him, without saying goodbye.

"Yes, I did."

He shouldn't push. He shouldn't ask. Because if she did care about him, he'd have to face the fact that he cared about her, too, and it would get complicated. "Because you care about me?" he asked, in spite of thinking better of it.

She bit her bottom lip, saying nothing. Then she nodded and he felt like he could take a deep breath again...and could possibly digest the cheese and soda without adverse consequences.

"I didn't do anything stupid," he said. "I let Sam take me to his place without even an argument."

"Because you were too drunk to protest?" she asked, turning her hand over and lacing her fingers with his.

"No, because you asked me to not be stupid. Arguing with Sam would be stupid. He's bigger than me."

She grinned. "It's good that you can take advice."

"Do you work tonight?" he asked, hoping the answer was no.

He had the strangest urge to buy her an extremely expensive dinner, take her to the theater or something else extravagant and then buy her a sappy gift. He had in no way missed how similar things had been for them growing up. His father hadn't been as obsessive as hers. Ben had owned video games and music tapes even in Africa, but he knew all about sacrificing for others and focusing time and energy on work. Jessica needed some fun and foolishness in her life.

"Yes," she said, regret in her voice.

He knew she would take on more shifts again now that he would be working at the coffee shop where Dolly could keep an eye on him. He also knew it drove Jessica crazy to not be the one making sure he behaved. But being away from the ER for more than a day at a time drove her just as crazy. "Twelve hours?" he asked.

She nodded.

That meant she wouldn't be off until seven the next morning. Damn. Looked like he was going to work that night at the coffee shop.

"Will you meet me at the center tomorrow?" she asked.

"Unless I can talk you into coming to my place and spending the day in bed with me," he said, wishing that could happen so badly it scared him.

She smiled. "Very tempting. But I'll need to sleep after my shift and I don't think a lot of that will happen at your place."

"You're damn right it won't," he told her, leaning in and giving her a quick, firm kiss on the lips.

She looked surprised but happy when he pulled back. "What will you do until tomorrow afternoon?"

He decided they'd had enough serious conversation for one day. He shrugged. "There are several adult channels on my cable package."

"You'll sit around all afternoon and watch pornos on TV?" she asked, obviously horrified.

"I'll have to get some candy bars and ice cream—oh, and I'm out of chips—on my way home."

He grinned at the look on her face as she processed the idea that he'd be watching drivel and ruining his health while she was working.

In actuality, he'd be at the coffee shop until closing tonight and then help out in the morning too. He still wasn't very good at sleeping in. He wondered if his body would ever adjust out of the trauma surgeon mode.

"Meet me at the center at four," she said.

He admired her restraint. She hadn't made one judgmental comment.

"That's a long time from now," he said, looking at his watch. "I could get into a lot of trouble between now and then."

She bit the inside of her cheek and he almost laughed.

"What are you doing right now? You don't work until seven." He still wanted to buy her sinfully expensive, delicious food.

"I'm going home to take a shower, eat some *vegetables* and change clothes for work," she said. "And I'm thinking about swinging by the church and lighting a candle for your soul."

He grinned. She couldn't hold it all back, after all. "You're not Catholic."

"God will understand."

"I don't suppose you need someone to scrub your back in the shower?" he asked.

She tried to frown at him, but he could see the corners of her mouth trying to lift up. "I've been scrubbing my own back for a very long time now."

He nodded. "Yes, I know. That's part of the problem we're having."

"We're having a problem?" she asked.

"Yes. The problem being that you don't even understand that you *want* me to scrub your back. You don't know what you're missing."

"If I did, everything would be fine?" she asked. "I suppose that sex with you will be so extraordinary that I won't care if you drink yourself to death? Or live sinfully with abysmal health habits?"

He laughed. "When I finally have sex with you, Jessica, I'm quite sure that I'll want to go on living for a very long time. And I'll want to be very healthy. It will make it easier to keep up with you all night."

She lost the battle with not smiling. "What about the

immorality?"

"No promises there. You're the best inspiration I've had for immoral behavior in a long time."

"Well, at least I'll be sexually satisfied as my principles plummet." She gave a very dramatic, long-suffering sigh.

Ben put a hand over his heart. "I promise that you'll never have a sexual urge or a junk-food craving that I can't take care of."

Jessica was extremely proud of the David Bradford Youth Center and the kids who ended up within its walls. However, it was not exactly a romantic setting.

It was basically a collection of various-sized rooms used for everything from studying and tutoring to relaxing and watching TV, a large gymnasium with attached shower rooms, and a basic kitchen. They had four twin beds for kids who needed a place overnight and a list of volunteers who would help overnight if needed. They received donations from time to time for supplies and food, but David Bradford's trust, along with occasional private, state or federal grants, allowed them to provide basic medical care, hygiene products, clothing as needed and one meal a day.

It was a great place.

But it was definitely not romantic.

Anticipating seeing Ben there with excitement that led to her regularly checking her hair and makeup and using breath mints one right after the other was ridiculous.

She was doing it anyway.

And when he wasn't there by four-twelve she started picturing him as she'd seen him the first night—disheveled, empty liquor glasses littering the table in front of him, his lap full of women.

She frowned into the mirror on the wall inside Sara's office door and applied another coat of lipstick. It wouldn't take long for a guy like Ben to get bored sitting around the house doing nothing. He didn't just work hard, he worked *long*. One surgery could take several hours. He was used to being on his feet with his hands and, most especially his mind, engaged. His system would surely protest being physically and mentally idle.

She just hoped his hands were not staying busy on *anyone*. He needed a hobby she decided. Better yet a *job*.

"Jessica?"

Ben's voice from down the hall made her sigh with relief.

She stepped into the hallway to greet him. "Hi."

He looked great—shaved and brushed.

He wore jeans and a casual cotton shirt but it was clean and wrinkle-free. It certainly hadn't been stripped off in haste and tossed onto the floor during a steamy sexual encounter recently.

Of course, he could have put on a new shirt and left the other shirt wadded on the floor.

He came to stand in front of her and Jess was glad he was there, even if it was late and no matter what he'd been doing on his way over. She also had the definite desire to make sure *he* was glad to be there.

She rose up, grasped the back of his head and kissed him.

His surprise lasted only milliseconds before his arms went around her and he pulled her up against him. The simple meeting of lips quickly became an erotic stroking of tongues mimicked by the way their hands stroked over shoulders, backs and buttocks.

"Don't mind me," a voice said.

Ben and Jessica pulled apart suddenly. Jessica somehow gathered enough sense to step back to let Sara into her office. She gave them each a grin, but passed without a word and sat behind her desk as if having people making out in her doorway was a completely normal occurrence.

Ben's attention was immediately back on Jessica. "That was a hell of a greeting."

She smiled widely. He didn't smell—or taste—like smoke, alcohol, or perfume. "You taste like coffee." And smelled like it. Not like he'd drunk a cup or two, but like he'd washed his clothes in it.

"I was at the coffee shop," he said.

She rolled her eyes. That coffee shop. Could he really like coffee that much? Or get along with Dolly that well? Or was there another woman? A regular? "I'm glad you're here now."

"Did you think I wasn't coming?"

"You're late," she pointed out.

He glanced at the clock over her shoulder. "A little," he conceded.

"Twelve minutes."

"Right..." Ben trailed off and glanced at Sara who pursed her lips and shook her head. "I'm late," he finally agreed.

Jessica frowned at the wordless communication between the two. She felt compelled to defend herself. "Twelve minutes late in a trauma means someone dies."

"But twelve minutes late in a coffee shop means that someone waits twelve minutes to drink coffee," Ben said with a grin.

Jessica propped a hand on her hip. "You could go out of business pretty quickly with that attitude," she said. "Making paying customers wait isn't good service."

"If I admit that you would make a better business owner than me, can we move on?" Ben asked.

Jessica thought she heard a little snort from where her sister was sitting at her desk but when Jessica glanced over, Sara's head was bent over her paperwork.

"Move on to what?" Jessica asked.

"*Anything* else," Ben said.

She definitely heard Sara snicker at that.

Jessica frowned at her.

Ben moved forward and cupped her face between his hands. "I get it. Twelve minutes matter to you. Duly noted."

She shrugged. "But you think I've got OCD."

Ben laughed. "I do not think you have Obsessive-Compulsive Disorder because you like to be punctual." He leaned close enough to kiss her. "But I do think you need a few interruptions in your schedule and a few bad influences in your life."

"And you'll very happily be an interruption *and* a bad influence for me, I suppose?"

His gaze intensified. "Yeah," he said huskily.

She wet her lips and had to take a deep breath before she could remember what they were talking about. Which was hard while he was still holding her, stroking his thumbs across the corners of her mouth. "And I should duly note that predictability is not a strength of yours?"

"Look at what I do for a living. There's nothing predictable about it."

"Don't you want something stable in your life? To even the rest out?"

He lifted a hand and ran it from the crown to the base of her head. Then he pulled her forward until their lips nearly touched. "If I'm your bad influence, will you be my predictability?"

Ben watched Jess swallow hard and wondered if she was as struck as he was by how right that seemed. Ben had never had a lot of stability in his life. A missionary's family moved a lot, sacrificed a lot, saw and learned a lot the hard way. The only thing predictable about the life of a missionary doctor and an ER surgeon was that there would always be more bodies to treat and patch up.

His mom had steadied him as much as anything could, but she was gone.

Looking at Jess now, Ben realized she was the definition of steady. Steady was what Jess did—for everyone. He suspected she'd become a nurse because she was drawn to the idea of being the rock for the victims in the ER, the calm eye at the center of the storm. She also seemed to want to be *his* rock. She wanted to steady him.

He needed that. He even wanted it. A little.

He also wanted to be the one who finally got to see Jessica uninhibited. She'd never truly let go. She'd never had a chance. She'd never experienced how exhilarating giving in to pure temptation could be.

Ben realized that it wasn't exactly noble to want to tarnish her reputation so much. But the passion he'd already felt with her, the way she abandoned her usual restraint when they kissed, made him want it all. He felt sure she would give him her virginity if he pressed the issue.

Unfortunately, he suspected that in her lucid, non-hormone-influenced moments, she felt that a guy who mixed lattes for a living and—more to the point—turned his back on sick people who needed him, wasn't quite worthy of being the one for whom she gave up her convictions.

In his own lucid moments, he agreed with her.

Which was screwing with his head.

Unable to deal with all of that at the moment—if ever—he gave her a quick kiss instead of the come-to-daddy kiss he knew she was expecting, then released her and stepped back.

"Where are the kids I'm supposed to be positively influencing?" Ben asked, clapping his hands together.

Jess blinked, seeming disoriented for a moment.

"Jess?" Ben snapped his fingers in front of her nose.

"What?"

"The kids?"

As expected, Jessica pulled herself together quickly. "They're um...doing their homework in the dining room."

Ben stared at her. "Homework?"

She put a hand on her hip. "You've heard of it?"

"Yeah, but," He shrugged. "Don't they come here for...fun too?"

"Yes."

"But they're studying?"

"Yes. They study, *then* play."

He tipped his head to one side. "Gee, whose rule is that?"

Sara snickered again. Jess glared at her, then back at Ben.

"It's a goal of ours to help them do their best at school. No one at home will hold them accountable, so we do. We have expectations. Homework will take them a lot further than being able to play foosball."

"So it's your rule," Ben concluded.

"Surely you agree school is important. You're a—"

"Doctor," Ben finished for her. "Yeah, yeah. We've definitely established that."

"It's—"

But he interrupted again. "How long has this been the routine?"

"As long as we've been here."

"What about mixing it up?"

"No," she said firmly as Ben started down the hall. "These kids need stability and predictability. They don't have enough of those in their lives."

"What about spontaneity? I think we need to shake things up. And not just for the kids." Ben pulled his cell phone from his pocket and stopped outside the door to the rec room. "You go on ahead," he told her, holding the door open. "I'll be right there."

He grinned at the look on Jessica's face. She was reluctant. She didn't want to trust him. However, she stepped through the open door and allowed him to close it behind her as he put the cell phone to his ear.

She might not want to trust him. But she did.

Being worthy might not be that far out of reach after all.

Chapter Seven

"Ben, there are a couple of guys here to see you!" Sara called to him from the doorway to the rec room an hour later.

Ben rose with a huge grin. "Be right back," he told the kids he'd been helping study for a history test.

As he passed her, Jess asked, "Everything okay?"

He nodded. "Definitely."

She was concerned anyway. Guys were coming to see him here? He looked happy about it so they probably weren't there to collect money for a gambling debt or anything. Were they drinking buddies? His excuse to leave?

But after getting on his case for being late she knew she couldn't demand or beg he stay.

Jessica watched him go and, in spite of herself, acknowledged the draw of Ben's take-it-as-it-comes attitude. It was tempting to let go the way he'd suggested. Even if it was just once—one night of recklessness, of unbridled passion and amazing sex.

But would she be able to walk away after it was over?

Would she be able to get back on her soapbox of responsibility and morality after such a far fall? Would she want to?

It came down to a choice between the way she'd always imagined her life—complete with the husband who was dedicated, and responsible, and of course had an amazing career that made the world a better place—or great sex with a guy whose biggest decisions were rum or beer and whose most important commitment was turning the TV on at the same time every day so as not to miss his favorite soap opera.

Ben returned with Sara. They were both grinning stupidly.

"Homework time is over," Ben announced loudly.

A collective cheer went up and Jess sighed.

"Ben has a huge surprise for you in the backyard," Sara said as the applause died down.

Ben caught Jessica's eye and he gave her a wink. Which made her nervous. What was he up to?

The kids surged toward the doors, with Mario, as always, in the lead. Even teenagers were suckers for surprises.

The so-called backyard was a slab of cracked cement about the size of half a basketball court with a netless hoop at one end. The concrete ended at the edge of a patch of grass approximately the same size.

Redoing the area was on their to-do list but with the indoor gymnasium in good shape it was not a huge priority.

The kids came through the back door and stopped, looking around with expectant expressions. Mario turned a full three hundred and sixty degrees, then looked at Ben.

"What?" he asked.

Ben walked to a huge plastic garbage can and lifted the lid with a flourish.

"Ta-da!"

Mario went forward and peered in. "What is it?" he asked after a long stretch of silence.

"You don't know what water balloons look like?" Ben asked, lifting a large green one from the top.

Jessica's eyes widened at that.

"Water balloons?" Mario asked.

"And," Ben added, crossing to where Sara stood next to a plastic crate. "Water guns."

Sara grinned at Jessica, evidently approving of the idea.

Jessica shook her head. "They don't have extra clothes."

"It's *water*," Ben said, gently tossing the green balloon up and down in one hand. "It's not going to ruin anything."

"We can just bean each other with them?" Reuben asked, moving forward.

Ben nodded and started to speak but Jess jumped in. "Don't you think we should establish some rules? Like no hitting anyone in the face."

"No," Ben said, tossing the balloon up again and catching it while watching her. "There are no rules."

"We just throw them?" Tony asked.

"Yeah, like this." The green balloon hit Jess in the right hip. She shrieked as it exploded, drenching her entire leg in cold water.

She looked at Ben in shock. Everyone around her was still and silent. Ben grinned back at her. Her eyes narrowed.

Sara handed her a large water gun. "It's full."

Jess didn't hesitate. She took aim and fired, continually pumping the chamber full of water with one hand while keeping a finger on the trigger with the other.

Ben's black shirt was soon plastered to him and he grabbed two balloons this time.

The game was on.

The kids grabbed balloons and guns and went at it, shrieking, yelling and laughing as they drenched each other.

Jess was hit a few more times and her gun soon needed reloading. Sara covered her while she knelt at the outside faucet, realizing what an advantage the refillable guns were to the balloons.

The kids quickly figured out that dividing into teams was best so they could have balloons and guns on both sides. They ended up with the boys against the girls.

Jessica couldn't help it. She was having a great time. She laughed and huddled into a crowd with the girls as the boys strategically circled them. She suspected that Ben had a lot to do with the scheme.

The girls tried to fend them off but they were now cut off from the water supply. The boys advanced, not firing, taking the shots from the girls, steadily closing in, the circle around the girls shrinking as they came. Eventually, the girls' guns were empty and they crowded even closer to each other, knowing they were about to get it. They giggled and called out pleas and tried to make deals, but the boys were stoic and closed in until they stood shoulder to shoulder only a few feet away.

They paused, doing nothing, saying nothing, just grinning, letting the girls worry.

"Ready!" Mario called out. "Aim!" The boys all lifted their guns and pointed. "Fire!"

War cries, squeals and laughter all erupted along with the cold water. In seconds the girls were dripping and laughing hard enough they were having trouble catching their breaths.

Suddenly, Ben strode through the ring of teenage boys.

In the midst of so many laughing faces, his look of serious intent made Jessica step back as he came at her.

"Come on," he said, his teeth gritted.

He took her upper arm in a firm grasp and turned her away from the group, toward the center's back door. The kids parted like the Red Sea before Moses.

Jess hurried to keep up with Ben's long strides. What was his problem? She tried to frown up at him, but he wasn't looking at her. They'd been having a good time. She'd even played in spite of the lack of rules. She hadn't said a word about drying off before they went inside and got the floor all wet, or about being careful not to slip on the wet concrete as they ran in bare feet. She'd been laid back, dammit!

"Ben, what is going on?"

He yanked the door open, pushed her in ahead of him and stepped in after her.

She turned to face him as the air conditioning hit her, and goosebumps broke out on goosebumps.

Ben's eyes dropped to her breasts. Her breath hitched at the look of hot desire in his eyes.

"I didn't want to share," he said, meeting her eyes again. "Especially not with underage kids."

She glanced down. Her blouse clung, the white fabric nearly transparent, to her breasts and nipples that stood erect in the cold air...and under Ben's gaze.

"I'm sorry Jess, I didn't even think about your white shirt until the boys had you on display and soaked."

Jess quickly tried to cover herself with her arms. "It's not your fault."

Ben caught her wrists before she could hide behind them.

"It's just you and me now."

Hearing the strain in his voice, she looked up. His hair and face were still wet, but he was oblivious it seemed. He was drinking in the sight of her.

"You're gorgeous."

And she felt it. She felt like the sexiest woman on earth with him watching her like he was.

She wanted him to touch her.

She racked her brain for anything to say other than that. The kids could walk in at any moment...

"Were any of the other girls wearing white?" she asked as the thought occurred to her.

"I wouldn't know," Ben said gruffly. "I was only watching you." He moved in closer and lifted a hand to her cheek. "You're so beautiful when you're having fun."

"You're just saying that because I'm nearly naked here," she said, trying for levity.

"I'm saying it because watching you laughing and genuinely enjoying yourself makes me want to get you naked even more."

"Ben," she said, her throat tight with wanting. "We can't."

"I know." He looked grim at the acknowledgement. "But I have to at least do this."

His hands came up as if in slow motion to cup her breasts. Jessica stopped breathing as much from the look on his face as he watched himself touch her as from the contact itself. When his thumb brushed over her nipples she had to grasp his forearms to stay standing.

"Ben," she moaned.

His face mirrored her arousal. "When was the last time a man touched you like this?" Ben asked, taking the tip of her left breast between thumb and forefinger and tugging gently.

Like this? She could hardly think straight. But nothing she felt with Ben was anything she'd ever experienced before. "Never," she mumbled.

His eyes darkened. "Never?"

She was breathing hard and had trouble focusing on the man in front of her, though if she closed her eyes completely she could picture him in detail, as well as feel, smell and *sense* him on every level.

Dang. What was it with this guy?

Even when she was wet and freezing, he could still turn her into a big pile of marshmallows. Melted marshmallows. Melted, toasted marshmallows.

She licked her lips. "Never like this."

Abruptly his hands were gone from her breasts. "Come on." She had been leaning in to him so she nearly pitched forward when he moved. He took her hand and pulled her down the hallway and into the first room with a door. It was the supply closet.

The door latch had barely clicked when Ben's lips were on hers, hungry and hot. He tunneled his fingers in her hair and pressed his thighs into hers. He walked her backward until they met the wall and he could press against her in all the right places.

It was like gasoline on a flame and for the first time in ten years Jessica wanted, no *needed*, to know if enticing boys was like riding a bike—something she would never forget how to do.

"Ben," she whispered.

She slipped her hand between them and pressed her palm against the rigid length that told her he wanted her as much as she wanted him. They both groaned at the contact and Ben's knees bent so she held him more fully. He stopped breathing.

Jessica felt the heady power that came with affecting a man like Ben this much. "I want you. All of you," she whispered.

She released the button of his fly and slipped her hand inside the cotton of his underwear and onto hot skin. She found the silky tip easily, circled it and then slid her palm down the hard, hot shaft. Maybe it had just been a long time, but all she could think was *big* and *wow.*

She found her voice, determined to make him as desperate as she was. "All of you. Every." She stroked up and down his length and he groaned. "Single." She pressed her hand more firmly against him and stroked again, making him suck in a quick breath. "Inch."

"It's all yours," he said gruffly.

The sound of the metal back door banging against the concrete wall that separated them from the hallway made them both jerk, then freeze. They heard laughter and shouts as the stream of teenagers rolled past the door.

After the last voice had passed, they both breathed again, slipped their hands from one another's clothes and stepped apart.

Jess stared at him, torn between laughing and crying. This was what they got for going at it in a supply closet. This was a *youth center*. It was named after her late father. Her dad had probably put the shelves up in here himself. She should feel terribly ashamed. But she didn't. The most overpowering emotion she was feeling was disappointment that they had been interrupted.

She ran shaky fingers through her hair to straighten it as well as she could.

Ben seemed to be trying to catch his breath as he fastened his pants.

"I'm not going to say I'm sorry," he said, meeting her gaze.

She took a deep breath. "Good."

He tucked his hands into his back pockets and took a step back. "And I intend to pick up where we left off as soon as possible."

She let the breath out. "Good."

He smiled at that. Then his eyes dropped to the front of her blouse again and his smile died. He pulled in a shaky breath and stepped back again.

"I'll go find something for you to put on," he said. "It's probably better that we don't both go out at the same time anyway."

Jessica nodded and Ben slipped out into the hallway.

He worked on getting his breathing back under control and his mind off of Jessica's hot body, hot mouth and hot little hands. He couldn't believe what he'd just done. Well, what he'd *almost* done. Jessica was not the type of woman to have a quickie in a supply closet.

She deserved better than that. It would be her first time and he'd almost taken her in the midst of rolls of toilet paper, bottles of disinfectant and jars of the stuff they used to clean up puke.

Nice, Ben. Really smooth. Really classy. Really considerate.

But it was her fault. His intentions had been pure, mostly, in bringing her inside when her blouse had gone see-through.

Then he'd wanted a quick feel and taste of the luscious breasts that had been taunting him since the morning in his bathroom. Heavy petting, necking, making out. That was all it was going to be. Honestly.

Then she'd touched him. And just like that, he was practically on his knees.

It was good the kids had come banging in.

Jessica deserved candles, rose petals, soft music and lots of foreplay her first time.

Her first time...her second time...every time.

Hell.

Ben stopped in the doorway of the small closet where they kept the extra clothes, a vise-like tension squeezing his chest. He braced his hands on the doorjamb, digging his fingertips into the wood as he let the truth expand in his mind.

It wasn't only that it was her first time that made him want to romance her. It was her. She was amazing. She was gorgeous and generous and dedicated and smart and...

First time or not, Jessica deserved even more than the rose petals—she deserved a declaration of undying love and a big ol' diamond ring for her left hand.

He was in so much trouble.

Ben swore under his breath and pushed himself back away from the support of the doorway. This was ridiculous. He wasn't the rose petal and candle type. He hadn't made any promises. He hadn't even said anything about it being more than casual, just-for-fun sex.

She wanted him anyway. It was her choice. She shouldn't be expecting lots of foreplay and sweet words.

He yanked a hooded sweatshirt from a hanger and stalked back to the closet where Jessica waited. If he had a condom with him, he'd go back into that closet right now and take her hard and fast. She'd like it, he'd *finally* be able to satisfy this crazy hunger for her. And he'd then be able to get the hell away from her before he went out and bought her the damn ring himself.

Yep. It was the lack of protection that made him stuff the sweatshirt through the barely opened closet door instead of going back in.

Three days later, Jessica was about to lose her mind. Ben was leaving her alone. Just like she'd wanted. Supposedly.

If they didn't sleep together, she didn't have to worry about falling for him any further and then being heartbroken when he didn't live up to her standards.

So, why was she so annoyed that he hadn't asked her to go home with him even once in the past three days?

Because of the supply closet.

The supply closet had convinced her that she wanted to have mind-blowing, I'll-never-fully-recover sex with him and she'd worry about the consequences later.

And *now* he was leaving her alone.

Kind of. He was definitely not ignoring her. They talked about everything under the sun. But he never even made an innuendo about sex.

It all made her want it even more. She was the type of person who—once she made up her mind about something— wanted to get it done. Ben was definitely something she wanted to do.

Since Russ insisted she do whatever necessary to keep track of Ben, she'd taken the last three days off. While Ben worked at the coffee shop for a few hours each morning during the rush, she worked on her to-do list at the center. Then, when Ben came to the center after his shift, she could spend her time with him. Purely to keep him out of trouble, of course.

That didn't mean she couldn't enjoy the time spent though did it?

She tried to enjoy it anyway. Ben just wasn't cooperating. She liked talking to him. She liked making him laugh. She liked watching him interact with the kids. But she would have preferred a lot more of his hands and lips on her.

She tried teasing and flirting with him, but he always changed the subject. Quickly and so bluntly it was laughable. Except she didn't find it funny in the least.

He'd give in to the kisses when she caught him alone, somewhere the kids wouldn't see them. In those moments he would hesitate for a few seconds, then all at once his lips and hands would be all over her, as if he couldn't get enough. Eventually, though, he would pull back, long before she was ready for him to, and he'd distance himself from her for a while, diving into a school project with some of the girls, or a game of basketball with the boys.

Oh, he was very sweet. He told her she was beautiful. He told her she was great with the kids. He brought her cups of her favorite coffee from Cup O' Joe. He brought more medical supplies for the clinic. He stitched up two more fight-night participants without argument or question, and he treated at least three patients a day who kept showing up when the neighborhood heard there was a doctor hanging out locally.

But he never asked her to go home with him. He never asked to go home with her. He never mentioned a hotel. Or even the backseat of his car. Or a return to the supply closet. He was a perfect gentleman.

Which was starting to tick her off.

She was restless. She craved so much more than the touches and kisses she stole. She imagined all kinds of things with the couches in the rec room, the showers in the locker rooms and even the pool table. She could hardly walk into the center without getting hot and bothered.

Which was sordid. It was a *youth* center focused on inspiring at-risk kids and bettering the world, for heaven's sake. How could she be constantly turned on while inside?

The answer was that, while the kissing was amazing, seeing Ben serving the needs of the people who showed up took her to a whole new level of awareness and it made her physical cravings for him all the stronger.

It was arousing—no, *interesting*, she meant interesting—to watch him with the people at the center. She'd seen him in the ER almost daily for six months. But there he was giving orders, working quickly and efficiently, making decisions as he went along.

At the center he was talking to the people, sometimes for an hour at a time. He listened to their stories, told a few of his own—not to mention a series of really bad knock-knock jokes—and accepted plates of cookies and cakes that were brought in appreciation. He took his time now and, if she wasn't mistaken, was enjoying himself. Too bad sitting around the center and goofing off all day didn't pay very well...or at all.

Not that he seemed to mind. He didn't say one word about the hospital and whenever she so much as mentioned the name of a co-worker he made an excuse and left the room.

She didn't like that he seemed so comfortable, and even happy, with their routine. Sure, she loved having him there, but he was supposed to be getting bored, or restless, or at least horny. He couldn't be simply enjoying himself at the center. That didn't make sense.

Which was why she avoided returning Russ's two phone calls. She knew she couldn't put him off forever, but she had nothing to report except that Ben showed no signs of wanting to return to work and she did not want to admit that her plan was backfiring. His interactions with the patients at the center didn't seem to be inciting any kind of desire to return to the ER and she couldn't even entice him out of his clothes for sex—how could she persuade him to take the jeans off and put his scrubs back on?

Finally, on Tuesday, she answered a call even though the display showed it was an ER number. She almost wilted in relief when it was a fellow nurse asking her to fill in for someone who was ill. They were desperate and she couldn't say no. She was surprised, though, how disappointed she was about it. The shift would completely disrupt their schedule at the center and she would likely not see Ben at all until tomorrow evening.

It was only polite to find him and tell him about the change of plans, she figured as she drove toward Dolly's coffee shop.

Jessica pulled up in front of Cup O' Joe and tried not to hate the little shop. Nothing that was going on with Ben was Dolly's fault or the fault of the patrons who were making the coffee shop successful enough to provide Ben a job. It certainly wasn't the fault of the coffee bean growers in...well, everywhere coffee beans grew, but Jessica found herself even annoyed with them on some level.

No, it wasn't exactly any of their faults, but she still wasn't going to buy anything. She loved white chocolate mochas but she couldn't get past the idea that her four twenty-five would essentially end up in Ben's pocket and allow him to keep paying his bills in spite of not working at the hospital.

A *ding dong* sounded as she stepped into the shop, evidently past the sensor that triggered the door chime sound. The bright, mid-morning sunlight splashed the old wooden floors, turning them to a warm honey color. The mouth-watering aroma of rich, freshly ground coffee beans and still-warm cookies and muffins floated through the air, enticing a deep breath and the hint of a smile from her in spite of herself.

She *really* wanted a huge paper cup foaming with white chocolate mocha with a brown cardboard ring around it to protect her hands from the heat. She wouldn't order one. But being principled sucked sometimes.

The sounds of milk steamers, blenders, metal spoons clacking against ceramic cups and conversation mixed with the soft sound of Harry Connick Jr. over the stereo system. Jessica squelched the thought that with a good book she could happily spend the day here.

She headed for the back coffee counter, her flat leather

sandals thumping pleasantly against the wood floor. She shouldn't have taken the time and effort to dress up to come see Ben. It shouldn't matter that she'd been scrubbing her tub when the hospital had called to see if she could come in to cover. She should have come down here in the sweatpants she'd cut off to mid-calf length and the ponytail she'd put on top of her head after rolling out of bed. But no, she had to take the time to shower, do her hair and dress in a red and white checked sleeveless shirt that tied above the waistband of the white Capri pants she wore. She was planning to spend a total of five minutes with Ben—just long enough to tell him she had to work tonight and wouldn't be at the center—and she'd spent twenty times that amount of time trying to look good.

Her skin tingled before she caught sight of Ben, like her body was aware of him before her conscious mind recognized him. Seemingly as in sync with her, Ben found her over the heads of the four twenty-something girls he was helping at the counter as she stopped to one side, watching him. The smile and wink he gave her made her want to climb over the wooden counter, wrap herself around him and pull him down onto the floor amidst the coffee grounds, splashes of milk and sprinkles of nutmeg.

Jessica was close enough now to overhear the conversation he was having with the girls. They were asking him to describe nearly every item on the menu, which he was doing with patience, humor and a smile that made Jessica immediately decide that the girls were asking endless, silly questions in an effort to simply prolong their chance to flirt with the good-looking new guy.

"The redhead has come in every day since he started. She's annoyingly cute and perky but every time she brings new friends with her and spends at least twenty bucks, so I can't be too put out."

Jessica turned to find Dolly behind the counter across from where Jessica stood. She was wiping her hands on a butter yellow dishtowel that matched the apron she wore over a simple white sundress. She grinned at Jessica. "Now don't you go over there and let on that he's yours. That girl is good for business and if she finds out Ben's taken she might go back to drinkin' Diet Coke at the Student Union."

Jessica smiled but she had to suppress the urge to shift

uncomfortably at the negative thoughts she'd been having about Dolly and her shop. They were both very nice. And why shouldn't Dolly take advantage of Ben wanting to work for her? He was smart, fun to have around, trustworthy and obviously good for business.

Dolly propped her hip against the counter and crossed her arms, watching Ben. "I wish he'd take me up on the partnership offer."

Jessica looked at Dolly with surprise. "Did you say *partnership*?"

Dolly chuckled. "Yeah. I offered him a partnership in this place. He's a natural at this."

Jessica said nothing rather than argue with the very nice woman Ben obviously liked a lot. She shifted her gaze back to Ben, who was making coffee and flirting with the customers. He was a *surgeon* who had operated on things that these girls couldn't even spell, not to mention identify on a cadaver. It was such a waste of time and talent.

He looked ridiculous with the white cloth apron tied around his hips over the faded blue jeans and New York Yankees T-shirt. Yeah, the jeans showed off his muscular thighs and trim butt and the T-shirt hugged his shoulders and pecs, making her palms itch to rub over the soft cotton. But these girls hadn't seen him in surgical scrubs. Yes, the denim showed more off than his loose-fitting scrubs. Still, there was something so sexy about a guy who saved lives. These girls had no idea how much sexy Ben could turn on.

"He's got a lot of great ideas," Dolly added.

Jessica looked at her again. Maybe her face had given away more of her skepticism than she'd thought. In that case, some sarcasm wouldn't get her into too much trouble.

"Great ideas about coffee?"

Dolly laughed. She didn't seem offended. "Not exactly. Great ideas about business."

Jessica knew Ben was incredibly intelligent and capable and a whole host of other complimentary adjectives. She would bet all of her savings that his grasp of the human anatomy and physiology was superior to all the other physicians at St. Anthony's. But coffee and biscotti were surely in a whole other category.

"Such as?" Jessica asked, curious about this side of Ben

Dolly seemed so enthralled with.

Dolly waved toward a bright orange sign on the bulletin board on the wall to Jessica's left.

Free Coffee the large black letters at the top yelled. How giving coffee away was a good thing for business was beyond her. She moved closer to the flyer and read: *to any designated driver for patrons of The Watering Hole.* It went on to explain how people agreeing to refrain from drinking in order to safely drive others home from the bar across the street could sit in Cup O' Joe and have free coffee until their services were needed. They were even given a pager to be used by their friends at the bar so they knew when it was time to go.

"Giving away your products for free is helpful?" Jessica asked.

Dolly smiled. "Nothing looks better than doing public service," she said. "Plus, these folks drinking free coffee get a chance to try our stuff, see our shop, and have a positive association with it. Then when their friends mention going out and doing something different for a change, they'll think of us and suggest it to their group. Or so Ben told me when he gave me the idea." She laughed. "Besides they might need to buy some cake or pie to go with their coffee."

Jess had to admit that was pretty good. "Ben's very aware of the problem with drunk driving from the ER," Jessica said, thinking in particular of Ted Blake.

Dolly nodded. "Oh, yeah, Doctor-Boy is going to set up some health talks too."

"What kind of health talks?"

"Once a month people will be able to come in for lunch or coffee and dessert from one to two p.m. and hear somebody talk about a health topic."

"Really?" That was interesting. And good. Dammit.

Dolly shrugged. "We haven't done it yet, but lots of people have commented on wanting to come to the one he's doing next week."

"What's the topic?"

"How caffeine works on the body."

Jessica smiled, then laughed, as did Dolly. Jessica felt better about all of it. "Ben's sticking to his first love, healthcare, after all I guess." Just in an alternate way. But she took it as a sign he still knew what was important and what his gift was.

Until Dolly spoke again. "Yeah. Though his idea for the moms group isn't exactly healthcare related."

"His moms group?"

"M. O. M. S.," Dolly spelled. "It stands for Moms Offering Moms Support." Dolly laughed at the surprised and confused look on Jessica's face. "He wants to get some women who have kids that are older together with some of these teenage mothers." Dolly shook her head. "Some of those young girls don't have any idea what to do about things like potty training and disciplining and finding good daycare. Who better to ask than a mom who's been there and done it well?"

Jessica stared at her. Good grief. Give him half a year and he'd have world peace nailed down.

"Is that something else Ben told you when he told you the idea?"

"Basically."

"How'd he think of that?" she asked, remembering his interactions with Sophie at the center.

Dolly looked directly at her, but her expression was soft. "He listens and pays attention to what people need. Then he's smart enough and generous enough to find a way to meet the need. It's his gift."

She moved off then to help a customer, as Ben was busy finally filling the order of his four admirers. Jessica watched him and felt her heart thump almost painfully in her chest.

He moved at ease behind the counter, competently doing three things at once, chatting and laughing and generally having a good time doing what he was doing. He moved with the same grace and confidence she'd seen a hundred times in the ER, but there was something different about this man.

She also knew right away what it was: he was happy here. The pressure and intensity and concentration that were such a part of him were missing.

Jessica checked herself to see if she felt any disappointment or fading of her attraction to him. That would actually be quite helpful. But she knew that answer immediately as well: no way. She'd been a sucker for heroes for a long time. But *this* Ben, this relaxed side of him, was as appealing as the savior side.

Which didn't do anything for her mental well-being. Whether or not she wanted to sleep with him, Russ was counting on her to keep him out of trouble and she knew from Sam that Russ had assured the lawyers, St. Anthony's CEO and the Board of Directors that things were being handled. If Ben did anything crazy or didn't report back to work after his suspension was over, everyone would know, and blame her.

It'd certainly be easier to be tough with Ben if she didn't *like* him so much. It'd be easier to resist his invitations to be irresponsible and it would certainly make it easier to not care that she'd never seen him smile this much at the hospital.

She was so screwed.

She wanted him, she liked him and she cared how he felt. Crap.

Ben came toward her then, his four devotees finally appeased. He had a wicked gleam in his eyes. That seductive, predatory look in the middle of the warm, pleasant shop made her think of a whole lot of other uses for the whipped cream and chocolate shavings that Dolly kept behind the counter.

"I'm glad you're here," he said. "I want to show you something." He held up the slab of countertop that lifted to let staff pass behind the counter from the public area.

"I came to tell you that I got called into the ER tonight, so you don't have to stop by the center."

Russ probably didn't know that she'd been called to fill in for a sick colleague, or he'd have found a way to cover the shift without causing her to leave Ben alone. But she'd been off for the last three days. She'd never been off for more than one at a time before. Not only were her co-workers getting irritated, *she* was missing her work. Besides, Sam was going to chaperone Ben tonight. The idea of Sam chaperoning anyone was the perfect illustration of how outlandish this was all becoming. Even Sam was concerned enough to behave.

"I told the guys I'd be there at four," Ben said with a shrug

"The guys?"

"Mario, Tony, Reuben... Those guys," Ben said.

Jessica blinked at him. "You're going to the center anyway?"

Ben grinned and crossed his arms. "You're not the only one at that center who has something I want."

Uh, huh. He hadn't been trying to get anything from her for days. Her eyes narrowed. "Is that right? What do Mario and those guys have?"

"A great basketball game."

All at once, strangely, and stupidly, she was choked up by the man standing in front of her. Liking him was going to be the least of her troubles. Wanting him physically was a no-brainer. But what was complicating things was wanting him as far more than just a friend. Which was definitely stupid.

When she'd barely known him, she could admit that having him as more than a friend or lover had occurred to her. He'd been the star in a number of daydreams that included a lot of great sex, of course, but also a couple of wedding rings and a joint checking account.

Yes, she'd filled in the blanks about him with her own appealing ideas. That was what having a really good crush was all about, wasn't it?

Now, though, she knew better and knew that his life's ambition seemed to include having as little ambition as possible. His professional dedication now started and ended with Styrofoam cups and flavored syrup. His sense of purpose now came from creating the perfect cappuccino foam versus performing, say, the perfect valve repair. Yet, she was beyond a crush. She was falling for him. For real this time.

Being married to someone who had no direction, no purpose, wouldn't work for her. She'd been without direction herself at one time, wandering all over without a road map. She didn't want to be in charge of the steering wheel for anyone else; especially a wheel that seemed so intent on veering off course.

Of course there were two things wrong with this whole train of thought.

One, she'd only spent a few days of real time with him and had no indication that he'd had one single thought of her beyond the bedroom. They were a long way from receiving Christmas cards addressed to Dr. and Mrs. Torres.

And two, it was possible that he was headed in a very specific direction. It just wasn't the one she thought it should be.

Her brain cramped.

She needed to go. She stepped toward the front door. "Um, I wanted to tell you about, you know, my work thing."

"No, you didn't."

She stopped and looked at him. "What?"

"You wanted to see me."

"Really, I—"

"Jessica, if all you wanted was to *tell* me something you could have called. But you brought your beautiful butt down here because you wanted to *see* me. So get back here and see me already."

"Ben, I..." she stopped. He was right. She'd wanted to see him.

She gave up and stepped through the barrier behind the counter.

As she moved past him he said quietly, "Yes, I would have missed seeing you too if you hadn't come down here."

She didn't admit it, but then she didn't have to, did she? Ben knew exactly what she was thinking and feeling. Great.

"You had something to show me?" she asked.

"Right in here." He took two steps, pushed open the swinging door into the kitchen and held it open.

She stepped through knowing distance was the only thing that was going to keep her sane. She was falling for him while she was *supposed* to fall for someone who was driven and heroic and had all those great Boy Scout qualities.

But distance was the last thing she got when Ben came through the door behind her.

He pulled her up against his chest and kissed her. He didn't lead into anything, either. It was a full-blown, hot, wet, deep, slow kiss that stole her breath and made her think that making cappuccinos was a brilliant way for him to spend his time.

Ben finally lifted his head and let her go and she found herself protesting with a groan. He grinned at her, cocky and full of himself.

"That's what you were going to show me?" she asked when she had some oxygen in her lungs again.

"Yeah."

"That you're still a great kisser?"

He slid his hands into the back pockets of his jeans and said casually, "That I can make you want to take off your clothes for me even in the middle of a coffee shop."

She frowned at him. "You don't have to convince me of that. I've been trying to take my clothes off for you for the past three days."

He looked surprised and amused. "How did I miss that?"

"Because you hightail it out of the room whenever I so much as brush against your arm." An exaggeration, of course, but she was irritated.

He suddenly crowded close. "Don't you know why?"

Her breath lodged in her throat at the look of hunger on his face. Mutely, she shook her head.

"Because I want nothing more than to strip you down, push you up against the wall and make you scream my name with your legs wrapped around my waist."

Still not breathing, Jessica swallowed hard as heat and moisture rushed south.

"But I can't do that at the center. So I have to get away from you and get some control back after you touch me."

More than ready for a little up-against-the-wall-screaming-his-name right then and there, Jessica said, "We don't have to spend all our time together at the center."

Heat flared in his eyes in spite of his answer. "I think we should."

Disappointment hit her hard. "Why?"

"Because if I go home with you, I don't know if I'll ever leave."

Oxygen swooshed out of her body and she stared at him dumbly. This was getting scary but she couldn't help what she said next. "I don't know if I would mind."

He took a deep breath and seemed to make a decision. "Then let's go."

"You're working."

"It's okay. I'm in tight with the owner."

Yes was on her lips when she remembered. "I have to get to the hospital." *Now* she was disappointed.

"I could say 'it won't take long' but that's not very romantic. And it's not true." He leaned in and brushed his lips over hers. "I intend to take lots of time. So I can taste every inch of you. Twice."

There went the breathing thing again. Jessica felt her heartbeat pulsing through her whole body. "Yeah," she said raggedly. "It's good to have plenty of time."

He grinned and held the swinging door open for her. "I'll see you after your shift." As she passed, he dipped his head near her ear. "Try not to accidentally stick anyone with a needle while you're busy thinking about all the things I'm going to do to you."

She turned and looked up at him, certain that all of her hunger was clear in her eyes. "It's all the things *I'm* going to do to *you* that might distract me."

He smiled. "I have a feeling I'm going to make lousy coffee and lose a basketball game today myself."

Well, that was just great, Jessica thought as she made her way to her car, her body still humming with desire. Was every plan she made going to blow up in her face? She'd gone in there to simply tell him she had to work tonight. Now she had a date for earth-shattering sex and she was truly concerned that she *would* accidentally stick someone with a needle tonight.

She'd planned to get him back to work, but he was happier steaming milk.

She'd planned to not become anymore enamored with him until he went back to work but here she was, halfway in love with him. And he was happier steaming milk.

She was impressed with him in any scenario and liked seeing him happy...even while he steamed milk.

This was not going according to plan at all.

She was pretty sure Russ was going to agree with her.

Two hours later, she wasn't any closer to solving her problem, so she'd chosen a different method for dealing with the whole thing...denial. Everything was going to be fine. She could have very nice sex with Ben and then walk away wanting nothing more and he was going to wake up tomorrow and realize that he simply couldn't go another day without repairing someone's duodenum.

Which was working well for her until Russ found her cleaning up trauma room two.

"He's working in a *coffee shop*?" Russ asked promptly upon entering the room. "Tell me Sam was messing with me."

"No. It's true." She threw the sharp instruments into the special red plastic container for disposal. "And he *likes* it." She stalked to the counter and slammed the container down.

"And what are you doing about it?" Russ asked.

Jessica whirled to face him, her own frustration making her not care that he was, for all intents and purposes, her superior. "What am I supposed to do, exactly? He's a grown man. He's not related to me..."

"Whatever it takes," Russ interrupted. "Pretty simple."

Russ maintained his composure, keeping his voice even, while his eyes told her he was not taking any of this lightly. "Ted Blake has dropped the charges. Thank God. We want and need Ben back but he won't return any calls. Even from his *boss*. You and Sam are the only ones who he'll talk to."

A fact that obviously irritated the hell out of Russ.

His I-can-order-you-around attitude needed some work when talking to people like her who he'd worked with and known for a long time before getting his own office and cherry wood desk. But his I'll-manipulate-you-to-get-what-I-want attitude was going strong and the fact he intended to use it to its fullest extent was clear in his eyes.

"You're the one who always gets things done, Jessica. You're the one everyone depends on. You're resourceful, smart, compassionate—you're the go-to girl."

Usually those kinds of things made her feel good. After all, that was pretty much what she'd been working for. She *wanted* to be dependable and prided herself on being resourceful. But this was different. She knew now that her feelings for Ben didn't have much to do with the hospital after all.

"That's in the ER, Russ. That's when people are lying on gurneys with their bodies in pieces."

"Think about those people," Russ insisted. "That's what I'm talking about. *They* need Ben."

"Do you think I'm stupid?" she asked, stalking across the room to inventory the med cabinet. "Don't you think I know that every day people come in here who need Ben, who could literally die because he's not here?"

"Then do something about it!" Russ snapped.

She turned around and put her hands on her hips. "I can*not* keep an adult, relatively sane man from making espresso, baking muffins and wearing an apron if he wants to."

She snatched two bags of laundry from near the table, unable to concentrate on inventory right now.

"He's baking muffins?" Russ was clearly appalled.

"Technically, Dolly makes the muffins, I suppose," Jessica conceded.

"But he's wearing an apron?"

"Definitely wearing an apron." She understood why it was so hard to believe. "And serving quiche and scones on china plates." She pulled the door to the trauma room open.

Russ stepped forward and pushed it shut again, almost on her toe, his hand staying on the door. "Jessica, think about what you just said. This is *Ben.* He's a surgeon. He's serving quiche and scones."

It was worth it all to see Russ's face when he said the word quiche like that. Jessica did, somehow, resist smiling.

"It's a complete waste," Russ went on.

Jessica agreed, but stayed silent. Russ seemed on a roll.

"We all go through rough periods. Everyone needs time off. But I'm starting to lose my patience with Ben."

Jessica sighed and shifted the heaviest bag of laundry to the floor. "I understand, Russ. But he's not acting like this is a tantrum or a vacation. I don't know what to do."

"Beg him," Russ said. "Give him whatever he wants."

The other bag of laundry hit the floor and she crossed her arms.

"Fine. I will do everything within my power to get Ben back here. But I expect to see a completed letter from you recommending me for the Director's position."

Russ Edwards didn't like being bossed around, but having lost the best trauma surgeon from his staff didn't look good, and being unable to entice him back looked even worse.

"Of course," he said with false graciousness. "And I'll expect a call from Ben regarding when he'll be returning to work."

"Of course." She could fake courtesy and compliance as well as he could.

Chapter Eight

Ben looked over the top of the *People* magazine at the other occupants of the ER's waiting room. Business in the department had been steady and these folks had been passed over for more emergent patients.

Of particular interest to him was the older woman sitting in a wheelchair near the soda machine. She looked queasy. She sat with an elbow propped on the arm of her wheelchair, her head resting in her hand, eyes closed. She'd been there when he'd come in twenty minutes ago.

He'd carefully chosen the far corner of the ER waiting area to sit until Jessica's shift ended. The basketball game had been a quick one. Evidently, Mario was spending more time in the rec room with Sophie than he was on the courts these days, and his team quickly lost to Ben's. Ben felt less than satisfied with the contest. He liked to win, but he liked to fight for it. Plus, it left him with more time to kill until Jessica was done. Which should be any minute now.

He wasn't here because he was bored, or had nowhere to go because all of his friends were working or involved with extracurricular activities or significant others. He just wanted to surprise Jessica.

He should get a hobby or something.

Or he could return to work.

Ben shook that thought off right away.

He'd received the phone message from Russ telling him that Ted Blake had dropped his assault charge. Russ had informed him that he was free to return to work whenever he was ready.

Ben hadn't returned the phone call.

But surprisingly, it had taken some real willpower to keep his seat when the first trauma had come through the doors from the ambulance. The adrenaline had started pumping and his brain and instincts had kicked into high gear the minute he heard the doors open. He'd automatically attended to all the information the paramedics had called out as the gurney came by.

The man had fallen nearly sixty feet from scaffolding. They would definitely need a surgical consult. Ben had literally grabbed the edge of his chair to keep from going in.

He couldn't let the reflexes that were still strong override the very sane decision he was mostly happy with. He hadn't made his decision to leave the ER in the heat of the moment with Ted Blake as many believed. It had been in the quiet solitude of his apartment three nights after he'd found out about what happened in Tanzania. It had been decided a week before Ted Blake's fateful decision to drive drunk. Ted had simply helped Ben decide when he was done and how he was going to make his exit.

However, the reflex to jump in and repair bleeding appendages was different—and evidently easier to suppress—than his ability to recognize someone with a problem and his desire to fix it.

Ben watched the woman in the wheelchair for another few minutes. She touched her forehead and he saw her hand tremble. He glanced down at the magazine he was reading and sighed.

He enjoyed the mindless Hollywood gossip. He'd lived for five years in a village where very little was mindless and for pure pleasure. There were occasional celebrations with the tribe, and the combination American and British medical group blew off steam with thrown-together, rag-tag parties from time to time. The music and books they'd brought, the Internet, and food and drinks sent from home had kept them all sane, as had the intermittent physical rendezvous with one of the female team members. But personal pleasure took a backseat every time to someone's medical needs. And some habits were impossible to break.

Ben stretched to his feet and dug in his pocket for a few coins as he crossed the waiting room. He approached the soda machine, jingling the change in his hand. Pretending to ponder the beverage selection in the machine, he observed the woman out of the corner of his eye.

She flexed her left hand open and shut a few times and Ben noted the thick knuckles of someone with arthritis. Then she shook her hand. Her eyes remained closed.

"Ma'am?" Ben asked.

She didn't answer or look up at him. She didn't even open her eyes.

"Ma'am?" Ben squatted next to her chair and put his hand on her arm. "What are you feeling?"

She shook her head.

"Can you look at me?" Ben asked gently.

She shook her head again. "When I open my eyes it's all blurry and I get dizzy."

He understood what she'd said, but the left side of her mouth didn't move as much as the right did.

Ben's heart rate picked up. "Why did you come to the ER today?"

"I fell at home. My daughter insisted I come in, but she had to go get..." She trailed off, then put her head back in her hand. "Her little girl."

"What's her little girl's name?" Ben glanced around for some help. Everyone was rushing around with no thought to the nice, quiet woman in the wheelchair who was conscious and not bleeding.

"Madeline," the woman whispered hoarsely. A tear slid down her cheek as Ben turned back to her. "I don't know what's wrong with me."

"What else are you feeling?" he asked.

"I have a headache. But I've had that for a couple of days."

"Okay," Ben said, stroking her arm. "We're going to take care of you."

She nodded glumly.

"What's your name?" he asked.

"Carolyn McDonald."

"Carolyn, can you squeeze my hand?" he asked, putting his hand in her right hand.

She squeezed it tightly.

"Now this one." He moved his first three fingers into her left hand. The grip was much weaker on this side.

"Do you use a wheelchair all the time?" Ben asked. He got to his feet and started to push her toward the admitting desk. Carolyn moved her right hand to cover her eyes.

"No. We got this when we got here. My daughter was afraid I might fall again. It took us ten minutes to get me back on my feet this morning when I fell at home. Sometimes I use a cane because of my right knee."

"Do you remember how you felt before you fell?"

"Dizzy."

Ben stopped by the desk and pretended to read the posted sign about the patient's rights and responsibilities, keeping his cap pulled down low on his forehead. He slipped a sheet of paper out of the top tray next to the phone and pilfered a pen from the counter.

Then he and Carolyn headed for the elevator.

As they waited for the car to arrive, he scribbled on the form, asking Carolyn for her date of birth and other pertinent information. At the bottom, under physician orders, he wrote: *CT scan, head and neck; rule out CVA.* He signed his name, though less legibly than usual.

It would work. The forms were for doctors transferring patients to other departments within the hospital and the folks in charge of the CT scan would assume that only a physician would know the process for transferring a patient, be able to obtain the form and fill it in properly. When they did read his name, he could only hope that they didn't know he was suspended or if they did, they would assume he was back to work.

"Carolyn, I'm sending you up to the fifth floor. When the elevator stops, you'll have to push yourself out, like this." He showed her how to maneuver the wheelchair by pulling it forward with her feet and legs. "When you're off, give this paper to the staff up there. They'll take it from there." He put the folded paper in her lap. "Can you do that?"

Carolyn nodded, opening her right eye slightly. "Tell my daughter where I am."

He promised to be sure she knew. Once the elevator doors slid shut he went back past the desk with his shoulders slouched and his hands in his pockets. No one spared him more than a glance.

In the men's restroom he pulled off a paper towel and

printed neatly: "Carolyn McDonald is in radiology. Her daughter will be looking for her."

The neat penmanship would ensure none of the staff recognized his handwriting. On the way back to the waiting area he slid the paper towel note onto the counter near the phone where Melanie, the desk clerk, would be sure to see it. He even returned the pen.

He was humming as he went back in to finish reading up on Bruce Willis's latest movie and girlfriend.

Almost as if Russ was trying to prove a point to her, Jessica found herself assigned to a nearly impossible task, as usual, within ten minutes of leaving their little chat.

The man in trauma four had fallen from scaffolding at work. Things were critical and Jessica's job was to find the man's wife and get her on the phone so he could talk to her before he... Jessica shut down the thought before it formed. It didn't matter what happened in five minutes or five hours. What mattered was right now. Unfortunately, right now the man's wife was somewhere between Japan and Omaha and the man was too dazed to know when her flights were to leave, where she was laying over or even for sure which airline she was on. He was "pretty sure" it was United Airlines.

Jessica hoped so. She'd been on hold for nearly ten minutes with someone from United who was checking passenger records for her. She could only imagine how long that might take and if, in the end, the answer was that the woman wasn't even flying United, Jessica was going to cry.

But she was the master of the impossible. At least that's what her co-workers believed. She would do anything she could. The worst was the waiting. Like now. Every minute that ticked by was one less that man in there had to spend telling his wife enough to last her for all the time she had ahead of her without him.

Shifting to put her other hip against the counter, Jessica tried to concentrate on positive thoughts and prayers. Once, she'd had a nurse from another floor pretend to be someone's sister when the real sister proved impossible to find in time. The patient had died peacefully, having said all the things she wanted to say, and the nurse was later able to repeat for the sister word for word what the woman had wanted to say. It wasn't perfect, but Jessica had to do whatever she could for the patients on the tables in St. Anthony's ER. That was why she was there. If the patient found some peace, then Jessica could sleep at night.

Jessica hunched over, putting an elbow on the counter top and her index finger's nail between her teeth. She watched through the window to trauma room four, willing the woman with United to come back on the line.

She could see that they were examining the fracture of the man's lower leg now and she took that to mean that his heart and oxygen had stabilized at least to the point where examination of a broken bone was important. If his heart stopped and couldn't be re-started, it wouldn't matter if his leg was broken or not.

Jessica's stomach clenched at the thought. She hated losing patients. Everyone in that room felt the same way, but she'd never gotten used to the fact that at times she was witness to a person's last moments on earth.

She supposed it came from being the one and only witness to her father's last moments, and not realizing it at the time. Now she was acutely aware of those precious, mysterious seconds at the end.

As she watched the team run the trauma, Jess prayed silently that the man would have at least a phone connection with someone he loved before those last minutes passed.

She could barely see the heart monitor from where she stood, but she could tell the line went up and down rather than straight across. As long as that rhythm remained there was hope.

"Ma'am?"

Jessica jerked upright at the sudden sound of the voice on the other end of the phone. "Y-Yes. Yes, I'm here."

"I'm sorry it took so long. Mrs. Abigail Snyder is a passenger of ours. She is on layover in San Jose, California. She goes from San Jose to Denver, Colorado and then on to Omaha. She is to board the plane in San Jose in about fifteen minutes."

Jessica felt tears stinging her eyes. "Thank God. Thank *you*," she added. The woman sounded tired. Jessica understood. She had explained the situation to her when they'd first been connected and she could tell the woman understood how important haste and efficiency were, but working under that kind of stress could wear a person out quickly. "How can I get a hold of her?" Jessica asked.

"The sure way would be for me to contact our hub office in San Jose. They could then connect us with the airport, then they could connect us with the gate and then someone there can page Mrs. Snyder."

"Wonderful. Will you do that for me?" Jessica asked. "Mr. Snyder is currently stable, but it is tentative at best."

"Of course. I'll have to put you back on hold."

"Thank you."

Jessica turned to put her low back against the counter now, preparing for another long wait. It would be better if she couldn't see the heart monitor on Ron Snyder.

As it was, she wasn't going to have a fingernail left on the index finger of her right hand.

Shifting to put her other hip against the counter, Jessica's eyes swept the waiting room. A boy with a homemade ice pack against one eye, a middle-aged woman with a not-readily-apparent problem, a man in a baseball cap hunched in the corner and a young woman with a crying baby.

Jessica's eyes flicked back to the man in the baseball cap. She couldn't see his face but that T-shirt with the NY Yankee's emblem on it looked familiar. Not that there weren't other Yankees fans in Omaha, but the man himself seemed familiar—a fact that her heart or subconscious mind or hormones or something recognized before she truly realized it.

"Ben?"

The desk was too far away from where he sat for him to hear her though. She glanced at the phone that she could not leave and then at the brilliant surgeon trying to pass himself off as a regular guy. What was he doing? He didn't even look hurt or sick.

She smiled at the little boy with the icepack. "Hi," she said.

"Hi."

His mother looked up. Jessica smiled reassuringly at her while shifting to be sure the woman could see her hospital ID badge. "My name is Jessica. I'm a nurse here."

"I'm Charlie."

"Charlie, do you think your mom would let you do me a favor? I have to stay on this phone, but I need some help."

Charlie looked at his mother, who asked, "What is the favor?"

"I need someone to take a note to that man sitting in the corner," Jessica said, pointing to Ben. "He's a friend of mine and I can't get his attention."

The boy's mother looked back at Ben, then down at her son. "I guess that would be okay."

The boy jumped up from his chair, abandoning his icepack. His eye was bruised and swollen, but he seemed to have forgotten about any serious pain.

Jessica looked around for a piece of paper. They were in a hospital. Paper was plentiful. But none of it was blank. She finally saw a paper towel stuck under the corner of the phone on the opposite counter. She stretched for it, leaning as far as her phone cord would allow but she still couldn't reach it. She lifted her leg and stretched her foot toward the paper towel, finally getting the toe of her shoe on the corner of it. She managed to wiggle it free and pull it toward the edge of the counter. Once it fluttered to the floor, she was able to stretch far enough to reach it.

She tore off the bottom half of the towel, leaving the message about somebody named Carolyn getting a CT scan at the top. She quickly scribbled, *what are you doing here?* on it and handed it to Charlie.

The boy ran from her to Ben, who he poked in the shoulder before handing him the note. Ben gave the kid a smile and said a few words she couldn't make out by reading lips, then glanced at the note. He didn't look at her, but said something else to Charlie, who then came running back to her.

"He doesn't have a pen."

Well, of course not. And he obviously wasn't willing to get up and walk across the room to get one—or to just talk to her for that matter.

She handed Charlie a pen and watched him deliver it to Ben. He wrote something on the back of the note she'd written.

I love those pink scrub pants. Are you wearing the red thong?

Her heart pounded at his words even as she was annoyed that he'd basically ignored her question and was sitting there as if he was relaxing in his stupid coffee shop rather than an ER where people were hurt and dying.

You should feel guilty sitting there thinking about my underwear while people here need you.

She didn't think Charlie was old enough to read, especially cursive writing, but she folded the towel over anyway.

"You're being really helpful," she told him as he took the note. "I'll buy you a juice if your mom says it's okay."

"Okay!" he said enthusiastically, and ran the note to Ben.

A moment later he returned.

I guess I'll have to find out about the thong myself. Trauma one or two?

"Ma'am?"

Jessica's attention was jerked back to the phone call she was supposed to be having.

"Yes?" She forced herself to concentrate on the man in trauma four, the man who needed her, instead of the man in the waiting room who frustrated her beyond reason.

"I've located Mrs. Snyder's flight. The staff in San Jose is trying to find her now."

"She's checked in though?" Jessica confirmed, turning away from the waiting area and the man who was driving her crazy. If Russ found out Ben was here and was sitting around reading a magazine she would certainly not be seeing any letters glowing about her competence in any situation.

"She is. They're paging her now."

Jessica prayed as she rose on tiptoe to see the monitor through the window to trauma four. Ben was crazy. They couldn't have sex in trauma one or two. They all had windows. "Hello?" This woman's voice was new.

"Mrs. Snyder?" Jessica guessed.

"Yes. I'm Abby Snyder." She sounded scared and Jessica realized the airline staff must have told her this was a call from a hospital, or at least an emergency call about a loved one.

"This is Jessica Bradford. I'm with St. Anthony's hospital in Omaha. Your husband, Ron, is here."

The woman on the other end of the phone barely made a sound as Jessica explained the accident, her husband's current condition and the importance of the phone call.

"You don't think I'll make it in time to see him...before..."

Jessica felt her chest tighten. "I don't know. Of course you should get here as soon as possible, but this way you'll have had a chance to say...whatever...in case things take a turn for the worse. He's in critical condition, Mrs. Snyder."

"I understand," she said softly. "I'm several hours away yet."

"We're doing everything we can," Jessica said.

"Thank you." There was a long pause, then the woman said, "I don't know what to say to him."

Jessica understood that. Words felt inadequate at times. Still, she knew how badly it hurt to not have the chance to say them.

"Just talking to you, hearing your voice, will be enough," Jessica said past her scratchy throat. "I know he wanted to talk to you."

"You know," Abby said after a moment. "Maybe it's more about what he needs to say to me. I guess I'll be the one still here to remember it." Her voice broke at the end.

Jessica couldn't breathe for a moment.

"I'm going to connect you to the room where he is, if you're ready. If he's able to talk, they'll take the phone to him."

"I'm ready."

Jessica punched the sequence of buttons to transfer the call. Stephanie, one of the nurses, picked up and assured Jessica that Ron could talk.

Jessica wanted to be in there. This was part of why she came to work—to make a difference, somehow. And she needed some real proof right now that the time and effort the ER staff had already invested in Ron Snyder was worthwhile. Maybe it was only to give him enough time to say goodbye. That still mattered. She knew that personally. To Jessica, goodbyes, I'm sorrys and I love yous had been precious to her ever since she'd had hers taken away from her by the boy who shot her father.

She ignored Ben. For now.

Twenty minutes later, Ron Snyder was on his way to the OR, his wife was on the plane to Denver and Jessica was satisfied. Ron had the chance to tell Abby where he'd hidden his gift to her for their twenty-fifth anniversary, in case he wasn't there to give it to her. Abby told him that their oldest daughter was pregnant and due around Christmas. Both were things that needed to be said and both people would have some peace now in case the worst happened.

Ron had squeezed Jessica's hand in thanks as they administered the medication that would start to calm him for the surgery. That hand squeeze had been real. It had mattered. All the time on the phone was worth it. The nail she'd chewed to a stub was worth it. Getting to know these people and care about them was worth it. Even if the outcome was painful she was glad she'd gotten involved.

She stomped to where Ben still sat, now nursing a soda, flipping through yesterday's newspaper.

"You should be ashamed of yourself!"

He glanced at his watch. "You were supposed to be off an hour ago." He rose from the plastic chair, stretching as he went, bending his trunk from side to side.

"I was *working.*"

"We could have been naked for forty-five minutes by now."

Heat spread from her scalp to her toes. The images rushing through her mind made her pause. Why had she stayed in the ER for an extra hour when Ben was waiting to take his clothes off?

Oh, yeah. Her *job.* "There is a man in there dying and I needed to find his wife so he could say goodbye."

"You're being dramatic." Ben tucked his hands into his back pockets.

"He fell from sixty feet," she said with wide-eyes.

"His vitals were stable within minutes," Ben said. "They caught the colon perforation and Mark Simpson is on it."

Mark Simpson was the second-best trauma surgeon in Omaha. The first-best actively working.

"The fractures aren't critical. The biggest concern will be the colon repair and monitoring him for spinal shock. It's amazing, but very positive, that he didn't have a skull fracture."

Jessica was stunned. "How did you know all of that?"

He shrugged. "I overheard the report from the paramedics when he came in. Right about the time you were supposed to be done with your shift, Dr. Martin did his dictation from the desk. And I happened to see his labs and CT scan."

Jessica processed the information, then felt smugness settle over her and knew her face showed it. "Just happened to see them, huh?"

"I'd been sitting here forever. I needed to have some idea how long it would be until you would be ready to go," he said smoothly.

"You were that excited to see me?"

The look he gave her made her wonder if her panties were fireproof. "Always," he said, his voice husky.

She loved that he wanted her as badly as he did. She loved that he was here because she was here. She loved that he'd been unable to keep from helping patients in the ER.

But she hated that he wouldn't admit it. She crossed her arms and studied him. "I was the reason that you looked at his chart? Not because of curiosity?" She looked at him closer. "Or concern?"

Ben continued to meet her eyes directly, but he didn't deny it.

"Can we go now?" he asked, feigning boredom.

"No." She wanted something more from Ben and she saw no reason not to ask for it. "Not until you admit that our work in there, on that man, giving him those few minutes he needed to talk to his wife, was worth it."

"He'd have been able to tell her all of it in the morning when she's here and he's awake and recovering from surgery."

"No. You don't know that," she insisted. "Not for sure. It was important that he have that time. Admit it Ben." She stepped close and took the front of his shirt in her hand, not to be aggressive, but to be sure she had his full attention and kept it. "Admit that even when the end isn't exactly what we want it to be, that the effort we give in there is worthwhile."

She couldn't explain why exactly, but she needed to hear him say it.

He stared down at her for so long she felt despair begin to settle in her stomach.

Finally, Ben wrapped his hand around her wrist. She released his shirt but didn't remove her hand. Instead, he pressed her palm flat against his chest. She could feel his heart beating fast.

"Jessica, I think what you do is amazing."

She could see that he was sincere. Was it enough? Maybe. For now.

"Excuse me?"

They turned to find a woman dressed in a yellow skirt and a white shirt looking expectantly at Ben.

"I was wondering..." the woman said. "You look like the man my mother described to me...Did you, um, did you sent Carolyn McDonald upstairs for a CAT scan?"

Jessica looked from Ben to the woman and back. "Ben?"

The look on his face was of resignation.

Ah. She smiled. "Did you send someone upstairs?"

"I don't remember."

"With an order?"

"I don't recall."

The woman looked confused. "Are you a doctor?" She took in his T-shirt and blue jeans. "Mom said the man who helped her was wearing a Yankees T-shirt. I didn't believe her."

"He is a doctor," Jessica assured her. The last thing Russ needed, and would totally blame her for, was a patient's daughter accusing the hospital of letting some guy off the street write medical orders for her mother.

"Oh." The woman smiled. "Well, they found something. I didn't understand everything they said, but they said that it was good they found it early. Still, there are some other things they're looking for. Anyway, mom wanted me to find you. She wanted to know if you agreed with the tests they want to do."

Ben didn't want this. He was sure they wanted to do an MRI, which needed to be done. They had to be sure that Carolyn's symptoms were coming from little strokes in her brain versus a tumor. It sounded as if there was something that made them suspicious on the CT scan. But this wasn't his call. She wasn't his patient. None of this was his deal.

But he'd stupidly stepped in, helped Carolyn out and now he was her hero.

He just wanted to make Jessica happy by playing basketball at the center and showing up here to take her on a surprise date.

Unfortunately, his years with his father, medical school and in Africa had created bad habits like being concerned about a sweet little old lady who had a suspicious CT scan.

He'd already seen the flicker of expectation in Carolyn's daughter's eyes. He'd felt the shiver up his spine, and not the good kind of shiver. It was so easy to get sucked in, so easy to fall into those habits of caring and trying to fix everything. But he didn't want to care. If he didn't care, he wouldn't get involved and he wouldn't feel frustrated, discouraged, or worse...guilty when it all went to hell.

Right on the heels of that thought was his heart's insistence that it wouldn't necessarily go to hell. There was a chance that whatever was causing Carolyn's headaches and dizziness had nothing to do with whatever was on the CT scan. It could be that she ate some bad fish last night. But his gut didn't care about all the other things it could be. It reacted to the person in front of him and what *they* cared about, as always.

Early on he'd believed he had the gift everyone insisted he did. He loved hearing that more doctors should be like him, that he would have a long, rewarding career because he was in it for the right reasons, that he reminded everyone of his father with his dedication and heart, that he saw the person not just the body—all that bullshit.

It wasn't a gift. It was a gut-wrenching nightmare.

It was the reason for a lot of sleepless nights; the reason for a stomach ulcer; the reason he'd talked his friends into staying in Africa...just long enough to get killed.

The reason he was now turning his back on medicine for good.

"The best neurologist at this hospital is a buddy of mine," Ben said. "I'm going to give him a call and have him check on your mom."

Steve could do this. Steve didn't have emotional baggage, or a bad attitude, or an intense need to stay on Jessica's good side.

"Ben?"

Dammit.

Jessica.

Ben almost closed his eyes and groaned out loud. Instead he looked down at the very woman he knew he should only picture naked, but who kept popping up in his mind, and in person, as the professional, capable, compassionate woman who was now looking at him with hope and happiness shining in her eyes. And neither the hope nor the happiness was because of his prowess at bringing her to orgasm. It was, as he should have expected, far more complicated than that.

He sighed. He should have known the minute he walked into the hospital that this would happen. Because the moment he saw a person as a patient, as someone who needed something he could give, he was like the rest of them, the rest of the people who worked in the ER and picked people up and tried to put them back together. He only thought about what could be. The option of losing, of quitting, didn't occur to him. The possibility of being wrong didn't enter in. He was trained, practically programmed, to keep the negative thoughts out.

Until it was over. Then, of course, he got to think all of it over, replay it, hate it.

Today had been good so far. Mrs. McDonald had gotten her CT scan before anything major happened. Jessica's guy from the scaffolding would very likely wake up to his wife's pretty face after his surgery.

But if it wasn't for Jessica and his insane need to be around her, he wouldn't even know there was a Carolyn McDonald to worry about. If Jessica had given in right at the beginning and let him make love to her, he'd already be over her and wouldn't be here, getting sucked in all over again.

He stomped to the phone on the admitting desk and punched the buttons he needed.

"This is Dr. Torres. I need the test results on Carolyn McDonald," he told the nurse who picked up.

He only had to wait a few minutes as she pulled the chart and read him everything he asked for.

"Thanks." He hung up. "Which room is your mom in?" he asked Carolyn's daughter.

"Six oh two."

He dialed the room. It only rang once.

"Hello?"

"Carolyn? It's Ben. The guy you talked to by the soda machine."

"Ben? Did Holly find you? I asked her to go down there—"

"Yes, she did. She's right here," Ben said. Even Carolyn's voice was sweet. He needed to get this over with. "Listen, Carolyn, I got your test results. They want to do an MRI. That's very appropriate."

"You think I should do it?" Carolyn asked.

"Yes, I do. You want to be sure to cover all the bases right?" he asked. "You put your trust in those folks up there. They're going to take good care of you."

"But I like you. Can't you do the test?"

Ben smiled in spite of himself. He was going to have to send Carolyn some flowers. When Jessica wasn't around to read too much into it, of course.

"You don't want me to do them, kiddo," he told her. "I don't even know where the on switch is on all those fancy machines up there."

"Oh, Ben—"

"Dr. Borchers is going to come see you tomorrow morning," Ben interrupted before she could say anything more complimentary or sweet to him. "He's a friend of mine. He's going to take over your case. You do everything he tells you."

He was going to have to call Steve before he called the flower shop. There was a long pause on Carolyn's end. Then she sighed. "I'll do whatever you want me to."

"By the way, you wouldn't happen to know where to get good peanut butter cookies in this city, would you, Carolyn?"

"Cookies?" she asked, obviously taken aback by his question. "Yes. I mean, I make wonderful cookies, if I do say so myself."

Exactly what he'd been hoping for. "Then I want you to make a huge batch of those cookies when you get home and bring them up here to all of the doctors and nurses and everyone who's going to be helping you out. Can you do that?"

Asking her to make plans for cookies would lead her to believe that things were going to be just as they were before she came to St. Anthony's, and in a relatively short time. He had no way of knowing that for certain, of course, but at least it kept her from asking, *will I be okay?* Besides, the staff deserved cookies once in a while and he had a feeling Carolyn McDonald could make some awesome cookies. Peanut butter was his favorite.

Ben frowned at that.

It didn't matter what kind of cookie he liked the best. He wouldn't be here to eat them. He chose not to change the order, though, when he heard the smile in Carolyn's voice.

"Yes. I can certainly do that."

They disconnected and Ben took a moment to gather his thoughts and emotions before turning to face Jessica and Holly. He already liked Carolyn McDonald and knew now that he'd be visiting her at least once, which meant he'd like her even more in a couple of days. He would also know in a couple of days if they had managed to stave off a stroke or if what they'd found on her scan was indeed a small brain tumor.

Son of a bitch.

He was worried, frustrated about being worried and pissed about feeling frustrated when all he wanted to feel was good and relaxed.

And there was a certain petite brunette with big, green, knowing eyes who was directly to blame for him getting tangled up in all of this.

He suddenly had a whole lot of steam to blow off.

And knew exactly how he wanted to do it.

"Holly?" Ben said as he turned. "Your mother is in good hands. She understands everything that's going to happen. There's nothing to worry about."

"Thank you for talking to her, Dr..."

"Ben," he said simply. "And you're welcome. Your mother is a lovely woman."

Holly's eyes filled up with tears, but she smiled. "Yes she is."

It was time to go.

"Come on," he said to Jessica. He turned and headed for the front of the hospital. Again. This time determined not to stop for anything.

He made it to the front doors before she caught up to him.

"Where are we going?" she asked, slightly out of breath.

"Out."

"Out where?"

"Wherever I want."

She stopped. "Is that right?"

Jessica's face registered apprehension when Ben pivoted to face her. "Jessica," Ben said, spreading his feet and crossing his arms, his eyebrows drawn together. "I have been playing basketball and talking to the kids, being a regular damn hero

181

down at that youth center. I've been waiting for you in that ER for almost two hours. I even stepped in and practically became an adopted grandson to Carolyn McDonald. Now it's my turn to get what I want. Get in the car."

He didn't wait for her to decide. He went through the front doors and took a right as soon as he stepped out of the building.

Ben was in his truck with the engine running by the time she arrived at his reserved parking spot.

"Are we going to your place?" she asked, snapping her seat belt across her lap. She was not going to comment on his mood. She was not. Ben seemed to be spoiling for a fight for some reason. But it wouldn't solve anything.

"We have to make a stop."

"Where?"

Ben pulled out onto the street and into the left turning lane, stopping at the light. He looked at her and his eyes ran over her from head to toe. "To get you into some slutty clothes."

Startled, Jessica looked down at what she wore. Light pink scrub pants and top with white tennis shoes.

"Why?"

"I look at you and see the in-charge, charitable, always-do-the-right-thing nurse who saves lives without even breaking a nail and thinks everyone else should give their heart and soul to that emergency room. What I *want* to see is you horny, barely dressed and so hot neither of us can think straight."

Ah. Even as heat suffused her body, she understood where this was coming from. Her scrubs reminded him of all of the stuff he wanted to walk away from. But he didn't want to walk away from her. So, he had to dress her up to forget all the things she made him think and feel, that went beyond physical attraction.

Which worked for her, because she didn't want him to walk away from her either and right now making it about sex was a lot simpler than everything else it was turning into.

She was going to concentrate on the physical and worry about the rest later. Much, much later. In fact, some new clothes might be just the trick, because when she was dressed in her scrubs, she also had a hard time separating herself from the do-gooder who would never think of having a flaming affair with nothing promised other than multiple orgasms.

"Barely dressed is better than *not* dressed?" she asked. "Because I'm okay with being not dressed."

He gave her that grin that made her sure he was picturing her not-dressed right that minute.

He leaned in. She felt herself move closer as well. "Jessica."

"Yeah?" she asked breathlessly.

He lifted his hand and ran this thumb along her lower lip. "We're also going to need to get some hooker boots."

"I..." She blinked, replaying his words and then pulled back. "Hooker boots?"

"You know—high-heeled, black, leather boots like Julia Roberts wore in *Pretty Woman.*"

"You saw *Pretty Woman*?" she asked, not sure what she was most stunned about.

"Not the point," Ben said with a roguish grin.

He put his thumb back over her lips, keeping them together. "I've been good, Jess. I haven't gotten into trouble, I've been following the rules."

He moved his thumb off her mouth and she wet her lips and swallowed hard.

His eyes dropped to her mouth and his gaze heated. "Now it's time to get naughty."

"Sounds like you have a pretty specific picture in mind."

"Oh, yeah," he said huskily.

"We're going to have to go shopping."

There had been a time when a simple stop at home would have been more than enough to fill Ben's order, but the black dress from the bar the other night was the only remnant.

Ben looked surprised for a moment, but quickly recovered. "I'm buying."

"That makes it even more fun."

Ben didn't say much on the drive, which left Jessica plenty of time to think about what the night ahead might hold. Sexual awareness hummed between them and Jessica felt like she was being wound tighter with every block that passed until she thought she was going to spring right out of the car through the moon roof.

Ben's hand came out and clamped down on her left thigh.

She gasped and jumped.

"Stop squirming," he said tightly, not taking his eyes off the road or his hand off her leg.

She frowned. "Why's it bothering *you*?" She was the one feeling bothered—hot and bothered.

"I can't concentrate on driving with you moving like that," he muttered. "Because all I can think is how it will feel to have you moving like that when you're underneath me. But I can't do anything about that right now. So sit still."

She didn't have a choice with him holding her leg down, but the heat from his palm on her thigh didn't do much to help.

Suddenly every reason to not sleep with him slipped her mind. She vaguely remembered that there was a reason, but she was pretty sure she could come up with a way to justify ignoring it.

"Maybe," she croaked. She cleared her throat and tried again. "Maybe we should just go to your place." It was closer than hers.

Ben shook his head at her suggestion, however. "I've got this vivid picture going. I need to get you into something other than what you wore all day as you made the world a better place. Then I'll be able to focus on all the delicious, dirty things you deserve to have done to you."

Oh, well, when he put it that way...

Then his thumb started stroking her thigh and she couldn't talk any more anyway.

They stopped at another red light and Ben's hand moved from her thigh to the back of her head, pulling her in and molding his mouth over hers. He kissed her hard, boldly stroking his tongue over hers. Jessica felt the heat and heaviness settle low in her stomach and between her legs. She wanted him to touch her, to counter the fullness building there, to stroke her like he was stroking her tongue. She wanted him to fill her, to rub against her, to reach a spot she couldn't even describe and that she instinctively knew only he could reach.

The honking car behind them finally got Ben's attention. He pulled back, breathing hard. "And that's what you do to me looking all nice and sweet."

Ben shifted the truck into drive and made the left turn with a little squeal of the tires.

"I like looking nice and sweet." Usually. In fact, she worked at it.

Ben's smile almost seemed affectionate. "I know. But you'll like this too. I promise to be sure that you like this too."

Jessica was inclined to believe him.

"What do you know about hooker boots anyway?" Jessica asked, as they drove toward the shopping district that catered to high-priced specialty shops.

He flashed her a grin. "I know that you've probably never worn them."

She hadn't. Stiletto heels sure, but she preferred shoes to boots. "You're right about that."

"And that's part of the appeal," he said, pulling up in front of a short strip of shops. "I've decided that you need to have some fun." He put the car into park and turned to face her. "And I don't want you to have this kind of fun with anyone else."

"The kind of fun that requires new clothes?" she asked.

"I've wanted you for a long time," he said. "The idea of rumpling your perfectly ironed clothes and smudging your perfectly applied lipstick has tempted me from the beginning. But now seeing how principled and altruistic you are even outside of the hospital makes me want to get you to do something...naughty." His smile was wicked.

Jessica opened her mouth and realized she was about to confess that naughty wasn't all that new to her.

"Why is it so important to you that I do something naughty?" she asked carefully. "Being principled and altruistic are generally good things." Things that she'd spent a lot of time and energy on.

Ben shook his head, his smile fading. "Take it from someone who's spent a long time being both...there are better ways to feel good."

He didn't let go easily, Jessica thought. Ben was as determined to shake off his hero status as she was to make up for her past indiscretions.

She wanted him to be the good guy she needed, the one to keep her out of trouble, the one to help her build the life that would have made her father proud.

Ben wanted a party, a good time...and to get her into

185

trouble.

Ironically, she had once been the woman Ben wanted her to be now. While he'd been off being the man she wanted him to be now.

Jessica glanced at the window of the store. The mannequins were dressed in short skirts and barely there tops.

She was shocked to feel a flip of excitement in her stomach. The foreboding she wasn't as surprised to feel.

She felt like an alcoholic staring at a no-drink-limit open bar.

Chapter Nine

Jessica stared at the shop. She knew exactly what Ben was going for—better than Ben did. Ben had his imagination. She had experience.

She'd loved to party. Of course, now she knew it had not been the rush or the fun as much the fact that the party was the one place Jessica could be selfish and superficial. Keeping it light, not knowing people too well, not worrying about tomorrow—that's what she'd wanted, and gotten.

Jessica got out of the car trying to squelch the butterflies in her stomach and the memories at the same time.

"How did you know about this place?" she asked.

"I bought some old records at that vintage music shop awhile back," Ben said, indicating the shop that occupied the space at the north end of the strip. "This place was hard not to notice."

Which was exactly the point to the sexy window display and the store's name—*Tease*.

"Let's go." Jessica slammed the car door shut and started for the store.

Her past followed her in.

In an attempt to make his children grateful for what they had and to instill his passion for bettering the world, Jessica's dad had made sure his son and daughters knew what the world was like. He didn't sugarcoat anything, he didn't protect them or hide them from the truth. In fact, he made them face the facts about what drugs did to people and families, what kinds of abuses people suffered, what desperation and hatred looked like, what crimes were committed every day. His heart was in the right place. He wanted to fight the things he saw wrong in the world. But he didn't know how to have fun or how to relax or how to enjoy what he had.

Jessica knew exactly where Ben was right now: tired of fighting a fight that seemed to have no end, tired of feeling depressed and angry all the time.

Which was why when she turned sixteen she decided to have some fun and enjoy life enough for both herself and her father.

A life she might have lost at age twenty if her dad hadn't gotten to her apartment that day before she did.

Ben joined her on the sidewalk. "This is going to be fun."

Jessica nodded and tried to smile, but the memories kept crowding in. She knew hard times personally now. She understood being scared and poor and desperate now. Ironically, all of those lessons had come once her father was gone.

She'd worked her butt off at school, for her siblings and to keep the center going. She'd finally gotten her dad's message loud and clear.

Didn't she deserve one night off?

She wasn't trying to prove anything now.

She could handle it.

Probably.

Ben held the door open for her. As they stepped through the front door of the shop, a saleswoman—or rather a sales *girl*—instantly greeted them. She introduced herself by name but neither of them caught it. They were too busy looking at the nearly transparent slip of white material she wore.

She was beautiful and definitely had a body worth showing off, but...wow. The material was certainly not effective in providing modesty, nor would it ward off any cold drafts. Even the tiny pink rose on the left hip of her white thong underneath was easily identified.

"We could take one of those," Ben said.

Jessica was impressed he could take his eyes off the girl, whatever her name was.

"Is there anything I can show you?" the girl asked.

"There's more to see?" Jessica asked wryly.

Ben stifled a laugh and said, "I can tell you exactly how you can help us." He handed the girl a fifty-dollar bill while explaining that he was buying Jessica an outfit as a gift, but that he needed her to try it on. He wondered if perhaps Jessica could wait in a dressing room while he picked something out and took it in to her. He added that he didn't think they would need any help other than that.

The girl took the fifty and waved in the direction of the fitting rooms seemingly bored with them already. There was no one else in the store but the girl didn't seem overly concerned about a commission or customer service surveys.

"You're choosing the outfit?" Jess asked Ben when the girl was out of earshot.

"I have a feeling we might have different tastes in this instance," Ben said with a smile, looking around like a kid in a candy store.

Jessica laughed. "Ben, there's only one taste that we're going to get here."

Like any good specialty shop, the store focused its display space on what it did best, which in this case was to put very little material and very large price tags on hangers.

"We've got classy-slutty," Jessica said, indicating the dresses to her left. "We've got fantasy-slutty." She gestured toward the costumes like the pink bunny with the fluffy white cottontail on the butt, the bright red satin devil outfit and the classic French maid's costume.

"And, of course, slumber-party-slutty," she said, nodding toward the various pieces of sleepwear displayed a few feet away. Of course, sleeping was in no way an objective for someone wearing any of those.

Ben looked around the store with a large totally male grin. "I am going to be very happy here."

Jessica sat on the plump upholstered chair, then paced across the relatively large dressing room and leaned back against the wall. That put her directly across from the mirror that took up an entire wall, which unnerved her, so she paced back to the chair and sat. In less than two minutes she was up pacing again. What was Ben doing out there?

At that moment, the door to the dressing room banged open. Jessica swung around to find Ben smirking triumphantly in the doorway, holding a shiny red gift bag that said, *Tease* on the front. "Are you ready?"

She had a very distinct feeling that she was, in no way, ready.

"Of course."

He moved into the dressing room and the space, which she had been feeling was huge, suddenly shrunk dramatically. Not only that, but it got considerably warmer as Ben kicked the door shut behind him, locked it, then advanced on her, a predatory gleam in his eyes and a sexy grin on his face.

He stopped in front of her, looking down, studying her face. His hands stayed at his sides but she felt like he was touching her. Her body strained toward him.

"We're doing this my way, Jessica."

It was a blatant dare. She knew it and she knew that he knew she recognized it for what it was. She used to love playing Truth or Dare. And she always took the dares.

Her heart raced as she lifted her chin. This was Ben. If there was one thing she knew for certain it was that he was a good guy. He would not hurt her or endanger her. There was absolutely nothing to worry about, which meant that all she had to do was enjoy.

She could totally do that. In fact, she could hardly wait.

"I'll do whatever you want," she answered, moving in closer to him, but keeping her hands carefully by her side as well.

That seemed to further stoke the fire she saw in his eyes.

"Jessica," Ben said, his voice low and gruff, "you are a dream come true."

He moved in even closer, one of his feet inserted between hers.

"Take off your shirt." The tone in his voice went from husky to commanding just like that.

It probably shouldn't have excited her, but it did. Jessica had always been the one in control in any man-woman situation. Whether it was who she let buy her drinks, or how close they danced, or how far she let the interested hands get, she always called the shots.

With Ben, though, she was willing to let go of that control, and that surprised her.

She wet her lips, but said nothing. There was nothing to say. She grabbed the hem of her scrub shirt and pulled it up and over her head. She knew exactly which bra she had on too. She'd put on the leopard print one, thinking of Ben that morning.

"Nice," he drawled.

She let the shirt drop to the floor.

"Now the pants."

His tone was firmer now and Jessica had difficulty breathing.

Ben's eyes were on her face rather than the body parts she had bared and he looked very aroused. Ironically, her nipples puckered in reaction. The way he watched her, she knew that none of her responses, physical or emotional, to him or his actions or words, would go unnoticed. She also knew that was his intention. He wanted to know everything that turned her on. Interestingly, *that* was a major turn-on.

Jessica undid the tie at the front of her pants, surprised to have no trouble with it in spite of the adrenaline making her hands shake. She jumped as Ben put a hand on either hip, sliding the pants down and letting them drop to the floor.

"I was going to keep my hands to myself," he said, before pressing his lips to her shoulder. He flicked his tongue over her skin. "I don't know what the hell I was thinking."

Ben was still completely clothed while she stood there in a satin leopard-print bra and panties. She definitely felt naughty.

And she liked it.

Ben found himself intensely aroused by the fact that his fantasy was playing out just as he'd pictured it. The undressing her in the fitting room part had come to him when they'd stepped into the store and found it empty of anyone but a sales clerk who he correctly guessed would be cooperative for money and lack of hassle. But the rest was right on.

"Now the bra," he said gruffly.

"The bra?"

"You can't wear one with the shirt I picked out," he said unapologetically.

"I'm going without?" she squeaked.

Ben smiled. Jessica had probably never gone braless in public and the idea that she would tonight, for him, made his already present erection pulse with anticipation. Jessica wasn't tiny on top but neither was she even a C cup. She was probably a B and her breasts were firm. She was going to look great in the top he'd picked out.

"Come on, give it up."

Surprisingly, she reached behind her, undid the clasp and let the black straps slip off her shoulders without another word.

She stood proudly before him in panties only and Ben knew if he didn't touch her he'd lose his mind. He stepped in, turned her to face the mirror and moved behind her, his chest against her back. She leaned into him and he wondered briefly if she was even aware of it. Then he had to touch her, it was that simple.

His hands came up and he cupped both breasts at once. Enjoying the soft fullness, the tips begging to be touched, the way she arched to get closer to his hands. But most erotic was the sight in the mirror. Jessica's eyes were trained on the reflection in the mirror, her hair tumbled around her shoulders and fell over the backs of his hands, her lips were parted as she breathed in quick, short breaths. Her hair slightly obscured the view, though, so he lifted one hand and gathered her hair back, out of the way. He took a moment to run his fingers through the warm, silky mass, loving the idea of messing up the style, giving an outward sign to the world that he'd touched her; that he'd pleasured her.

But her breasts beckoned him, her excited, short breaths quickened his own breathing and he moved his hand again, this time taking her nipple and tugging gently.

She gasped and moaned and Ben smiled.

He teased both breasts similarly, loving how her eyes slid shut and how she pressed back against him and the sounds she made. Then he flattened his hand on her ribs and slid it down over her stomach.

Her head tipped back to rest on his shoulder and the short little pants stopped as she held her breath.

"We've got to take these off too," he said near her ear.

Her head came up fast, but he kept her shoulder blades against his chest by keeping his hand on her breast, her rock-hard nipple peeking between his middle fingers. He squeezed and she breathed in deep.

Feeling smug, he dropped both hands, hooked the

waistband of her silky panties with his thumbs and pulled. They slipped easily over her hips and he let them drop to the floor on top of her pants.

As she stepped out of them, Ben paused, eyes glued to the mirror and the sight of Jessica bare-assed naked on display for him under the bright lights designed to show every detail of what the room's occupants wore—or didn't.

"Jess," he said hoarsely. "You're gorgeous."

He brushed his hand over the curls between her legs before she could complete even a word. She gasped as his palm cupped her mound and his middle finger slipped into the hot, silky folds that parted in welcome. "Damn, you're wet for me," he murmured with approval.

Her hands came back, grabbing the material of his slacks along the outer seams for support as her head fell back onto his shoulder again. He stroked in and out of her, closing his eyes in pleasure, then quickly snapping them open so as not to miss the exquisite sight in the mirror.

Jessica's back arched, pressing closer to his hand, her eyes pressed tightly shut. She moaned softly as he stroked her. But Ben didn't want soft responses. He wanted loud, hard, unrestrained.

He slipped another finger into her and his thumb found her clitoris, rubbing over it with enough pressure to cause her hips to buck. He held her steady with his other hand on her hip and watched his hand move on her, incredibly turned on by being able to watch in the mirror and wondering why the hell he'd never thought of this before.

"I want to touch you, too," Jessica said in between gasps.

"But this isn't about what you want," he said. "I want you to see this. Open your eyes."

He could tell that having someone else take command—of anything—was new to Jessica, and that she liked it. He loved that it was him she felt safe enough with to be adventurous. It shouldn't matter, probably. In a casual affair it didn't matter how the other person was feeling as long as everyone had a good time. But it did matter. She met his eyes in the mirror and wet her lips. He reached up and tugged on her nipple while he caressed her deeply, keeping his eyes connected with her.

"I can't walk out of here without taking you," he said gruffly against her ear.

"Good," she said emphatically. She pushed his lower hand away, pivoted and grabbed the front of his shirt, pulled him forward, and kissed him deep and hard with lots of tongue.

He gripped her hips in his hands, pulling her up against him, settling her mound right against his painfully hard erection and then rubbing.

"Yes," she breathed as she pulled her mouth free. "Yes, right there."

He obliged, grinding into her, even as he smiled. "What about right here, right now?" he asked, fully intending it to be right here, right now.

"*Yes.*"

He appreciated her enthusiasm.

Jessica slipped a hand between them and pressed her open palm against his erection. "I want you, Ben. As deep as you can possibly get."

Damn. Her words, her voice, her hand... It was all better than he'd imagined. He cupped the back of her head and brought her in for a long, deep, hot kiss.

Jessica had never been this turned on in her life. While Ben was very good with his hands and fingers, she wanted the hot, steely shaft that could fill her in a way that nothing and no one else could.

She unbuttoned and unzipped his pants and slipped her hand inside, needing to be skin on skin. He groaned and she grew even warmer with the sound.

Ben pulled back as she stroked up and down his length.

"I did not mean for it to go this far when we came into this store," he said, his voice tight. "But I swear, if I don't get inside of you soon I'm going to explode."

Jessica smiled and opened her mouth to reply when a tentative knock sounded on the door.

"How are you doing in there?" the salesgirl, what's-her-name, asked.

Ben had to clear his throat before replying and Jessica smiled watching him try to form a coherent answer as she squeezed and stroked him.

"Great," he managed, though he sounded like he had strep throat.

"Do you need anything?" the girl asked. "Another size,

maybe?"

Jessica bit back laughter, running her thumb over the silky tip of Ben's rock-hard penis. "No, this size is perfect." She rubbed again.

"Okay," the girl said slowly.

"And you're in for a huge commission," Ben added, closing his eyes and pressing into Jessica's hand. "We are taking all of it."

"Okay," she said again, even slower. "I'll be out here if you need me."

"Do you think we'll need her?" Jessica asked Ben.

Ben's eyes were closed, his jaw tight and he was breathing raggedly as she put both hands around him.

"Hell, no," he said through gritted teeth. "All I need is you, bent over in that skirt." He pointed at the bag he'd set on the floor when he'd first come into the dressing room.

Wow. She gripped him tighter, wanting him moaning, groaning, begging like she was on the verge of doing herself. She looked at his face and saw that he was on the edge with her. And he was all hers. At least for tonight. For now. In this moment she wanted nothing more than to take over every one of Ben's senses, to make him unable to focus on anything but her. She wanted to possess him

She pushed his jeans down and pulled him free of his underwear as she went down on her knees and ran her tongue over the tip of his penis, fully intending to take him in her mouth.

Ben jerked back and swore, his hands going to her head and pushing her away.

She looked up at him from the floor in confusion.

"No," he said firmly.

"No?" she repeated. Her eyes dropped back to his rock-hard shaft.

"Quit looking at it like that." Ben's hands in her hair forced her to look up at him.

"Like what?" She licked her lips.

Ben frowned. "Like you want to suck on it."

"I do."

"*No.*"

"Why not?" Now she was concerned. Why was he being

weird about this? "You don't like...this?" Was he a human male?

Ben looked pained. "Of course I do."

"But not from me?" The idea hurt. She had never wanted to do this to another man and now the one she did didn't want her to? She'd barely gotten started. He didn't know if she was bad at this. Heck, neither did she. She'd never done it before. But she definitely had the general concept and she wanted to make Ben feel good, the way he did her.

"Get up." Ben reached down and pulled her up from the floor. "I can't think with you on your knees in front of me."

She propped a hand on a hip. "What's your problem?"

"If you knew how many times I've fantasized about you going down on me," Ben said tightly. "You would be amazed I was able to get anything else done at work. But if you do it now I'm going to lose it."

She believed him. She could see the raw desire on his face. And it thrilled her. She wanted him to lose it. "Okay."

"No. That isn't how I pictured this."

"Oh," she said breathlessly. "How did you picture it?"

Without taking his eyes from her face, Ben kicked his pants and briefs off, reached into his pocket, pulled out a condom, ripped it open with his teeth and rolled it on. Then he put his hands on her butt and lifted her. She wrapped her legs around his waist and Ben thrust upward, sliding into her in one bold stroke.

She had *never* felt this good ever before in her life. She'd never even imagined being able to feel this good in her life.

"Jess," Ben groaned.

He took two steps forward until her back was against the wall next to the mirror.

She couldn't even manage to moan his name. Ben pulled out slightly and then entered her again in a deep, swift thrust and she came just like that.

"*Yes*," he muttered.

He thrust forward five more times, deep, hard and fast, and then came with a deeply satisfied "Ah!"

Shivers of pleasure raced up and down her body knowing that she had put Ben into a frenzy of passion and then satisfied him.

She leaned forward resting her forehead on his shoulder.

Several seconds passed as they waited for their breathing to calm and their bodies to stop quivering and contracting.

"Wow," she finally said.

"Yeah."

He pulled out and let her slide down until her feet touched the floor, then cupped the back of her head and kissed her deeply, then hugged her close, her cheek against his chest. He ran his fingers through her hair and she felt tenderness from him in sharp contrast with the way they'd just gone at it.

"I'm sorry our first time was like this."

Startled, she pulled back and looked up at him. "You are?"

He grinned. "Not as much as I should be."

"Why should you be sorry at all?" she asked. "I'm not."

His fingers ran through her hair again. "I won't say it can be better because that was damn good, but it could be more romantic."

He looked abashed and she wanted to kiss him for the sentiment, but she had a nagging suspicion that the reason behind the sentiment was something they needed to talk about.

"I liked it," she said, moving back. "I don't need a lot of romance."

He shook his head. "You're going to make those boots look even better than I imagined. But I promise I am not going to take you like this again."

Oh, that wasn't good. She stepped forward again, earnestly. "I want you to."

"I know I said I wanted to dress you like this, but I know this isn't you." He lifted his hand and cupped her cheek, a tender look in his eyes. "And I like you, Jessica Leigh."

He tripped her heart in one second and then made it plummet to her toes the next. He liked her. But he thought this wasn't her. They might have a problem here.

"Ben, I am okay with this. *Really* okay," she insisted.

"I'm glad I didn't shock you," Ben said with a self-deprecating grin.

"Ben, I—"

"Jess," he interrupted. "I'm not exactly sorry. But you bring out this side of me that makes me think of red thongs and deep thrusts and being naked all the time. Even in the middle of surgery."

Whoa. Well, she hadn't known that. It was probably inappropriate to feel smug about that.

"Ben—"

"But I can control myself for your sake," he said quickly, as if thinking she was going to protest the naked-all-the-time bit. "We can play out your fantasies, too," he said. "If you want rose petals all over the bed, or to make love on a private beach, or under the stars, whatever. And you can wear whatever you want," he added with a sheepish grin. "I'll find you attractive in anything."

Dammit, maybe she didn't want to be ho-hum attractive. Maybe she wanted to be ball-busting hot. And, it may very well shock Dr. Torres to know that she already knew how to do that.

She stepped close, took his face between her thumb and fingers and forced him to look at her. "Ben, I *love* that you marched in here, stripped me down and took me up against the wall. Got it? I *love* that you were that out of control. I was too."

"But maybe you'll like..."

"*Ben*, stop. I already know what I like. I've had rose petals, I've had fancy dinners and champagne, I've had the attempts at romance. Soft music and silk sheets aren't what great sex is about."

Ben had paused in the midst of tucking himself back into his pants and zipping up, apparently speechless.

She reached into the red *Tease* bag and pulled on the itty bitty black T-shirt that didn't even cover her belly button and the hot pink skirt that fell to mid-thigh and tied on one hip.

"You weren't a virgin?"

She looked at him, balanced precariously on one foot while she put her other foot into the first black hooker boot.

"No."

Jessica watched him process that information. "How not-a-virgin are you?"

"Very not-a-virgin," she admitted.

He thought that over as well. "Do you have any clitoral warming gel?"

Her eyebrows shot up. "What?"

"They make this gel that warms up with friction and it goes..."

"Yeah, I get the idea. But no, I don't have any."

"Oh." He looked a little disappointed.

"But I know where we can get some."

Ben practically threw Jessica into the driver's side of his truck. It was either that or back her up against it, hike that skirt up and start all over again.

Lord, he'd thought he was going to explode. She'd made him crazy enough when she was sweet and serious. This new side of her—that liked having sex in semi-public places and wore hooker boots like they were custom made for her—had made him redefine everything he'd previously believed about lust.

The not-a-virgin information was new, but he found that he was not completely shocked. Jessica exuded a sexual energy that spoke of a confidence that went deep. The fact that she had some experience behind it made sense too. He was, however, jealous. Jealous of the man, or men, who had experienced the Jessica he had just discovered. Of course, those men were clearly idiots. None of them were still around and Jessica Bradford was not a woman a guy let walk away easily.

That realization should have made him stop cold. And panic. But...it was true. Jessica was the whole package and any man should want to have her in every way a man could have a woman.

"How many guys?"

He didn't care. Not really. She was all his now and he knew, could somehow tell, that any intimacies with other men had been less than stellar. And she responded to him like he'd never had another woman respond. It was addicting. He wanted to make her respond over and over, in different ways, various positions...

"Only two," she said. "But with John—"

She stopped talking abruptly.

There was silence in the car for nearly twenty seconds.

"John?" he prompted. Oh, he was definitely going to hear about John.

"John Shepard," she finally said.

Ben waited for another ten seconds, but she didn't

elaborate.

Fine, he did care about the other men. But it wouldn't change how he felt about her. And he was sure he'd find some way of *never* again thinking about another man touching her. Eventually

"Who is John Shepard?" There was something in her voice, and her face, that made him certain that him knowing about John Shepard was important.

She sighed, then said, "My greatest rebellion." She smiled, but didn't seem truly amused. She also didn't go on.

"You don't think I'm going to let that go, do you?" he asked.

She took a deep breath, then glanced at him. "No, I know you're not going to let it go."

"Tell me about John-boy."

He was going to be patient and laid back about this. He was. Ben settled back in his seat. He even crossed his ankles. Though he couldn't quite convince his stomach, which twisted, and his heart, that pounded, that he was nonchalant.

"John Shepard was someone my friend Marcy introduced me to," Jessica said. "He was worth sixty million dollars when I met him."

Ben didn't respond with the *holy shit* that crossed his mind.

"And he offered me the chance to travel the world with him."

"And you took it." He sounded bitter and realized that crossing his ankles and leaning back in his seat didn't help him feel even a little laid-back.

She looked at him. "Yes. For ten months. Parties every night. Only the most exclusive clubs and resorts. Posh hotel rooms. Shopping and eating and anything I wanted. No holding back, no guilt, no regrets. It was the exact opposite of what my father wanted from me."

"Just a shot in the dark, but I'm guessing John wasn't interested in your views on world disarmament policies."

"He was mostly interested in making everyone who'd ever doubted him, especially his ex-wife, see that he was better off and happier without them."

"And a beautiful, spirited young woman who wanted to piss off her dad was perfect."

Jessica shook her head. "I wasn't trying to piss my dad off. I was trying to convince him."

"Of what?"

"That I was serious about rejecting the lifestyle he was forcing on me. Humility, poverty, sacrifice, chastity. All of that."

Jessica snuck a look at Ben. He looked like he couldn't quite decide on one emotion. He was frowning and his jaw looked like it was clenched, but he seemed to be pondering something.

"So," she went ahead with the point she'd been thinking of keeping from him indefinitely: that she was a hypocrite. "While you were in Africa making the world a better place, I was spending enough on manicures and shoes to fund your entire project."

And she wasn't exaggerating.

Ben nodded, watching the road in front of them intently. But he didn't look at her.

He was disappointed. She gripped the steering wheel and bit the inside of her cheek. She had expected it. She was the one who kept insisting that he was a good guy under all the rebellion, and a good guy would not approve of her time with John, and more especially the motivation behind her time with John.

"And what did John expect in return for the nice nails and fashionable footwear?"

Ben's voice was low and had a note of danger to it, like challenging her to give him the truth, knowing he wouldn't like it and knowing that she wouldn't like his reaction.

She licked her lips, not daring to look at him as she answered. "The rules were simple. Always look great and always be available."

"What did being available mean?" he pressed.

"It meant that if he had a party to go to and I wanted to go to a show, we went to the party."

"Dammit, Jessica!" Ben finally snapped.

She jumped but still resisted looking at him. She couldn't stand seeing the judgment in his eyes.

"Did it mean being available for sex too? Did you sleep with him?"

She felt Ben's eyes on her, hot, angry and determined. She

knew he would want every detail from her and not hesitate to push until he got it. He was used to drama and trauma. In his world there wasn't time for gently asking for clarifications. He had to storm in, take control and demand details and explanations.

"At first."

Ben muttered something under his breath that she did *not* want him to repeat so she could hear it more clearly.

"Not very often," she said, instead of leaving it alone like she should have. "And it wasn't very good."

"The sex with John the billionaire?" Ben asked in a tone that made her seriously consider not saying another word about John Shepard. Ever again.

"Don't you dare even think the word prostitute," Jessica said in warning.

It was nothing she hadn't thought of herself but she couldn't let Ben think that it was that simple. It had been about rebelling, about showing her father that she would make decisions on her own whether he liked it or not. The money had only allowed her to be more dramatic about it.

"You object to the term?"

"Emphatically."

"Was that before or after the shoe shopping?"

She gritted her teeth. She knew how it looked. She understood. But it still pissed her off. "Do you think that I am the type of person to have sex with someone for money?" she asked.

"How about for manicures?"

Jessica had nothing more to say. Her time with John had been what it had been. It had been strangely simple and terribly complicated at the same time. She still felt like crying when she thought about Ben assuming the worst of her, though.

Total silence stretched between them, thick with disappointment and bitterness.

Which further irritated her. Where did he get off being judgmental? So he'd saved lives and spread the word of God in a third world country. He wasn't perfect, either.

"Why are you so disappointed anyway?" Jessica finally demanded. "It's not like you're my father, or my minister, or John's ex-wife."

Ben was scowling at the road in front of them when she glanced at him.

"Because I'm jealous as hell," he muttered.

"You're...what?" she asked, glancing at him again.

"Jealous." he said. "I'm thinking of all the things that Johnnie got to do to you and I want to do him bodily harm. Then I want to take you home and do everything ten times better and harder and deeper and..."

"Okay," she said quickly as every inch of skin started to burn. "I've got the point."

He looked over at her. "I'm serious."

She reached forward and turned up the air conditioning. "I know."

He was jealous. That was much better than judgmental.

"You don't have to try too hard," she told him.

"What do you mean?"

"What I said before. The sex with John wasn't all that great."

"I want to try too hard," he said, almost under his breath.

"Fine with me," she said. "But I want to be sure that you understand how things were with me and John. I was inexperienced enough to not know what I wanted or what I was missing. And he quickly figured out that spending time with a girl half his age isn't as interesting as it's built up to be."

Ben didn't speak at first, but Jessica felt his outrage slowly building as her words sunk in.

"What do you mean half his age?"

She swallowed. She was pretty sure it was going to get worse before it got better. "John was forty when I met him."

"And you were *twenty*?" Ben demanded, pivoting in his seat.

"Nineteen. He threw me a huge party for my twentieth birthday four months later."

"What in the hell were you thinking?"

"Hey!" she shot back, her index finger up in front of his face. "It was legal. It was consensual. He didn't mistreat me. He was good-looking, charming..."

"Rich," Ben spat.

She gave him a frown, then had to look back at the road. "Yes. Rich. I already admitted that his willingness to spend money on me and my whims was a main attraction." She took a deep breath and tried to calm down. "I saw the world, did everything I'd ever imagined..."

"I'll bet a few things John imagined too," Ben said acidly.

Jessica pressed her lips tightly together. She was used to this reaction, but it stung more from Ben. Especially when he was intent on doing plenty that *she* disapproved of. He should understand her desire to break away from the pressure of living up to her father's expectations. Wasn't breaking away from pressure what Ben was all about lately?

Still, she felt the need to explain, somehow, that things weren't exactly as he was picturing them.

"I was his trophy. He liked having me on his arm and didn't mind having me in his bed, but there comes a point in ten months of being together almost twenty-four-seven where you have to *talk*. That was where things fell apart."

She looked over at Ben but it was getting harder to read his expression as they headed farther into the residential area south of the city, where the street lights glowed with a softer rosy light than the bright yellow of the main business area.

"And when you can't talk to each other, you don't get to know each other or like each other," she went on. "That makes the sex...blah."

"Blah?" Ben repeated. "You're telling me that you didn't enjoy the sex because you didn't know him well enough?"

He sounded disbelieving, like she was just trying to make him feel better.

Well, she wasn't. This wasn't about Ben.

And suddenly Jessica got mad.

Things had been about Ben for the past few days. She'd been trying to help him, support him, make him see his potential, build him up. But this wasn't about how Ben felt about her past. If he didn't like it, somehow couldn't accept it, or couldn't get over it, then too bad. She couldn't change it and she didn't need him to make her feel bad about it. She'd spent plenty of time beating herself up about it without any help from him.

She frowned and took a hard right turn. "Look, we weren't in love. We weren't even friends. When we did spend time together it was almost always with other people, so when it was only the two of us, we went through the mechanics of sex and then went to sleep. It was just something else to cross off my to-do list every day. I never even had an orgasm with him."

Ben had been frowning at the spot on the road in front of the car that was illuminated with the headlights. But her last sentence made him jerk his head around to stare at her.

"You never what?" he demanded.

She scowled at him. She didn't want to badmouth John to her new lover, but it was too important for Ben to understand what her relationship with John had been, and what it had not been.

"I never had an orgasm," she repeated.

"Did he know?"

"I faked it."

His frown darkened. "Why?"

"Got it over with faster."

She could hear Ben grinding his teeth together.

"You won't be faking it with me."

She nodded. She was sure she would never need to, but she had a feeling Ben would know if she did. "I know."

"I mean it. I won't have it. If there's something you don't like, you tell me." He sounded very angry. "If there's something else you want, or something you want different, you tell me."

"You're upset that I faked it with another man?" she asked. "You should be glad I didn't enjoy it!"

"I should be glad that you gave yourself to a man who couldn't even give you an orgasm and who you couldn't be honest with?" he asked. "I should be glad that you had this long-term, physical relationship with a man you couldn't even talk to?"

"You would have rather had me be madly in love with him and have multiple orgasms every night?" she snapped.

A few seconds of silence followed and then Ben replied, sullenly, "I don't know."

Good Lord, she didn't understand men at all.

They drove several blocks without another word.

"Why did you break up?" Ben finally asked.

Ben's tone of voice was certainly not casual and when she glanced at him again, she could see the tightly clenched jaw and the spark of jealousy in his eyes. Too bad.

"It was never intended, by either of us, to be a long-term

thing," she said. "But, eventually, I got tired of going out all the time. And John realized he was more attracted to women who shared his interests. It burned itself out."

She thought about John with the same emotion she always associated with him. Affection. Nothing more or less.

She'd had a lot of time since John had dropped her off on her father's doorstep from his stretch limo to think back on the relationship. What it boiled down to, no matter what angle she approached from, was that she and John had each come to the relationship for a multitude of reasons other than sex. But they'd both assumed that sex was supposed to be part of it, and that the other was expecting it, so they went through the motions.

"Were you a virgin for John?" Ben asked caustically.

Ben's tone suggested that she had saved herself for John...or had stolen from Ben the chance to be her first. Again, all about him.

She frowned. "No. Tim Hubert took me to prom my junior year and I jumped him on the couch in his parents' basement afterward."

She glanced at Ben to find him studying her as if trying to figure out if she was telling him the truth. She rolled her eyes.

"If I was trying to bother you I would have made up a bigger number of victims and made things a bit more exciting than on a plaid couch in a prom dress, don't you think?"

Ben didn't look amused. At all.

"And was it blah with Tim, too?"

That annoyed her. "You know what, Ben? Why don't you shut up?"

Chapter Ten

Ben looked at her in surprise. Up until that moment, Jessica had been encouraging and positive, even when she was being firm and sassy. She didn't say things like shut up and she certainly didn't say them with such petulance in her voice.

She'd been frustrated with him before. He knew that. But she had never dismissed him. Her tone now was of dismissal, like she did want him to shut up and leave her alone.

But that was simply not going to happen.

"Pull over."

She looked at him. "What?"

"I said, pull over," Ben repeated, more firmly. "Now."

"Ben, you're being grumpy because I—"

"Jessica, pull the damn car over right now!"

She took her annoyance out on the car brake, bringing his truck to an abrupt stop.

"What are you—"

"Pull in there."

He pointed ahead to a dirt alley about a hundred yards from the massive house that sat up a slight rise off to the right of where they were stopped.

Jessica followed his instructions, turning in and bumping along the narrow path for about twenty feet before stopping.

She shoved the gearshift into park and turned to face him. "I don't know what you're trying—"

"Turn off the lights."

She did, angrily.

"Anything else?" she asked with fake sweetness.

"Yeah. Come here." His command was soft, but very firm.

Her frown deepened. "Excuse me?"

Ben couldn't have put to words exactly what he was feeling. Jealousy seemed to be the most logical, but that seemed too simple an explanation. This woman was important to him and he wanted to be important to her. He knew that John Shepard, no matter how much money he'd spent on her, hadn't appreciated her. It didn't sound like he'd even pleasured her. Which, strangely, made Ben happy and pissed him off at the same time. It wasn't just the other guy. It was that Jessica had been cheated and she deserved the best. With him.

"I said come here."

"Where?" she asked, looking less irritated and more wary now.

Ben spread his arms. "Right here. Now."

She hesitated long enough for him to grow impatient. He reached out, looped his arm around her waist and pulled her onto his lap.

Round eyes met his. Her skirt hiked up high as her legs spread to straddle to his. "What are you doing?"

"I can't take you to Paris tonight and I can't give you thousands of dollars to spend on shoes, but I sure as hell can give you an orgasm."

He held the back of her head in one hand as he took her mouth with all of the frustration and jealousy and anger he felt. But most of the anger was on her behalf and he was a very smart man. He knew he was holding one of the sexiest, smartest, best women he'd ever met and he was going to savor every minute.

He gentled his mouth and kissed her until she was breathing hard and had the front of his shirt clenched in her fists.

"Did John-boy ever do you in a car?" he asked against her mouth.

She tried to shake her head, but Ben wouldn't let her head move enough. "No," she whispered.

"Up against the pyramids in Egypt?"

He felt her small smile against his lips. "No. It was always a bed, always dark, him always on top."

Ben moved his hand to her thigh and moved it to cup her buttock. "That's great. I don't know how I'd top the pyramid thing."

And the angry tension left her body all at once. She melted into him, moving her mouth against his, her tongue stroking across his bottom lip until he opened and took possession of her mouth.

She pulled back two minutes later. "It's not a competition. With you it's—"

"It's going to be different in every way," he interrupted. "It's going to be everything it wasn't with him."

"It already is," she said with a soft smile.

But that wasn't good enough. Ben was pretty sure he was already one up with the dressing room stunt earlier, but he wasn't finished. When he was done with her, she wouldn't remember how to spell John Shepard.

"Tell me what you want me to do to you."

She sat back in his lap. "What do you mean?"

"You've never told a man what you like, what you want, what will give you the most satisfaction. Tell me." Just thinking about her telling him where she wanted to be touched was enough to make him hard. But more, the idea of giving her pleasure she'd never come close to made his heart pound.

She bit her bottom lip, watching his face and Ben wondered if she'd be too embarrassed to say her thoughts out loud. Or if she wouldn't know what she wanted.

"Jessica, I can—"

"Lick my nipples."

He almost swallowed his tongue. He watched, speechless as she stripped the tiny T-shirt off and arched her back, bringing her breasts to his face.

"You've got the best nipples I've ever seen," Ben said gruffly, cupping one breast in his hand.

"Yeah, we might have to talk about your sexual past too, eventually. But right now I want that orgasm you promised me," she said, letting her head fall back.

He lifted her breast, bringing her nipple to his lips where he obligingly licked. Again and again.

She went from holding her breath to breathing raggedly.

He moved to the other breast, but licked only once before sucking gently, then more firmly as she put her hand at the back of his head to urge him on.

"What else?" he asked, somehow.

"I don't know if I'm going to be big into foreplay," she said, breathlessly.

"Whatever you want." Ben ran a thumb over one of her stiff nipples.

She moaned and wiggled on his lap. "Touch me..."

"Where?" he urged as she shifted.

"You know," she whispered.

"Say it."

"I'll show you instead."

Part of him wanted to hear it, but he certainly wasn't complaining when she moved his hand between her legs, shifted her knee so he could better reach and then pressed him against her heat.

"There," she purred as he slid a finger under the edge of the thong and inside of her. "Right there."

How any man could have had her all to himself for ten months, every night, and not managed to take the time to fully enjoy her was beyond him. But he wasn't complaining about being the first and only.

Or was he...

"Did you have an orgasm with Tim Hubert on his basement couch?" Ben asked, stroking in and out even as he spoke.

She shook her head. "No. Not until you."

He'd wanted it. He'd assumed it for a few minutes. But hearing it, *not until you*, made him harder than he'd ever been in his life. He wanted to be her only everything.

"Hold on tight, darlin'," he said, increasing the pressure and rhythm.

The yard light about ten feet from the car spotlighted her breasts and face, the sexiest sight he'd ever seen.

She slumped against him a moment later. He smiled against the top of her head, feeling more content than he could ever remember feeling. He ran his fingertips up and down the bumps of her spine, loving the soft heat of her naked body, her breath warming his neck as her breathing returned to normal.

"See, I think this has got to be better than up against a pyramid," she finally said. "Those stones have to be rough."

He chuckled. "I fully intend to show you how it can be against lots of surfaces."

She shivered. "When?"

He laughed and she lifted her head. "I might be able to make it until we can get to my apartment."

She glanced out the window. "Where are we exactly?"

"You were driving."

She brushed her hair back and frowned. "I was thinking so much about our conversation that I might have made a wrong turn. Or two."

Ben suddenly kissed her deeply and with a fierce tenderness. Jessica felt tears sting her eyelids and blinked rapidly against them. How dumb to cry at a time like this. Especially because she hadn't felt this good in ten years—or ever. She laughed before she could help it though.

Ben looked down at her, a smile that she let herself imagine tugged at his lips.

"I've never inspired *laughter*."

"I was thinking that Sam might have been right."

"About?"

"Maybe I did need to get laid. I feel great."

Ben gave a snort of laughter, as she slid to her seat.

"I intend to keep you feeling great," he said and the low promise in his voice made her shiver.

"Tonight?" she asked hopefully.

"And then some."

"I'll have Sam send you a nice thank you gift."

Ben smiled and leaned forward, looking into her eyes directly. "He already did. He sent it to Charlie's bar a few nights ago."

Her heart expanded and she realized that the sex was good because Ben was awesome at this, but it was incredible because she was in love with him.

A sudden sharp rapping against the window made them both jump.

Jessica grabbed her shirt and held it against her breasts as the dark shadow of a person moved to the window next to Ben and a bright beam of light hit him in the face.

"Hell," Ben muttered.

Jessica's heart was pounding and her thoughts were spinning but she reached for and pushed the button to lock the car doors.

The shadow rapped on the window again. "Police. Lower your window."

Police? She glanced at Ben.

He reached for the window control.

"Ben! You don't know..."

"Relax." He lowered the window half an inch. "Can I see some ID?"

The man produced a badge, which he shone his flashlight on.

"He's legit," Ben told her. "Put your shirt on."

"I'm going to need to ask you to step out of the car," the cop said.

Jessica tried three times to get her shirt turned right-side-out and on before she accomplished covering the breasts the policeman had to have already seen.

Both policemen, she corrected as she got out of the car and faced two uniformed officers. She went to stand beside Ben. He took her hand.

"This is a private driveway," the first cop informed them. "Were you aware of that?"

Jessica looked up at the back of the house on top of the hill. "We thought it was an alley, at best."

"It's not," the younger of the two officers said. "It's the service drive to Mr. Benson's estate. Those are his prize-winning strawberries." The cop pointed to the patch of green leaves that they were parked in the middle of. "And that's his son's room. His son who just got a telescope for his birthday. A telescope he was using when you all pulled in."

Jessica closed her eyes and groaned. Of course. She would have to pull into the service driveway of some guy whose son had a telescope.

Twenty minutes later they were sitting in a jail cell.

Evidently they'd not only been cited for public indecency—in other words, the bad influence they'd inadvertently had on the young Mr. Benson—but trespassing and destruction of property. In fact, the older Mr. Benson was much more irritated by the loss of his famous strawberries than he was about his son's view of Jessica's naked breasts. But he was irritated enough by all of it to press charges.

The worst part, it turned out, was being cooped up in the

jail cell with Ben.

It wasn't only the pleasant, sitting-in-jail-is-no-big-deal tone of voice he was using, though she found that incredibly annoying. Jessica swore that if Ben shared one more piece of Hollywood trivia with her from the year-old gossip magazine he was flipping through, she was going to beat him with one of her hooker boots.

Her short temper was also fueled by being caught half-naked, having sex in a car like a horny teenager.

"Did you know that Brad Pitt dumped Jennifer Aniston for Angelina Jolie?"

"Of course. Everyone knows that!" Jessica snapped. "It happened forever ago."

"What's eating you?" he asked over the top of the magazine.

"Being arrested!"

"We did do all the stuff they said we did," Ben said casually, flipping the magazine page.

"It was harmless!"

"Not to the strawberries." Ben's eyes stayed on the page in front of him as he made the flippant comment.

She didn't want to fight with him, especially on the very night they'd finally become lovers.

But she reconsidered beating him with one of her hooker boots when he started to whistle "Jailhouse Rock".

"Dr. Torres, you are a man among men," a voice boomed down the hallway. A familiar voice. An obnoxious, I'm-lovin'-this voice. "You're seriously up for Man of the Year."

Jessica groaned. "I thought you called Sam."

"Sam said he'd handle it," Ben said with a shrug. He laid the magazine aside and got to his feet.

He smiled over her head at the men coming down the hall.

Without even turning around she knew that Dooley led the way. Mac was there too. Dooley rarely went anywhere entertaining without Mac. When she reluctantly turned she saw Kevin was with them too. At least he looked concerned.

"Hey, guys," Ben greeted. "Where's Bradford?"

"He was working when you called. Picked up an extra shift so he could hang out with that new nurse," Mac said with a grin.

"She's not even twenty-one yet!" Jessica exclaimed.

Mac's grin widened. "I know."

Jessica rolled her eyes. "Why didn't he tell us he couldn't come?"

"Because he likes us." Dooley wrapped his big hands around the metal bars of their cell and peered in. "He knew we'd want to see this."

Jessica was grateful that she'd been able to grab the scrub top out of the Tease bag before they were hauled in to jail. Though it covered her breasts and stomach, most of her skirt showed and all of the boots. She would have gone barefoot, even on the questionable cleanliness of the jail floor, if she'd known Kevin would be here. He was likely shocked at her.

"Are you okay?" Kevin asked.

She nodded, not meeting his eyes. She was fine if they didn't count humiliation as a problem. And Dooley and Mac didn't.

"I'm impressed, Ben. Seriously," Dooley said with sincerity. "Not only did you get into her pants—you got rid of the pants all together. You deserve a trophy or something."

Jessica's cheeks burned. "We were shopping," she said, not exactly denying that she and Ben had been doing exactly what the guys thought they'd been doing, but not admitting it either.

"Must have been before you climbed on his lap in the front seat of the car."

Jessica's eyes widened. "How did you—"

Mac grinned. "Wes Foster and I are buddies."

The cop who'd arrested them. Of course.

"Are you going to get us out of here?" she asked wearily, realizing the story of this night was going to spread through the ER like crazy. This was far worse than the night they'd seen her dressed up in front of Charlie's bar. That had been their idea and she'd been doing a favor for a friend—and her brother. As far as they knew, that night she'd been acting a part with honorable intentions. Tonight was real and not-so-honorable.

"Wes is on his way. He had paperwork to do for the bail." Dooley smiled.

Finally, the door at the end of the hall opened and keys jangled as Wes came through it.

"I'll write you a check for the bail," Ben said to the guys as they gathered on the sidewalk in front of the police station.

"We know you're good for it," Dooley said, checking Jessica out again.

Ben sighed and stepped forward. Dooley was about an inch shorter, but twenty pounds heavier. Still, Ben leaned in. "Your eyes don't go below Jessica's chin again and nobody at the hospital hears about tonight. Got it?"

Wow. Jessica smiled at Dooley's wide-eyed stare.

"You don't want the notoriety, the reputation, the acclaim?" Dooley asked. "The trophy?"

Jessica rolled her eyes. Dooley would actually get Ben a trophy for getting Sam's uptight, conservative, bossy sister naked.

Ben dropped his voice a notch. "Something to keep in mind about that trophy," Ben said. "I can put foreign objects *in* bodies as easily as I can remove them. And without anesthesia."

Whoa. Jessica wouldn't have blinked for the world. She waited to see Dooley's reaction.

Slowly, he grinned. "You just ruined an awful lot of fun for me, man." He slapped Ben on the back.

Jessica sighed. She should have known Dooley would admire Ben's threat rather than be intimidated by it.

"That was impressive," she said as the guys headed for Kevin's car.

He looked at her. "I did it to stay on your good side—why go for Man of the Year when I could potentially be Man of the Decade."

She raised an eyebrow. "Of the Decade? For what?"

"If getting you naked gets me Man of the Year, imagine what I'll get when I take you to bed twice in one night."

She laughed. "We haven't been in *bed* together. And we've already done it twice."

Ben moved close and ran his hand up and down her arm. "I'd like to make up for your first point. An oversight on my part. As for the second, I'm going for too many to keep track of anyway."

Heat tingled along her nerve endings. "I'm not complaining about past locations." She shivered in pleasure at the memories. "But a bed does sound nice."

"Yours or mine?" he asked, his voice gruff.

"Which is closer?"

"I like it when we're on the same wavelength," he told her before hauling her up on tiptoes for a hot, wet kiss that left her thinking that the brick wall of the police station was as far as she was going to make it.

What the hell? It was firm. And here.

Just then her cell phone rang. Damn. "It has to be Sam checking on us," she muttered, rooting in her purse for the phone.

"Or wanting details," Ben said wryly.

"Or wanting to tease me and congratulate you because he already got details from Dooley," she said, finally pulling the phone from under her day planner.

"Jess, it's Sam. I—"

"Why don't you wait and get *all* the details from Ben tomorrow. I'm taking him back to my apartment right now to do a whole bunch more dirty stuff to him."

Ben gave her an amused, heated look. Sam was, amazingly, speechless for a moment.

"Mario collapsed at the center. They're on their way in."

Her brother's words were like a bucket of ice water in the face. "We'll be right there."

Ben's expression was instantly sober and his only question was, "Where?"

"St. Anthony's."

They broke into a run together.

Twenty agonizing minutes later, they finally screeched to a halt outside of the ER. Ben was out of the car by the time Jessica's hand reached for the door handle.

"You can't park there!" someone shouted at Ben as they sprinted toward the ER entrance.

"So tow it!"

They ran through the automatic glass doors, but Jessica stopped abruptly on the other side. Ben almost plowed into her. He saw right away what had stopped her. Sam was coming toward them, in uniform. His crew must have been the ones to respond to the call. Ben felt Jessica tense as her sibling approached and knew she was hesitant to hear the report about Mario.

"Where is he?" Ben asked.

"Exam two," Sam answered. Then filled in the rest so they didn't have to ask. "He was at the center. Sophie said that he was quieter than usual, but otherwise seemed normal. Then he fainted when he stood up."

"Vitals?" Ben asked.

"He's shocky. Blood pressure is low. He's weak."

Ben couldn't stop his mind from playing over all of the possibilities. But they were numerous. He needed to know more.

Son of a bitch.

He took a deep breath as the realization set in—he was going to go in.

Son of a bitch.

He just couldn't leave it alone. He couldn't stand out here while they worked on Mario.

There were a whole lot of reasons getting involved was a bad idea—and probably just as many why he was doing it anyway. But he wasn't going to analyze what he was doing or why.

He was going to act on instinct and reflex and pure intellect. To hell with emotions, and complications and cans of worms opening and slithering all over the fucking place.

"Dammit." He stomped in the direction of the exam room. He hit the swinging doors with two hands, both doors flying open.

"Gown," he barked to the first nurse he saw.

She grabbed one and he practically ripped it from her hands.

"Torres, what are you doing?" Chris Burnham, the attending ER physician, asked with a scowl.

Of course Burnham would have to be the attending. Chris Burnham was controlling and pompous and jealous, especially of Ben.

"Your surgical consult is here," Ben told him grimly, pulling on a pair of gloves. "Where are we at?"

"Like hell," Chris objected sharply. "You don't work here."

Chris struggled between trying to intimidate Ben and

keeping his attention on the patient on the table.

"I do work here." Ben approached Mario, much more worried about the low blood pressure on the monitor than Chris Burnham's ego.

"You were suspended and haven't been reinstated," Chris snapped.

"Ultrasound is here, Dr. Burnham," Linda, one of the nurses, said coming through the doors. She stopped and looked at Ben. "And Dr. Torres."

He moved aside as the ultrasound machine was rolled past him and reached to take the x-ray report Linda had brought in as well. Chris beat him there.

"You're not reinstated," he said again, trying to shoulder Ben out of the way.

"So reinstate me," Ben growled.

"Sorry. I can't do that." Chris looked smug.

"But I can."

Both men turned to find Russ Edwards watching them, his arms crossed over his chest. "Dr. Torres, you are officially on the job. Try not to hit any patients."

Ben gave him the slight nod of acquiescence that Russ was expecting. Burnham snickered.

"But Burnham isn't off limits?" Ben inclined his head toward the other physician.

Russ didn't answer, but he gave Chris a pointed look.

Chris waited until Russ turned his back to look pissed.

"Get that ultrasound going," Russ said, taking the x-rays from Linda himself.

He hung them on the viewer and Ben and Chris moved in on either side.

"Three ribs fractured," Russ said.

"Uh, Dr....all of you," Linda said behind them.

The ultrasound was going and Nadia, the ER resident, was running it over Mario's abdomen. Ben moved in. Mario's stomach was distended and bruised where his ribs were broken.

"It's his spleen," Ben said, pointing to the ultrasound screen. "Dammit, he's bleeding internally. We'll have to go in."

He'd have to go in. He was the trauma surgeon on the case.

For better or worse.

"What took you so long?"

Jessica looked away from the trauma room doors to see her sister coming toward her. Sara's eyes were red and her mascara smudged.

"We just got here. We were..." She couldn't tell her sister the truth. "Where have *you* been?" Jessica asked instead.

"Restroom." Then Sara's eyes went wide. "What are you *wearing?*"

"Forget that," Jessica said quickly. "How's Mario?"

"Ben's here too, right?" Sara asked.

"Yes. He was with me." Jessica grabbed Sara's arm. "What happened?"

"I have no idea." Her sister's eyes went to the doors of the trauma room. "Oh, Jess, he looked so bad at the center." Sara's voice broke and she sniffed.

"How is he?"

"He was so pale. His eyes fluttered when Sophie was talking to him, but he didn't really wake up," Sara said.

"How is he *now?*" Jessica asked, trying to be patient.

"I tried to take his pulse, like you showed me. And I made sure he wasn't bleeding anywhere. Then I tried to be sure he was breathing. He was, so I knew that meant he didn't need CPR, but I kept checking every few seconds to be sure. It seemed like it took the ambulance forever to get there."

Jessica pulled in a long breath.

In spite of the fact her nerves were wound so tight she felt like she'd drunk three pots of coffee, eaten four candy bars and had a vitamin B12 shot in the past fifteen minutes, she tried to be patient.

Sara was sweet, compassionate, gullible...prone to dramatics.

Jessica was as close as she'd ever been to shaking the nicest person she knew.

"How. Is. Mario. Now."

Sara shook her head. "I don't know. No one's told me anything. Sam's been in there the whole time I've been here."

Jessica looked toward the doors to the room where Mario was being worked on. She could go in too...

Actually, she couldn't. She couldn't distract Ben. His full attention had to be on Mario.

"I wish we knew what was going on." Jessica started to pace. Thank goodness she had two pockets on the front of her scrub top. She had to do something with her hands.

"Well, now that Ben's here, everything will be all right."

Jessica stopped and looked at her sister. "What does that mean? We don't even know what happened."

Sara shrugged. "Ben will figure it out." She looked at Jessica. "Right?"

She was completely serious. Of course, Sara was seeing him from the base of the pedestal that Jessica herself had put him on.

Sara was watching Jessica closely.

"Sara, Ben's a great doctor, but..."

"The best trauma surgeon in Omaha." Sara crossed her arms. "Or so I've been told."

Had she really run at the mouth this much about Ben to her sister?

"The best in the Midwest," Jessica corrected.

"Exactly," Sara said, nodding in satisfaction. "Mario's in great hands. He'll be fine." She smiled and took a deep breath. "Thank God."

But what if he wasn't fine? The thought came automatically and Jessica's heart cramped in her chest at the thought of voicing that to her sister. Or worse, the news that Mario definitely wasn't fine.

They didn't even know what had happened. Ben was in there working on a mystery, with the clock ticking.

That kind of pressure, the constant reality that he might have to give someone news that would change their life forever, the frustration of trying to fix something without knowing the cause...and that was on strangers. Jessica stared at her sister as the thoughts bounced around in her head.

He had to face this every day. He knew that he might disappoint someone every time he walked into the ER. Bad things happened all the time. He couldn't prevent them all. She knew this. As a nurse, she experienced it too. And it was the same for every one of the doctors.

So, why did she expect so much of Ben? Why couldn't she

understand that he might want to walk away from such stressful, difficult circumstances?

She knew the answer almost instantly. Ben was more to her than an amazing physician or a wonderful co-worker. He was the man she wanted in the role of confidant, friend and lover. Always. And she wanted him to be perfect at all of it.

She wanted him to make everything good and right for *her*.

Being the hero of the ER was simply representative of all the other ways she wanted him to be a hero.

"Of course he's in good hands," Jessica acknowledged. "But," she went on. "Ben isn't a magician. He can't fix everything." She needed to remember that, too.

Sara shook her head. "But...Ben's the best. He'll figure out what's going on and then he'll be able to put it back together."

Jessica closed her eyes and rubbed the middle of her forehead. All of this was getting so complicated. It was so unfair. Ben would give his all, but it wasn't fair to expect so much from him. He was a man, human, not omniscient, not able to turn back time, no magic wand. Strangely, as worried as she was about Mario, she was just as worried about Ben. This wasn't what he wanted. He hadn't chosen this. He had come tonight because of her. While he was trying to escape situations exactly like this, she was nagging and pushing. Forcing him back into the hospital, the ER, the situations that made it impossible for him to fail without losing a part of his soul.

"Sara, sometimes—"

"Mario's just a kid," Sara stubbornly interrupted. "He can't die."

"Ben will do everything he can." She knew that for certain. Ben would put everything he had into this. No matter how it turned out, or how he felt afterward. Just like he would for her.

"Then everything will be fine," Sara said resolutely. She glanced over Jessica's shoulder. "Sam!" Sara stepped around her sister to go to her brother. "How is he?"

"They're still working on him." He slipped an arm around Sara's shoulders. "They found some broken ribs and a lacerated spleen."

"What's that mean?" Sara asked.

"One of the arteries to his spleen is torn. They'll have to operate to fix it. He fainted because of the internal bleeding." Sam turned his eyes to Jessica now. "Ben's going to operate."

Sara sighed in relief. Jessica barely squelched the urge to say *No!* Instead she frowned at her sister and her irritating adulation.

Ben was going to operate on Mario.

Jessica's heartache got worse. A symptom of what she was beginning to suspect was guilt. Ben was here because of her. He was about to face something incredibly difficult, potentially devastating, because she'd dragged him into the center, Mario's life and, tonight, the hospital.

"Is it true you got Ben arrested?"

Sam's words took a few seconds to sink in. Jessica gaped at him. Of course he knew because Ben had called him from the police station. Sam had sent Dooley—an act she fully expected to get retribution for. But she couldn't believe Sam was bringing this up here and now.

"You couldn't wait to get back to your apartment?"

"He told you *why* we were arrested?" she exclaimed.

"I guessed. But he did confirm it."

She frowned at him. "You have a dirty mind."

Sam grinned. "I know."

"He should be working on Mario, not talking to you," Jessica said, trying to turn the conversation.

"He didn't talk. He just had to nod."

Sam was still smiling and Jessica knew that meant he intended to get all the details from her. "How much was the bail?" He was far too entertained.

"None of your business," Jessica snapped.

Sara frowned at her. "Wait a second. You did get him arrested?"

"Hey, I got arrested too!" Jessica said.

"For having sex in public," Sam made sure to add.

"*What?*" their younger sister practically shrieked.

Jessica glowered at him. Sara looked from Jessica to Sam to Jessica. Then Jessica got huffy. "It wasn't *public*," she said. "It was some guy's backyard. It was dark. And a total accident." She crossed her arms and tipped her nose into the air.

"You got *arrested?*" Sara asked, her eyes wide. "Having *sex?*"

"Yes!" Jessica shouted throwing up her hands. "We got arrested having sex in the front seat of Ben's truck. Okay?

Don't forget that you were the one, Miss Sara Jo, that informed him you and Sam thought that's what I needed."

She stopped for a deep breath and then noticed Russ Edwards coming toward them.

Of course.

Jessica sighed and ran a hand through her hair as her pseudo-boss stopped in front of her, his hands casually tucked in the front pockets of his slacks. His expression, however, was anything but casual.

"Explain to me how getting him arrested is keeping him out of trouble."

"Russ, it was...a mistake..."

"Does my top surgeon now have a police record or not?" Russ demanded.

"Russ—"

"Explain to me how going out with him dressed like *that*—" Russ swept his hand up and down in front of her, "—and doing what I understand you were doing to him is supposed to deter him from acting like this."

Jessica felt herself blush but she looked Russ straight in the eye. "It's none of your business, Russ. But remember, you asked me to keep track of him."

"Not just keep track of him, Jessica. Keep. Him. Out. Of. Trouble. Convince him that he wants to go back to work as a *conservative, responsible, upstanding* physician that makes this hospital look good." Russ paused and took a deep breath. "You seemed like the perfect choice. It seemed too good to be true, since you are the only person Ben will spend significant amounts of time with—though tonight certainly helps clarify why."

Jessica bristled. "Russ, you are overstepping here. I understand you're frustrated and worried and under a lot of pressure from the Board and staff to get Ben back, but how Ben and I spend our time outside of this hospital is none of your business."

"That's not entirely true," Russ said. "Do you remember the Code of Conduct you signed when you started working here? Ben signed one as well. Everyone does. It says, among other things, that our employees will not do anything outside of work that will reflect negatively on the hospital. Like assault. Or getting arrested."

Jessica vaguely remembered something like that, but she'd been working here so long—and at the time would have been completely convinced that she would never do anything that would violate a code like that—she could barely remember it.

"My job is in jeopardy?" Jessica asked. Russ wasn't even being subtle. He was telling her this right in front of her sister and brother. Witnesses. He wasn't trying to intimidate or manipulate her. He was stating facts.

"None of us want that. We don't want to lose you or Ben. The Board can come up with some disciplinary action other than termination. But we have to control this. So far we've kept things quiet. Ted Blake's lawyers have agreed to be sure that the story stays out of the papers—"

"The papers?" Jessica interrupted. "What are you talking about?"

"A physician punching a patient while he's laying on the table in the ER? That same physician getting arrested having sex in a car parked on a prominent citizen's lawn? Come on, it's not hard to imagine that a reporter might find that interesting."

She hadn't thought of any of that. In actuality, she hadn't thought about much beyond Ben and the moment all night.

"Don't let him enjoy himself so damn much away from work. In fact, don't let him enjoy it at all."

She felt the need to defend herself to her boss and her siblings, who she had wanted to be a role model for, but her argument sounded weak when she said, "We've been having some fun. Mostly harmless fun."

"Well, knock it off." Russ wasn't smiling as he said it. "And act like you want to continue being a nurse in this ER," Russ said, turning on his heel and heading toward the elevators.

Frustrated with Russ getting the last word, Jessica turned to her sister and brother. Sam looked from one sister to the other and, without a word, headed toward the cafeteria.

Sara, on the other hand, was watching Jessica with undisguised censure.

It was almost funny that Sara disapproved of her. Jessica had spent the past ten years doing absolutely everything she could to be approved of by everyone, especially the little sister who needed a positive female role model.

"You have something you want to say to me?" Jessica propped a hand on either hip.

Sara pressed her lips together, looking very prim and proper. "Not really," she finally said. "I'm just..."

"What?" Jessica pressed, scowling now.

"Disappointed."

Jessica stared at her sister, letting the word roll around in her head.

Then she got mad.

"You're *disappointed*? Because I'm not perfect after all? What about all of the things I've done *right*, Sara? What about all of the times I did exactly the right thing at the right time? I don't get credit for any of that?"

Sara looked upset and Jessica had to fight the urge to apologize and tell her everything would be okay. She shouldn't be sorry. It was all right for her to have a bad day, to show some not-so-pretty emotions, to make a couple of not-quite-responsible choices.

She also didn't know if everything *would* be okay and for once she couldn't bring herself to say the words to make Sara feel better.

Sara crossed her arms. "You're making choices that are negatively impacting other people. That's not like you."

"I'm..." Jessica trailed off, speechless. For one, Sara suddenly sounded just like her. For another, all she'd done for the past ten years was make decisions specifically to make things as good as possible for everyone else, no matter how she felt or what she wanted. This was one night, one instance, and she couldn't figure out how this was the end of the world.

"How is this affecting you, other than mild embarrassment at being seen with me in this outfit?"

"I wasn't talking about me. You're messing things up for Ben!" Sara's eyes dropped to the toes of Jessica's boots. "You're getting him in trouble."

Jessica was torn. Part of her admired her sister's blunt honesty. Another part was insulted.

"Is it possible that I'm not to blame?" she asked, defiantly.

Sara's gaze never faltered, but her cheeks got pink. "Maybe. But no matter what he's going through, you're supposed to be the one we can count on. You should be talking him out of...whatever. We need him. We need you to make sure he's here."

He was here, all right. But she was feeling torn—she felt more than a little guilty about him being here, yet she was also relieved that Mario was in Ben's care. "Why do *I* always have to be the one doing the right thing?" Jessica crossed her arms, feeling hurt and unappreciated. "Why can't I have some fun for a change?"

"Because!" Sara exclaimed. "That's what we depend on you for. That's why Sam called you that first night. It's obviously why your boss asked you to be the one to watch over Ben. That's who you are."

Suddenly Jessica understood Ben. People had decided who she was and now there was no room for error. Just like she felt about Ben. Yes, they'd both worked to be the person everyone else saw, but now they were expected to never falter, to never mess up, to never change.

Changing didn't have to be bad.

"I'm still me, Sara," Jessica said wearily. "One night, one mistake, one uncharacteristic act doesn't change who I am underneath." Jessica felt like something was trying to make itself clear in her head, but whatever it was had to swim through quite a bit of emotion and fatigue. Why did all of this seem like it should be familiar?

Sara looked at her for a long moment. Then she nodded. "I'm sorry."

"I'll always be there for you, and for everyone who needs me. I'll always do my best. I just might not always do it the same way I've always done. And I might not always succeed."

And the realization finally found a clear spot in her brain.

Ben was still him too. He wasn't in the OR every day, but he was making a difference anyway—at the coffee shop, at the center. He was the man she wanted because of the man he was behind the changeable moods and moments. She wanted the man he would be no matter what.

"I know," Sara said quietly. "I know I can always depend on you."

"Thank you," Jessica said with a huge smile. She leaned in and kissed her sister's cheek. "I love you, you know."

Sara looked wary. "I know."

Jessica tipped her head to one side and regarded the beautiful woman in front of her. "I did a good job with you."

Sara smiled. Then chuckled. "Thanks. I guess."

The door to the trauma room burst open just then. Jessica whirled and all levity left the immediate area. Sara stepped closer and took Jessica's hand as Mario was wheeled out to the elevator. He was deathly pale, a tube in his mouth and down his throat to help him breathe.

Jessica swallowed hard.

He had to live. So she could at least say goodbye.

Ben caught her eyes on the way past. He slowed next to her. "I'll see you later," he said.

She nodded. She would be here when he was done in surgery.

"No promises," he said, low enough for only her to hear. "But I'll be in there."

She looked him straight in the eye. "That's enough."

He looked like he wanted to kiss her. But of course, he followed the gurney into the elevator.

He was still watching her when the doors slid shut.

Three hours later Jess had a pounding headache from worrying, pacing the hard tile floor in high heels and the after-effects of the longest, most emotional twenty-one hours of her life.

Sara slept against Sam's shoulder, Sam slept propped up in the corner of the waiting room couch.

Jess paused and looked at her siblings and her heart swelled. Sure, they'd pooped out, but they were here.

And she knew the fact that they were asleep did not reflect on how they felt about Mario. They were worried too. But Jessica was the pro in that area. No little detail like sleep would get in her way.

Sara had finally learned from some of the other center kids that Mario had sustained his injuries fighting. The fight had even been arranged outside of the regular fight-night schedule. Jessica's heart had broken hearing that. Mario had been the biggest champion of ending the violent competitions. However, the story went on. Mario had developed feelings for Sophie, and vice versa. The father of Sophie's baby wouldn't leave her alone and Mario finally asked him what it would take for him to never bother her again. The baby's father had said he would leave

Sophie alone forever if Mario, the reigning fight night champion in spite of not participating for over a year, would fight him...and lose. Mario had agreed for Sophie, sickened that the other boy cared more about his reputation as a tough guy than he did about his unborn child.

Unfortunately, the fight was not fair. The other boy had brought friends, who jumped in to help him ensure that Mario would not walk out the champion. Or walk out at all.

Mario's friends had showed up just in time to drag him, unconscious, to the center, where Sara called 9-1-1.

The whole scenario made Jessica want to cry. There was plenty to keep her pacing.

Mario had tried to do what he believed to be honorable, protecting the girl he loved and the baby that wasn't even his, but at a terrible cost. Mario's friends were here tonight, more worried about him than they were about getting retribution, but that didn't mean there wouldn't be another night for revenge. Sophie was feeling guilty about dragging Mario into this, and worrying about losing the boy she'd just realized she loved. Sara would have to worry about the fights becoming more personal and potentially coming closer to the center.

And now Jessica had Ben in there to worry about too.

She wondered how he was holding up. Surgery like this was strenuous, even without an emotional attachment to the person on the table.

Ben cared about Mario, knew him, had spent time with him. How much harder was it to concentrate on that surgery without being overwhelmed by the fact that his life was literally in Ben's hands?

And if Mario died, Ben would blame himself.

It was almost enough to make her go into the surgical suite and pull Ben out, before *he* could get hurt. She chewed on the thumbnail of her right hand.

Who was she to tell him that he had to keep going into the fight? Who was she to be upset when he said he'd paid his dues?

She should just love the fact that he had a soul that could be touched by his patients and their suffering. She should be overjoyed to find someone who could care so much about a stranger.

Jessica wanted him, whether he was making coffee or

saving lives.

Obviously, he wouldn't walk away when things got tough. He didn't have to be the one with his hands on Mario. But he was. Because he chose to be. How much more would he be willing to endure for the woman he loved?

She frowned into the fish tank near the windows.

Did he love her? She supposed that was the real question, the one that needed answering before anything else mattered. But no matter what else—she loved him.

"Jess?"

She heard the intense fatigue in his voice before she turned and saw it in his face.

She went to him, her heels clicking against the tile, the only sound in the room besides the hum of the fish tank and the soft snoring from her brother.

"How are you?" she asked.

He looked terrible and her heart ached. She wanted to take him in her arms and hold him and tell him everything was going to be okay. And it broke her heart that she wasn't sure she could honestly say that. Seeing Ben's pain was worse than feeling her own and she decided right then that she didn't *want* him in medicine—not if it hurt him like this. She didn't want him to do anything that made him unhappy.

"I'm fine," he said. He ran a hand over his face. "Mario's in recovery."

"How is he?" She grabbed his arm, a bubble of hope rising in her chest.

Ben sighed. "Stable. For now anyway."

Jess almost couldn't breathe as emotion constricted her throat.

"Thank you," she said sincerely.

Ben swallowed hard, then cleared his throat twice. "He won't be awake for a while."

"Then let's go home. To my place." She wanted to be with him, to take care of him, to try to ease the fatigue and stress from his face. She wanted to tell him how she felt about him.

"No. I'm staying for a while. You go."

"But..."

"Go, get some sleep. You'll be a lot better for Mario if you're rested. I just want to stay until he wakes up."

He was obviously emotionally and physically drained. But she was in love with him and wanted him to know *now*.

Jess figured the hospital's surgical waiting area was probably fitting for the two of them, but she wanted this moment to be a bit more romantic. She'd imagined telling the man of her dreams that she loved him too—because of course she'd imagined him saying it first—with candles and soft music in a restaurant with floor-to-ceiling windows overlooking the city skyline.

But the waiting room with the harsh fluorescent lighting and the smell of disinfectant and coffee would work too, she supposed.

"I was hoping we could talk," she said.

Ben shook his head. "Not now, Jess."

"It won't take long." Saying the three words wouldn't anyway, and that was what was most important to her right this minute.

"Jessica," Ben said firmly. "I am so far from being my best right now that I can't even explain it. Don't push. Please."

If it wasn't for the *please*, said with a weary sigh, she might have pushed anyway. Instead she paused and thought about what Ben had just come through. While she'd been out here pacing, face-to-face with her fears and desires and her love, he'd been concentrating on Mario. As he should have been. So he wouldn't be able to say it back to her right now. That was okay.

Three little words, then she'd let him go.

"Ben, I..."

He took her gently but firmly by the upper arms. "Jessica, *don't*. Not now. We're both emotional and tired. I do not want to talk anymore, at all."

"But I..."

"*Jessica*," he said, exasperated. He looked into her eyes in that way that made her certain he knew every thought in her head.

"Fine," she said, frustrated, but accepting defeat for the time being. "Can I go see Mario quickly before I leave?"

"I'd rather you went home. It's hard for me to concentrate with you here."

She didn't know if that was a compliment or a concern. She

chose to simply agree. "I'll go home for a few hours."

Ben lifted his hand and her breath caught as he traced his index finger down her face from her cheek to jaw.

"Sam will take you home?" he asked simply.

She tried to find a smile. "Sara will. Sam's the first one to stay for Mario. He won in rock, paper, scissors."

Ben smiled back. Then leaned in and kissed her on the forehead before turning and heading for the doctor's locker room.

There were no words of when they would talk or see each other again.

Chapter Eleven

The break room was blissfully empty of people and Ben headed straight for the refrigerator, then the short sofa along the wall by the window. He propped his feet on the beat-up coffee table in front of the couch and leaned back, popping the top of his orange juice bottle. He wasn't nearly as tired as he should be, feeding off of emotion and adrenaline like he was, but he could probably expect a crash at any point.

Out of habit, his brain began replaying the night behind him.

The little boy with the appendicitis was in pre-op right then and the risk for rupture of his appendix was small.

The young couple he'd consulted with had finally been able to leave about five minutes ago. The husband had been using a nail gun and put a nail through his foot. Somehow he'd missed damaging anything major and would be fine in the end.

Two out of three cases he'd worked had turned out. Thank God, that was more usual than not. He didn't know about Mario yet, but the repair of the laceration to his spleen had gone well. He could very well be three for three. Overall, it had been a good night.

In fact, most nights were good. For every one trauma that turned out badly, at least two, and probably more, turned out well. When had he turned into a person who remembered only the bad stuff?

His pager erupted in his pocket and he jerked upright, pulling it from his waistband in a move so habitual it was like tying his shoes. The readout said *post-op*. He looked at his watch. It was five-thirty a.m. It was about Mario. It had to be.

Ben headed for the stairs, taking them two at a time to the

second floor. He strode down the hall, his lab coat flapping behind him. The scrub pants and shirt he'd changed into after surgery felt so familiar, so comfortable. He'd spent more hours dressed like this than he had any other way since he'd started his residency.

"What?" he asked when he was still several feet from the nurses' desk.

"Mario Riccio," Kati, the charge nurse said. "He's developed some left-sided paralysis, Dr. Torres." She handed him Mario's chart.

Ben stared at her. "When?"

"Just now. He's been in and out, but we finally got him awake enough for assessments. He isn't able to move his left arm or hand to our commands."

"What are his vitals?"

"Blood pressure remains low. Temperature is normal. Pulse is weak. He's also confused and complaining of a headache."

"Son of a bitch," Ben muttered. There was more going on. "We need to get him to CT now," he said to Kati. She nodded and moved to get the order going.

Fifteen minutes later, Ben watched as the scan of Mario's brain confirmed his fear. There was a slow bleed in Mario's brain. It explained everything from the headache to the drowsiness and trouble moving his left side.

"Call Steve Borchers," Ben said, referring to his friend, the best neurosurgeon in the city. Steve would have to consult, but it looked like Mario was going back into the OR. If they didn't relieve the pressure on his brain, the damage could be irreversible.

He wanted to be relieved. He wasn't a neurologist or a neurosurgeon. He couldn't do anything about this now.

But he wasn't relieved. He was pissed and restless. He wanted to *do* something; he wanted to be the one operating, in control, knowing exactly what was going on at every second.

Either that, or he had to get the hell out of here. Before he lost his mind and decided to return to work for good.

Turkey was supposed to make people sleepy.

Jessica sighed, feeling somewhat betrayed by all the

turkey-hype. She'd had two turkey sandwiches and still couldn't sleep. The glass-topped coffee table also held half a cup of hot chocolate, an empty mug with a used teabag in it—decaf of course—three-fourths of a cup of now tepid milk and a glass with only a drop or two of wine left in the bottom.

So far, the wine was winning for taste but she was still wide awake. In fact, she was so wound up that she didn't know if she'd ever sleep again. She was however, very full.

Hot sex, figuring out she'd fallen in love, getting arrested and pacing hospital hallways all without any food was a great way to work up an appetite if nothing else. But she should be exhausted too.

The knock on her door made her jump. It was a quarter to nine in the morning. She didn't think the paper boy knocked or that any of her neighbors would be asking to borrow anything at this time of the day, but she was thrilled at the idea of having another human being to talk to and something to do other than try to convince herself to sleep.

When she opened the door, Ben was standing on the other side of her threshold, his hands braced on either side of the doorframe, his head hanging.

He looked as tired as she should have been.

He was dressed again in the T-shirt and jeans he'd worn on their night out.

"Hi," she said, stepping back to let him in.

He didn't move right away. Instead he just looked at her, his gaze roaming over her face. She got nervous.

"Ben, are you..."

"He's okay."

It took her a moment to understand what he'd said. "Mario?" she asked. He nodded. "I was asking about you." She reached out and took his hand, pulling him into her apartment. "How are *you*?"

"He woke up with left-sided paralysis. They did a CT scan and found a subdural hematoma. Steve Borchers went in right away. He's stable again."

He headed toward her living room without her.

She followed him, trying to keep up with what he was saying. "Ben..."

Ben slumped onto her couch, tipped his head back and

covered his face with his forearm.

Jess stood in front of him, her knees mere inches from his, hands on her hips. "And how are *you*?"

Of course, she cared about Mario and his status. But Ben had told her about that and it sounded good. And Ben was *here*. If things were too touchy he would have stayed. Besides, Sam was at the hospital and he would have called if anything terrible happened.

Ben leaned forward, grasped her hips and pulled her toward him until his forehead rested against her stomach.

Surprised, she slipped her fingers through his hair, her palms resting against the warmth of his skull, and waited for him to speak.

He drew in a deep breath. "He's stable, but barely. To go back in so soon...and on his head...damn."

Her chest throbbed. For Mario. For Ben. This was hurting Ben so much too.

"Do you see why I hate my job?" Ben asked, still not moving. "Why did you have to pull me into this?"

But he didn't sound or act angry with her, and he continued to hold her as if he needed her comfort.

"I'm sorry," she said, her throat tight. "But if you hadn't already been with me, I would have called you. *I* would have needed you there."

And having him here now made it painfully clear that it wasn't because he was a doctor. She'd wanted him there because he could make *her* feel better just being in the room with her. Ben would do anything in his power to make things right in the world. He was a warrior, a hero, a fighter. That's all she needed. Not the victory necessarily, but the man willing to do battle for the right reason.

Ben rubbed his forehead back and forth against her abdomen, his hands still splayed on her hips, the gentle but firm pressure keeping her against him. She became aware of how thin the cotton of her pajamas was. The heat from his hands spread and her stomach tightened as she felt the hem of her pajama top pull up as he rubbed, exposing a strip of skin about six inches wide.

"I don't want to talk medicine right now," he said hoarsely. "I want to forget all the bad stuff. Just for a while."

She felt his breath on her skin a millisecond before she felt his lips. He kissed her three times along the waistband of the pajama pants and she reflexively tightened her fingers against his head. He must have understood the invitation to continue.

Her eyes slid shut as she felt a lick along the side of her belly button.

"You taste as good as you smell," he murmured against her skin.

Her breasts tightened, the nipples prominent under that soft cotton. If Ben looked up he would see how much she wanted him. But he seemed content to trace the bottom edge of her ribcage with his tongue.

The power his mouth had on her was incredible.

She wanted to strip off every stitch of her clothing—then start on his.

"Ben, maybe we should talk about what happened and how you're feeling."

His lips hardly lifted from her skin. "You're not a damn psychiatrist, Jess," he growled. "I'm not here for psychoanalysis."

"What are you here for?" She knew, even as she asked. He needed a distraction, an outlet. Could she sleep with him for those reasons?

Absolutely. If she could make him feel better, in any way, she'd do it. Not that there weren't perks to being his therapy right then. His hands and lips were hot on her and she, too, wanted to do anything but talk.

"I want to feel good. I want to forget that there's any pain or disease or sadness, even if it's just for a while." He looked up at her with a wanting she had never seen, even in her fantasies. Because what he needed from her was so much more than physical.

His grip on her hips tightened. "I did the hero thing and now I want to be the bad guy." He ran his chin over her bared stomach now. The roughness of his stubble sent goosebumps skittering in every direction.

"You're overdressed, Dr. Torres."

He paused, as if surprised by how easily she'd agreed. "I don't believe I've ever taken my clothes off for anyone who addresses me as Doctor."

"Then maybe there will be a few firsts for you too," she

replied. She really, really wanted that to be true. It was silly, and probably impossible, to think that she might be Ben's first anything, but she was sure she would do anything he wanted her to if he told her she was the first to ever do it.

His eyes darkened. "I have a feeling everything about being with you will be a first for me."

She so wanted that to be true. She loved this man and she wanted all of this to be as special and wonderful and earth-tipping for him as it was for her.

Ben grasped the front of her pajama pants and tugged, pulling her forward and onto his lap. Then he slid his hands under her pajama shirt and swept it up and over her head. His hands cupped her breasts and he kissed her deeply, his mouth and fingers both moving slowly and sensually on her.

Eventually, he tipped her over and then rolled her beneath him, his body fitting against hers perfectly. As he pressed into her, Jessica arched up.

"I..." She caught her breath as he moved against her. "I..."

He slipped his hands under her buttocks and lifted her more firmly against him.

"Ben, I love you," she gasped, pulling away from his mouth.

Ben froze, his heart pounding so hard he could barely hear over it.

"What did you say?" he asked in a hoarse whisper.

She kissed him. "I love you. And though the circumstances seem to prove otherwise, it's not just about the sex."

She loved him. His heart stopped pounding. In fact, it seemed to stop all together.

Then a rush of heat that was passion and relief and joy and amazement and probably a tiny bit of fear streaked through his body. Just when he thought Jessica couldn't do anything else to make him want her more...she went and fell in love with him.

"Say it again," he told her gruffly.

"Um..." She paused, her lips hovering over his left shoulder.

He bent his head and kissed her neck. "Say it again, Jessica," he whispered against her ear.

"I love you, Ben."

He shuddered and closed his eyes, replaying the words in his mind twice. "Okay, darlin'," he said, pushing himself up and off of her and then pulling her to her feet. "Let's see if we can make it to a bed this time."

Jessica led him down a short hallway to her bedroom and he nudged her to the edge of the bed. Once she sat he swept her pants from her, then shucked out of his jeans, and rolled a condom into place. He gently pushed her to her back and knelt on the bed between her knees but looked into her eyes.

"Say it again, Jessica Leigh."

He slipped her panties off. She rolled her head back and forth on the comforter. "Ben, this isn't fair."

"But it's very, very fun."

"Ben, please..."

"Just say it. Three little words. And I'll be *sure* that you're happy you did."

He stroked a finger over her clitoris, relishing the bucking of her hips.

"I love you, Ben." Her voice was softer now. "I love you, I love you, I love you."

Ben pressed forward as she was still telling him the sweetest words he'd ever heard.

A few minutes later, they both came with fast, furious climaxes, calling each other's names.

"Tell me again," he said before even catching his breath.

"I love you," Jessica said, snuggling close. "I love you."

After three days of waking up in Jessica's bed, Ben was completely addicted. But waking up from a sound sleep at four-thirty a.m. to hear Jessica talking to another man in the next room was not something he wanted to become a habit.

On his way out of bed to see what the hell was going on, Ben rolled over and inhaled deeply of Jessica's scent on the pillow next to him. He'd never been with a woman who smelled so good all the time. Then again, there were a lot of things about Jessica that were a first for him.

For instance, this whole waking up thing was different with Jessica. He hadn't truly slept deeply in years. His study and test schedule in medical school had made for screwy sleeping habits and in Africa things like strange nocturnal animals, the occasional detonation of rebel explosives and middle-of-the-night medical emergencies kept him from sleeping deeply. Then, of course, the crazy hours of being an ER doctor kept his system perpetually out of balance.

But with Jessica he'd slept. For the third night in a row.

Ben sat up on the side of the bed, amazed at how good he felt. Oh, the sex was unquestionably a part of it, but this had been a deep, restorative, dreamless sleep that he suspected had even more to do with the woman who had lain beside him.

And who was no longer lying beside him.

He heard male laughter from the other room and scowled. A woman having another man over just after making love to Ben was a definite first. While Ben was still naked in bed in the next room.

Ben was still zipping his pants as he stepped into the living room.

The first person he saw was Jessica.

Of course.

They could be on opposite ends of Times Square in New York City on New Year's Eve and he knew he'd still find her, even if he didn't mean to.

It was like he had radar for her.

She was sitting in her wide, overstuffed chair, in a silky, peach-colored short robe, her feet tucked underneath her, looking tousled and sleepy, but smiling...like she'd spent the better portion of her normal sleeping time having amazing sex instead and she was simply too relaxed and contented to do anything more than sit and smile.

Something very male and primitive inside of Ben reared its head at the sight.

That contented, exhausted-but-happy look was because of him.

He wanted that to be her everyday look from now on.

And it could be.

She loved him.

Her words replayed in his head and it was all he could do not to walk over to her, pick her up in his arms and take her straight back to bed.

Or drop his pants, pick her up, pull her robe to one side

and sit her right on his lap—and newly invigorated erection—in that chair.

Guest or not.

Who happened to walk in just then.

Of course, it was Sam.

Ben leaned a shoulder against the doorframe, nearly knocked over by the fact that hearing Jessica say she loved him, even in his memory, was as much an aphrodisiac as the hooker boots. Even now, three days after she'd first said it—and he'd made her say it repeatedly since then—it still almost knocked him on his ass.

He slid his hands into the front pockets of his pants, pulling the fabric away from the evidence of how affected he was physically. When Jess and Sam looked over they'd be able to tell right away that he was ready to go. At least they wouldn't be able to see how affected he was emotionally.

"You know, your sister might have had sex on that couch."

Ben was very entertained watching Sam catch himself halfway into sitting on the couch. He balanced the plate in one hand, somehow keeping the bacon, eggs and pancakes centered, and his coffee cup in the other, only a few drops slipping over the edge as he quickly straightened, almost losing his balance backward.

He moved to set his plate and cup on the coffee table and Ben said, "She might have had sex on that too."

Sam froze with his plate only inches from the table surface. He glared at Ben, then glanced at the breakfast bar between the living room and kitchen.

"Is there any place in here that's safe?"

Ben shrugged. "I can't kiss and tell."

The throw pillow that Jessica had been leaning against hit Ben directly in the stomach. "Ben!"

He grinned. "What? It's Sam. You can't be embarrassed about sex in front of Sam. He's done everything embarrassing and degrading that you can think of."

"See, now this is the disadvantage to spending time with my brother's friends," she muttered. "Way too much information."

"You're embarrassed?" Sam asked.

Jessica scoffed. "No."

"Then why'd you hit me with the pillow?" Ben asked.

"Because I would never have sex on that coffee table."

"Too risqué?" Sam teased.

"Too rickety. That table would never hold up under the sex Ben and I have. We need big, sturdy surfaces."

Both men stared at her for several seconds, mouths hanging open. Then Sam started laughing.

She frowned at him. "What? We could have gotten hurt on that table."

Ben was positive then and there that he had never liked another woman as much as he liked Jessica. He laughed too, a true, from-the-gut laugh, using abdominal muscles he hadn't used in far too long.

"And by the way, all of the aforementioned surfaces are fine for eating," Jessica informed her brother.

Sam raised a suspicious eyebrow at Ben but set his plate down on the coffee table.

Ben laughed and pushed away from the doorway. "I said she *might* have had sex there."

Sam looked from his sister to Ben and then to the hallway behind Ben. "Thank goodness she's having it somewhere."

More of his coffee sloshed out of his cup as she hit him in the stomach with another throw pillow.

"Hey!"

"Sit down and eat," she ordered, but she was smiling.

"Or better yet, take it with you and eat it in the car," Ben suggested as he moved toward the kitchen, fully intending to help himself to pancakes.

Sam settled himself on the couch, retrieved his plate, crossed his ankle over his opposite knee, and stuck his fork in his pancakes.

"Oh, I'll have this gone by the time I leave."

"Which will be when?" Ben raised his voice to ask from the kitchen.

"After I eat," Sam called back.

Ben rolled his eyes as he put four pancakes onto a plate and slathered butter and syrup on them.

He poured coffee and went back into the living room.

"What did you say you were doing here?" Ben asked.

It wasn't that he didn't like Sam. Sam just wasn't Ben's

favorite Bradford. He especially wasn't Ben's favorite naked Bradford. And Ben had a strangely strong urge to spend a lot of time naked.

"Eating breakfast," Sam said around a mouthful of eggs.

"You have an apartment," Ben said, sitting on the arm of Jessica's chair. She shifted so that her shoulder was against his thigh and he smiled at the casual yet obvious contact. She wanted to touch him as much as he did her and strange as it seemed, this touching was enough. It didn't have to be sexual to be pleasurable. Interesting.

"My apartment doesn't have eggs." Sam said. He chewed said eggs, then added, "Or pancake mix."

"Or bacon?" Ben asked, amused.

"I have bacon. But I'm out of coffee."

Ben laughed and handed Jessica his coffee cup so he could cut his pancakes. She sipped from the cup before cradling it in her hands and Ben felt warmth spread through him at the intimacy he felt at the action. It was just coffee. Her mouth hadn't even touched the same part of the cup's rim. But he felt stupidly pleased by this strange, almost tangible feeling of contentment and happiness, sitting in Jessica's living room, with her and her brother, his best friend, sharing breakfast and giving Sam a hard time that Ben knew Sam would take in the affectionate, if slightly put-out, way Ben meant it. Put-out only because he was less than fifty feet from a bed that was still rumpled from his making love to Jessica and he could easily put a few more creases in the sheets before the sun came up.

But he was content to sit here too, and have coffee and talk and just be. It was as new to him as waking from a real sleep, but Ben knew he could easily come to crave this. Even after the last few days at the hospital with Mario, he still felt good. He could deal with Mario's condition if he knew that he could come here and relax—another relatively new concept to him—even laugh and later hold Jessica.

Hell, if he could spend his nights in Jessica's bed maybe he could even handle spending his days in the ER again.

The bite of pancake he'd taken seemed to swell in size and lodge at the back of his throat, making it impossible to breathe or swallow.

He coughed, trying to dislodge the blockage, to think and to not panic.

He grabbed the coffee cup and drank gratefully, feeling the mass soften and move down his throat. He coughed again and drank once more.

Was he seriously considering returning to work?

He glanced at Jessica and found her watching him with concern, her mouth moving even though he couldn't hear what she was saying.

She got up on her knees, putting her face closer to his and it hit him that yes, he could go to work and do what he loved in spite of the pain and disappointment if he had this woman to look forward to. Jessica would support and encourage and celebrate his work with him, but would also help him make his life about more than what happened at work.

His ears felt like they'd suddenly popped open after yawning on an airplane. "What?" he asked.

"Are you okay?" she asked. "You look...weird."

He felt weird. But not bad weird. Confused weird. Weird weird.

"I'm fine. Who's with Mario?" Ben asked to change the subject.

Sam, Sara, Jessica, Ben and several people from the center had made sure that Mario was rarely alone in the three days since his surgeries. Ben didn't want Jessica to go back to the hospital just yet and knew she would if someone else wasn't there.

"Sara should be soon. She was coming at five-thirty," Sam said, stretching to his feet. "He was fast asleep when I left. He got up tonight and sat at the table to eat the McDonald's hamburger and fries that somebody brought in. It wiped him out."

"He got up?" Ben asked. That was great progress. Mario had steadily improved over the last few days but he was still very lethargic and easily lost his energy. "That's good news." At least the boy kept trying to do more.

Jessica grinned at him and plopped back down in the chair, evidently satisfied that Ben was all right. "I'll have to take him some of those ice cream sandwiches he likes so much when I go over later."

"Later?" Ben asked.

"This afternoon, probably," she said.

"You're going to wait that long?" He was surprised that she was able to wait to see Mario up and moving around for herself.

She looked up at him with a small, almost sheepish smile. "He won't be alone."

"No. But I figured you'd want to be there."

"I want to be here more right now." Her expression changed minutely and her voice only dropped slightly, but Ben knew exactly what she was talking about and felt equal measures of arousal and flattery.

She was staying here because of him.

"I'll go with you. Later," he said.

She smiled and opened her mouth to reply but suddenly her cell phone rang from the black bag that sat on the breakfast bar. Then Sam's cell phone started singing and Ben's pager started beeping from where he'd laid it on the end table.

They all looked at each other, eating, drinking and teasing suspended.

Two rings later, Jessica was the first to speak.

"Oh, crap."

Jessica scrambled for her phone while Ben headed for his pager.

"It's a hospital number," Jessica read from her caller ID.

"Me too," he said, retrieving the call-back number on his pager. "Who are you talking to?" he asked Sam.

Sam seemed distracted when he looked up. "Sara," he said simply.

Ben felt his stomach cramp. This didn't feel good at all.

He grabbed the phone that sat on the end table and punched in the number from his pager.

"Dr. Torres," he told the woman who answered.

"This is Mary, Dr. Torres. I'm the head nurse tonight."

"What's going on?"

"I'm calling about Mario Riccio."

"What's the problem?" he asked shortly.

"We can't find him."

Ben paused, processing what she said. "What the hell are you talking about?" His volume drew both Sam's and Jessica's attention.

"He's gone," Mary answered simply.

"He was discharged?" Ben asked tightly. There was no way that kid was medically stable enough to be discharged. Somebody was definitely going to get yelled at.

"No. He left AMA."

Against medical advice. What the hell...

"When?"

"We're not...exactly sure," Mary said hesitantly.

Ben pulled his hand over his face. "He snuck out?"

There was a pause then Mary said, "He must have."

Terrific. Just fucking perfect.

Surprisingly he sounded calm when he asked, "What were his last vitals?"

Mary recited the numbers for him and Ben kept from swearing. Barely.

"You've notified Dr. Borchers?" Ben asked.

"He's the one that asked me to call you. He said he was very concerned and hoped that you would know where Mario might be."

"I will be in touch," Ben said. "I want to know the second *anyone* knows *anything*."

He folded the cell phone shut, took a deep breath, gripping the phone tightly, then relaxing his hand, hoping the action would relax the monstrous ball of frustration and worry that was knotting his shoulders and his gut. It didn't work.

Mario had left the hospital AMA.

"Son of a bitch!"

Ben hurled the phone against the living room wall.

Sam looked at him with raised eyebrows and told Sara he needed to go. Jessica jumped about a foot and whirled around, her eyes wide. Seeing Ben's furious expression she disconnected without a word to whoever was on the other end.

Ben shoved both hands through his hair, glared at the phone in pieces on the floor near the corner of the couch and didn't feel one damn bit sorry...or one damn bit better. He wished he could break it again. And maybe a lamp or two.

"Ben?" Jessica asked.

Without answering her, he stalked across the room, then spun on his heel and stalked back, feeling claustrophobic.

"What the fuck is he thinking?" Ben demanded when he ran out of living room space. "He's barely stable!"

"I know."

Ben turned on her. "Where is he?"

Jessica stared at him. "I have no idea."

"None?" he demanded stalking over to where she stood. He saw her step back, but didn't let up. "You must have some idea."

"The center—"

"Sara said she's been talking to the kids—everyone she can think of. Nobody's seen him," Sam interrupted. "But she can't find Tony or Reuben."

Ben felt his chest tightening. "They helped him leave."

"Probably," Sam agreed.

"Three stupid kids," Ben muttered. "Good God." He scowled down at Jessica again. "He doesn't go anywhere else? Come on! Think!"

Jessica glared right back at him. "Knock it off. We're just as worried as you are."

He felt like a jackass yelling at Jessica like she had snuck Mario out of the hospital, but he couldn't calm down enough to say anything close to *I'm sorry*. He was pissed off. He was worried. He was frustrated. And the only thing he was sorry about was getting involved in this whole mess to start with.

Which *was* Jessica's fault, as a matter of fact.

"What the hell is the matter with that kid?" Ben asked, pacing again, clenching and unclenching his fist. "He could *die*. He isn't stable. He could hit his head on a cupboard door and drop over dead!"

"I know," Jessica replied.

Ben paced the other way. "He could pull stitches and bleed internally. There could be another small bleed that we missed. He could *bleed* to death!"

"I know," Jessica said, more firmly.

Ben turned on his heel again. "Was he hit that hard? So hard that he can't comprehend something like 'you could die'? I'm surprised he could walk out of there in the first place. I'm surprised he could figure out which direction to go. He could *die*!"

"I know!" Jessica finally shouted.

Ben stopped and glared at her. He knew he was ranting but he couldn't stop. At least the yelling and pacing was getting rid of some of this energy.

"The ungrateful little shit!" Ben went on. Mario skipped out the minute he was able to move around, without acknowledgement or thanks. Certainly without thought to anyone's effort or sacrifice on his behalf. "We spent all that time putting him back together so that he could go out and fuck it all up again!" He didn't have words to express how truly pissed off and insulted and disappointed he was.

"Mario doesn't know his risk. He doesn't know what you did for him," Jessica said, coming to him.

Ben gritted his teeth so hard he almost ground his molars flat. "He didn't notice the IV tube stuck in his arm, or the hospital bed he was laying in, or the bandage around his head? He didn't know that there were doctors and nurses working their asses off to keep him comfortable and healing and...alive?" Ben asked sarcastically. "He basically gave the finger to everyone who worked on him! And your sister who called the ambulance," Ben said, pointing at Jessica. "And you who rushed down to be there with him. And your buddies," he said, turning to point at Sam, "in the ambulance. All those people who spent their time trying to make sure he gets more time and how does he thank them? By walking out like he doesn't give a shit. I don't know why I bothered."

"You don't mean that." Jessica almost couldn't find her voice.

Ben was upset. She understood that. She wasn't real thrilled with the situation herself. In fact, she was nearly scared to death wondering where Mario was and why he'd walked out.

Ben rounded on her. "I don't mean it?" he repeated.

He studied her for so long she shifted her weight from foot to foot and tucked her hair nervously behind her ears. As he stared, she became increasingly aware of the fact that Ben could look at her and really see her. He knew her body in a way no one else on the planet did and he could likely conjure images of every detail fairly easily. It hadn't even been seven hours since they'd last been joined as intimately as two people could be.

She shook off the feeling that Ben was trying to see her

very thoughts. "You sound like you did that day in the ER with Ted Blake," she said, crossing her arms.

One of Ben's eyebrows went up and he came toward her. "Maybe that's because that's still me. And I'm still sick of helping people who won't help themselves and who don't give a shit about people who try to help them. What do you think of that, Jessica?" He stopped directly in front of her, leaned in and stared her down.

She tried not to let her lip tremble or her eyes fill as Ben leaned back, put his hands in his pockets and narrowed his eyes.

"See, I wish I'd known it...the fact that Mario would basically tell me to fuck off. Because those hours I spent at the hospital making sure he was taken care of, assisting in saving his life, I could have better spent here, with you in bed. Or getting drunk. Or seeing a movie. Or scrubbing my damn bathtub. Any of that would have been more fun and more worthwhile."

Jessica pressed her lips together, not wanting to cry and not wanting to say the first few things that tried to come out of her mouth.

"Easy, Ben," Sam said, his voice low with warning.

But Ben didn't even blink. Jessica put her hand up to halt her brother as he came to his feet, obviously willing to step in if Ben didn't back off.

Ben was upset. He was being rude to upset her, to start the fight he was obviously spoiling for. He was lashing out at her because she was a safe outlet for his emotions. That didn't make her any happier to be that outlet, however. She was worried and frustrated too. She was mad at Mario for his foolish decision to leave the hospital too. She just wasn't taking that decision personally.

"Not everything that needs to be done in life is fun and worthwhile," she said.

She knew that statement was true for a fact. She couldn't count high enough to number all the things she'd done that were neither entertaining or rewarding, but that needed doing, that were her responsibility to do.

"And, as I've told you before, over and over, I am done with those things."

The force and finality of his voice made her believe that he really believed he could turn his back on this crisis, on Mario, but there was one flaw in his plan. To walk away from this he had to turn his back on her too. And she couldn't, wouldn't, believe that he would do that.

What about the times when *she* was the one who had screwed up? Who did something he didn't agree with? Who made the wrong choice?

She had to know that Ben would be there beside her, unconditionally, when the chips were down. If she couldn't trust that then...

She shut that train of thought down. She couldn't deal with that right now on top of everything with Mario.

"We have to find him. He needs to know what the risk is. He needs to know what's going on."

Ben stared at her for several seconds, his eyes probing hers, before he took a deep breath, then slowly shook his head. "No."

Jessica blinked several times. "No, what?"

"I'm not going. I know that's what you're thinking. But I'm not doing it."

"You have to." She needed him. She needed him to tell her it would be okay. He didn't have to find Mario, but he sure as hell had to hold her hand while they tried.

"No, I don't." Ben crossed his arms over his chest and looked at her defiantly. "When he walked out of that hospital, he took himself out of my care."

She shook her head as her stomach tightened. "Ben, he needs you." *I need you.* She wanted to say that, but the words stuck in her throat.

Because she was afraid it wouldn't matter and she didn't think she could face that right now. Or ever.

"I know he does. But he should have thought of that before he walked out."

"He's just a kid. He needs us to find him, to make him do the right thing."

"I don't care."

She felt the knot in her stomach solidify into a lead ball. "You do," she insisted, feeling the sting of tears. "You swallowed your pride and went in to work on him even when you didn't want to before, because it was the right thing to do."

Ben's frown deepened and she saw the muscles in his arms tighten. She could feel the anger radiating off of him in waves.

"And what if I hadn't?"

"What do you mean?"

"What if I hadn't gone in there that night in the ER?" He came forward, his eyes stormy. "What if I hadn't taken over Mario's case?" He came closer until he was towering over her, his frustration nearly palpable. "What if I'd said no...like I should have?"

Jessica met his eyes and stood straight even when his aggravation nearly pushed her over. In a flash that took her breath for a moment she found herself in her father's shoes.

How many times had she stood defiantly in front of him, telling him exactly the opposite of what he wanted to hear? Many. Too many.

Tears pricked at the backs of her eyes. Dammit. This hurt. Even more than she'd known.

And what had her father always done? When she'd said *I'm leaving anyway. I don't care what you think. No.* He'd always said that he loved her. And he'd always been there when she'd come home.

She took a deep breath. "I would still love you," she said. "Even if you'd said no, even if you hadn't gone in."

It was true and she could tell he needed to hear it. Just like she needed to say it. Her love for Ben wasn't about what he did with his hands, his time, his career. It was about what he did with his heart.

Which was why she really freaking needed him to come with her right now.

"You're not angry?" he asked, his eyes telling her he didn't believe that for a moment.

"Yes. I'm definitely angry."

"Disappointed?"

"Very."

"But you don't want to take back any of the things you've said?"

It mattered to him. She could tell. She didn't know how things were gong to turn out with them. She didn't know how things were going to turn out with Mario. But what she did know, firsthand from her dad, was how to love someone no matter what. "Of course not."

He stared at her for several seconds. Then said, "You can't take it back."

"Okay."

"I'm going to shoot some pool."

Her stomach dropped. He wasn't going with her. He wasn't going to be holding her hand. "Okay," she said, fighting her tears.

She didn't point out that it was before the bars or pool halls would be open. She also didn't say a thing about drinking, gambling or other women.

Her dad had tried talking her out of the things she'd insisted on doing. He'd given her all the reasons she should do what he wanted. It hadn't worked. It had made her more determined to show him that he didn't get a say. Then the guilt had made her resent him.

She didn't want Ben to do anything out of guilt. Or even because he loved her. Or for any other reason than because he chose to do the right thing.

And she wanted a say in Ben's life. But only if he *gave* her that privilege. She wouldn't just take it.

She also had to keep hoping that she had inherited her father's stamina for loving someone in spite of being disappointed in them repeatedly.

Finally, Ben rammed a hand through his hair, swore under his breath and turned toward the front door. He grabbed his shoes from the floor by the door before yanking it open and disappearing without a look back.

Chapter Twelve

Ben wanted to have a huge, raging hard-on.

For someone other than Jessica Bradford.

Someone like Amber, for instance.

He watched her bend over the pool table to line up her shot in the very short, very tight, red skirt.

It should have been working and then some. She was totally his type. Curvy and brunette and completely aware of exactly how to use her assets to the max.

She also wanted Ben. There was no way he, or anyone in the general vicinity, could have missed that—and that's all she wanted. She wasn't concerned about him eating junk food or drinking too much and she sure as hell didn't expect him to spend day and night combing the streets for some punk kid who wasn't smart enough to keep his ass in the hospital after a major surgery.

Amber made her shot and gave Ben a sultry smile over her shoulder.

And he wasn't tempted at all.

Even though he was doing everything he could to be tempted. He was watching her every move, flirting, letting her touch him, even doing some touching himself. Reluctantly. Which was damn stupid.

But it didn't mean anything. It was probably her perfume or something that was turning him off. Eventually, he would meet someone that would make him lose his mind with lust and passion, that would make him laugh and make him feel more contented by simply being with her than he'd ever felt before.

Well, someone besides Jessica.

Until then, he needed liquor.

Lots of it.

He'd contemplated starting the annihilation of several brain and liver cells right after leaving Jessica's apartment. No bars or pool halls were open that early but there were a couple of all-night liquor stores between her place and his.

But he'd gone home and hit the workout room in his apartment complex instead. He hadn't wanted to play pool in the first place. It was just the first thing that came to mind when he was pushing Jess.

It was only fair that he push her, since she was constantly pushing him.

Pushing and testing and challenging him. Then what had she done when he'd tested her? She'd said she loved him anyway. And he believed her.

What drove him to drink after the bar did finally open was the disappointment he'd seen in her eyes.

She loved him and Ben knew that to Jessica that meant she would never tell him to get the hell out of her life, no matter what he did.

Look at how she was with the kids at the Bradford Center. They screwed up, repeatedly, and Jessica was always there to patch them up, tell them they were important and give them what they needed.

She would do the same for Ben.

But that didn't mean she wouldn't hate how he acted sometimes. That didn't mean he wouldn't drive her crazy. That didn't mean that she wouldn't sometimes wish she'd fallen in love with someone else.

He could be with her. All he had to do was be okay with breaking her heart over and over again.

He reached for his glass as he watched Amber move to the other side of the table. Why couldn't he be with *her*? The whiff of whiskey made his stomach lurch. He'd had the same glass in front of him for almost an hour. The other people around were too far into their drinks to notice, but Ben was feeling like the wuss they would have accused him of being. Maybe he should try beer.

But the beer in the glass of the guy sitting next to him reminded him of a urine sample.

Rum, vodka, brandy—nothing else sounded good either.

The music from the jukebox sounded obnoxious, the pool game was boring, the jokes were stupid and the pretzels were stale.

Ben leaned his elbow on the bar and turned to survey the room. This was exactly what he thought he wanted. He didn't have to go to work tomorrow, he had a bar full of people willing and able to party, women willing and able to get naked, and a bartender willing and able to pour as much liquor as he could handle.

And Ben felt lonely, restless, bored and empty.

Empty.

Shit.

It was Jessica's fault. He kept seeing how she'd looked at him when she'd realized he was letting her down.

If he went to her apartment she would let him in. She'd let him into her bed, her life, in spite of it all. But could he be with her knowing that he would see that look on her face again? Could he live with that? Could he handle knowing he was breaking her heart over and over?

The answer was simple. No way.

He loved her, wanted her, was miserable without her.

One of the things he loved about her was the way she stood by the people she believed in, whether they deserved it or not.

But he couldn't just take her love. He had to be the man she deserved, a man who deserved her.

And he was even more screwed than that.

He missed the hospital.

That morning with Jessica, he'd been focused on how pissed off he was at Mario for not taking care of himself.

But being at the hospital over the last few days, analyzing tests, putting together the pieces that led to a diagnosis, executing a plan to fix the problem, the clockwork of the team, even the noises and smells had slammed into him and made him like being in the damn place.

He hadn't used that kind of brainpower in so long that it felt like the endorphin high from a hard workout. And the triumph of finding the problem and fixing it had rekindled something in his soul—as corny as it sounded even in his head.

It wasn't his fault. He'd practically been born a doctor. His dad had taken him along on his rounds at the hospital when Ben was barely old enough to walk; he'd been holding a stethoscope before he could throw a ball; he'd helped with cleaning and bandaging wounds in Africa before he could drive.

He hated losing patients, he hated that some people would always take their health and the American medical system for granted, but the truth was, there wasn't anything else he'd rather do. The good days were good and he now knew that Jessica could make the bad days better.

Jessica.

She'd forgiven him when he acted like an ass.

Maybe he could forgive Mario. And the others who didn't make good choices, who screwed up, who didn't always meet *his* expectations.

Yeah, Jessica was a pro at forgiveness. She'd teach him how.

Ben tossed back a soda and then threw two twenties on the bar to cover his eight dollar tab.

He knew how he needed to start.

Twenty minutes later he strode through the doors to the ER. The personnel around the front desk all froze for several seconds, then everyone started talking at once. With only half a mind on what they were saying and asking, Ben scanned the assignment board and then turned toward room three.

On his way he pulled his cell phone from his pocket. He'd turned it off when he'd stormed out of Jessica's apartment, but now turned it back on, ready to be responsible again and back in contact with the real world.

He had nine voice mail messages.

Eight were from Sam. He didn't want to be preached at by Jessica's brother, especially after his friend had witnessed him being such a prick.

The other call was not Jessica, so he ignored it too.

Ben tossed his cell phone to Rita, the front desk clerk. "Answer that if it rings."

"Sure thing, Dr. Torres." Rita had been a fan of Ben's ever since he'd worked on her grandson after a snowmobile accident.

As he came through the swinging doors of room three, trauma physician Matt Taylor looked up from intubating the patient on the table.

"Your surgical consult is here," Ben said simply.

A nurse held a gown suspended toward Ben out of habit, but paused to look at Matt.

"You're..." Matt started.

"Back," Ben filled in.

Matt looked at him for a long moment. Then he gave a single nod. "About damn time."

Two hours later, someone knocked on and opened the door to the film viewing room. "Dr. Torres?" a female voice asked hesitantly.

He didn't turn from the x-rays hanging in front of him. "Yeah?"

"Your phone, Dr. Torres," the woman said. "It's Sam Bradford. He's... rather insistent about talking to you."

He could only imagine.

"Fine." He held out his hand and the nurse gave him the phone. He took a deep breath before putting the phone to his ear.

He prayed that Sam was calling about Mario. Ben had already checked with all the ERs in the city, hoping Mario had wised up and checked in with a doctor when he realized he'd left the hospital too soon.

So far, no one had seen him.

What bothered Ben the most was that he knew Mario was a smart kid. Now that Ben had calmed down some he realized that Mario might have had a good reason to leave.

That didn't mean that it was any less dangerous though.

"Did you find the kid?" he asked in lieu of a standard greeting.

"Where the hell are you?"

"Did you find him?" Ben repeated. "If not, I'm too busy to talk."

"Yeah, we found him. He's at the hospital. When he found out Sophie was in labor he went to be with her. But he blacked out."

Ben's chin dropped to his chest and he squeezed his eyes shut. "Dammit."

"Get your ass down there," Sam said. "I'll be there in ten

minutes."

Ben shook his head back and forth even though his friend couldn't see him. "I can't do anything, Sam."

"Bullshit!" Sam barked. "I'll come drag you down there if I have to. This kid deserves the best surgeon I can find and Ben, trust me, I'll find you." Sam's tone was ominous.

"I'm not a damn neurosurgeon, Sam!" The sentence was still traveling over the phone line to Sam when Ben realized that he wanted to be the one. He wanted to be the surgeon for Mario. But this was a neuro case.

They would let him scrub in though.

Ben switched off the light to the viewing box and headed for the door.

"No, Ben," Sam was saying in his ear. "It's not his head. They found more internal bleeding."

"Damn," Ben breathed. "I missed it."

"It was small. The spleen. It was..."

"Has he regained consciousness?" Ben interrupted, not wanting to hear condolences. He'd missed a small splenic tear. It wasn't uncommon. He'd found and repaired the two major lacerations. Then there was the hematoma. But still, he'd missed the small tear that had continued bleeding. Son of a bitch.

"I don't know. I doubt it. They were taking him straight to the OR after they found the bleed."

Ben didn't remember turning toward the elevators but when the doors didn't open immediately, he headed for the stairs, taking them two at a time.

"You have to be there," Sam said, his voice having lost some of its earlier heat.

"I'm already here." He pushed the door open from the stairwell and stepped onto the surgical floor.

"Where?"

"The hospital. It's a long story."

"But you'll be there? You'll go in with Mario?" Sam asked, clearly not caring why Ben was there.

"Yes."

"You're sure?" Sam pressed.

"Sam," Ben said seriously as he located Mario's name on the assignment board. "There is nothing that could keep me out of that OR. Trust me."

Open-toed, flip-flop sandals were not any better than stiletto-heeled boots for pacing a waiting room, Jessica realized only fifteen minutes into the wait during Mario's third surgery.

The bright orange plastic was cute by the pool but not at all for comfort. They had simply been the first shoes she'd seen in her closet. She'd kicked the shoes off for pacing but her bare feet on the hard, thinly carpeted floor wasn't much better.

Her feet hurt and her toes were cold. She was exhausted, and hungry and her heart hurt. But more than anything, or rather adding to *everything*, was the fact that she was here alone.

She should be used to it. She'd been going it alone ever since her dad died. Sara had been too young to help out with more than some dusting or dishes once in a while and Sam had never been the type to jump in and give respite. He also responded very poorly to threats and guilt, though bribes had worked from time to time.

Until now, though, she hadn't realized how much she'd trusted that Ben would be there with her at times like this.

Jessica rested her head against the window, the glass cool from the air conditioner vent above where she stood. Whether or not she should be well-practiced in being on her own, she was nevertheless right in the middle of wanting some company.

"Jessica?"

She whirled to find Sara coming from the elevator.

The two women met in the middle of the waiting area, hugging one another tightly.

"How are the kids?" Jessica finally asked.

Sara pulled back and took a deep breath. "Dealing. A couple of the volunteers came down to sit and talk with them so I could come over here. They brought burgers." She shrugged. "That can't hurt."

Jessica smiled. "I'm glad you're here."

"So, what do you know so far?" Sara asked, moving toward the coffee pot.

"Nothing."

Sara frowned. "What do you mean?"

"Nothing. No one's been out to tell me anything."

"But Ben's got to know how worried you are. I would think he'd send someone out to give you an update." Sara poured a cup, her back to Jessica.

Jessica frowned. "Ben? What are you talking about?"

Sara turned, frowning too. "Ben. Ben Torres. The surgeon you're sleeping with."

Jessica felt tears sting her eyes and she pressed her lips together for a moment. Ben was so much more than that. At least he had been. She wasn't sure what he was at the moment. "Ben isn't here, Sara. He..." This part was tough to explain. "He refused to come when he found out that Mario left against medical advice."

Sara looked confused. "But he didn't leave AMA. He was upstairs with Sophie."

Jessica sighed. "I know. But Ben doesn't know that. And he's not answering his cell phone and he's not at home. Ben was angry, and hurt, by what he thought Mario had done and he stormed out of my apartment this morning."

Sara's jaw dropped. "Seriously? He walked away?"

Jessica nodded, trying to block the memory of the look on Ben's face as he'd left her apartment. It was that look of *just try to stop me* that she'd worn so many times herself.

"He was upset. It's complicated."

"But Mario needed him. It shouldn't matter if Mario left or not." Sara's voice rose slightly and her coffee seemed forgotten. She gestured with her other hand as she spoke. "Ben's a doctor. He's Mario's doctor. He can't just walk away!"

Jessica frowned. "Ben's not perfect, Sara. He's just a man. He has feelings too. He worked his tail off for Mario. And he thought Mario was throwing it all away. We all did until we heard where they found him."

"That's no excuse!" Sara declared. "Mario needed him. Wow, I thought Ben was a good guy; that we could count on him, but now—"

"Knock it off!" Jessica snapped. "Of course we can count on him."

Sara stopped talking and stared at her sister.

Jessica wasn't done. "Ben is one of the best guys I know. He cared enough about Mario to be upset that Mario was putting himself in danger. So, he got mad. Ben doesn't just do a job, Sara. He gets involved. And that sometimes takes a lot out of him. But I would rather he be like that in his heart and serve coffee, than be a surgeon who doesn't know or care about who's on the table."

Sara nodded, her eyes wide. "Good. I'm...glad. Maybe I spoke too soon..."

"Jessica?"

She turned away from Sara to find Russ Edwards coming into the waiting area. Jessica was breathing fast, adrenaline pumping from the confrontation with her sister and from the realizations about her feelings for Ben.

"What?" she asked, bordering on rudeness and not caring.

"About our agreement..."

She couldn't take any more of this. She'd blown the promotion and she didn't care. She spread her arms wide. "I don't know where Ben is. I didn't convince him to come back to work and I know you expect to hear that I'm sorry, but I'm not." She took a deep breath. "Ben is a wonderful physician, one of the best, in fact. But more importantly he's a wonderful man. The best I've ever known. And I'm done trying to do anything other than love him." She pointed a finger at Russ and narrowed her eyes. "Leave him alone. He'll figure it out."

"It?" Russ asked, composed in spite of her finger pointing at him.

"What he's supposed to be doing," she said.

"And what if he chooses the coffee shop?" Russ asked.

"Then he'll be the best at that too."

Russ reached inside his jacket and pulled a long white envelope from the inside pocket. He walked forward and handed it to her. "You're going to be a hell of a head nurse."

The envelope had the hospital's return address and insignia in the upper left hand corner.

"This is..."

"Your recommendation letter from me for ER Director."

Oh.

Jessica looked up at Russ, her cheeks burning. "I thought..."

"I know," Russ said.

"Russ, I..."

"Don't worry about it. It will be a pleasure working with you."

Luke Pierson, one of St. Anthony's trauma surgeons, entered the room, pulling a scrub cap from his head.

Jessica and Sara turned in unison, momentarily forgetting Russ.

"Is he okay?" Sara asked, rushing to Luke's side.

"He's a tough kid," Luke said of Mario. "He's back together and his vitals are stable."

Jessica nearly crumpled the precious recommendation letter in her hand. "Thank you, God," she breathed.

"It's early, but I expect to see him doing well over the next few hours."

Jessica grabbed Luke in a spontaneous hug. "Thank you. Thank you."

"I didn't..." Luke stopped as he stepped back and cleared his throat. His eyes flickered over her shoulder to Russ, then back to Jessica. He gave her a small smile. "I'm part of a whole team. We're just doin' our jobs."

Jessica smiled back. She knew that team. None of this was just a job to them.

"You need to go home now," Luke said. "You look ready to drop. We'll call you with any news."

Jessica let herself breathe deeply in and out for the first time since she'd gotten the phone call that Mario was missing that morning. The morning that seemed an eternity ago.

Fatigue and relief combined to bring tears to her eyes. "Is he awake?"

"I don't expect him awake for a while. We're going to monitor him in recovery a little longer, then ICU."

She was anxious to see Mario, but she trusted these doctors and nurses to take care of him right now. And she wanted to go find Ben.

"We'll talk later," Luke said.

"Thanks again." Jessica watched him leave. Then she grabbed her purse and the sandals near the couch. "Sara, I have someplace I need to go."

Sara smiled. "Bring me a white chocolate mocha."

Jessica knew exactly what she had to do. She'd always been more of a do-er, anyway. Words didn't mean a lot without action to back them up.

For years she'd put her creativity and energy into *showing* her father that she was her own person. His actions had always spoken loudly to her as well. He'd told her he loved her, but she was convinced by how he always welcomed her home with open arms. She'd known where his heart was by what he did.

Over the past ten years her actions had been focused on proving that she could be the one to take care of her siblings and the center. It didn't matter what she said, but what she did that got noticed.

She'd told Ben that she'd love him no matter what.

Now she needed to *prove* it. Imagination, energy...and a quick pit stop were all she needed.

The same girl was working when Jess rushed through the front door of Tease fifteen minutes later.

The electric blue dressed molded to every curve. A two-inch thick strap covered her left shoulder, but the neckline dove dramatically to dip under her right arm, with a sharp point cutting low between her breasts so that a hard sneeze would reveal *all* her secrets. Not that many were left. The back of the dress plunged shamelessly to end in a V at the base of her spine. The right side of the dress had three inch squares cut out at one inch intervals from underarm to where it ended just short of mid-thigh, letting skin and curves play peek-a-boo with anyone looking.

And they *would* look. It was like being wrapped in neon saran wrap that screamed *Look at me!*

It was as far away on the spectrum as she could get from the image she'd been trying to project for the past ten years. Which made it exactly what she wanted tonight.

Jessica had never actually stopped traffic before, but she did stop conversation when she stepped into Dolly's coffee shop.

But she didn't notice the attention she was drawing as she scanned the shop for Ben. The only thing that registered was that the faces staring back at her were not his.

"Jessica?"

For a moment her heart skipped, but even before she turned she knew it wasn't Ben. Instead she found Dooley, Mac and Kevin sitting at a table about five yards from where she stood. They all looked like they'd been kicked in the groin.

"Holy shit!" Mac exclaimed, breaking the stunned silence that let Frank Sinatra perform uninterrupted from the stereo system.

"Oh, my..." Kevin, of course, didn't finish the expletive. The strong Christian looked a bit guilty around the edges, but he didn't look away from her as she approached.

"What are you guys doing here?"

Coffee with foam, music from the 1940s and women older than them—and unimpressed with them—were not usual ingredients in an evening out for her brother's friends.

They all continued to stare at her.

"Where's Ben?" she asked, growing impatient with the struck-stupid looks on her friends' faces.

"Where's *Sam*?" Mac finally found a voice to ask. "Does he know you're wearing that?"

She frowned down at the dress. "No. He's working. Where's Ben?"

"At the hospital," Dooley answered. "*Damn*, Jessica. You sure can make a guy feel stupid for respecting the fact that you're his friend's sister all these years."

She sighed and propped a hand on her hip. "Thanks, I guess."

Kevin, Jessica was amused to note, was the only one who hadn't yet blinked. She put a hand on his shoulder and leaned in. She needed to know where Ben was and she didn't have time to be subtle. Kevin was a Christian man. True love, devotion and sacrifice were right up his alley.

"Kevin, have pity on me. I'm in love with Ben and need to find him right now. Do you know where he is?"

Kevin pulled his eyes from her breasts, slowly, impressing her with his fortitude. Of course, Dooley and Mac weren't trying to *not* look. They were taking in the view like avid baseball fans on opening day. She was sure they'd buy popcorn if a vendor happened to come by.

"He's at the hospital," Kevin told her, obviously struggling to keep his eyes on hers.

She shook her head. "Not Sam. I need to find *Ben*. You know, the guy who works in this coffee shop?"

"I know I should feel bad about picturing you naked, Jessica Leigh," Mac interjected with a big grin. "But honestly, that dress doesn't leave me a lot of options. You don't want to drive clear over to the hospital again, do ya? When I'm right here and very willing to do pretty much anything you want? Or you could debase Kevin there." Mac gestured at his friend with his coffee mug. "Doesn't look like he'd mind."

"And that's a huge compliment," Dooley said with a chuckle. "Kevin hasn't thought about being debased in a long time."

"I have too," Kevin muttered, picking up his cup. "I just *try* not to."

Jessica rolled her eyes. She loved these guys. They were good guys, even if they were *guys* in every sense of the word.

She straightened abruptly. "Cut the crap," she told the men in front of her. "Where's Ben?"

"I don't think we're going to talk her out of going," Dooley said to Mac, openly ogling her some more. "At least squeeze her ass," he said to Kevin with some disgust. "She's right there. How can you stand it?"

Jessica moved a step further away from Mac and Dooley's side of the table. "Stop it," she insisted. "Where. Is. Ben?"

"The hospital," Mac said. "We keep telling you. He's at the hospital."

She was stunned. "He is? To see Mario?"

Kevin looked up at her, *just* at her face this time, with a small smile. "Be sure to tell him you're in love with him *before* you tell him you're glad he's back to work."

She stared at Kevin. "He's back to work? What do you mean?"

"He went in even before he heard about Mario," Dooley explained. "He was there when Sam called. Working. Reinstated. The whole shebang."

Jessica vaguely recognized that she was stunned. But her brain did compute that she now knew where Ben was. She could worry about why later.

"Wish me luck," she told the guys.

"You got him out of that bar in the black dress," Dooley

said, his eyes sliding up and down her body unapologetically. "You'll have no trouble getting whatever you want in *that.*"

"Are you going to wear that to the hospital?" Kevin asked, eyes wide.

She certainly wasn't stopping anywhere between here and Ben. Besides, the thing had cost her over two hundred dollars. And the point was, she had to show Ben that he was the right man for *her.* Not the super-organized, go-getter ER nurse who had been intent on finding—or creating—the perfect man. But the woman, who now knew that the man for her was not perfect, but was just right.

Ben was pacing the Emergency Room at St. Anthony's— something he'd never done before. Generally, his time in the ER was filled up with patching holes in people. There wasn't time for pacing. Of course, that wasn't the only thing he'd done for the first time since getting involved with Jessica.

Where the hell was she?

His gut had clenched into a knot of hope and anxiety when he'd come to the surgical waiting area to find Sam alone. He'd instantly decided to go after her, but Sam's phone had rung before Ben could get his locker open. Sam had run in, telling him that Jessica had showed up at Cup O' Joe looking for him and was now on her way back to the hospital to find him.

He was nearly climbing the walls waiting for her. He was in love with her. He hadn't looked for it, hadn't thought he wanted it, but there was no denying it. Nor was there any sense in denying the fact that it was good for him. Great for him. He was a better person because of her and, if that didn't scream *marry her, dumbass,* he didn't know what did.

The stretch of hallway linoleum ended and he pivoted to go back the way he'd come, but stopped short.

He was in love with Jessica and he would never want another woman, but there wasn't a man on the planet who wouldn't take a moment to appreciate the female form that had just graced the ER department with the most delicious combination of blazing blue leather and creamy, satiny skin.

Nancy, the receptionist, pointed in his direction and the woman turned.

His heart nearly stopped. It was Jessica.

Love and lust, heat and happiness all raced to be the first thing to register in his mind.

What finally won first place was *what the hell is she doing wearing that dress out where other men can see her?*

He knew the moment she saw him. Her eyes widened and her mouth formed a little O. He assumed it was from the look of pure, unadulterated possessiveness on his face. Or the fact he was literally stalking toward her.

"Ben, I—" she started when he was within a foot.

He cut off whatever she was going to say by stooping and swinging her up into his arms. He headed for exam room six. It was one of only two rooms in the ER with walls and a door instead of just curtains.

After her initial gasp of surprise, she wrapped her arms around his neck. "Where are we going?"

"Exam six." He didn't dare look down at her. The heat of her skin was seeping through the amazingly erotic dress and he was about to strip the damn thing off of her. But they needed those walls and the door. Oh, yeah, and he needed to say a few things first.

"Um, Ben?" she asked, wiggling enticingly in his arms.

"Yeah?" He still didn't look down, but he definitely felt every curve. When had they moved exam six so far away from the front desk?

"I really want to go to exam six, but I have to tell you something first."

"In a minute," he said. After *he* talked. In private.

"Ben, seriously, I need to say something." Jessica wiggled to get down.

"Then you can tell me just like this," he said, still walking, and still holding her. He wasn't sure he was ever going to put her down.

"But I want you to get the full effect," she argued, wiggling harder.

He stopped in the middle of the hallway intersection that led off to the cafeteria in one direction, the parking garage in another, the third hallway to the ER and the lab down the fourth.

The trauma team had just shipped a patient up to surgery and was wearily leaving the room to Ben's left. They also stood in between the nurses' locker room and the staff entrance. It was time for the next shift to start work, which meant they were in the middle of a crowd of people coming and going. All of them knew Jessica and Ben well. It was the most un-private spot in the hospital.

He loosened the arm under her knees and let her slide down until her toes touched the floor. "Believe me, Jessica, I got the full effect," he said gruffly. "The first time I ever saw you."

She smiled, but stepped back, spreading her arms. Ben looked around and noticed that the trauma team looked much less tired suddenly and the nurses on their way home were obviously less anxious to leave. They had an audience.

He smiled at their stunned expressions. They saw a lot of interesting things working in the ER, but their little general in bright blue leather and stilettos, being carried down the hall by their star, recently suspended surgeon was one for the books.

"I've spent a long time trying to make things in my life go a certain way. I thought I had it all figured out. I thought I knew what I was supposed to do." Jessica had tears in her eyes now and Ben reached out, but she stepped further back. "And the funny thing is, I knew you were a part of it, even before I realized that I didn't even know what it was."

He reached out again, *needing* to touch her. The crowd around them was silent, at least as silent as a hospital ever got. "Jess..."

She stepped back again, holding up a hand. "Wait. I'm almost done. And if you touch me, I'm going to start taking off my clothes and not be able to finish what I need to say."

He felt the heat shoot through him, even as he heard the startled and amused murmurings from the crowd around them.

"Jess, I—"

"I love you," she interrupted. "And, I don't care—"

"Excuse me, could I get some help here?" A man of about fifty pushed through the group, holding his forearm against his stomach, a bloody towel wrapped around his hand.

Ben looked around the group of emergency personnel gathered. They all glanced at the man, but no one seemed inclined to leave the mini-drama going on between him and Jessica.

"What happened?" one of the residents asked.

"Lawn mower blade," the man said. "I think I need

267

stitches."

None of the staff's eyes had left Jessica and Ben. One nurse took a long pull on the straw sticking out of a paper cup from the cafeteria. Another was passing out sticks of gum. It was a real-live soap opera and no one seemed inclined to miss even a minute.

"Everything still attached?" the resident asked.

"Yeah." The man shrugged.

"You in a lot of pain?"

"I have ice on it so I'm doing okay."

"You think you could wait a bit?"

"What's going on?" the man asked, looking at the middle of the semi-circle formed by hospital staff, with Ben and Jessica on display. He did a double-take as he noticed Jessica, his shoulders turning to face her more squarely.

"Jessica is talking about taking her clothes off and—"

"The one in the blue dress is Jessica?" the man asked.

"Right."

"Yeah, it can wait." The man took a place next to one of the med techs leaning against the wall.

Jessica turned back and smiled at Ben. "I don't care what you do for a living. I don't care if you do nothing for a living. You've helped me realize what living is."

"Jessica!"

Ben nearly groaned in frustration as the small crowd of co-workers parted to let the latest addition to the chaos through.

It was Sara.

"Jessica, I'm—" Sara stopped dead in her tracks, taking in her sister's dress and heels. "What in the world..."

"I'm trying to propose to Ben," Jessica explained, obviously exasperated. "What's going on? Why aren't you upstairs with Mario?"

"Oh." Sara's eyes darted between the two of them. "I wanted to tell you that he's awake and Sophie's with him."

"Great news." Jessica smiled and once again turned back to Ben. "I love you. I want you to be happy. Whatever that means, whatever you need to do, is good with me. As long as we're together."

Ben smiled down at her, knowing exactly what he wanted and where he should be for the first time in a very long time.

"Isn't there something you were going to ask me?" he asked, moving forward.

"Will you please take me to exam room six?" she asked promptly.

Ben smiled, but shook his head. "Everyone's already heard everything else. They might as well hear the proposal too."

A cheer of agreement went up from the group around them.

Jessica's smile was sly as she said, "Oh, the proposal is a given. Like the answer. But we still need exam six."

He liked the look in her eyes. "Oh?"

"Yeah. It so happens that I have a very specific fantasy about you in surgical scrubs, in this hospital's ER department."

"Thank God." He swept her up in his arms and strode quickly down the hall even as their crowd of fans booed at being left out. Jessica laughed as he fumbled with holding her and turning the exam room's doorknob at the same time.

She reached down and turned it for him.

"You will marry me, right, Ben?" she asked as he set her on the edge of the exam table and kicked the door shut behind them.

"You're damn right, I will," he said, his fingers already on the zipper at the back of her dress. "But for the next several minutes, I'd prefer it if you called me Dr. Torres. It makes me think of all those times you were bending over in that thong."

"Hey, I thought this was *my* fantasy." Her protest was weak as Ben's lips traveled from her ear to her collarbone.

"You're right," he said, lifting his head. "Sorry. Go ahead. Tell me your fantasy. In detail, please."

"You," she said, her eyes tearing up in spite of her smile. "You're my fantasy. You loving me no matter what."

"Done," he said, looking into her eyes. "I love you. More than anything. No matter what."

"Then maybe you are perfect after all." She sniffed and grinned at the same time.

"Nah." He kissed her. "That'd be no fun." He kissed her again, longer this time. "But with you, Jessica, I *am* perfectly happy. Finally."

And she knew just what he meant. Finally.

About the Author

Erin Nicholas has been reading and writing romantic fiction since her mother gave her a romance novel in high school and she discovered happily-ever-after suddenly went a little beyond glass slippers and fairy godmothers! She lives in the Midwest with her husband who only wants to read the sex scenes in her books, her kids who will *never* read the sex scenes in her books, and family and friends who say they're shocked by the sex scenes in her books (yeah, right!).

For more information about Erin and her books, visit:
www.ErinNicholas.com,
http://ninenaughtynovelists.blogspot.com/,
or
http://groups.yahoo.com/group/ErinNicholas/

HOT STUFF

Discover Samhain!

THE HOTTEST NEW PUBLISHER ON THE PLANET

Romance, fantasy, mystery, thriller, mainstream and more—Samhain has more selection, hotter authors, and everything's available in ebook.

Pick your favorite, sit back, and enjoy the ride! Hot stuff indeed.

Breinigsville, PA USA
22 March 2011
258171BV00001B/56/P